USA TODAY BESTSELLING AUTHOR

SARAH M. CRADIT

ISBN: 978-1-958744-43-7

Cover and Interior Design by The Illustrated Author Design Services
Map by The Illustrated Author Design Services
Hardcover Art ("Squish and the Scholar") by Stephanie Brown of Offbeat Worlds
"F*cking for Science" Art by Nora Adamszki of Adamzki Art
Aesylt and Rahn Portraits by Steffani Christensen of Art by Steffani
Editing by Novel Nurse Editing

Publisher Contact:
sarah@sarahmcradit.com
www.sarahmcradit.com

For all my fellow geeks and nerds.
Never let anyone tell you learning isn't sexy.

PRAISE FOR THE HAND AND THE HEART

"The Duke and The Disciple is an enthralling read with witty characters. Sarah Cradit creates an amazing multi-layered world full of banter and tension. It was downright addictive to read!"

~Lucy Smoke, USA Today Bestselling author

"An academic study in sensuality? Yes please! The Duke and the Disciple is everything you want in a darkly seductive forbidden romance!"

~Tessonja Odette, author of A Rivalry of Hearts

"Sarah never misses and the Duke and the Disciple is no exception! I will never not brag about Sarah and her work, and the beautiful way in which she writes. Anything she writes, I'm going to read it!"

~Ky Venn, author of Justice in Magic

"Golden retriever in the streets and Daddy Wulf in the sheets. Lord help me, this book was HOT! I love forbidden love and this had me so giddy. Throw in some denial, magic, and a coup and this is a book you definitely need to pick up."

~Rachel, @rachelsbooktea

"This enrapturing book will have you feeling all types of emotions, whether it is swooning over the romance, sobbing because of the angsty heartbreak or cheering for this forbidden love that is as bright as the stars in the sky!"

~Pia (pias_bookshelf)

INTRODUCTION

There exists a kingdom set upon an isle, surrounded by a sea no one has ever traveled beyond. The Kingdom of the White Sea it is called, or simply the kingdom, for they have no other name for it.

While most of the realm lives under the watchful laws of the crown, the Vjestik of Witchwood Cross observe their own traditions and have formed their own code. Nomadic by nature, they've called several places home but have been in the far northern outpost for almost two hundred years by the time this story begins.

The Wynters, the stewards of the Cross, have indoctrinated themselves into Northerland politics to the extent it serves them. They pay taxes to the capital, Wulfsgate, and enjoy a cordial relationship with the lord of their Reach. But each winter, when supplies are allocated and food rations become meager, their allies are nowhere to be seen.

This self-sustaining resourcefulness is the root of the tradition that defines their entire culture to everyone on the outside, and sustains it from the inside: the Vuk od Varem, or the Season of the Wulf.

Witchwood Cross belonged to the wulves long before the Vjestik showed up in search of a new home for their people. Darek Summerton, as the legend goes, parlayed with the wulves and came to an agreement. The men could build their village, but the forests were off-limits as a food source unless the men earned their right to hunt, a right they had to re-earn year after year by sending one of their sons into the forest to face off against a wulf, with nothing more than food, drink, and a dagger. If the wulf survived, the forests were theirs to stalk, unbothered, until the next winter season. If the boy survived, the forests were theirs to hunt and restock their meat stores.

Most winters belong to the wulves.

But every now and then a boy emerges a victor.

Drazhan Wynter, current steward of Witchwood Cross, was one such boy. But his victory was forever marred by his return home, when he found his village burned and his family massacred by the crown, the terrible night afterward referred to as Nok Mora. The Nightmare.

His little sister, Aesylt, was the sole Wynter survivor of the attack, left alive by the king's men as a witness. And for years after, while Drazhan channeled his grief into rage on a vengeance quest, she was the one who led her people through the greatest crisis in their history, with her closest friends, Valerian and Niklaus, at her side.

Two years ago, Drazhan returned home with a bride and an unwelcome protectiveness for the little sister he'd left behind. All she wants to do is spread her wings and fly, but fear of losing her compels Drazhan to keep her close and safe, even at the expense of her happiness.

Soon after arrived the studious Duke Rahn, who joined Drazhan's wife, Imryll, in her endeavor to create an encyclopaedia for the realm. In Rahn, Aesylt sees the same curiosity and passion for the world that has burned in her heart her entire life, and she excitedly joins him in his research, ready to throw herself into something with true meaning.

But just around the corner is another Vuk od Varem, and once more, someone close to her is chosen. Someone who has always been there for her. Following a tearful good-bye, she prepares herself for the worst, but not even a full day later, Valerian returns. The manner of his return throws the entire village into chaos, and thrusts them toward the verge of their first civil war.

A war with Aesylt at the center.

She did this, the villagers chant. *She cursed us.*

Drazhan has no choice but to bar the gates of Fanghelm to protect his family. He directs Rahn to keep his little sister busy with research, oblivious to the next subject in their curricula.

To meet the burden of requirement, the researchers must conduct the experiments themselves—illicit, sensual experiments that leave nothing to the imagination and everything to be explored. If they refuse, they'll be giving the powerful Reliquary exactly what it wants: failure and exile.

But to proceed as required is utterly unthinkable. Rahn is nearly thirty, and Aesylt's mentor. And while she is yet unmarried, thanks to her overprotective brother, she hopes to be a wife someday. In a moment of desperation, she even promises herself to Val before he ventures into the forest to his uncertain fate.

With no clear path ahead of them, Aesylt proposes a different way. As a starwalker, she has been secretly visiting the celestial realm her whole life and has learned how to take others with her. It's a place with no consequences, she believes, but will it be enough to allay his heavy conscience?

And can something so intimate truly come without consequence?

As tensions rise in the village, Aesylt and Rahn race a clock and their inhibitions. If they want to finish the curricula, they'll have no choice but to lead with the science and put aside their forbidden, budding feelings for each other.

For if Drazhan ever discovered what his baby sister and the esteemed scholar were *really* doing behind closed doors, there would be no mercy. No second chances for the man he trusts to keep her safe.

With war on the horizon and another tempest brewing between teacher and student, only one thing is certain.

Not everyone in this story will make it out alive.

WITCHWOOD CROSS

Reach
Northerlands

Steward & Stewardess
Drazhan and Imryll Wynter of Fanghelm Keep

Children
Aleksy, 1

Steward's Family
Aesylt, 20 (sister)

Tindahls
Duke Adrahn, 29

Farrestells
Teleria, 40
Tasmin, 22

Barynovs of Hoarfrost
Baron Esker
Marek, 25
Valerian, 21

Petrovashes of Hibernal
Anton
Niklaus, 20

Castels of Castellan
Baron General Fezzan
Baroness Asa
Uli, 28

Voronovs of Howlestra
Baroness General Brita
Baroness Jasika
Tessa, 22
Emira, 18

Others
Elara Cantor, 19
Maia
Kilgore
Cassius

WULFSGATE

Reach
Northerlands

Lord and Lady
Lord Rustan Dereham and Lady Felice Dereham of Wulfsgate Keep

Children
Pieter, 27
Nyssa, 18
Hadden, 2

Others
Halifax
Kezza

VJESTIK TRANSLATIONS

ahen vodah: "fire water" / hot springs
auvjek: evermore
dobranok: good night
dobryzen: good morning
frata: brother
grimizhna tea: contraceptive drink
hej: (greeting) hello
hejka: (parting) good-bye
hvala: thanks/gratitude
kahk si: (greeting) How are you?
koldyna: pejorative term meaning "evil witch who communes with demons"
kyschuna/kyschun: archivists, keepers of histories and storytelling
nien: no/negative
Nok Mora: The Nightmare, referring to the massacre on their people led by Carrow Rhiagain, at the behest of the Meduwyn Mortain
oma: mother
onkel: uncle
opros: sorry
ota: father
pjika: (term of endearment) bird
pros: please
sostra: sister
stranjak: (friendly term) outsider / anyone who doesn't have Vjestik heritage
tak: yes/affirmative
uljez: (pejorative term) outsiders who are not friendly
vedhma/veduhn: shaman/diviner
Vjestik: traveler community of witches who immigrated to Witchwood Cross hundreds of years ago
Vjestikaan: old language of the Vjestik

volemthe: love / I love you
vozhdae: spiritualists assigned to male leaders
vozhd: assembly of the vozhdae
Vuk od Varem: Season of the Wulf
zolvha: spiritual adviser
zydolny: "the touch"

HOWLING SEA
MIDNIGHT CREST
ICEBOLT MOUNTAIN
MIDWINTER REST
WITCHWOOD CROSS
WHITECAP
FOREST OF LYCANA
NORTHERLAND RANGE
WULFSHEAD HAVEN
TORRIN'S PASS
WESTPORT
EASTPORT
DUNWOODE
DARKWOOD RUN
SALTHILL
WULF'S NECK
MAYKE
SALEEN
ASGILL
DRUMAIN
BYTHESEA
TERMONGLEN
RUSHWOOD
WHISPERING WOOD
VALLEYBROOKE
STREAMSTOWNE
EVERLEIGH PIKE
WILDWOOD FALLS
EVERHART THICKET
PARTH
RESPLENDENT RELIQUARY
THE SEPULCHRE IN THE SKIES
THE SEVEN SISTERS
GAP OF EVER
BRIARHAVEN
RIVER RUSH
WINDWATCH GROVE
GREENFEN
PINE BLUFF
WHITEWOOD
OLDCASTLE
FIONN'S PASS
OAK HILL
WHITE SEA
EAST DERRY
IRON HILL
BLACKPOOL
STONE MAWR
NEWCARROW
SANDYMOUNT
GREENCASTLE
GOLDTHORPE
SANDYCOVE
LEECASTER BAY
HORNSEA
PORT WORTHING
CAMP ATONEMENT
GREYSTONE ABBEY
WHITECLIFFE
CAMP RESTITUTION
N
S
E
W
1.) NORTHERLANDS
2.) HINTERLANDS
3.) WESTERLANDS
4.) SOUTHERLANDS
5.) EASTERLANDS
6.) ISLE OF BELCARROW
7.) DUNCARROW
8.) WASTELANDS
9.) WULFSGATE
10.) LONGWOOD RUSH
11.) WARWICKTOWN
12.) WHITECHURCH
KINGDOM OF THE WHITE SEA

AS IMITABLE
AS THE STARS
IN OUR
INTERMINABLE SKY

ONE
TELL ME ABOUT THE STARS

Adrahn raced half-blind through the darkened, snow-dense forest, deeply regretting his choice to participate in the utterly arcane tradition with every lumbering, strenuous step.

Sweat trickled down his brow and over his nose under his musty, untenable mask, his strained breaths creating garbled echoes inside the hot leather. He felt as ridiculous as he must look wearing a hulking wulf's costume and chasing an unknown woman, also in disguise, but he'd come to the forest for one reason and one reason alone.

Aesylt was out there, somewhere.

Before the chase had begun, he'd searched for her in the sea of curly brunette wigs, peeling, plaster masks with garish rosy circles to mark the cheeks, and shapeless sack dresses, but the young women were dressed identical.

Once the horn had cut through the last of dusk, the night had become a blur.

A flash of brown appeared in a gap between the trees ahead. She was his "damsel," as the young women taking part in the

Dyvareh were called. She could be any of the dozen girls who'd signed up, but if the night was on his side, it was Aesylt.

If anything happened to her on the debaucherous night, he would never forgive himself.

The young woman ahead broke off to the left. Rahn slid across a fallen log and pushed himself harder to keep from losing her. Regardless of who she was, he had no intention of letting her be caught by some drunken imbecile using a wulf costume to justify his miscreance. The "wulves" weren't supposed to chase any "damsel" except the one wearing the same color paint slash, but he'd heard more than enough stories about how the forest became a lawless place on the night of the chase. It was his first year participating, and he'd only agreed when he'd learned Aesylt intended to join for the first time as well.

The mask limited all except what was immediately in front of him, so Rahn had to turn his head all the way up to see the sky. Fat snow plopped into his eyes, hazing them. Scarce light remained beyond what the crescent moon provided, the reflection of snow offering an eerie glow. *The wulfing hour,* he'd heard one of the other men say to a fellow wulf, with a roguish laugh that had made Rahn's peaceful blood boil.

He thought of the books piled on his desk in the library, how he'd rather be reading, studying. There was an almost sentient demand to the research awaiting his cohort, but even if he wasn't concerned about Aesylt, it would have been ill-mannered to decline to take part in the annual Dyvareh after everything the Wynters had done for him.

The Chase, he translated in his head, as he always did with the modest amount of Vjestikaan he'd learned over his past year and a half in Witchwood Cross.

But for all he'd learned, he still had a long way to go before he understood. In what society was it agreeable to garb the bachelor men and unmarried young women in dilapidated costumes, in the dead of midwinter, and force them into a sybaritic chase that could end any number of dreadful ways?

The same one that sent one of their sons into the forest every midwinter to face off against a wulf for the right to hunt the forests in the coming year, he supposed.

Rahn pushed on through lofty, grueling banks. His panting was louder than the forest sounds, so he focused on slowing it, on listening. But other than the harried steps of the young woman ahead—

Rahn seized, stilling. There *was* something else.

Crunch.

He shuffled sideways until he was partly hidden by a broad pine. From there he spotted a fellow wulf scaling a fallen log. The man nimbly landed on the other side, darting his head around, and took off in the direction of the young woman.

Rahn reached up under his mask to wipe the sweat before peeling away from the tree. The wulf and the damsel appeared to know each other, engaged in a seemingly cordial conversation Rahn was too far away to hear. He continued to hold his distance, trying to get a better read on the situation, but then they disappeared from view, so he relinquished his hiding place and started after them.

Several moments passed and then a shrill scream tore through the forest.

Rahn took off running.

Aesylt was proud of herself for not screaming. She was hard to scare, but she'd always been jumpy, and Valerian often exploited that for his own amusement. So when he'd come up behind her, surely bargaining for *some* kind of reaction, with great delight she'd simply tilted her chin with an impudent grin and said, "Lost in your own woods, are you, V?"

Valerian groaned, long and deep. His hands went to his hips, a flare of patchy fur. "Come on, Aessy. I don't believe for a second you were expecting that."

She hadn't been expecting him to stalk her, no, but she *had* heard him coming. Knew it was him by the gait—smooth, cocksure. Even in the snow it was unmistakable. "Your attempt was actually quite boring and uninspired." Her mask hid her grin. Her gaze swept his costume in what might have been disbelief, had he been anyone else. "Your color is *yellow,* Val. Mine is red." She tapped her thick sack dress, groaning. "Wrong damsel."

"What if I say it's the right one?" He stepped closer.

Aesylt shook her head. "The Dyvareh has only just started, and already you're breaking the rules?" She felt her own wulf behind her, holding distance and biding his time, probably salivating over his free night of stalking a helpless female. She'd been hoping to lose him near the quarry, but getting Val to leave her alone was going to take some effort.

Val clapped his wulf hands over his ears and made an obnoxious singsong sound. "What rules? Afraid I didn't hear them."

She quirked a brow. "Only a fool closes his ears when Drazhan Wynter is speaking."

"I'm not afraid of your frata." Val scoffed. "What rules am I breaking anyway? I can't talk to my oldest friend?"

She ticked them down on her fingers. "Nien chasing a damsel who doesn't match your color? Nien *talking* and giving away your identity?" The third rule she didn't speak aloud. *If you catch your damsel, no behavior beyond what they allow.* She'd let Val kiss her before, and even enjoyed it. But he'd enjoyed it more. Enough that he'd thrown around the word *marriage.* What had followed were tense closed-door talks between the Barynovs and her brother and then... nothing. Drazhan wouldn't allow her to marry, nor even court, because he claimed none of the men in the Cross were good enough for her. And though she'd certainly imagined what life might be like with Valerian Barynov, she'd not seriously entertained it.

"When do we ever get to be alone like this anymore?" Val stepped forward again when she shivered. The night was as cold as always, but she usually wore a heavier fur than the costume allowed for. "Someone is always there. The cohort. Your vedhma. The scholar. Nik. Your fucking frata. Besides, if I'm here, your damned wulf can't get any foul ideas."

"It's not appropriate." She choked on her distaste for the refrain. Val and Nik had been her dearest friends since she was crawling around her nursery, but only since Drazhan had returned to the Cross had it been deemed unsuitable for the three to do what they'd always done.

She was grateful to have her brother home after all those years, but sometimes—

"You know what else isn't appropriate, Aessy?" He swung his hairy, costumed arms around. There was a dark edge to his voice. "This. The village acting like the Dyvareh is *anything* like the sacrifice they expect me to make in a week. This is just a *game*, a silly, stupid game. When I enter the forest with nothing but a dagger, some dried meat, and a pelt, the games are over. I either kill the wulf or he kills me, and we know who usually wins."

"I know." Aesylt crossed her arms to hold back the chill, shifting in place. Valerian's upcoming turn in the Vuk od Varem wasn't something she'd allowed herself to think about. The idea of him never coming home was unbearable. She'd watched her oldest brother and father massacred in front of her, but it was that same trauma keeping her from addressing the one awaiting them. "You could refuse."

"And be the first? You're not that naïve."

"I'm not naïve at all." She wondered where her wulf was. Watching, perhaps? Waiting for them to finish so he could strike? She had no intentions of getting caught on her very first Dyvareh—no matter how thrilling the idea had seemed before the chase started.

Aesylt rotated her head and took a deep breath through the stuffy mask. She coughed, sputtering dust and layers of Ancestors knew what else. It was still better than inhaling the icy cold into her lungs. "Who ran Witchwood Cross while my frata was off on his vengeance quest?"

She could almost see the smirk behind his snout. "I'd like to think Nik and I helped."

"You kept me sane." Aesylt smiled even though he couldn't see it. "*Look,* I need to find a place to hide, so go. Go!" She shooed him. "Go, Val!"

"Fine... Fine..." Val raised his hands in surrender. "I'll *guess* I'll *go.* I'll—" He froze, snapping his attention to the left.

"What?" she whispered. "What is it?"

"Stay still."

"Val—"

"It's a wulf. A real wulf. And he's coming slowly our way." He grabbed her by the shoulders and shook her, spinning her away from the forest. "I'll handle it. Run!"

Aesylt stumbled sideways. Her foot caught on something, causing her to flail, but her next step tried to land on air. She was flying, out and down, thrashing through blankets and blankets of pine needles assaulting her face and arms as she clamored for anything to slow her fall.

Her ankle smashed into something solid and unyielding, and she screamed.

Rahn tripped over something he couldn't see in his limited vision and the ever-darkening night, landing in an ungainly crouch in the middle of a snowbank. He recovered and pounded through the deep drifts, aware not only of the damsel's screams but of another voice, one he recognized as well as he did the young woman's, yelling at her to *stay still* and *don't move.*

Valerian Barynov.

And Aesylt.

Both were members of Rahn's research cohort, but only one had learning on their mind when they joined the group in the Fanghelm library every morning after breakfast. Aesylt was all business when she walked through those doors, and so was Valerian, except his business was her.

"Fuck. Fuck! Opros, opros, opros, opros, Aessy. I thought..." Valerian kicked at something in the snow, his fists balled at his sides, before inching closer to a cliff. He was standing at the edge of the quarry, looking down.

"Stop apologizing and get help!"

"Can you hold on if I leave? Are you... Are you gonna fall?"

"Just *go* already!" Aesylt cried. Panic girdled her shaky voice.

Valerian staggered back a few steps. He tugged at the patchy fur on his mask until it slipped away and disappeared in the snow.

"Valerian, what *happened*?" Rahn demanded, pulling up beside him. He started toward the edge, but Valerian tugged him back.

"Careful, man, unless you want to join her." Valerian drew an unsteady breath. "Wait, Scholar *Tindahl*?"

Rahn shed his own mask and the ridiculous furry overdress, wrenching them to the side. "Speak. Quickly and clearly."

"I, ah..." Valerian turned and revealed his flushed, sweaty face. "I just wanted to scare her. I told her there was a wulf, but... fuck."

"And?" Rahn asked, both eyes on the edge of the quarry.

Val shook his head. "There was no wulf."

Rahn inhaled a bracing breath. "I'm asking what happened to *her*."

"I didn't realize she was so close." Valerian scrunched his face with a tight roar. "She's... Go look, but be careful."

Rahn glared at him before inching toward the cliff. Even had Valerian explained that Aesylt was caught on the upper bows of a tall pine, it wouldn't have prepared him for the sight of her arms spread around the broad trunk, both feet splayed across different branches.

"Aesylt, it's Scholar Tindahl."

"Scholar?" She was breathless.

"I realize this is a strange question, under the circumstances, but are you all right?"

She nodded against the bark, then shook her head. Her wig had fallen off at some point, and her pale blonde hair was a sweaty, matted mess.

"Are you injured?"

"Tak. I mean, yes. My ankle, and... I don't know how long I can hold on. Tell that ill-born to close his jaw and get help already!"

"Val," Rahn said with a swat of his hand. He couldn't even look at the boy. It was the same story, all the time. Val was always getting her into trouble. "Barynov!"

"I don't want to leave her." The boy had gone pale. "You go."

I don't know how long I can hold on. "Are you prepared to climb this tree and help her?"

Val laughed without humor. "*How*?"

Rahn couldn't remember ever having even *seen* a tree beyond books until a year ago, when he'd left Duncarrow for the kingdom, but it took only a second of deliberation before he was sliding down the treacherous embankment, maneuvering snow and plant roots to slow his fall. He hit the bark with a thud, but Aesylt's scared voice asking if *he* was all right, when she was the one dangling from a treetop, was all the courage he needed to act.

Hazarding a quick glance upward, he assessed his path. The conifer reached the bottom of the quarry, but Aesylt had fallen into the uppermost boughs, a good twenty feet up from where he'd landed. Twenty feet. Just over three times his own height.

I can do this.

He reached for the branch nearest him and gave it a sound tug, ensuring it could hold his weight. With a disgusted glance back up at Valerian, he dug his boot into the rough bark and swung up.

"*Go*," he commanded with a grunt. "Valerian Barynov, move your legs and go! Find Drazhan. Find anyone."

"You aren't really going to climb that..."

"Go!"

Rahn paused only long enough to confirm the crunching of snow signaling the boy's departure, then reached for the next branch.

"Scholar?"

"Don't worry about me, Aesylt. Just focus on breathing and holding on."

"My arms are shaking. I can't... I can't see anything. I'm afraid I'll fall if I look for a better place."

"I'll find one for both of us. Just—" Rahn grunted when his hand slipped from a branch. Blood beaded along his palm. There wasn't time to do a thing about it, not with the way the confidence in her voice slipped with every word. "Why don't you tell me about the stars?"

"The stars?" Aesylt sniffled. His heart shattered at his bursting-with-life researcher sounding so small.

Rahn gripped another branch and hoisted himself higher. "When we started studying astronomy, you told me the stars were the Ancestors of the Vjestik. The eternities of your people." He gathered his breath and resumed climbing. He'd never in his life done anything so reckless, but he couldn't remember a time he'd ever been so scared.

That wasn't true. He could remember, if he were ever brave enough.

"It's just a thing we say..." Aesylt whimpered. "I feel so foolish. It was a damn *chase*. I should have been ready for it."

"*He* shouldn't have scared you like that." Rahn breathed deep. *Almost there.* "And Valerian wasn't your wulf, Aesylt. I was."

She said nothing for several long seconds. He feared she'd lost consciousness, but then she finally spoke. "Tasmin said you weren't going to come tonight."

"I wasn't." Rahn gritted his jaw, ignoring the tremors taking over his sore arms. Once he reached her, what then? Climbing up was one thing, but climbing down? *Doesn't matter. She won't be alone.*

"What changed your mind?" Her voice was louder, clearer.

You. "I'm a guest of your family. It would have been disrespectful to decline a second year in a row."

Her laugh was idyllic, crystalline, reminding him of the ice shimmering off the branches when the wind blew. It sounded nothing like the fear bloating in her voice. "*Drazhan* doesn't even want to do this anymore."

Rahn tried to remember how much time had passed since Val had left for help. Regardless, they'd be waiting a while. He couldn't fathom how the rescuers would get them down safely. Climbing down themselves would introduce the same risk he was hoping to avoid by joining her. *Keep her talking.* "No?"

"He's never cared about tradition. He's only doing what the people want." She paused, then said, "But I understand. For some, this is an important night. All the damsels who evade their wulves get a feast, paid for from the village's thin coffers. The wulves who catch theirs get one as well. Do you know how long it's been since *any* of us have had a proper feast?"

The last time he'd had one had been on Duncarrow, so he could imagine. The Wynters only lived slightly better than the rest of the Vjestik, but they lived half as well as their counterparts across the Northerlands. "Tradition shapes cultures. Their memories. Their hopes. This one also fills bellies, and that might be a better reason than any." Rahn didn't have to agree with them to understand the appeal. He recalled how giddy and excited Aesylt had been in the costume room. "I'm sorry this night hasn't gone the way you'd hoped."

"Who says it hasn't?"

Was that mischief in her voice? Couldn't be. She was holding onto a damned tree for dear life. "Enjoying yourself up there?"

"You won't believe the view, Scholar."

Rahn chuckled to himself.

"I had a pet squirrel once. I thought he was my pet anyway, because he kept coming back, following me into the keep. Not very smart, I thought, because Vjestik eat squirrels, aye? Further south, they'd turn their nose up at such a meager ration, but we take what we can get. Anyway, when he'd come to my bedchamber, he'd sleep right on the stones in front of the hearth. My oldest brother, Hraz, the one who... Well, he named the thing Squish and agreed not to tell the kitchens about my new little friend. Said he was small enough that if he got caught under the wrong boot though…" She made a *splat* sound. "But I liked the name. The way it sounded. Squish the Squirrel. He was smart for a rodent and a right good climber. Best I ever saw. Resourceful little creature, he was. *He'd* know how to get down."

"Squish," Rahn mused aloud. "Resourceful, smart. Sounds like someone I know."

Aesylt snorted. "I notice you didn't include the part about being a right good climber."

He grinned to himself. "Have I ever lied to you?"

Her laugh gave him the last bit of vigor needed to reach for another branch and heave himself up. He strained and squirmed up onto a thick blanket of needles, carefully slithering on his belly, and huffed out a triumphant sigh.

Aesylt whistled. "I'm impressed. Did *not* figure you for a tree climber, Scholar Tindahl."

"A reasonable assertion, given this is the first one I've ever climbed," he answered, winded from a combination of exertion and shock, and scooted himself closer to where she was gripping the trunk. "And hopefully the last." He made a conscious effort not to look down as he surveyed the situation. Behind her was a cluster of thick arms they could both sit on without fear of them breaking, but now that he was close to her, he could see her bantering had been a cover for pure terror. Her shoulders were pinched and trembly, her knuckles bone white from her bloodied fingers digging into the bark. He'd need to proceed carefully. "I want you to let go, one arm at a time, and slowly turn toward me."

Her laugh was shaky, forced. "You must be joking."

"Come on, Aesylt. I have a better sense of humor than that." He waited for a giggle or some sign she was easing, but all he got was a garbled sigh. "You can let go. I have you."

"What does that mean, have me? Could you perhaps elaborate, offer specifics? Run through your personal definition of this particular combination of words?" Aesylt turned her face to the side but then snapped her forehead back toward the tree.

"It means there's plenty of room for you to move around here without falling. You told me once you liked to climb trees."

"When I was eight!"

Rahn eased himself onto the cluster of branches, working to position himself behind her. "How high did you climb?"

"Never this damned high." She snorted. "I was adventurous, but I didn't have a death wish. Then..." She exhaled and rolled her head along the bark. "Val... He was always the one who wanted to climb in the first place, the one who pushed me to go as high as... but he never could do it himself. He always gave up halfway and watched me finish, cheering like it hadn't been his stupid idea to begin with."

"Maybe he believed in you that much," Rahn replied, a far more charitable assessment than the boy deserved. But he was trying to keep her calm, not get her more riled up.

"Always getting me into trouble. Even now." She squeezed tighter. "I'm not... I wish... I rarely get this scared, Scholar. About anything."

"I know."

Aesylt was fearless in a way he couldn't fathom being. It had been his first impression of her, and a lasting one.

"But as far as fears go, dangling from the top of a very tall tree isn't one to be ashamed of. Even Val knew it. It's why he froze."

"He's... doesn't matter." Aesylt angled her head sideways. "You're right behind me, aren't you?"

"I am." Rahn braced one hand on the trunk to show her.

"You're insane, Scholar. Unreservedly mad."

"I wasn't leaving you up here alone, Aesylt. Not for a moment longer than I had to."

"Why?" Another forced laugh escaped her. "No reason to risk your life for mine."

There was no answer he could give that would make sense to her, or even to himself. He could say he was doing the right thing, the only thing, but in truth, he hadn't thought about it at all. There'd been no chance of him leaving her up there alone. "Do you trust me?"

"The only time people ever ask that is when they're about to suggest something no one in their right mind would ever agree to," Aesylt quipped. Her spread arms shook and one hand lost purchase, causing her to yelp.

"Reasonable," Rahn said with a light laugh. "But I wouldn't ask if I didn't know everything was going to be all right. If you can't make yourself turn, then I'm going to slide my arms around your waist and peel you away slowly. Do you understand?"

Aesylt shook her head wildly.

"I promise you won't fall."

"I thought you never lied to me?"

Rahn moved one hand to her lower back. "I am *right* here, Aesylt. There's enough room for us to turn fully around, even to lie down, if you were motivated enough. Let go."

"I can't." Her voice quaked again. "Think less of me if you want, but I can't do it."

Rahn made a split-second decision. He wrapped both hands around her waist and tugged. With a scream, she went tumbling into his arms, but he pressed her close to his chest with a weighty exhale, whispering the reassurances she needed. "You're fine. I'm here. You're fine."

Aesylt shook in his arms, sobbing, but her response was so short-lived, he wondered if he'd imagined it. She peeled back. Her startled gaze darted back and forth, drinking in their surroundings. "Wow. I..." Her eyes rolled back, so he quickly reached for her shoulders and guided her back against his chest. She slid lower, her head falling into his lap as she struggled to breathe.

"All right, just..." Rahn's hands danced over her arm, unsure whether to prop her back up or let her lay across his legs. If Drazhan saw, he'd no doubt think he was being untoward with his little sister, but Drazhan wasn't there. No one was. Rahn wouldn't punish Aesylt for her vulnerability, no matter how confusing it felt.

"I'm fine," she said softly. She curled her legs up toward her arms, wiggling in his lap. "Opros. Opros."

"There's nothing to be sorry for." Rahn's hand landed on her arm. He traced it along its length, the way someone, in another life, used to do for him. She slowly calmed. "You're safe. Help is coming."

Aesylt laughed, sniffling. "Don't count on it. Val probably ran home."

"He cares about you. He wouldn't do that." The words grated, but they were true. Val was a lot of things—brash, selfish, wild—but he loved Aesylt. If he hadn't been chosen for that year's Vuk od Varem, the boy's father might have eventually worn Drazhan down about a proper betrothal.

"Maybe," Aesylt replied, conceding. "But it's not Valerian Barynov comforting me at the top of a giant tree, is it?"

Rahn grinned to himself. "If I'd stopped to think about what I was doing, it wouldn't be Adrahn Tindahl up here coddling you either."

"Shocking behavior from Witchwood Cross's foremost scholar, I must say."

"Has your esteem of me been damaged?"

"No, I rather think it's gone up after your foolhearted climb." Aesylt turned her head upward at him and smiled. Her crystal-blue eyes sparkled with old tears. "Thank you, Rahn."

Everything within him skidded to a halt. His pulse. His breath. His resolve. Rahn. Not duke. Not scholar. "Of course." He swallowed and tried again when his voice broke. "Of course, Aesylt."

She rolled her face back toward his leg and breathed deep. "I suppose Drazhan will be relieved to find my honor is still unblemished. All the real action is happening in the forest. Not much I can get up to at the top of a tree."

"Was it ever in question?"

"I *wish,*" she said, and they both laughed. "You know how impossible he is."

"He'll relent one day," Rahn said, shocked at how hard the words were to say, to hear. "He wants you to be happy."

"I am happy," she said. She drew her hands up and propped them under her head. "I'm happy with you, in the library. I'm happy to be learning something new every day, to be spreading the knowledge to others. There's just something missing is all, a piece of me I'm bursting to share with more than just Draz and Imryll. To be close to someone..." She shook her head. "Oof, forgive me. You didn't climb a tree in the dark to hear me whine."

A knot formed in his chest at how familiar, how aching her confession was. To be close to someone... He'd given up on that dream a long time ago. King Carrow had offered him several brides, perfectly wonderful women Rahn had known all or most of his life, who would have made perfectly wonderful wives. But none of them *saw* him. They smiled patiently at his passion for learning but never shared it. They warmed his bed but never his heart. Even Teleria, who hadn't been much older than him when she'd taken him in as a young orphaned duke and had mentored him, loved him but didn't fully understand him. "It's a privilege to listen to you whine."

She removed her hands from under her face and swatted his knee. "You think I don't know when someone is messing with me?"

"I wouldn't presume anything to get past you," Rahn said and squeezed her arm. "It never does."

He felt her smile form against his thigh. "I don't know what I expected from this evening, but I can say with certainty, I never would have imagined *this*."

Rahn chuckled. "Nor I."

"But you know, Scholar? There's no one I'd rather be stuck up a tree with."

"Not Nik or Val?"

"Val *ran*." She shifted. "Nik... He wouldn't have run, but he's not built for this kind of excitement either."

Aesylt's two closest friends could not be more different men, in or outside of the library. But Rahn would take sensitive, thoughtful Niklaus over hothead Valerian any day. "And we are?"

"We're here, aren't we?" She leaned her head upward to look at him. "You were right. This is fine." Her eyes closed. "I might just..." Her words faded, her shock becoming a crash.

Rahn traced his hand once more along her arm, eyes pointed at the forest and the gentle silence blanketed by an eerie veil of fresh snow. A few rogue flakes landed on them through the gap in the bows, restoring peace to his harried thoughts. "Rest, Squish. I have you."

You don't bother trying to figure out who your wulf is. You don't care because he will not catch you, right? Run. Run hard and far. You know these forests better than most, and you'll know where to hide until the time runs down.

It's not like it used to be, Draz. No one has to marry the wulf who catches them.

But you'd be alone with him, and there will be no one to... look after you. None except yourself.

And I cannot look after myself? Have I not, for most of my life?

Aesylt's consciousness danced between past and present, the boundaries so distorted, she couldn't anchor herself to any point in time.

She was both at the top of a tree and in Fanghelm Keep.

With Rahn. With Drazhan. With Tasmin.

She was accustomed to living between realities, being the only individual in the Cross to have the curse of starwalking. But this was not that.

You are as inimitable as a star in our interminable sky. Rahn's words, but not from that night. He'd said them months ago, before the others had joined in their library endeavors. When it had only been the two of them—the duke and his eager disciple—and their thirst for mining and sharing knowledge.

Aesylt moaned and twisted. A warm hand stayed her from shifting into danger.

Draz didn't want me to go, but he's worried about the unrest if he exempts his own sister.

There's already unrest. Tasmin.

More of it then.

She strained to recall the conversation from earlier that day, when she'd gleefully bedecked herself in costume, secretly hoping to be caught. She and Tasmin had been talking about the rising pressure from some families to put an end to the long-standing Vuk od Varem, which had always been controversial, from the very first season the Vjestik had settled into the village, centuries past. They were tired of losing their sons to wulves every year, just for the chance to safely hunt the forests for a season. It had been almost two hundred years since the accord with the wulves had been made, and it was time for a new one, a new way, they said. Drazhan's own son, Aleksy, would probably one day face a wulf, and the odds were no more in his favor than any who had come before—even if Drazhan himself had bested the wulf when it had been his season.

Aesylt had no intention of having children of her own, because she refused to offer even more to such a taking forest.

Her breath hitched.

Val.

Val was this year's chosen son.

The one she prayed and prayed would buck the overwhelming odds and win… but was more likely to lose, like most sons of the Cross.

No matter how heroic the sacrifice, Drazhan could never know Valerian was the reason his little sister was stuck in the bows of a towering timber in the middle of the night, or he'd have his testicles for breakfast.

Soft snow dusted her face. She swatted her cheeks, but a soothing voice told her to relax, that everything was fine.

Scholar Tindahl.

Could it be that he was *really* at the top of a pine tree with her?

Surely she was dreaming.

If your wulf catches you, it won't matter if he does nothing, Aesylt. Everyone will assume he's done whatever he wants. And then I'll have to kill him, right? So don't get caught.

Later, Tasmin had accused her of wanting to get caught. She wasn't wrong, but it wasn't for the reason her friend supposed. The past decade Aesylt had thrown herself into crisis after crisis, hoping to feel *something*.

Rahn. Duke Rahn Tindahl was the one cradling her in his arms. The scholar who had reignited her life when he'd come to Witchwood Cross—the man who had said she was inimitable as the stars in their interminable sky.

I know how these traditions must seem to you, Scholar, coming from royalty as you do. Like we're savages.

Rahn had set down the quill, removed his spectacles, and met her eyes. He always gave her his full attention. *I don't think you're savages.*

Then you'll come?

I have so much work to do. But I promise to try, Aesylt.

She'd started the chase so full of excitement. There'd only been the briefest hesitation at the start, when the horn had blasted. Her wulf had placed a hand—Rahn's hand, though she hadn't known it then—between her shoulders to stir her from her daze, and she'd bolted, ready for anything the night had to offer.

Ready for the freedom Drazhan seemed determined for her never to have.

The last clear memory she had before losing her footing was of the foothills of the Northern Range, how they colored the tops of the trees like one continuous painting, stretching higher until they joined with Icebolt Mountain in the Northeast. Behind her, Fanghelm Keep had loomed high on the cloudy horizon, but she'd been looking ahead, not back. If she'd been looking *sideways,* she wouldn't be stuck in a tree.

In the distance, a horn sounded.

The Dyvareh was officially over.

"When we don't return, they'll come looking," Rahn said, more to reassure himself, it seemed. Had he really climbed a *tree* to save her? The tenderhearted, studious duke who had come to Witchwood Cross to learn and teach, and had given her purpose?

She should tell him her ankle was broken. It had happened when she'd landed, and if she hadn't managed to catch hold of a firm branch on her way down, she'd have broken everything else too. Even the thought of putting weight on her foot sent her stomach churning. She was too tired to shift into the celestial realm and heal herself—and too scared the return might somehow create instability in their little haven of branches—so she'd have to wait to address it. Once she was safe, she'd have to let the vedhmas heal it up for her, or Drazhan would know she was still starwalking when she'd promised not to.

For all Rahn Tindahl had taught her, she knew so little about him. He was one of the handful of people in the kingdom who had come from Ilynglass, the mythical land beyond their kingdom no one had ever been capable of traveling to. His family had perished in the same shipwrecks that had eradicated most of the Duncarrow refugees, and he, only a little boy, had been taken in by Duchess Teleria Farrestell, a young widow who had lost her husband and infant in the same disaster. The king and his court hadn't known what to do with the child duke, the sole heir to House Tindahl, so they'd given him the task of teaching the children born on Duncarrow.

Whatever had happened over the next two decades was a mystery. Even *why* he'd left the royal isle was unclear, only that he'd shown up in the Cross one day, unannounced, and decided to stay.

He never called himself a teacher in their small learning cohort, and he disliked the term *student* for his research assistants. *We're all equals in this endeavor*, he would say, though everyone but him seemed to know how untrue it was.

Rahn Tindahl was a god among men, even if he didn't know it.

"A god," she muttered, rolling her face along the warmth of—

Aesylt froze when her mouth connected with something thick and solid.

Oh, for the love of the Ancestors.

The poor man was rock hard.

Rahn gently adjusted her toward his knee without a word.

"Aesylt," he said softly. He brushed her hair from her eyes and said it again. "Listen."

What she needed to do was lift her head, move away, and give them both some dignity, but she was too horrified to do more than nod against his trousers.

"I hear someone." Rahn's voice sounded dense, almost choked. "Several someones." He adjusted forward, straining. "Oh, thank the gods. They brought ropes and ladders. You see?"

Aesylt dragged herself up with a tight, inward cringe. She'd never be able to look the man in the eyes again after rutting around in his crotch, delirium or no. And what would Drazhan think? He might have been joking about having a chastity belt forged for her, but his next stop would be the foundry if he knew she'd had the scholar's appendage pressed against her mouth, clothed or no.

"How..." She squinted at the large group moving their way. If she focused on the rescue, perhaps she could distract herself from the horror of what she'd carelessly done, which was somehow even more crushing than the throbbing pain in her ankle or the skinned flesh of her palms. "They're not going to pull the tree down with the ropes..."

Rahn shook his head straight ahead. "Do you remember what you told me when I asked you what you wanted to achieve in the cohort?"

The question surprised her enough to make her do the last thing she wanted to do, turn toward him. "What?"

His cheeks were rosy from the cold, softening his smile. A bang of his dark, wavy hair dipped over one eye. "You said you would take any adventure, in whatever form offered."

"Well, *yes*, but..." She laughed and gestured around. The way his grin persisted made her realize he was trying to show her it was all right, that nothing had happened that couldn't be forgotten when they stepped through the library doors tomorrow, ready to embrace the truths of the world.

How she prayed it was true.

Rahn reached for one of her wrists and angled her palm upward with a tight frown. "Gods. Let me wrap this before we do anything else—"

Drazhan's booming voice cut through the quiet forest. "Aesylt? Can you hear me? Rahn?"

"We're here!" Her voice cracked with her scream. She pulled her hands back in case her brother could see. "We're here, Draz!"

"Oh, glory be to the fucking Ancestors." Whatever he said next seemed to be for the men with him. Then he yelled, "Don't move. We're coming up."

Aesylt shook her head. "If we all get stuck up here..."

"We won't, cub. Sit still, and it will be over soon."

She huffed a hard breath.

Rahn leaned close, enough for his breath to send a fresh chill ripping through her, and whispered, "When they ask you if your wulf caught you, what will you say?"

Aesylt's heart almost burst through her chest. The way he'd said it, roguish and playful, was far from the way she felt it. It wasn't the first fluttery pull she'd felt toward her mentor, a man a decade her senior, but all she'd had to do before was remind herself she was with him to learn and enrich herself, not act like a lovestruck maiden.

The same reminder now only made her pulse shoot to the same stars he'd tried to distract her with.

"Aesylt?"

“I don’t know.” Her attention was torn between Rahn awaiting her response and the melee of men in the snow below. “What do you think I should say? You scaled a mighty tree for me, but is it the same thing?”

“I don’t think anyone could ever really catch you, Aesylt, any more than a man could catch a cloud in his hands.”

You are as inimitable as the stars in our interminable sky.

Aesylt let his words be the blanket that kept her warm and safe as she waited for their rescue.

TWO
ORGIASTIC DEN OF HEDONISM

Rahn strode into the Fanghelm library just past noontide two days after the Dyvareh. Jasika and Anton were already seated at the round table near the row of windows, sipping tea in silence. He didn't see Imryll, which was unexpected, as she was usually the first to arrive to a council session.

They'd begun their tradition of weekly meetings at Imryll's Book of All Things Society in the village, but over the intervening months, student attendance at Book had increased enough that the council had had to repurpose their assembly room into another research laboratory. Moving their sessions to the Wynter keep, Fanghelm, had been posed as a temporary measure, but Imryll had also been under the weather as of late, and though she'd made no announcement, he suspected she was again with child.

"Stewardess. Dobryzen," Anton said, and he and Jasika both shifted to their feet in deference. Rahn turned to see Imryll enter, fluster dotting her cheeks and an empty child sling dangling off one shoulder.

"Dobryzen." Jasika echoed his greeting.

"Forgive my tardiness, friends," she declared in a rush, storming across the stone floor with a strained smile. "Aleksy is still recovering from a brief illness, and he'll only calm for me or his father."

"We can meet another time, Imryll," Anton said as he settled back into his seat.

"If we delayed a meeting anytime one of our children was ill, we'd never meet, would we?" she said pleasantly, peeling the sling away and setting it on a bench. Her eyes fluttered fleetingly closed, then opened as she inhaled a slow breath.

Rahn escorted her to the table, reading the sidelong look she gave him. It was more than exhaustion. She'd come with something to say, something that couldn't wait.

"Are you all right?" he asked, loud enough only for the two of them. He'd known Imryll her whole life. He'd been her teacher on Duncarrow, the royal isle. The *only* teacher on Duncarrow. The late King Carrow hadn't cared a whit if the children learned anything; he'd actually preferred they knew as little as possible.

"You and I should speak after," she muttered from the corner of her mouth. "Before Drazhan calls you in."

"Calls me in?"

"About Aes. And the Dyvareh." Imryll's smile broadened as they approached the table. She took her usual place, and Rahn, still pondering her words, took his. "Let's do a full report and then I have another matter to discuss. Anton? Would you like to start?"

Anton cleared his throat and sifted through a stack of documents. "My cohort has completed their final notes on balms and will have the full package for submission within the week. We've also begun the pre-work for the arduous task of classifying the beasts of the Northerlands. It's a fairly comprehensive list, bigger than we originally anticipated when we sent our time estimate, so I predict this will take us the next three seasons to complete, not two, especially since many are hibernators. Unless we expand the cohort again, of course. Depending on how thorough we want to go with the notes, we may even want to transition this one to an ongoing topic rather than a closed-ended one."

Imryll nodded. Her gaze was fixed on the wall of windows and the snowy valley beyond. "We knew this would be a sizable area of focus, but this is important work. Take the time you need. We'll either add a fourth cohort to stay ahead of schedule, or we'll adjust our expectations on the timeline. I'd like us to get started before we propose making it an ongoing subject, so we have figures to support the request."

Anton nodded in gratitude. "I was hoping you'd say as much."

"Good work on balms, Anton. I'm excited to see what you do with beasts." Imryll turned to Jasika. "Jas?"

Jasika tapped her fingers along the edge of the table. "We still only have the three of us, Imryll, so we're working as fast as we can to wrap up coastal patterns."

"How much longer?"

"Two, three weeks?"

Imryll nodded. "That'll be fine."

Jasika sighed through her teeth. "But... After that, we're approaching a sensitive topic that I'm uncertain how to... how to complete without corrupting our researchers."

Rahn quirked a brow.

"I'd like your guidance on how to proceed."

Imryll lifted a hand. "Remind me."

"Coitus."

Anton snickered into his fingers.

"Coitus. Right." Imryll nodded in thought, her eyes turned to the side. "We knew we'd have to sort this one eventually. How long is the curricula again?"

"*Extensively* long." Jasika's round cheeks darkened in a flush.

Anton did nothing to hide his growing amusement, releasing a side-of-mouth snicker that drew a scowl from her.

"I don't suppose you've reviewed it?"

"I haven't had the opportunity with everything going on down at Book these days," Imryll said. "Whatever the prospectus, we'll make it work. The Reliquary may not want to play nice with us, but our agreement to follow their lead was nonnegotiable if we want their support."

"But it's not a reasonable prospectus, Imryll. By *any* standard."

"Forgive me, you'll have to speak plainly, since I haven't read through the notes yet. What's the concern?"

Anton raised a finger. "I have no concerns tackling coitus."

Jasika glared at him.

"Don't you remember when my cohort had anatomy?" Rahn asked.

She said nothing.

"The Reliquary made us go through all those preposterous exercises about using our own bodies for diagram purposes, which we did, grudgingly, amid no shortage of anxious giggles, and after all the awkwardness of that, they had the audacity to accuse us of falsifying the diagrams and sent us an 'official' warning. They're having a go at us again. That's all." Rahn almost laughed, but the sick expression on Jasika's face stayed him.

"Rahn, respectfully, their warning almost got us kicked out of our own program. We cannot afford another one, and you know it. And you have not seen this curricula. It's not just a bunch of silly diagrams. It is almost entirely..." Jasika wedged her tongue between her teeth and groaned. "Participatory in nature."

"Participatory, you mean..." Imryll shifted in her seat. One hand gripped the seat of her chair so hard, it was bone white.

"It means in order for any report we submit to meet the burdened requirement of official research, there must be *actual* experiments run. Do you... Must I say it?"

Imryll's relieved laugh cut through the room. "Jasika, gods, it doesn't mean *you* have to perform the experiments. There are dozens of households in the Cross. Select a few randomly, give them predefined questions to answer, interview them a few times..."

"Well, I thought so as well, but when I wrote for clarification—"

"Agh, we never write for clarification!" Anton interjected, shaking his head.

Eyes narrowed, Jasika finished. "When I wrote for clarification, they stated that while we are expected to collect practical observations from citizens as well, and that the Reliquary has in fact sent this curricula to others in the realm for a variety of responses, the cohort itself must be part of the experiments in order to validate any claim made regarding the body's physical and emotional response to the various stimuli they've outlined. Without the official cohort's validation of these actions and reactions, the Reliquary won't accept our research as complete. We cannot get around this rule by increasing our cohort artificially for this topic. They have the names of all our researchers. I have the letter, Imryll. I don't think this is a question of misinterpretation on my part. Aside from the obvious concerns here, my cohort is all young women."

"Sexy," Anton muttered.

Jasika flung a hand toward him in the air. "Muala," she hissed, which Rahn took to be the word for *mule* in Vjestikaan.

"I used to think the Reliquary sent us the topics they had no desire to explore themselves, but if so, this was definitely an oversight." Anton chuckled, tracing a hand down his thick beard. "You can't convince me that cabal of repressed scholars wouldn't jump at this one if they could."

"This is a test," Rahn said slowly, sighing. The Reliquary was intentionally making it hard, trying to push them until they surrendered and abandoned their own idea, their own work. The Reliquary had strong-armed its way into the project and taken it over, relegating Witchwood Cross to an annoyance to be dealt with. "They think they've backed us into a corner with this one. We just need to be creative enough to find a way out of it."

Imryll's face pulled into a frown. She glanced at Rahn. He'd been the first to offer aid and embrace her vision, and their dynamic was more like a partnership. Jasika Voronov had come next, and not long after, Anton Petrovash. Their addition had meant more resources, more legitimacy, but neither was as feverish about the success of their endeavor as Rahn and Imryll were.

"Rahn, where are you with your cohort?" Imryll asked.

"We're only partway through astronomy," he said. "The observatory is expected to be ready in springtide and then we'll need another season or two to complete the remaining prospectus. But as we're held up until we can do more intensive study, we planned to take a detour into our next subject: atheism."

"Well, you won't find many atheists in Witchwood Cross," Imryll said wryly. "You said we just need to be creative, right? Perhaps your cohort can handle coitus until the observatory is built?"

Rahn's words caught in his throat. A deep heat seized him from head to toe as all three watched him in anticipation of his response.

"It's clearly a test, as you said. They're having one on with us," Anton said, still laughing.

Imryll shook her head at the table. "We *all* know what happens if we tell them we cannot handle one of their assignments. They never took us seriously to begin with, and they're *looking* for a reason to discredit our work and become the sole claimants. Work *we* started."

Rahn spun sideways to face her as the blood rushed away from his face, plummeting toward the floor. He'd backed himself into his own corner. "Imryll, I agree with what you're saying—"

"You're a clever man, who will find another way that doesn't break the Reliquary's very clear guidelines on research but also does not put any of our young academics in vulnerable and compromising positions." She exhaled a long breath. "I trust you to figure it out."

Rahn said no more. Imryll rarely ruled with authority, but when she did, her decision was not to be mistaken for an invitation to debate.

"Jas, your cohort will continue their study of coastal patterns for now and then move on to your next one, whatever came after coitus. Conifers, was it? Anton, keep all your focus on the classification efforts for beasts, and when you have time, draft a proposal for shifting the topic to continuous research, and I'll run it by the Reliquary. Rahn, you'll put a pause on astronomy until the observatory is ready for use and focus on solving this coitus dilemma until that time. Everyone in agreement?"

Anton snickered as he nodded. Jasika sighed, muttering her gratitude.

Rahn smiled tightly and prepared for the meeting's end, but Imryll breathed deep, readying to say something else.

"It pains me to bring this up, but I feel we must approach the upcoming Vuk od Varem with hope but pragmatism." She pulled both hands onto the table, folding them. "Valerian Barynov is one of our academics. There is a very real possibility he will enter the forest a week from now and never return to us."

"Imryll, we don't talk like that about our sons when they are chosen," Jasika said in a low, cautious rush. She and her wife, Brita, had adopted only daughters for a reason. "We know what the odds are, but we don't surrender our hope before we have reason to."

"Keep your hope, if it brings you comfort," Imryll said. "But we are women and men of science and learning. Val will have to defeat a wulf with nothing but his wits and a measly dagger."

"Your own husband won the Vuk od Varem when it was his turn," Anton replied.

"And his experience was not typical, was it?" Imryll's mouth twitched. "Drazhan may be more beast than man."

"Won't argue that," Jasika said. "But we *need* this springtide. The imports on meat are prohibitive for most of the villagers. The forests south of us have been sparse of game ever since the disease spread through the elk-kind population there. And after last year's crop rot, illness is on the rise."

"A matter for my husband and his counselors," Imryll replied curtly. "As for us, we are realists. If Val does not return, we need to consider who might replace him." She tapped the table and stood. "We don't have to know the answer today. You may think my broaching this, in the manner I chose, is heartless, but if it were up to me, we'd never lose another son to this tradition. Keeping our funding and interest from the Reliquary is my concern. So have a think on it, and when the Season of the Wulf is behind us, we'll know our direction, one way or another."

Rahn still didn't understand the traditions of the Vjestik. The Vuk od Varem was an agreement Drazhan's ancestor had made with the king of the Icebolt wulves many years ago, when the nomadic Vjestik had fled to the far north for a new settlement. The wulves were not keen to give up their safe roam of the forest so that men could hunt, but to avoid a war, they came to a compromise. Once a year, a son of man and a son of wulf would have a week in the forest to decide who the land belonged to for the hunting season. It was simple: whoever lived, won, but to win, the other must die. The wulves rarely lost, and even when the men prevailed, they could never hunt enough to make up for the dry years ahead. As a result, most families spent their gold on the heavily taxed imported meats from Wulfsgate and farther south, and they had little left for anything else. Many Vjestik were tired of losing their beloved sons and believed it was time to challenge the wulves once and for all. Others feared such an act would spell the end of their people.

Rahn waited for Jasika and Anton to leave before retaking his seat. "Has something happened?"

Imryll sighed and squished her face in mild exasperation. "Rahn, my husband is a stubborn, stubborn man. He asked me to thank you for what you did for Aesylt, and to make clear the debt he owes you for keeping her safe until help arrived. If you had not... We don't even want to consider what might have happened. Because of you and the vedhmas, she will be perfectly fine. And as you and I know, if he were fully aware of how she ended up in that tree, Aesylt would never see her friend again, so we'll protect the small white lie, for her sake." She sighed, her mouth quirked into a sardonic grin. "Now, after lavishing you with praise, I'm to remind you his sister is unmarried and far too young for you."

Rahn exhaled a stilted laugh. "Of course he said that."

"I don't need to tell you how ridiculous he is about her. He said even Val, her oldest friend, wouldn't climb the tree to save her, so you must have strong loyalty to Aesylt to put your own life in danger," Imryll said. "But... Aes thinks the world of you. You know that?"

He lowered his head, his thoughts reluctantly returning to the hour or so Aesylt had spent sleeping in his lap as he'd held her to protect her warmth. "I did only what either of you would have done for her. For anyone."

"Of course." Imryll nodded. "Of course, but just... Be cautious, is all I wanted to say. I don't know where the man got it into his head that you've become sweet on her, or how he turned your bravery into something else. I'm not surprised she looks up to you. I always have." She smiled and reached a hand toward him. He took it, and they both squeezed before letting go. "But if you sense there's more than admiration at play, do yourself and her a great favor and quash it."

"You needn't worry." Dread crept across his bones. Nothing she'd said should have been alarming, but he felt very much alarmed. He hadn't even been to see Aesylt since the vedhmas had tended her wounds, but he should have. He wanted to, and maybe that was the problem. "If anything, Imryll, I've been harder on her than the others."

Imryll cocked her head, watching him. "Why?"

"She reminds me a little of you." He chuckled to himself before growing serious. "She has so much potential, and people don't reach their potential if they're not challenged. I, myself, am still chasing mine."

Imryll traced her finger along the table. "I could see her being another you in a few years." She offered him a sleepy smile. "Do you suppose you'll take a bride someday?"

Rahn whistled. It wasn't that he hadn't thought of it. He and Teleria had even thrown around the advantage of a union between them. But it would be a matter of practicality, nothing more. He'd not been in love, and he wouldn't know it beyond words on a page. "Marriage is the last distraction on my mind at present."

"Hmm." Imryll pushed back, and he did the same. "Go see Aesylt. She's asked about you. Oh, and... about the research. You know I made that decision because I trust you'll find a way to work with *and* around the Reliquary's intemperate guidelines?"

"I know why you did it," he said as he followed her to the door. "And it's going to keep me up a fair number of nights trying to figure out a way around it without disqualifying us from inclusion."

Imryll reached for the door but hesitated before opening it. "Do you remember telling me I was too clever for my own good?"

Laughing, Rahn shook his head at the floor. "I don't recall saying it, but it's true."

She gave him a quick, tight smile. "I didn't inherit that from my selfish parents. I learned it from the man who was like an older brother to me. The man who showed me the path to curiosity. Rahn, what we're doing here... It *matters.*"

"I know." He nodded solemnly. "I believe in it just as much."

"There exists no true compendium of knowledge in this kingdom. Not one. Scattered scrolls and documents, patchy histories. That's all. That is *all* the people of this realm have to guide their learning. The Reliquary wants to steal our idea for *The Book of All Things* and claim it as their own. They have more money and resources than we ever will here in the Cross. The crown is funneling gold their way, fast enough to feel suspicious. None of that I have any control over, so I try not to let it wound me too deep. But I will be *damned* if I let them ice us out altogether." She clamped a hand atop his shoulder. "Find a way."

Rahn felt the same about their ambitious endeavor, which half of the village thought was a silly waste of time and the other was curious but cautious toward. The Vjestik had their own history keepers, the kyschun, who, using the magic of the Ancestors, stored their people's histories in their minds to preserve across the generations. Each society had their own way of holding onto the past, he supposed, but nearly all of it was limited to selected words passed down lines. Crafting a true compendium classifying every beast, plant, phenomena, disease, geography, peoples, and everything else that made up their thriving world had been his passion since he was a boy, and that Imryll had run with it, inviting him in, was a dream come to life. Sharing the passion with other eager researchers was leaving his heart full and happy.

He would find a way because he refused to give up. "I will."

Aesylt was itching to get out of bed. She felt fine. There was only a dull ache where her ankle had been broken, almost no evidence of the dozens of scratches she'd earned, and the matter of her frostnip was becoming harder to imagine with each passing hour.

Drazhan refused to hear any of it. He'd stationed sentries in the hall to keep her from—what? She couldn't guess. Did he expect her to fling herself back into the tree for another round?

She'd protested enough about it that he'd broken one of his own rules and allowed both Niklaus and Valerian to keep her company in her apartments while she had pretended she still needed to convalesce. *My guards will hear if anything untoward happens inside.*

The eyeroll she'd made as he'd left hurt more than the phantom pain in her ankle.

She was old enough to decide who was and wasn't allowed in her bedchamber, but as long as she stayed at Fanghelm, she was subject to his rules.

Val, lying next to her on the bed, turned toward her with a pensive, faraway look. Niklaus practiced his sword work, sans sword, by jabbing wildly toward the wall.

"You didn't do it on purpose," Aesylt whispered, studying the minute tics appearing across Valerian's face. She whispered because sometimes Nik wasn't the best person to pour her heart out to. "Val?"

"Doesn't make it better," he said, digging his face against a pillow. Still, he wouldn't look at her. "I couldn't even climb a fucking tree to save you."

Aesylt sighed and reluctantly turned toward Nik. "You still haven't said how the Dyvareh went for you."

"He caught Emira, but she screamed her head off before he could even come near her. Drew all sorts of exciting attention," Val said, perking back up. "Impressively subtle, Nik."

"Emira," Aesylt said, whistling. "I thought she liked you, Nik?"

Nik took a break from his shadow stabs to shrug and sigh. "Emira is..."

"Aye, well he has a cock between his legs, doesn't he? Wrong part for her." Val cupped himself over the covers. A near smile tickled his mouth. "All he did was say, 'gotcha,' and she shrieked like a banshee until she had the attention of the entire forest. Even if he had been turned on..." He made a slicing gesture.

"She really wanted that feast," Aesylt said, laughing.

Nik groaned. "And what do you know about it, other than twisting what I told you? I never would have touched her. She knows it."

"One word from Emira, and Draz would have freed you of your balls," Aesylt agreed, thinking of Val's comment about his parts.

Nik shrugged and struck his invisible opponent. "I only went because my uncle made me."

Val slithered under the blanket. His long, dark hair pooled around his face. He caught her staring and grinned.

"You never told me how you knew it was me," she said.

Val's eyes darkened. He dragged his teeth across the center of his lower lip. "I always know when it's you, Aessy."

"Get a hold of yourself," Nik muttered.

"Nik's right," Aesylt said. "I don't believe you."

With a laugh, Val inched away. "I paid one of the vedhmas to tell me your color."

Aesylt was shocked. "Nien, you did *not*. Or, I should say, *they* did not. They cannot be bought."

"Not with gold." He winked.

"Disgusting."

"What I want to know is what really happened in that tree with the duke?" Val's focus on her was total.

Nik used his sleeve to wipe his sweat and turned their way. "Yeah… Anything you're not telling us about *your* adventure in the forest?"

Aesylt nestled back on the pillow, staring at the candelabra hanging above the end of her bed. There was the accidental face-roll into his groin, which was still horribly mortifying. The familial, brotherly hug after they were rescued… the way he'd held her close yet with distance, worried for her but also for the message he might send.

It was a mess, all of it. And he hadn't come to see her at all, which only confirmed he was drowning in the same discomfort.

"You mean *other* than Val sending me hurtling into a tree?" She shook her head. "Ra—the duke clambered up like a squirrel and waited with me for help to arrive. Humiliating and painful. The end."

Val leaned in close, his eyes narrowing. "You almost called him by his given name, didn't you?"

Aesylt groaned. "I'm exhausted."

"That's not what you told your frata," Nik said from across the room.

"Because Draz is insufferable."

Val craned forward and kissed her cheek. "Your mysterious scholar won't stand a chance as long as I'm here."

Something foreign and strange stirred between her legs. Their long-standing friendship had come with few boundaries. She'd seen both Val and Nik without their clothing and had swum with them in the ahen vodah—the warm springs—in the nude, enough that it was nothing special. Other than the relatively innocent barn kiss with Val, after a bit too much mulled wine, she'd never felt more than familial love for either of them.

But the idea of Val and Rahn facing off for her was unexpectedly arousing.

And wrong.

Very wrong.

"Course, he may get his chance when I don't come home."

"V." The air left Aesylt's lungs. "Don't say that. You *are* coming home." She reached for his hands under the covers and gripped them in hers. "You *are* coming home."

Val snorted, his eyes fluttering dramatically. "Be realistic. No one comes home. Your brother has more wulf than man in him, and no one has come home since his victory. Not once."

Nik watched them both with a dark look. He turned back toward the wall but didn't resume his phantom swordplay.

"Don't tell me what to say, or to think, you rapscallion," Aesylt spat. "If I say you're coming back, Valerian Barynov, then you are."

"Only if you'll marry me when I do." His grin didn't quite reach his amber eyes.

"That is far from up to me." Aesylt snapped a finger at Nik. "And I can see you glowering in the window's reflection, like you have any deep thoughts about marriage. You're going to join the kyschun under the mountain and forget all about us common village folks."

"Not by choice," Nik muttered. "I should just do what Onkel Anton did and refuse. Everything turned out fine for him."

Val snorted. "I'd come back just to see that. Niklaus Petrovash, growing a pair? Wonder of wonders."

"You want to see this pair, Val? Feel them in your mouth?"

"Foul creatures, the both of you," Aesylt protested.

"And you love it," Val teased.

Aesylt smiled. It did little to soften the crippling ache in her heart that had started the day Val's name had been read in the village. The chosen son could refuse, of course, just as Nik could refuse his destiny as a history keeper. But no son ever turned their back on the Vuk od Varem. No son could muster the damning courage to commit the village to another hard year without hunting, despite knowing their odds of victory were slimmer than a thread.

"I love you both," she said softly. A rare wave of nostalgia passed over her. The Nok Mora, the massacre of their village and families by a vengeful, tyrant crown, was a decade past, but the wounds still ran deep. Her armor rarely cracked, but the past days had been unusually taxing. "You're like fratas to me. I should remind you more."

Val's brows shot upward. "Brothers? Really?"

Nik smirked. "We love you too. But I *very* much dislike my actual sister."

Aesylt laughed. "Neriah's only ten."

A knock drew their attention. Maia, Aesylt's personal vedhma, opened the door and peered in. "Scholar Tindahl would like an audience with you, but only if you're well enough."

Val threw a shoulder into Aesylt with a teasing scoff. "Your hero has arrived, princess. Shall we leave you two alone?"

Nik crossed his arms and fluttered his eyes.

Aesylt's breath caught, her focus divided between Maia and her friends. She knew why he'd stayed away, but it didn't explain his change of heart. "He's here now?"

Maia nodded. "Just there in the hall." She thumbed behind her.

"Come on." Val groaned as he peeled away from the bed. He smacked Nik in the arm when he didn't move. "Come *on.*" Over his shoulder he said, "Don't fuck him, Aessy, or I'll feel slighted."

"Ancestors keep us," Aesylt hissed. The moment they were both gone, she squirmed out of bed and hastily shrugged a robe over her sleeping gown. Her arm caught in the dense fabric, bending unnaturally, and she practically screamed her frustration.

"Everything well?" Maia asked from the door.

"Tak." All she had time for was a quick mirror glance, but what she saw was an exhausted woman staring back at her. Nothing would fix her except rest. She had no reason to be so fussed about her appearance around the scholar anyway. He was her mentor. More than likely, he was there out of a sense of duty. "All right, Maia. Send him in."

Maia stepped aside and Rahn swept in. He wore the same dark-green dressing cape he'd been wearing when she'd met him a year ago, and the effect it had on his matching eyes was no less startling. His dark hair was combed, as always, but there was a harried look to the style, as though he'd done it in the dark.

His cheeks flexed, dimpling. "Aesylt. How are you?"

"Perfectly fine," she said, with a shrug so ungraceful, she couldn't even discern how it had happened. "Drazhan is overreacting, but the Howling Sea remains blue and choppy, so what else can we expect?"

His mouth hitched at the corner. "He's very protective."

"Is that what you'd call it?" Aesylt's nostrils flared with her sharp inhale. "Thank you for checking on me, just the same. It wasn't necessary."

Rahn glanced briefly at the ground. He took a step into the room and turned back, as though readying to close the door, but stopped. "It *is* necessary. I should have come yesterday. I could..." His mouth twisted. He looked not quite at her but past her. "I could ply you with the falsehood I was irrecoverably detained by work, but the very honest truth is..." One of his hands twitched at his side. "I feel a sense of shame for my part in what happened to you."

Aesylt withheld her frown. He was acting peculiar, and she was no longer so sure it was awkwardness from her mortifying transgression in the tree. "You weren't the one who made up some ridiculous story about a wulf."

"Yes, but I was *your* wulf."

Something in the way he said it—*I was your wulf*—had her mouth watering. "You didn't know that until you found me stuck up a tree."

"No." He nodded. "But I intended to ensure my damsel, whoever she was, would enjoy a night without miscreance from some oversexed young man. I offered too much distance, and the result was..." He gestured around.

Both of Aesylt's brows lifted at the word *oversexed*, but it was no difficult task to recover herself when she remembered the first thing he'd said. *Whoever she was*. She was interchangeable, apparently. "Consider your conscience suitably cleared." She dusted her hands with a tight smile. "I sincerely appreciate what you did. I'll not forget it. Nor... Nor will I hesitate to return the favor, should the opportunity arise."

His smile was a warm current, melting the ice keeping her heart safe. "You were my first researcher, Aesylt. The first of our cohort to truly embrace our vision of an educated realm. There's nothing I could do for you that would ever be monumental enough to require anything further."

"Ah." She crossed her arms tighter, pinning the openings of her robe so far to the sides, she was nearly swaddled. "I should be able to return on the morrow."

Rahn shook his head with a light frown. "We'll resume after the season. You have enough to occupy you, and I'd never take Valerian away from his family in these final days before he leaves for the forest." He scratched the back of his neck with an odd look. "Besides, I need a few days to compose my thoughts on our next subject."

"We still have months left on astronomy."

"We've been asked to pause until the observatory is ready. There's... another subject requiring our attention in the interim. It's nothing." He cleared his throat and half turned. "Will I see you at supper?"

"What? What other subject?" He was keeping something from her. *Have I ever lied to you?*

No, he hadn't. It was time to put his claim to the test.

"I should let you rest—"

"I told you, I'm fine." She released her robe with a groan, shrugging it down off her shoulders. "This thing is as hot as the fires of the demon realm. What subject, Scholar?"

His hands opened at his sides. With a drawn sigh, he said, "Coitus."

Aesylt choked on her spit, bowing forward. "What did you say?"

Rahn wore a stern, flustered look. "I believe you heard me just fine."

She had no doubt whatsoever that her cheeks were big red apples. "I'd like you to repeat it, to be sure."

His mouth drew in, then his eyes closed and he said, "It's a participatory experiment, requiring the researchers to actively contribute to the studies, which of course is *ludicrous,* but Imryll has tasked me with finding a way to meet the requirement without compromising our cohort."

Aesylt was dumbfounded. Participatory. There was only one conclusion she could draw from that. "We're certain those are the parameters?"

Rahn's exhale was abrupt and breathy. "I've read them myself. Five times." Before she could rebut, he shook his head. "*This* is why I was hesitant to tell you. You'll worry needlessly before I've found an alternative that meets their requirements. And I *will* find a way. As... enticing though it may sound to some, I'm not keen to turn our cohort into an orgiastic den of hedonism."

Aesylt could think of nothing more intriguing than an orgiastic den of hedonism, but it would surely only add to her visible mortification. "No, that would be un... uh, unproductive."

Rahn cocked his head, watching her. Then he laughed. "I rather think the problem is that it would be *too* productive." He grinned and turned again. "Don't waste another thought on it. I'll have a new curricula for us when we resume."

Oh, she'd waste a thought. Maybe a hundred thoughts. The words *oversexed* and *orgiastic den of hedonism,* said in Rahn's stoic delivery, would live gleefully unfettered in her mind for all of time. "No. Of course not."

"Until then." Rahn bowed, nodded with a quick lock of eyes, and left.

When he was gone, Aesylt plopped onto the bed, her thoughts buzzing. “Coitus, eh?”

No matter what Rahn Tindahl had said, she’d never met a problem she wasn’t aching to solve.

THREE
AND ANOTHER WITH ME

Aesylt had pretended the day couldn't possibly arrive, and she hadn't prepared herself at all for seeing her dearest friend off to an uncertain fate.

It felt like the coldest day of the season, but Aesylt couldn't even trust her own senses that morning.

Everyone else had already had their turn. Val's family. Nik. It seemed wrong to her that she should be his witness, the last person he saw before venturing alone into the forest. But a chosen son could make three requests before they left on their Vuk od Varem. One for his family, one for the handling of his body, and one for the safe and smooth passage of his soul. The village was honor bound to grant them.

For his family, Val had requested they have first pick at the meat storage for the next season. That was tradition anyway, for families of the chosen sons, but Val wanted it recorded. He was leaving nothing to chance.

For his body, he'd requested the flames, followed by a scattering of his ashes in the Howling Sea. Vjestik, unlike others in the north, did not entomb their dead.

And for his soul, he'd requested Aesylt to be the last face he saw before he surrendered himself to the forest. His final witness.

She huddled near the half-open barn door, waiting for him to finish assaulting the hay with his steel. The sun was already setting, and heavy clouds darkened the late-afternoon sky. He'd want to be settled in his encampment by nightfall. He wouldn't be the first son to perish before the contest had fully begun, but she wasn't about to let that happen.

"V." She dug the toes of her boot into the splintering frame. The nausea in her belly competed for prominence with the delirium sweeping over her head. "I could happily stand here with you forever, but it's going to be dark soon."

"Yeah?" Val lunged forward in a violent thrust, rattling the hay. He stepped back and wiped his brow, then looked her way. "So it is." He returned his attention to the bale.

"You don't want to be looking for a campsite when it's dark."

"What would you know about it, Aessy? They send sons, not daughters."

"I know enough." She took a single step in, to dodge a hard swirl of snow. It was getting dark *and* stormy, and every second he lingered was one closer to his doom. Even thinking about it... She couldn't. That wasn't what he needed to dissolve his angry fugue.

Aesylt knew what to do, but if Drazhan—if anyone—found out she'd been in the celestial realm again, she'd be in terrible trouble. She'd promised not to do it again, and *definitely* never to bring someone else with her, and she'd kept the promise... mostly.

Val shrieked a battle cry and made another decisive jab.

With a sigh, she leaned out of the barn to make sure no one was watching, closed it, and threw the bolt. Val was so consumed, he didn't notice either, nor her moving toward him. It wasn't until she whispered the words "and another with me" that he looked up.

The colors of the barn dulled, no longer vibrant, and the air had an ethereal quality that made it seem thinner, hazier. Anyone who came in would see an empty space where she'd stood only seconds before, though if they looked close enough, they might notice the shimmer marking the place she'd return to.

She waited until his entire corporeal form had transitioned before throwing herself into his arms.

"It's all right, V. It's just us here." She pressed her mouth tight to the flesh of his ear. Everything seemed and felt as it did in the real world, but heightened. His breath in her hair sent an imperious wave of shivers through her. The clamp of his hand, buzzing with heat, had her nearly twisting to get away, afraid of how *alive* the sensation made her feel. "You chose me for a reason. Stop taking your agony out on the poor hay and *talk* to me."

Val gradually relaxed. His hand clenched in the middle of her back, then softened. "You know I hate it here."

"You didn't always." She craned her head up to smile at him. Tears glossed his eyes. She wished she hadn't seen them. "You used to beg me to come here. Remember?"

"That was before Drazhan told us you could get *stuck* here and never be able to leave." His brows fused. "You know I'm not much for rules, or your damned brute of a brother, but I have to agree with him on this. You *shouldn't* be coming here anymore. No one in this village has the magic to come find you if you lose yourself."

Aesylt made a *pfft* sound and averted her eyes. "Our world is far more treacherous."

Val shook her once. "Promise me this will be the last time."

"It would be a lie." She forced a smile, reaching a hand toward his cheek. Fear bubbled up from her chest, clogging her throat. This was it. In minutes, he would walk away from her, and the odds were she would never, ever see him again alive. Never hear his laugh. See his smirk. Feel his hand on her arm, guiding her both toward and away from trouble. "I could keep you here with me, and we could stay forever. We don't need sustenance in the celestial realm. We don't need anything."

His mouth turned at the corner before spreading into a smile. "You know why I chose you as my witness? I wanted to ask you for something. Two things."

Aesylt waited for him to tell her.

"A good-bye kiss," he said, grinning broader. "I want *you* to be the memory I take with me into the forest."

Her mouth parted in surprise. She nodded, but before she could add voice, Val had both of his hands wrapped along the underside of her face. A gasp was the only sound she made when his tongue slid across hers, their moans colliding. She lifted for more, unsure whether her desperation for his touch came from love, fear, or both.

"Mm." He nibbled her lip as he drew away. "Aessy, Aessy, Aessy."

Her mouth tingled, humming. "And the second thing you wanted to ask me?" she asked, breathless.

"No one expects me to come back." He looked off to the side, scorn scoring his dark expression. "But do you know why they send boys into the woods?"

She shook her head.

"Because *men* have something to come home to." He dragged his thumbs along her temples. "If I come home, Aesylt, I want you to be my wife. Don't worry about your brother. If I win, I'll be a hero. The village won't accept his shallow excuses anymore."

"You're a man now," she said distantly. Certainly they'd *played* happy families as children, the two of them husband and wife, and Niklaus—quite reluctantly—their child. Always fun, always a laugh. Never real. "I don't even know if I want to marry."

His touch faltered. "You always said you did."

She searched for the right words, excruciatingly conscious of the way he was hanging onto her silence. Did she want to marry him? Could she see it as something real, tangible, desirable? She *did* desire him, but was it love? Was how she felt for him the foundation of a marriage?

Moments from him walking away from her, probably forever, did *any* of it matter? Were objections the words she was going to leave him with, weakening him before the greatest battle of his entire life?

"Tak," she blurted. Her heart fluttered in her chest. "When you come home to us, I'll marry you."

Aesylt gulped when he suddenly lifted her in his arms and spun her, ending the joyous outburst with a drawn, ardent kiss.

He broke away, trailing his mouth toward her ear. "Volemthe, Aesylt. I always have."

"You know I love you as well, Valerian," she answered. Her heart pounded hard enough that if she were in the outside world, it would have rendered her lightheaded. The twisted, well-intentioned lies turned to molasses in her belly. Her justification for them was no relief. She was either saying good-bye to her dearest friend in the world or she was waiting for a husband to return.

Both outcomes hollowed her beyond belief.

"Can we get the fuck out of this creepy place now?" Val's larger-than-life smile was back. He brushed a band of hair off her face. "Please?"

Aesylt laughed, but the thought of staying there, forever, nagged at her. If it saved him, she could be anything Valerian Barynov needed her to be. Approaching the last moments before his departure, she was desperate enough to say words she knew she didn't mean. "Stay, V. Stay with me. We can run. It isn't too late. We can go... anywhere, really. This realm is big. It's big enough for people to get lost in, if they want, and I have the gold my mother left me—"

"No. *This* is our home." He glanced at the doors with a heavy sigh. "And I won't purposely subject our village to another awful year."

She wouldn't have either, in his place. "You can't fault me for trying."

His smile brightened the entire barn. "I *love* you for trying. And I will come back to you. You gave me every reason to return victorious. So I will."

Aesylt squinted away tears. "That simple, is it?"

"If I say so." He kissed her again. "Don't worry for me. I know what I need to do, and I know I can do it." He fingered the necklace she'd placed on his neck the day before. It was her mother's, one of two left after the sacking of the village. The ruthless cowards had taken everything else of value, but Aesylt had been wearing both, huddled under her bed as she listened to screams without end, breathing the rancid, unforgettable stench of bodies burning in the village square. "I have everything I need now."

"Come back to us." Her voice cracked. *Say it. Give him everything he needs, for he'll need everything he can get.* "To me." She closed her eyes and whispered the words to return them both to the real world. "And now we return."

Val glanced around in powerful relief. "All right then, beautiful. By the wings of this life or the bones of the next."

Aesylt repeated the Vjestik refrain. He kissed her as the last word left her, held his hand to his mouth, and went to the barn doors.

"Better start picking out materials for a gown." Val grinned, winked, and then he was gone.

Aesylt was bent over the hearth in the library, heaving, when Tasmin walked in.

Tasmin quietly approached and chose the chair Rahn usually sat in. "He's gone?"

Aesylt breathed out through a small gap in her mouth, choking back emotion. Her sour belly constricted, churning. She inhaled, eyes closed, and turned.

"I won't ply you with reassurances. You're Vjestik. You've lived here your whole life. You'd see right through them." Tasmin leaned closer. "But if you'd like to talk, I'd be honored to listen."

Aesylt had chosen the library for solitude. There wouldn't be another cohort session until the Vuk od Varem was over, and depending on the outcome... No, she couldn't let her mind wander such a path. But Tasmin, who had come to the Cross with Duke Rahn and her mother, Duchess Teleria, was easy to talk to. She had a natural warmth and wisdom that surprisingly paired well with her blunt assessments of everything. She and Aesylt had become fast friends, and even confidants. "I don't even have words, Tas. I feel like a great void has opened up within me, one I'm neither capable of closing nor motivated to try. Letting it swallow me would be easier than standing on the edge of the abyss, waiting to fall."

"You're not one to wax morose," Tasmin said lightly. "But if anyone has a right to, it's you. I won't tell you what I think about the Vuk od Varem, but I will pray to the gods for Valerian's safe return."

The gods. The Ancestors. The Guardians. There were so many deities in the realm, it was hard to lay accountability at any of their feet. "I know how it all must seem to an outsider, Tas, but I've heard some of Imryll's stories from Duncarrow. Every culture has traditions no one else understands. Every culture understands brutality. It's a rather universal language, don't you think?"

Tasmin nodded at the fire, tucking her mahogany hair behind her ears. She was remarkably beautiful, in a way Aesylt struggled to define. There was an "otherness" about her that men and women alike found immediately appealing. Aesylt had never concerned herself much with her own reflection, but Tasmin's arrival had her scrutinizing herself about things that had never mattered before.

It wasn't just Tasmin's arrival though. It was Rahn's. No one had ever challenged her the way he had. Before he'd come along, she hadn't even realized there were more challenges to be made.

Before his arrival, she hadn't been living, so much as existing.

"You're right. And I was born on Duncarrow, unlike Rahn who was old enough to remember Ilynglass when he came to our realm. Despite that, he remembers nothing. As you know, even raising the topic turns him into a cornered animal." Tasmin shrugged. "Whatever world Rahn came from, whatever it looked like, I know it couldn't be any more civilized than ours."

Of their cohort, only Tasmin ever called the scholar by his given name. It made no sense why it rankled Aesylt, just like their easy way with each other shouldn't be so maddening, but it did and it was. It didn't matter that Rahn and Tasmin had been raised like siblings.

But they *were not* siblings, and the way Tasmin sometimes smiled at Rahn from across a room made it clear there were no familial boundaries between them.

"What aren't you saying, Aesylt?"

Aesylt pushed off from the hearth and dropped into the chair next to Tasmin's. "Val asked me to marry him before he left."

Tasmin pitched forward. "Did he now?"

Nodding, Aesylt drew her legs up under her.

"Your answer?"

"What else could I say but yes to a man embarking on..." She couldn't finish. "Even if he comes back, Drazhan would put up a fight about it, and..."

"He might not," Tasmin said. "The boys who return from the woods are heroes, no? It would be an honorable match."

"You're assuming my brother is reasonable."

"Oh, I *know* the man isn't reasonable. I was there for his entire illicit courtship with Imryll. He may be a gentle giant with her now, but we can't forget he went to Duncarrow to extinguish the Rhiagain line."

Aesylt could have defended her brother, but instead she closed her eyes and sighed. "Val is... He's so dear to me, Tas, but I cannot see making a life with him."

"Well, I imagine he'd be a proper beast in bed," Tasmin said with a cheeky grin, which had Aesylt unexpectedly smiling too. "Listen to his chaos. It's a symphony of unbridled promise."

"What a way with words you have," Aesylt teased, envious at how easy it was for Tasmin to speak of such things. If anyone heard them... but no one would. And she trusted Tasmin enough to know she didn't even need to ask her not to repeat any of what was said to Drazhan or Imryll. "But I need more than that." She frowned. "I think."

Tasmin pulled her dark-cherry waves over one shoulder. "Many women get stuck with a man who fulfills none of their needs. Very few can manage to please you both inside *and* outside the bedroom."

"And you would know this how?" Tasmin had once inferred that Duncarrow was an island of lechers, but she had not implicated herself in the accusation.

Tasmin smirked instead of answering. "You could do worse, Aesylt. He's brash and a bit... uncouth, but he's gorgeous and has only ever had eyes for you."

"It's not as if Witchwood Cross is teeming with options." Aesylt leaned back in her chair with an inaudible sigh. She let her eyes slowly close, taking in the soft warmth of the crackling fire, which was still no match for the fire raging within her. Her heart hadn't settled at all, not in hours. "Val isn't the first person I cared about who went into the forest, but he's the only one I've been tempted to follow."

"Wouldn't it break the alliance with the wulves? If he had help?"

"I didn't say I was going to." Aesylt lolled her head to the side, searching for a subject change. "Did Scholar Tindahl tell you about the curricula change for our cohort?"

"Haven't had the chance," Rahn said from the doorway. Both women startled at the unexpected intrusion.

"Well, don't hold out on me, Rahn," Tasmin said with a teasing grin.

Aesylt clenched, feeling foolish for her jealousy of a relationship that had nothing to do with her. She reached for the quilt on the back of her chair and pulled it over her, sad and ashamed and a slew of other emotions she was too out of sorts to put name to.

"Another time," he said pleasantly. His focused steps echoed as he approached. "I'd hoped to speak with Aesylt, actually. Alone, if you don't mind."

Tasmin's brow creased in surprise. "Does Drazhan know you want to be alone with his sostra?"

"If you're suggesting my intentions are untoward..."

"Not at all." Tasmin leaped from her chair, pointing a quick wink at Aesylt before sauntering toward Rahn. She squeezed his arm as she passed.

He stood stock-still until the library doors whooshed closed and then settled into the chair Tasmin had vacated. "How are you holding up?"

Aesylt tugged the quilt tight around her neck and shrugged. "Perfectly recovered."

"That isn't what I meant."

She could feel his eyes fixed on her, but her nerves kept her own gaze pointed at the fire.

"You were Val's final witness."

She nodded.

"I can't imagine the convolution of emotions you're experiencing after that." He tapped the arms of his chair. "I may be an outsider and don't fully understand the Season of the Wulf, but I've been told I'm a good listener."

Aesylt smiled to herself. "You've certainly endured a fair dose of my whining without complaint."

"No reason to complain about something I chose to do."

"I appreciate your concern, but I'm fine. I'll be fine." She twisted in the discomfort of her lies. She wasn't remotely fine. Thinking... even *breathing* was a chore. The scholar's presence made both of those things inexplicably more challenging, like she had to be conscious of what every part of her was doing, the precise path of each inhale and exhale. "In fact, I may head on to bed now."

Rahn's presence was heavy beside her. "You must be exhausted."

"Not especially."

He hesitated a moment before saying, "Have you an appetite for adventure then?"

The suggestion was so unexpected, it made her laugh. "Does said adventure involve trees?"

"Gods, let's hope not." His mouth parted in shocked disgust, and they both laughed. "It's just I... I had a cart prepared to journey up to the observatory to see the progress. The road up the mountain has been cleared, and the skies are fairly open—a good night to go up and test out the telescope. I'd hate to waste it."

Aesylt turned toward him. She'd only been up to the spot once, when construction had broken ground. Rahn usually went alone—or with Tasmin. "Are you asking because you feel bad for me? Do I look pitiful?"

Rahn pursed his mouth in amusement. "There's nothing pitiful about you, Aesylt. Not a single thing."

"Well, you've answered one question," she quipped, shifting again under the blanket.

He leaned close. "I'm asking because I want to know what you think."

"About the construction?"

"Yes. I value your perspective." Rahn straightened his jacket and stood. He extended a hand to her. "Will you accompany me?"

Aesylt narrowed her eyes at the strong hand calling her name and tried very hard not to think about her dream the night before, when she'd ridden the poor scholar into oblivion at the top of that ill-fated tree. At least he couldn't read minds. "No one put you up to this? Like Tas or Nik?"

He withdrew a little. "Do you really believe I would ask you if I didn't mean it?"

Aesylt lowered her eyes and sighed. "Opros, Scholar. I'm just not good company tonight."

"Let me be the judge of that." His hand waved again.

She curved her mouth to the side in cool regard. "You'll regret this. Deeply, I suspect."

Rahn grinned. "I look forward to adding it to my ever-growing list. Come on."

FOUR
STARWALKER

The ride up the steep, winding path took twice as long as usual. Rahn was typically accompanied by workers on these ventures, who managed the driving and tended the cart and pack mules, and though he'd been learning to manage on his own since arriving in the Cross, it was the first time he'd ever journeyed up the mountain road alone.

Except he wasn't alone. Aesylt sat beside him on the small bench, huddled near her end with a desolate look into the gradually thinning wilderness.

It had been on his return from the livery earlier that night when he'd spotted her emotional good-bye with Valerian. Aesylt had waited just long enough for the boy to disappear beyond the forest line before collapsing to her knees in soundless, tearless sobs.

Rahn had never wanted so desperately to go to someone and comfort them, but his instinct told him she wouldn't want him, or anyone, to see her like that. So he'd waited for a better opportunity to offer his friendship. Visiting the observatory wouldn't cure what was ailing her heart, but it might distract her long enough for her to find her footing again.

Rahn shivered, casting a grin at an unbothered Aesylt. He'd bedecked himself in three layers of outerwear, compared to her one, but he was still ready to throw himself into a fire. "You're not cold?"

"I'm a wulf," she said, smirking from the side. "Or so they say."

"You have the temperament of one at least." He angled the mules into the last switchback. They moved slower at the higher elevation, giving the chill air more opportunities to wrap around them. "You believe there's veracity to the tales of your ancestor speaking with and mating with wulves?"

"There *are* those who can communicate with animals. It's called zydolny. The touch. Unique among the Vjestik, but rare." Aesylt wiggled and sat straight. "Darek Summerton spoke with wulves. It's an established fact. Whether he..." She snorted. "Who knows?"

"I may only be an aspiring scientist, but I struggle to imagine any real compatibility between the races."

"No one even understands what biological phenomenon causes children to look like their parents, Scholar. And if you cannot explain something, then you cannot rule out anything, however improbable."

Rahn's mouth puckered in amusement. "Did I teach you that?"

Aesylt gave a petulant shrug, but he caught her proud smile buried in her fur collar.

They scaled one last hill, short but sheer, and then they were there. Rahn pulled the cart under a long, covered area where the workers had parked their supplies. The row was empty at the dusky hour, but there were piles of empty crates and scraps, evidence of another long day of construction.

Aesylt slowly climbed out, regarding the half-built observatory in silent awe. Though he'd been visiting weekly since the workers broke ground, he turned to witness the progress through her eyes. Her mouth opened as she approached the half-built dome. The colossal glass panels had been installed along the back half, but only the beams had been built on the front side. A tarp dangled from the middle to keep snow from blowing in. Wood had been laid as temporary flooring, but when construction completed, it would be stone, like most other structures in the Cross.

He marveled at her reactions, a tad jealous he couldn't experience seeing the behemoth structure in its evolving form for the first time.

"I know you asked for my opinion, but I don't know where to start." Aesylt wrapped her arms around herself and stepped closer to the platform, dodging thickly packed hills of snow. "It's far beyond anything I could have imagined, but that isn't helpful."

Rahn chuckled to himself as he unloaded the wagon. "It's helpful." He checked his baskets: fire and kindling for the hearth inside one, and a blanket, a cask of ale, and some bread in the other. "Go on in. The floor is solid, though probably damp, so step carefully. Once you're under the domed section, you'll be protected."

He followed several paces behind to let her discover each detail for herself. There were boards and nails everywhere in the unfinished half, but once they stepped under the glass, an eerie calm descended. A glance up revealed the dusting of snow on the panels, but the moon, sky, and stars were on full display. The auroras danced along the peaks and valleys of the mountain, emerald and gold and a hint of violet.

Aesylt spun around, taking it all in. She stopped when she spotted him. "I've never seen anything like this. Ever."

"It will be an exceptional place of learning and discovery when it's finished." Rahn set the baskets on a worker's table and emptied the contents.

"The hearth works?" she asked, sneaking by him to snag an armful of kindling and logs. She smirked at his indignation and pranced away without waiting for his answer.

"You want to attempt to light it with magic, or shall I save you the trouble?"

Aesylt arranged the logs and tossed the kindling in. She snapped her pale fingers without turning. "Give it to me."

"Where I come from, 'please' is not undervalued," he teased but brought her the flint. Their hands connected with a soft brush, passing like strangers in a market, and he experienced his first pang of self-doubt for bringing her there alone.

"I was only thinking of you, Scholar, and your delicate royal disposition." The fire took and then roared to life. She stood, sanded her hands, and turned. "I'll take some of that ale."

Rahn poured two mugs and handed her one. As she downed hers, he removed two of his furs and carried them to the far edge of the dome, where the best views of the mountains and sky were, and laid them down. He arranged them so they weren't too close together. "Grab the bread and come join me."

Aesylt made her way over but didn't immediately sit. He glanced up and caught her staring through the thick glass.

"We see the auroras all the time. But never like this," she whispered. She passed him the bread without looking at him. "And the stars... It's like you could reach up and hold them in your hand if you were clever enough."

"If anyone is clever enough, it would be you, Squish."

Aesylt whipped her gaze at him in mild affront. "That's the second time you've called me a squirrel."

Rahn raised both hands in surrender. "I didn't call you a squirrel. I merely implied you have the same practical traits as your beloved childhood pet. Resourcefulness, clev—"

"You're not making this any better," she said but plopped onto the other fur. "I no longer wonder why you've never married, Scholar. You are clearly incapable of speaking to women as anything but specimens to be studied."

Rahn burst out laughing. "I could have told you that. Why do you think I'm at my best with my nose in a book or a quill in hand?"

"And how many books have you offended without realizing it? The trail of carnage must be unceasing," she said as she settled in. "You made a mistake bringing me here. Waiting will be torture."

"You can always come up here to visit."

She took a swallow of ale and pointed at the glass with her mug. "Thank you for the distraction tonight."

He nodded, sensing her darkness return. "The stars are brighter up here, don't you think?"

"They sure seem so. I know you don't believe they're Guardians or Ancestors, so what do *you* think they are?"

Rahn leaned back on his hands and gazed at the colorful sky. "Whatever they are, they're so much bigger and more complex than anything we've come up with as a theory so far. I fear we'll never know until we have the technology to reach them ourselves."

"So, never?"

He chuckled. "There's another, unintended casualty of us having no accounting of your histories, no glimpse into the past. We cannot know how far we've come because we don't know where we started."

"The rest of us, sure. You started in Ilynglass."

Rahn's blood cooled. Speaking, or even thinking, of his homeland threw him into a swirl of melancholy. Although he'd been nearly eight when the Rhiagains and the Noble Houses had fled a realm on fire, he remembered next to nothing about it. Just the fires and the screams. The shipwrecks. The chaos. "Duncarrow forbade unsanctioned writing and had no interest in documenting facts. As for Ilynglass..."

Aesylt seemed to read something in him, because her tone turned soft. "I shouldn't have brought it up. I'm sorry."

"You needn't apologize. Everyone wants to know about it, but few believe all my memories of the place are gone."

"I believe you," she said. "If it matters."

Rahn tried to smile. He fixed his gaze on the dance of light in the sky. His mind was already feeling the effects of the ale, which was far stronger than he'd realized when he'd packed it. "It matters."

She refilled both of their drinks and leaned back onto one elbow. "Is that why it's hard for you? Because no one takes you at your word?"

"I stopped concerning myself with the uninformed opinions of others years ago."

Her laugh returned the smile to his face, but realizing what he meant to say next dulled it.

"I lost both my parents and my little sister that day. Grandparents. Cousins. Aunts. Uncles. And the saddest part is I hardly remember them at all. I can't even picture my mother's face anymore." He glanced down at the intrusion of warmth, finding Aesylt's hand on his arm. "I've never told anyone else that. I don't know what compelled me to tell you now."

Aesylt tossed back a generous swallow of ale. "Confessions of the unintentionally inebriated," she said lightly, but her smile was joyless. "Would you feel better if I offered one of my own?"

Rahn rolled his hands over the cool mug. "You don't have to do that."

Aesylt finished her drink and flopped back. Her light hair spilled out on all sides, blending with the fur. "It's not the kind of secret no one else knows, I'm afraid, but very few do, and they're just as guarded about it as I am. Drazhan. My other frata, Hraz. My ota knew too. Nik and Val." She sighed. "We may practice magic openly in the Cross, but even among the Vjestik, there are forbidden magics. They won't ship you off to the Reliquary like the rest of the realm does when one of their children manifests something they shouldn't. We deal with our troubles ourselves."

Rahn turned to his side in alarm. "You possess forbidden magic?"

She nodded, her head rolling away from him. "When I was born, I... wasn't *there*. They delivered me, but then I was just gone. Disappeared into thin air. My oma started screaming for me, and my ota was ready to have every last nurse's head if they didn't explain what was going on. But then I was back. And no one ever spoke of it again until after my oma died, and I started going *elsewhere* again."

Rahn's mind continued to spin as she spoke. He was torn between wanting to stop her before she revealed something she wasn't comfortable sharing and letting her finish.

"My childhood vedhma, Saskia, called the place I went the celestial realm, and Ota sent her away for it. I think because he was scared for me," Aesylt said. Her tone took on a dreamlike quality. "She called me a starwalker."

Rahn tucked his chin down in confusion. "A starwalker?"

"When I go into this realm, everything is the same but different. The sky... It's like it's right on top of me, and I'm one with the stars. Like land and air are one. Some things follow me there; others don't... It's different every time. I can see and feel and do everything I can do in the real world, except nothing I do there has consequence here. If I die in the celestial realm, I just wake up here again, like nothing happened."

"If you... *have* you *died* there?" Rahn was aghast. His pulse had started to pound, bolstered by an unmistakable sense there was more danger to her words than she was letting on. "Aesylt?"

She nodded, her head tilted back. Her mouth parted, then closed. She exhaled. "A few times. Hraz, maybe a dozen." She smirked to herself. "Drazhan? Probably fifty."

Rahn shook his head, trying to understand. "You all go to this celestial realm, as you call it, to *die*? To experience death with no consequence of death?"

Aesylt propped herself up for another refill. "I haven't had this much ale in so long." She quaffed it back in one impressive throw.

He knew what she was doing and why. "Then maybe it's time to slow down a bit."

"Vjestik are born knowing how to hold their spirits, Scholar." She tilted her head back toward him. When her wide eyes implored him, his heart issued a betrayal, skipping wildly. She pressed a hand to her golden hair, twined with the dark bear pelt. It was the way she said *scholar*... perfectly ordinary. Perfectly indecent.

Perhaps I'm the one who has over-indulged himself.

"I stand corrected," he said hoarsely. He'd brought her to the observatory to take her mind off her fear and grief, not introduce a complication to her life. And his. "You were saying how you enjoyed murdering your brothers for sport?"

Aesylt chortled. "Well, I did enjoy it. In my defense, they begged me to take them. It was a safe place to practice. Hraz, for fun, I suppose. Drazhan for... everything that came after Nok Mora."

Nok Mora. The Nightmare. Rahn's heart ached for the village that had lost so much in one terrifying night and was still recovering from. "What about your own deaths?"

Her shoulders lifted against the fur into a shrug. "I prefer to face death and know it than wait for it and not recognize it."

Stories of that night filtered back to him. Whispers of the little girl who had hid under the bed as her father and eldest brother were massacred in front of her... as the village and half its inhabitants burned to ash upon the order of a vengeful king.

Just as swiftly followed more unwelcome visions, of waking, sodden, upon foreign rocks, bleeding and confused. Waiting for a family that would never arrive. "I understand, even if I wish I didn't."

Aesylt tapped the fur with the hand closest to Rahn. "I could take you there."

"To the celestial realm?"

She fought a yawn, but the urge won. "Yeah," she said sleepily. "Only if you want."

Rahn pressed his own yawn into his arm. *Did* he want to go? Even if the answer was yes, *should* he? His academic mind spun around the possibilities of such a place, but if there was one unspoken but powerful truth, it was that if something offered endless potential, expect danger in equal measure.

"Another time, perhaps," he said, but she was fast asleep.

FIVE

NEITHER ALIVE NOR DEAD

Aesylt was jolted awake, surrounded by the clangs of armor and the scrapes and squeaks of leather. Dawn pierced through the thick glass.

Scholar. She whipped her head toward his fur, but he wasn't there.

"Up," Drazhan commanded, but he didn't leave it to chance, gathering one of her hands in his with a rough, effortless tug. She staggered to her feet, readying for some obnoxious rant, but when she looked up at him, the rage she expected was absent.

Beyond him were several dozen of his men fanned out in a semicircle. All were armed, like him. The way out was blocked.

"Draz, what is this?" She couldn't stop staring at the line of men ready for battle.

"I won't ask you what the fuck you were doing spending the night here with the scholar because we have a much bigger problem, Aes." He released her and turned toward his men, raking a hand through his stubble. "Are you all right?"

She crossed her arms and took a step back from him. "Why wouldn't I be?"

Drazhan nodded to himself. He looked around with hard, wide-eyed blinks. *He's anxious. Unsettled.* "It was just the two of you up here?"

Aesylt closed her eyes, groaning. Of course Drazhan would make a big deal of nothing, just as he'd been doing ever since coming home. He loved to forget she'd had all the freedom in the world when he was away, and had managed just fine. "Yes, and *nothing* happened, for the love of—"

He shocked her with a silencing, crushing hug. "Doesn't matter." He pulled back, sweeping a guarded gaze over her. "Gather only what you need right now. We're leaving."

Aesylt blindly stepped backward, raising her arms at her sides. "Nien. Not until you tell me why you came marching up here at dawn with an *army*." She searched around again for Rahn. "And what you did with Scholar Tindahl."

"Your scholar is on his way back to the village with the other caravan. He's fine." Drazhan almost spat the words. His mouth twisted in scorn, but it didn't hold. None of his reactions were lasting more than seconds.

"You mean your men *dragged* him back, don't you?"

He shook his head and then rolled it back, facing the sky. "Aesylt, you just need to come with me now. Please."

"Draz—"

"Please!"

Only once before had she seen desperation like that in her brother's eyes: the night he'd returned from the Vuk od Varem a victor, only to find Witchwood Cross had been razed, their father's and brother's heads greeting him as he stepped through the village gates.

"All right," she said quietly. She darted her eyes around at the men, looking for signs of the answer, but they were solemn monoliths. "All right, wulf."

She waited until they were settled in the cart and driving down the mountain before she asked another question. "It's not Imryll and Aleks?"

Drazhan stared forward. He shook his head.

"Tas? Duchess?"

"Nien."

"It's not... Val?"

"Aes." His voice creaked. "I just need to get you back to Fanghelm. We can talk there."

"Get me back to Fanghelm?" Her restraint slipped away. He was acting as though she was in danger, like he expected an ambush on the road and for her to be taken. The wagons of guards ahead and behind weren't making it easier to discard the notion. "I really think you owe me an answer now, Drazhan."

His stubbornness was immutable though.

Aesylt bundled her furs tighter and stared into the forest on the side of the path, which grew denser as they neared sea level. The fog splitting the range disappeared, and soon they were on the more-traveled section of the road.

The bustle of the village trickled in bits and pieces. The closer they got to town, the deeper the ripples in her brother's tense, thick muscles as he directed the mules through closed-jaw commands and white-knuckle tugs of the reins.

Her own heart hadn't moved from her throat.

When he guided the cart onto the main road, villagers on all sides stopped to watch. They exited their shops and stalls or slowed their wagons and horses. An entire range of sentiments played out across their faces, from curiosity to sadness to disgust.

"Eyes. Ahead," Drazhan ordered.

"What *happened*?" she whispered, struggling to follow his order. She faced forward, but her eyes flicked toward the sides, trying to read in the villagers' eyes what her brother was refusing to say. "Why are they all staring at us like that?"

Me. They're staring at me.

Drazhan reached over and yanked her away from the edge of the bench to bring her to the center.

Aesylt twisted out of his grip, her confusion turning to anger. "If you want me to fall in line, you're going to tell me, and you're going to tell me right now."

"Almost home," he muttered, grinding the words.

"You're deliberately withholding things from me, because you think I can't handle whatever it is." Aesylt slid hard to her right, gripping the far end of the bench, and leaned half out. "Drazhan, I will jump out of this wagon right now if you don't—"

Drazhan snaked a hand out and slammed her back down, but when he spoke this time, his deep, confident voice had a crack down the center. "Aesylt..." His hands loosed up on the reins, and the wagon slowed. "It's Valerian. He's returned."

Aesylt's entire body seemed to coil inward, tightening around her lungs, her heart. She tried to breathe before speaking, but her throat constricted around the words, which came out in a rush. "Returned... like he won? He bested the wulf?"

"I just need to get you home, cub."

Her heart plummeted toward the cold wooden floor. "Did he abandon his post? Did he already... Is he..." Aesylt shook her head and grunted. *Don't say it.* "Drazhan."

"He's alive. But so is the wulf." Drazhan's throat jumped in a hard, protracted swallow. He spurred the mules on, sending Aesylt and himself slamming back from the force. The cart made a sharp turn onto the long approach to Fanghelm Keep. There were dozens teeming around the gates, but when Aesylt craned forward to see better, her brother pinned her back with one arm. Gentler this time, which was worse.

"Fuck," he hissed. The guards in the cart ahead tried to clear the way, but the gates were completely covered with a swarm of villagers. "Don't move."

"What? Where are you going?"

"Don't move." Drazhan hopped out and marched toward the gathering scene. Aesylt looked on in horror as he was circled by angry men, shouting demands she couldn't make out. She started to climb out anyway, but Fezzan Castel appeared on her side of the cart and shook his head at her to stop.

"Fez, what is going *on*?" Aesylt reached out and grabbed the man's armored arm. "Why are you all wearing your metal? Why is everyone acting like this?"

Fezzan screwed his mouth tight. His nostrils flared. "Better for your brother to tell you, cub."

"I *will* find a way out of this cart if you don't tell me!"

He stepped closer, his focus still on Drazhan and his other men trying to thin the crowd so they could open the gates. "We don't *know*." His teeth scraped over his bottom lip, his eyes wide and wary. "I was meeting with your brother about allocations for the meat stores, and we heard shouting near the north end of property, at the forest line, and out from between the trees comes..." He stopped when someone threw a punch at the gates. "Shite. That's Esker Barynov. Stay put."

"Fezzan!"

Aesylt clambered out after him, bursting through the thick crowd of onlookers to get to the center of the melee.

"She was his final witness!" someone cried. "She spelled him!"

Someone grabbed her around the waist from behind, whisking her feet off the ground. She threw a low elbow and they released her, but then someone else had her from the left, pinning her against one coming in from her right. She twisted and squirmed, dropping into a crouch, but a boot crashed into her face, and she went sprawling onto her back.

"Grab her! Grab the koldyna!" someone said, muted and distant, as she clawed along the ground, dodging boots and mud and legs. Her head swam from the kick, but if she could get to the gate, she could climb, and maybe she could finally see what had caused so much violent confusion.

Something grabbed hold of her foot and swung her upward until she was dangling, her hands grasping for the ground. She screamed and wriggled, but more hands came to help her assailant, until she was surrounded and pinned, her breath ripped away with every crush and press of their fevered hold.

Aesylt spat blood into the dirt. She watched it sink into the mud as she was carried away from the gates, from the carts, from her brother. She screamed again and again, squirming and swinging her arms wildly to strike everything she could.

"Draz—" The word was choked by the leather of someone's leg. She tightened her knuckles and swung as hard as she could into the shin. Her vision filled with stars from another swift kick.

Then she was crudely dropped, and she landed on her neck, tumbling sideways. She took in a mouthful of cold rocks and spit, scrambling, but then the darkness of her flock of kidnappers spread away, revealing the bright morning sky.

And Drazhan.

He knelt and scooped her up with one arm, pointing his ancestral sword, Stormbringer, with the other. "No one else has to get hurt today, but the next man who touches my sister meets the Ancestors."

Aesylt buried her face in his chest and breathed in the comfort of his strength.

"None of us know what happened out there, but we are not solving it like this." He backed them slowly toward the gates. Most held their distance, but a half dozen or so followed, bloodlust imprinted in their hungered gazes. Aesylt recognized all of them. They were good people, friends of theirs. None of it made sense.

She remembered the dagger in her boot and swung her leg up to catch it, drew it, and wielded it out to the other side.

"You wouldn't be protecting her if she weren't your sister," Esker Barynov said, pushing through the crowd. He'd drawn his sword as well, circling them from the side. "She was his final witness, Drazhan."

"*Steward Wynter.*" Drazhan threaded the correction through his teeth. "If you want to act like a savage, Barynov, disrespect my house and blood, then you'll address me as your steward."

"She was his final witness! And we all know she's just like her mother! I know all about how she can travel—"

Drazhan pressed the tip of his sword against the hollow of Esker's neck. Gasps ripped around them, the only sound other than the heavy, labored breaths of a cooling mob. "One. More. Word."

Esker's nose flared, his eyes trembling as they narrowed into catlike slits. "My son is neither alive nor dead. He's an abomination. A failure. Someone must answer."

Drazhan twisted his sword, and a stream of thick blood poured from the superficial wound. "If you want to speak like men, then we'll speak like men. But I can just as easily remove your venomous head from your shoulders."

"I didn't do anything to Val," Aesylt croaked. She reached for her throat but recoiled at the budding bruise. "I swear to you. I don't even know what's going on right now."

"You were his final witness, girl, the one who sent him into the forest filled with foul magic. And now the wulf has brought him back to us. Dishonored before the entire village!"

Aesylt's jaw trembled. Tears blinded her. "What?"

Esker's smile was dark and dangerous as he leveled it on her. "You're a koldyna, Aesylt. Just like your mother was." As soon as the word spewed from Esker's mouth, everything around her returned to chaos. Clangs of clashing steel rang in her ears, drowning out any sense of coherence. She clung to her brother, her eyes closed, and prayed for a reprieve.

She was jolted when the gates swung open, but she hardly had time to register that before she was transferred from her brother's arms to the embrace of another.

"Take her to your apartments. Lock the doors. Quickly!" Drazhan barked.

"I have her." Rahn. He leaned down and gathered her legs under his opposite arm, then swept her against himself like she weighed no more than a feather. "Hold on, Aesylt."

"Go!" Drazhan screamed. It escalated to a grunt as Stormbringer crashed against another sword.

The shrill clangs and screams faded with every jostling step. Aesylt buried her face in the scholar's neck and blocked out the world.

Rahn kept his eyes on the window as he poured some tea. Drazhan and his men had subdued the rabble, but the trouble was just beginning. He replayed the word in his head, *koldyna*, a terrible slur for witches who communed with the demon realm. In Vjestik culture, there were few things more dangerous or reviled. And now Aesylt had been branded with it, and Rahn had a dark, sickening feeling such an accusation wouldn't be so easily forgotten or set aside.

Aesylt lay curled on his settee, under the thick blanket he'd lain over her when she'd started shaking. She hadn't said a single word from the moment he'd swept her from Drazhan's arms. Little color had returned to her cheeks.

"Here." He put the mug on the table and lowered himself onto the armchair across from her.

"Not thirsty," she muttered. She stared at the fire with a vacant gaze, her breathing slow but unsteady.

"Maia brought it by. Said it would help your nerves."

Her eyes fluttered closed as she pulled herself up with what seemed to be great effort. He started forward, but she tucked her chin and shook her head. She cupped the mug with both hands, apparently unbothered by the steaming heat, and after a slow, drawn swallow, she said, "You're going to tell me what you know, Scholar."

Her face was smeared with fading abrasions, her clothes torn. He'd cleaned and dressed her wounds, and her vedhma had healed them. The memory of that morning, however, would leave none of them soon. "Unfortunately, I don't know very much, Aesylt."

"Then tell me what little you do."

Drazhan might have been trying to protect her by not explaining things, but Aesylt was not someone who would be satisfied by half-truths. He breathed deep and began. "From what I understand, just before dawn, a wulf came from the forest dragging... dragging Valerian by the ankle. He was unconscious and badly injured but alive. I heard Fezzan talking to your brother, and they said nothing like that has ever happened before. Either the wulf lives or the boy lives, but never... this. There are whispers that either Val or the wulf was spelled. Most seem to believe there's some sort of dark magic involved. No one can explain it, and so they fear it." He inhaled deep and breathed out. "That's all I know. I'm sorry."

"Was spelled by me. That's what you're not saying."

Rahn frowned. "Once cooler heads prevail, they'll know how ludicrous the accusation is."

Aesylt winced but nodded. "Thank you for telling me." She took another sip before setting her tea aside. "I suppose visiting Val is out of the question."

"Undoubtedly."

"Where are Imryll and Aleksy?"

"In their apartments. Tas and Teleria are with them. Everyone is safe."

"Everyone inside, you mean." She contorted and tucked her legs under her. "Why weren't you there this morning?"

Rahn glanced again at the window. The thinning crowd provided some relief, but he'd never seen such fear as he'd witnessed in the eyes of the villagers when they'd stormed Fanghelm, desperate for answers and consolation... anxious and afraid of the repercussions the entire village would suffer as a result of the unprecedented event. "I was outside for a morning stretch when the carts came up the hill. Drazhan sent me back with several of his men to help secure the keep. He didn't allow me the opportunity to tell you myself. I'm sorry if my absence caused you any distress."

Aesylt picked at the fresh bandage on her arm. "In Vjestik culture, wulves are omens. Messengers. Everyone will try to decipher their message, and the guessing, the supposition, will bring this village into civil war if Drazhan can't get a handle on it."

Rahn studied the tight flex in her cheeks, where her dimples bedded, and the same motion at her temples as she must have bitten down on her tongue. Her questions so far had skirted the one she should have asked, the one he knew she wanted to. "Your brother offered to have Val convalesce here at Fanghelm, where the Wynter vedhmas could set him to rights, but the Barynovs wouldn't hear of it. They won't even dispatch their own vedhmas. They're refusing any healing at all, until they have answers. The irony is Valerian is the only one who can provide them."

"I didn't ask about Val."

"I know."

"They've branded me a koldyna."

Rahn breathed out. "I know."

"There is nothing worse to the Vjestik. We take it so seriously, even accusing someone is a crime, without proof."

"Well, they can't prove it, can they? Because you aren't a koldyna, Aesylt."

She looked down at her hands, her head shaking. "Whatever the wulves are playing at, it has nothing to do with me."

"We both know men are rarely rational when they're afraid," he said. "When Valerian wakes, he may be able to fill in the missing pieces of this strange tale."

"I just don't understand..." Aesylt bowed forward and raked her hands through her hair. "Nothing like this has *ever* happened before."

"All things can be explained eventually," Rahn said. "And heads will clear in time." Even as he said the words, he wasn't sure he believed them. Drazhan Wynter was not a man who feared anything, but when he had placed his sister into Rahn's arms, the men's eyes connecting for the briefest moment, Rahn had seen pure terror there.

"You don't even believe that," Aesylt said, scoffing.

"Read my mind, did you?" he said lightly.

"I need to go find my brother." She pushed forward, trying to rise, but fell back with a swoon.

Rahn shifted quickly to the settee, one arm behind her in case she lost her bearing again. "He wants you here. Whatever's going on out there, he needs to focus without worrying if you're in danger."

"Didn't take you for a Drazhan fan," she muttered but then relaxed, leaning against him with a defeated sigh. She pulled her knees to her chest with a shivering sigh. "This is a proper mess."

Rahn nodded, exhausted. Whatever sleep he'd garnered at the observatory had been used up in the past hour. "It seems so."

"You know how I know it's a mess? Drazhan asking *you* to lock yourself away with me. Oh the scandal if others find out."

His brows lifted. "It's not a scandal if there's nothing to talk about."

"You think that ever stops a wagging tongue? Why do you think we're in this mess?"

"It's just until he can clear the trouble at the gates. He'll be back soon."

She looked up at him, her crystalline eyes heavy and dark. A soft pause scored the air between them. "I had an idea for how we can solve your curricula problem."

Rahn gave her a light squeeze and stared into the crackling hearth. "I'm not worried about our research right now."

"You should be. The support from our Vjestik elders is just as critical as the Reliquary's endorsement. If we fall behind, they'll pull their sons and daughters from the cohorts. When the village turns on something, their shunning is total."

With one researcher near death and another being accused of dark magic, their studies were the last thing on his mind, but if talking about it kept Aesylt grounded, he'd listen. "What's your idea then?"

Aesylt sat up and met his eyes. She reached for one of his hands, breathed in, and whispered, "And another with me."

Rahn gasped at the startlingly abrupt change in his surroundings. His rich furnishings blended with everything else into a dull sepia. A violet settee had become a muted lavender. The gold tapestry on the wall was a haze of soft bronze and blurred design. And there was a shimmer in the air, one that inexplicably made him think of stars and sky. Everything was like that, everything except—

Except him and her.

"Is this..." He turned his hands over before his eyes, but they were the same as they'd always been.

Aesylt nodded. She pivoted until she was facing him head-on. "Welcome to the celestial realm, Scholar."

Rahn ran his hands through the air in wonder. He couldn't decide what to focus on. His thoughts were a blur. "I've never been confronted with so much I can't explain."

"I can bring you here whenever you want." She glanced to the side. "As I told you last night, nothing anyone does here has consequence in the real world."

Rahn shook his head, struggling to catch up as he tried to confront what had happened, what *was* happening.

"If you and Tasmin need a place to conduct your practical experimentation for the upcoming curricula..." Her throat bobbed with a brief glance away. "I can bring you both here. Give you a safe place without worrying about anyone crying indecency. You can do everything here that you can do out there, but nothing you do here follows you into the real world."

"Tasmin and me?" Rahn's head spun between the surrealness of sitting in a world not his own and Aesylt's stunning offer. "No, no that's not... Besides, she's leaving for Whitechurch soon. I'll find another way."

Aesylt moved to her knees and lifted up until they were eye level. Without warning, she kissed him. Her smooth lips brushed softly over his with a gentle whimper that lighted something in him long dormant. Something dangerous. "You see? That didn't happen."

Rahn, breathing hard, backed away. "How can you say it didn't happen?" His hand traveled to his mouth, his disbelief still forming.

"Because it only happened here."

"Are you saying my memory won't return with me to the real world?"

"You'll remember, but it won't matter. It happened in a place where nothing matters." She lowered onto her heels. "You *must* continue the work, Scholar. Drazhan is going to pull me away from the cohort—I know it in my soul—and I need to know *you* will continue. This is a dark moment. That's all. It will pass, and when it does, we still have important work to do."

Rahn stood and paced toward the window. The sepia land beyond was devoid of people, unlike the one they'd left behind. They had the entire world to themselves. His lips buzzed, still drawn to the recent past, the warmth of a young woman who had left an indelible mark on him the moment he'd met her. But it was wrong to feel that way. Wrong to desire what could never be his. To even think of Aesylt in those terms, to have or not to have, was wrong.

She was wrong as well. It mattered.

"Scholar?"

"You're upset. You have every reason to be. Every damned right to be." He dragged his hands against his mouth to erase the imprint of her. "But that can't happen again. In here or out there."

Her laugh was short, humorless. "But it didn't happen. That's my point."

"This isn't the way," he said, tossing his head. He reached for the windowsill and saw his hand was trembling. The taste of her lingered despite his efforts.

"Have I crossed a line?"

"No. No, you were... You were making a point. But the point has been made, and we need to—"

"And now we return."

Rahn pitched forward when the world shifted again. The color and vibrancy returned, sending his mind reeling and fighting to catch up.

"I wasn't sure, but I had a feeling," she muttered.

Soon enough, he understood why she'd brought them back so abruptly.

"Cub." Drazhan slammed the door and charged in. He tossed a glance at Rahn and then moved to Aesylt and knelt before her. "I'm sorry I scared you. Val is alive but gravely wounded. His pigheaded family won't allow any vedhmas in, not even their own, and I don't know what it means for his future. But the Barynovs are out for blood. *Your* blood. And they can't fucking have it."

Rahn caught Drazhan's eyes. In the quick connection, an understanding passed between them. *The danger to her life is very, very real.*

"I swear to you, Draz, I didn't—"

Drazhan reached for her face and brought it to his, pressing their foreheads taut. "I know. I know you didn't. But the Barynovs are telling anyone who will listen that you did. It's not safe for you beyond Fanghelm, Aes. Not right now." He kissed her nose and stood. "Adrahn, I need something from you."

Rahn inhaled a shaky breath and nodded. "Anything."

He flicked a nod at Aesylt. "You and I both know this one won't keep still unless she has something to occupy her."

"If you're going to talk about me like I'm not here, I'll leave," Aesylt snapped.

"How can I help?" Rahn asked, hiding a smirk.

"Val is out of the cohort, clearly. Nik's family needs to maintain their neutrality. Tas has decided to move up her trip to Whitechurch. Elara is being moved to Jasika, for reasons Imryll explained, but I can't remember now." Drazhan swished his mouth. "So my sister is your partner now."

Rahn squeezed the sill, nodding. The kiss hammered his thoughts from all sides. *Never again.* "You want Aesylt and I to continue working? Together?"

"That's what I said."

Imryll's secondhand scolding came back to him. Drazhan, for all his gratitude about the matter of the tree, still saw Rahn as a threat to Aesylt's honor. His heart sank, realizing how bad things must be for him to suggest they spend hours and hours together, alone. Drazhan must have felt the best option was to keep Aesylt occupied with something productive—and rightly presumed Rahn would have more sense than to cross a line. "If that's what you need from me, then of course."

"Good." Drazhan broke his gaze and clamped a hand atop Aesylt's shoulder with a tight smile. "Focus on your research, cub. Leave the rest to me. It will blow over."

"I don't get a say in this?" Aesylt asked. "You're just going to keep deciding for me, like I'm eight?"

Drazhan's brows furrowed. "I thought you'd be happy you get to continue."

"It's fine." She crossed her arms and retreated onto the couch. "I'll be a good little soldier, wulf. Don't worry about me."

Drazhan sighed. His eyes fluttered back toward Rahn. "I'll sort this mess out. She's your responsibility until I do."

"Fucking archaic notions of men," Aesylt hissed under her breath.

"What's that?" Drazhan asked, though he'd clearly heard.

"Nothing." Her smile was saccharine. "Don't worry about me, frata. I have a stalwart protector here, a strong and powerful *man* to keep this little damsel from doing anything foolish."

Drazhan shot her a bracing look and started to turn. "Ancestors be with you, Adrahn," he muttered and stormed out. His armor echoed down the halls and then disappeared.

Rahn leaned against the window with a sigh.

"You're relieved of Aesylt duty," she said with a flippant shrug of one shoulder. She tossed the quilt away and jumped to her feet. "I'm going to the Barynovs to sort this out. If something happens, I'll be sure and tell my brother it wasn't your fault."

"No." Rahn massaged his throat when the word creaked.

"What did you say?"

"No." He found his voice again. He said it again, more firmly. "You're not going anywhere."

Aesylt spun on him. "Excuse me?"

Rahn marched to the door, digging in his pocket for his keys as he swept by her. He locked both bolts, turned, and found her wearing a flushed glower that was part surprise and part indignant rage. "If Drazhan needs me to help keep you safe so he can work matters out with the Barynovs, then it's what I'm going to do." When she lifted onto her toes with a menacing glare, he didn't back down, not even when her face was close enough for him to feel her breath. "I'm not a man who walks away from his responsibilities, Aesylt."

"I am *not your responsibility,*" she said through clenched teeth. "And we can't continue our research anyway, can we? The other women are out of the cohort. The men too. If you think anyone is sending more to join us after what happened this morning, you don't know the Vjestik. So who are you going to conduct practical experiments with? Yourself?"

Nothing we do here matters.

Rahn swallowed a hard lump. "I don't know. I haven't had enough time with my thoughts."

"And when we have nothing to send to the Reliquary in a fortnight, when the next report goes out, what do you think will happen?"

"I said I need time with my thoughts." He dusted his hands along her tense shoulders, sighing. "But I *will* think of something. I promise."

"There is one answer," Aesylt said with a proud tilt of her chin. Her eyes seemed to shake in their sockets, narrowing in a challenge issued. "The question is whether your commitment to the science is bigger than the man inside of you... whether you're capable of removing emotion and moral and ethical inhibitions from the equation." She rose higher on her toes. "But most of all, it comes down to whether you have the courage to defy my brother for the greater good of the realm."

Rahn's heart pounded against his ribs, ready to burst. What she seemed to suggest, it went beyond scientific boundaries. If he could find his words, he might explain it in a way she would understand, but he couldn't speak at all.

"I've died a dozen deaths while starwalking. I've kissed. I've hunted. I've climbed mountains. I've killed. I've done things I never could or would do in this world, and I am who I am because of it. Sometimes I think those experiences are the reason I'm still alive at all."

Aesylt lowered back to the ground with a light sigh that was quite the opposite of her charged delivery. "So I can put the emotion, the ethics, the morals aside for the sake of the research, Scholar, because I've been doing it my whole life. Can you?"

THE DARKER SIDE OF LEARNING

SIX
STIRRING LECTURE

Two days had passed since Valerian had returned under frightening circumstances. Two excruciatingly long days since Drazhan had swept out of Rahn's room, brimming with vengeance and rendering Aesylt a veritable prisoner in the hands of Scholar Tindahl.

But what really had Aesylt's nerves on edge day and night was the silence. The lack of news, of any kind. She'd tried probing the kitchen staff when they passed meals through Rahn's service gap, but they either knew nothing or would say nothing. Maia was no more forthright. The only thing she could offer was that Imryll and the others were still in the same situation as Aesylt, sequestered in their apartments and waiting for the same news.

The world beyond their row of fogged panes was snowy and quiet. Dusk had descended an hour ago, darkness imminent.

If there was a skirmish underway, it wasn't happening at Fanghelm.

Aesylt unenthusiastically stabbed at the congealed remnants of her stew. She'd eaten as much as her sour belly could tolerate, and only because she'd need her energy for what she had planned.

Rahn sat in a rickety wooden rocker at the corner window, one leg propped over the other, his notebook resting against his trousers. His quill tapped the paper as he divided his attention between the night sky and his notes. His spectacles, the ones he needed for reading and writing, balanced on his nose, and there was something about the man in those moments that—

"Aesylt. Come look at this."

"I'm fine over here," she said crossly, slopping her spoon through the sludge in her bowl.

His sigh was delayed. "Were you not the one who proffered a stirring lecture on putting emotion aside for the betterment of science?"

Aesylt flickered her eyes upward, her muscles clenching. He wanted to talk about her *stirring lecture* but not the reason she'd given it?

She braced against the chair and pushed to her feet, cursing under her breath as she shuffled toward him. He glanced up with a gentle smile that made her feel unreasonable for her anger. But it didn't go away either.

"What am I looking at?" she asked, lifting a hand to the side in poorly acted disinterest.

"You see that cloud cover over the range?" He pointed his quill and glanced up to make sure she was following. His tenderness with her was maddening, but it was also an unexpectedly warm hug. "If I could get to the observatory, I'd be able to confirm this, but..." He rifled through his notebook, flipping page after page. "That cluster of stars we've been studying. The bowman?"

"Mhm," she said when he waited for her confirmation.

"You know how we've been puzzling over its appearance on some nights and not on others? How our predictions have all been wrong?"

"I suppose," Aesylt replied with a dismissive shrug, but her curiosity was officially piqued. She could turn her nose up at anything else, but not the research. Months their cohort had been charting the elusive bowman, and they'd found no discernible pattern or cycle to its waning or waxing presence in the sky. It was seemingly random, but randomness, as Rahn had explained, though not unheard of in nature, should never be used in lieu of searching for the truth.

"Bonfire nights." He waved his quill at the sky, grinning back at her. "In the village."

"And?"

"All that smoke... It goes somewhere, doesn't it?" He adjusted in excitement. "I read a pamphlet once on smoke and fire, and well, I won't bore you with all of it, but what I found fascinating was the revelation that the reason smoke and heat rise is that they're both less dense than cold air. The decreased density allows them to spread apart and move faster, thus rising—at least if the surrounding air is cooler." He paused, his look reminding her of a little boy showing his parents something he built.

Her mouth hooked into a half smile despite her temperament.

"The air is *always* cooler here. Even in springtide. So the smoke goes up. It eventually dissipates, as all gaseous matters do, but not before creating a haze." He flipped through the pages once more, pausing every few with a hard tap. "Every third, eighteenth, and twenty-seventh day is a bonfire night in midwinter, but in wintertide, it switches to every second, sixteenth, and twenty-ninth. Look at these dates."

Aesylt leaned in, but he was flipping too fast. "You're saying the nights we couldn't see the bowman were bonfire nights?"

Rahn nodded, visibly restraining a burst of elation.

Bonfire nights were a Vjestik tradition, a reason to gather as a community. Warmth, food, ale, and conversation. Some joined to cast salt or other spices into the flames, to invite protections against their family or business. Others used the bonfires to dispose of unwanted items. Most came for the community. But those nights were always a spectacle. Five, six, sometimes seven pyres would burn down the main road, enough to warm the entire stretch, leading to ashy mornings that put a burn in even the strongest villager's lungs. "Contaminants in the air create obfuscations..." Aesylt made a *huh* sound. "Well it seems so obvious now."

Rahn loosed his spectacles from his face and let them fall with their chain against his chest. It was then she saw the gleam of keys in his lower vest pocket. "We were looking for the wrong patterns. And yes, it does, doesn't it?" He shook his head. "Of course, to validate, we'll need to visit the observatory on those nights."

Aesylt wanted to share his enthusiasm, even if she couldn't find the desire to express it. But the way Rahn had been acting like nothing was amiss, deftly dodging any attempt she'd made to argue the merits of defying Drazhan's ridiculous order, was all the armor she needed to keep her giddiness to herself.

And there was still—like a festering sore—the matter of the proposition she'd made, which he was pretending hadn't happened. He'd said not a word until he'd smoothly called her to task for being a hypocrite.

"Can't very well do that locked away in your apartments, can we?" She spun away, ashamed of her lack of restraint... her insolent tone. It was impractical and worked against her plan, which needed to happen *soon*, or she'd be forced to wait another night. Without knowing what the devil was going on outside their doors, or when it would stop, she couldn't afford to delay.

"It's not forever." His eyes locked onto hers. The way he treated every person speaking like they were the only other individual in the room had always disarmed her, but she was impervious in her current state of annoyance. His gaze swept downward briefly. "I can have your vedhma bring more clothing for you. You could wear mine, though you'd be swimming in it."

Aesylt patted herself in indignance. "What, am I too filthy for you, Scholar? Is there a stench?"

"Neither question requires an answer, as I'm sure you knew before you asked." He grinned and stood, setting his notebook and quill on the small table. With a stretch and a yawn, he turned toward the room.

Stop goading the man. You need his concern pointed anywhere but you. "Fine. Send for clothes. Trousers and blouses though. I'm tired of gowns."

"I will then. First thing." He reached for his implements and carried them to the armoire where he kept his ink blots and paper.

It's now or wait another night.

When she was sure he was fully occupied, Aesylt carefully slinked to the other side of the room, opposite of where his back was turned. She started a slow tiptoe toward him but froze midway, when he looked over his shoulder.

"Look... I know you're frustrated. I'll send word to your brother tomorrow and see if he'll at least give us... something. Perhaps he'll see fit to expanding your borders so you're not stuck with me day and night. Even I would consider it torture."

She could almost feel him grinning to himself at his flat attempt at humor.

Aesylt muttered her response from the side of her mouth, praying it was enough to obscure her location, and he returned to sorting his cabinet. Flitting forward another few steps, she breathed deep and stretched a hand slowly forward, then stopped when it looked like he was going to speak again. When he didn't, she said a silent prayer and reached forward, this time hooking her pinky under the thick ring of keys poking from the top of his vest pocket. He tensed, but something else drew his attention, and the danger passed.

She squinted, bracing from head to toe as she slowly lifted. Her hand shook, so she went even slower, until she had them fully extricated from his pocket.

Rahn startled again. When he started to turn, Aesylt swiftly shifted into the celestial realm.

She couldn't stay any longer than it would take him to search his apartment and discover she wasn't there. But if she phased back while he was still standing at the cabinet, he'd see her and the stolen keys and know precisely what she'd done. She'd never be able to hide them fast enough. And he'd certainly never be so careless again.

Panting, she took a moment to recover herself. Starwalking had limited function as a stealth ability. She could only return to where she'd left. She couldn't shift into the celestial realm and stalk the halls, learning their secrets, because she could only see those who were in the realm with her. Rahn could be anywhere. She'd only find out where upon returning, and if she did at the wrong time, it was over.

She had no choice though. He'd be looking for her soon, if he wasn't already.

Aesylt counted to sixty, phased back...

And stumbled sideways from the force of her relief.

The cabinet was closed and latched.

The scholar wasn't in the room at all anymore.

"I'll be finished dressing shortly and then the bedchamber is yours for the night," Rahn called from the distance. "I may turn in soon actually, if you don't find it terribly rude."

"Hvala, Ancestors," she whispered, stuffing the keys inside the bosom of her gown. It was the one place his gaze wouldn't travel. The man was far too concerned with proprieties. "Of course not, Scholar," she said, louder, grinning in the nascent dark. "I think I may just do the same."

Aesylt crouched behind the split of a double-trunked evergreen at the edge of the courtyard of the Petrovash estate, Hibernal. There were only a couple of guards she could see, both swaying on their feet. It was otherwise unsurprisingly quiet, reminiscent of the Petrovashes' famous neutrality on all matters.

Escaping Fanghelm had been easier than she'd expected. Only the Wynters were on lockdown, but Fanghelm was otherwise operating as usual. Cloaked in a man's dress—almost comically swimming under Rahn's bulky fur cloak—she drew minimal gazes, and none lingered. People saw what they expected, and no one expected Aesylt Wynter to be traipsing about in her scholar's clothing.

But all it would take is for Rahn to wake. To notice the unlocked door. The missing keys. The missing *girl.*

She perked when one of the Petrovash guards started speaking to the other. She waited impatiently for their conversation to end, but what happened instead was even more fortuitous. They both started toward the east side of the keep, leaving the courtyard unguarded. There wouldn't be a better opportunity, not unless she wanted to risk being out at dawn, so she gathered the hem of the teeming cloak in both fists, lifted, and ran as fast as she could with the added weight.

Niklaus's apartment was on the ground floor of the west wing. He always slept with one window cracked, even in the winter. He liked to say the Petrovashes ran hot because they were bred for living under the mountain, as many kyschun did. But Aesylt knew his family subscribed to old Vjestik superstitions about always leaving a way for the Ancestors to get in.

Aesylt stretched up onto her tiptoes and slapped the frame until she found the right spot to push. She winced when the window creaked, cutting a sharp sound through the silent night, and waited for her pulse to even out before digging her boots against the stone wall. With a muffled grunt, she hoisted herself until her forearms draped over the sill. She wiggled as quietly as she could, but the thickness of the furs kept her from going any farther.

A slice of steel cut through the air. She arrested, trying to retreat, until she heard, "*Aesylt*?"

"Keep it down." She hissed in relief and dropped to the snowy ground with a crunching thud. She waved a hand. "And put that away before you cut your own hand off."

Niklaus held his suspicious gaze on her as he sheathed his dagger. He retreated into his room and returned with a candle. "Where's your brother?"

"At Fanghelm," she said irritably. "Come down here."

He leaned out and glanced around with a shaky sigh. "You shouldn't be here. Have you gone mad?" He smirked. "Madder than usual?"

"I need your help." She shivered under the cloak, thinking of how long she'd already been gone, how much longer she'd need before she could return. "I need to see him, Nikky."

Niklaus's face crumpled in horror. "Oh, nien. Nien, nien, nien. That's a terrible idea, Aes, trust me. The Barynovs do *not* want you anywhere near him. Hoarfrost is teeming with guards, and there's no... No, there's no way."

"I'm going." She plied him with a searching look to disguise her own fear. "With or without you. But it will be easier and safer if you come with me and help me find a way in."

"There isn't a way in!" His face crumpled, and he lowered his voice, craning out again with another nervous glance to each side. "The Barynovs are expecting war. They're preparing for war. You cannot just stroll onto Hoarfrost like you did Hibernal and expect anything but chaos."

"I *need* to see him." She pulled down her ungainly hood and implored him, sputtering through a caught mouthful of hair. "I didn't do that to him, and I need to know what really happened. I can't go another night without knowing."

Niklaus dragged his hands down his face. "*No one* knows. You won't get anything from his family except accusations. We aren't getting any answers until Val wakes up and can tell us himself. From what Onkel Anton told me, we shouldn't be getting our hopes up."

"He might wake for me." Aesylt lifted her chin with false pride. She couldn't tell him about the last conversation between her and Val. What she'd promised. Despite her denial and fear, she finally realized she'd truly believed the good-bye had been forever. But he was alive, and there was no reason to expect he wouldn't still mean the words when he regained consciousness.

Betrothal was a problem for another day.

Niklaus peered behind himself with a yielding shrug. He sounded almost hostile when he responded. "Tak, I suppose he might. For you. But do you really want to risk your life on a maybe?"

"The Barynovs won't hurt me," she stated. "They want to, but they won't. Their fear of Drazhan is greater than their hatred of me. And they once dealt with me as an equal, when it was me in my brother's seat."

He watched her in intense silence. "You better hope you're right. Because your brother isn't here to intervene this time. He doesn't even know you're doing this, does he? Don't answer. I already know there's no chance."

Aesylt sighed, shifting from one foot to another as a cold gust ripped through the courtyard, sending a mournful song threading through the pines. "Look, I don't know how long I have before the scholar finds I've given him the slip. He'll go straight to Draz, which won't be good for anyone."

"I can't talk you out of this, can I?" he asked, but it wasn't a question. He waved a hand and muttered for her to give him a minute. She waited in bittersweet relief.

Moments later, he was dressed and sliding out the window to join her.

When he landed, he pulled her in for a ferocious hug. "I'm *only* doing this because I know you're stubborn enough to go without me." He pulled back to regard her more closely, his head shaking. "I would never forgive myself if something happened to you."

Aesylt cupped his face in her hands and kissed his nose. "Volemthe, Nikky. Hvala."

"Don't thank me yet, madwoman." Niklaus grabbed her and aimed her away from the keep with a soft shove. "We'll go the back way. Less chance of someone seeing us."

They moved in silence through the garden and then climbed out through an adjoining pasture, until they were on a familiar forest path.

"So what happened with you that day at Fanghelm? After Val came back?" he asked. The trail was speckled with fresh snow, but the older piles had been plowed into banks on either side.

Aesylt shrugged under Rahn's furs. "I don't know. Drazhan was acting strangely when he came to the observatory with his men. He only told me about Val right before the mob came for us."

"Everyone is saying you..."

"Spelled him." Her breath furled before her in a dense white cloud. "It's not true."

"I never thought it was. But you know our people. They smell a koldyna; they're ready to ride."

"Mm."

"Are you going to tell me what you think going to the Barynovs will accomplish? He's not going to wake up, Aes. Not anytime soon."

She didn't have a satisfying answer. All she knew was she needed to see Val. To lay hands on him and listen to the stories of his flesh. "Has there been more fighting?"

Nik shook his head. "Just your brother and Esker trading prickly letters that go nowhere."

"I wonder why he has me locked away with the scholar then."

"Indeed." Niklaus chuckled without humor. "Was wondering the same."

"It's been nothing short of imprisonment, I assure you," she said, eyeing him from the side.

"Oh, I'm sure." He snorted. "And the cohort? What's going to happen with that?"

"It's just him and me now, until you can come back," she said with a hard breath out. "But we won't let the research suffer. We'll... figure it out."

"Figure it out?"

"It's just this upcoming subject. It's... never mind."

Niklaus came to an abrupt stop. "What?"

Aesylt kept walking, but he hadn't budged.

"Tell me."

She slowed and turned. "Jasika's cohort was supposed to be handling it, but Imryll wanted Rahn to take it instead because it requires participatory exercises rather than just documentation, and they're all women now on her cohort, and..."

"Say it already."

Her gaze lowered. "Coitus."

Niklaus cocked his head all the way to the side. "Sex?"

Aesylt shrugged. "We're working on a plan."

"You're working on a *plan*?"

"Can we keep moving?"

"Aesylt!"

Aesylt craned her neck to look up at him. "We'll do what we have to do, all right? There are ways around the... ah, problem. But we can't refuse. You know that. The Reliquary is looking for any reason to kick us out of our own study, and we won't let it happen."

"You absolutely can refuse!"

"Tak," she said softly. "But then it all ends, doesn't it?"

"So you're going to..." Niklaus brought both hands to his nose. "Fuck the scholar?"

She shrugged, but her heart launched into a sudden race. Was she? Rahn was the one who needed convincing. "You're making this out to be something personal when it's not. It's science."

Niklaus cackled, throwing his head back. "Fucking for science. That's a new one to me. Don't recall reading that anywhere in our charter."

"For the love of the Ancestors, you're making this far more than it is."

"Am I?" His smile was gone. "Never mind that if your brother even had a *whisper* of suspicion about this, he would murder the man, how exactly are you going to explain who compiled the research notes and how? The Reliquary has the cohort's names. We can't make them up."

"I don't have all the answers now, and frankly, I'm exhausted, and this isn't—" She lifted and lowered her shoulders with a weighty sigh. "I can only focus on one problem at a time."

"Is it a problem though, Aes? I see the way you look at the man. Science, eh?"

A hot flush flooded her cheeks. "If you cannot speak about this like an academic, then we're not going to speak of it at all."

He shook his head and continued without her.

Aesylt took a quick moment to gather herself and followed.

SEVEN
HOARFROST

They heard Hoarfrost before they saw it. Aesylt had been expecting its extraordinary guard force, but the Barynovs could have been hosting a party for all the village, for as loud and raucous as the sounds were, carrying up to them on their way down the tree-lined slope.

"Told you," Niklaus murmured. He pulled to a stop at the start of their descent down the forest hill overlooking the modest keep at the north wood's edge. "There's no way in, Aes. You can see for yourself now."

She squinted through the fog, trying to add visual confirmation to everything she was hearing. Red was the color of the Barynovs, a bright and bold color that contrasted with the icier blues and silvers of her home. The color was everywhere, on all sides of Hoarfrost. Standards, uniforms, painted posts... Against the stone and snow, it reminded her of the gory splash that had followed carnage. Of the Nok Mora.

With a shiver, she straightened. "How about the root cellar?"

"What about it?"

"They have six cellars, remember? The others are detached from the keep, but not the root cellar. You really don't remember that was how Val would sneak us in after dark?"

Niklaus gazed at the ground. He toed his boot against a rotting log. "If they catch you, they might not kill you, but they will take you hostage. The war you asked me about? It will begin. Over you."

Aesylt balked. "But I haven't done anything *wrong*, Nik. Val asked me to be his final witness, and I was. Nothing happened that could have caused whatever... whatever he went through out there. And if I don't see him, if I can't figure out what happened, this will only get worse for everyone."

"I thought reading whispers didn't work anymore."

"It does... sometimes."

What Nik wasn't saying, because even in his anger he still loved her, was that her ability to receive messages from laying hands had gone away after the Nok Mora—not because the magic had left her but because it had been years before she'd let anyone touch her in more than a passing way. Before she'd dared touch anyone else. When she finally allowed it again, she was careful to close her thoughts off from receiving information. Wandering through the smoldering village alone, checking for breaths and heartbeats, reading their deaths in reverse... It was still just as real. The scent was never far from her nose. The horrors gripped her heart in perpetuity.

The truth was she had no idea if she could read Val or not.

"Even if you could, who in there will believe you? If you tell them you *read* the truth in his flesh, that would only make it worse. Ancestors save you if they ever knew what you used to do. The starwalking." He jutted an arm toward the keep. "They've already decided. You're a koldyna to them, and we both know how our people deal with dark witches."

Niklaus was right, but she had no choice but to try. Drazhan would raze the Barynovs altogether in his fear of losing her, and they would take everything they could with them as they burned.

Aesylt crossed her arms and turned back up the hill. Hot tears burned her eyes but didn't fall. They wouldn't. She'd cried exactly twice since the dust of the Nok Mora had settled: once when Drazhan had returned home after many years away and then the other night, when she'd been certain her doom awaited her at the top of a damned tree. "You and I could go in circles about this for hours. But I'm going. It would be easier if we went together, but..." She lifted her shoulders and started down the hill.

"Wait!" he cried, part whisper, part scream. "Aesylt, for the love of the Ancestors!"

Aesylt wove a path between the trees, pausing at each to verify she hadn't been spotted. Niklaus was close behind, grunting his displeasure under his breath but keeping pace. They continued this way until they reached the edge of a small garden, where the Barynovs grew winterberries and hoargrapes they made into wines. They could hardly get anyone south of Witchwood Cross to stock their harvest, for all its bitterness, but to the Vjestik, it was a sigil of their resilience. If they could suffer through a Barynov varietal, they could withstand anything.

She ducked between two rows and gestured for Niklaus to join her. "Here's what I'm thinking. We get as close as we can. If we can't... If we can't reach the cellar on our own, I'll create a distraction to draw their eyes away and you go for it."

"The fuck you will." Niklaus's eyes flashed wide in fearful anger. "You stay here, and I'll go take a look around. *Stay* here, Aes. I'm not asking either, so unless you want me to get Drazhan involved, you'll calm your blood for a few more minutes. If I get caught, I'll say I was coming to see Val, and no one will say a word to me, other than wondering why I'm here so late, but I can explain that. If you see anyone coming... Can you still... starwalk..."

Aesylt nodded, glancing away. It had been years since she'd taken Niklaus starwalking, long enough that he'd evidently tucked it into the back of his thoughts. How would he feel if he knew she'd been to the celestial realm with Val just days prior? And the scholar after.

"Good. I think." He frowned. "I'll be back."

The keys. Rahn's first thought after waking abruptly.

Gods, she played me for a fool. His second.

He searched his apartment, but it was strictly performative, confirming what he already knew.

She'd given him the slip.

Rahn dressed in a rush. As an afterthought, hopefully an overreaction, he grabbed his sword and scabbard and fastened them onto his belt.

But when he reached for the open bolts, he didn't know where to go next.

Drazhan was the sensible choice, but Rahn only had suppositions, not facts. Aesylt would never forgive herself if her brother went ballistic on her behalf. It would be deeply unfair and inappropriate to put Imryll in a position to either lie to her husband or betray her sister-in-law.

He needed to get a read on the situation before involving them.

Tasmin then.

Rahn slipped out of his apartment with a reasonable gait, but once he passed the guards in the hall, he bolted.

It was a half tick of the moon before Niklaus returned. Aesylt crouched in the knobby root system of a large tree.

"You were gone a while," she remarked. "How bad is it?"

"Bad," he said, keeling forward to catch his breath. "But you were onto something with the root cellar. There are two guards with a partial view, and quite a few more once you exit into the keep, but… I remembered something. We don't need to go through the halls at all once we're inside the cellar."

Aesylt brightened, standing. "The hoists!"

Niklaus grinned. "I remember the middle one stops in his apartment on the top floor. Only trouble is someone needs to be at the top to run the pulley. But if *I* head to his room, the way any welcomed guest would, then I can go inside and pull you up. It's late, and they might question it, but we used to come and go at all hours. If anything, I'm overdue for a visit."

Aesylt didn't hesitate. "Let's do it."

"Adrahn Elezhar Tindahl." Tasmin spun away and lifted a hand, her gold robe flapping, as she stormed back into her bedchamber. Her tight smile appeased the guards, and then she slammed the door to a rustle of fabrics. "How could you let this happen?"

Rahn groaned as he slid his fingers down his face. "The question deserves an answer, but finding Aesylt is more pressing at the moment."

"You have blinders on with her. You're incapable of objectivity." Tasmin emerged with her hair piled hastily into a ribbon, a dense cloak covering her wrinkled gown. "And I'll be insulted if you deny it. To others, fine, but to me?"

He threw out his hands in weary surrender. "I won't argue that. But if we don't find her before Drazhan realizes she's gone, then..." There was no point in finishing.

"Fine." She fastened the leather straps on her cloak, starting at the neck. "How long has she been gone?"

Rahn stared at her in blank shame.

"No guesses whatsoever?" Tasmin blinked.

"At best, an hour." Rahn breathed deep. "At worst... three."

Tasmin blurted a laugh. "She could be halfway to Wulfsgate by now."

"But that's not where she went." He grimaced before speaking it. "Hoarfrost."

Tasmin's smirk disappeared. "Rahn, if she's there, we *have* to wake Draz. This is not something you and I can handle ourselves—"

Rahn reached for her arm. "Please. Not until we know for sure. You and your mother are the only ones I trust to keep this between us. Every other person in this keep has sworn a vow of loyalty to their steward. I could wake Teleria, but—"

"No, don't." Tasmin wrenched away with a tight scowl. "For the love of the gods. Aesylt. She's just like Imryll, you know. Obstinate. Incorrigible. I love them both, but only miracles can account for them still breathing."

Even the words sent his heart into a discordant flutter. "Perhaps." He glanced at the window, into the darkness. "I'm not much of a tracker, but if we can retrace her steps..."

"We'll rule Fanghelm out first. First the keep, then the courtyard, barns, and livery," Tasmin said. She checked her pocket for her keys. "There's no reason to go storming into a lion's den without being absolutely sure our little lamb has wandered where she doesn't belong." She turned and met his eyes. "But if she did go to Hoarfrost, we have no choice but to wake the beast."

They had no trouble reaching the cellar or climbing down the dark, narrow stairs. But Aesylt had her first pang of doubt when she considered the row of hoists.

The cellar had a dank putridity to it from the roots that had gone to rot and been left to decay. The long table centering the room was scored with knife marks and stained with vermilion and ocher hues. Ends and other discarded bits were gnarled and dried, and the cobwebs stretching over the lift doors had her wondering if they even worked anymore or if they had fallen into the same disrepair as the rest of the fetid room.

"Did you test it?"

Niklaus ran a finger through the table's dust. "*Now* you're concerned about the viability of this plan?"

"Not concerned," she lied. "Just mindful of all the details we need contingencies for."

He laughed. "You sound like the scholar."

"He's thorough. As we should be." Aesylt moved to the middle door and brushed her sleeve along it. She turned the creaky latch, wincing, and the door yawned open, revealing the tray and pulley. With a hard breath out, she turned and said, "*Should* we test something first?"

Niklaus scanned the room with an exasperated air. "All we'd be doing is drawing more notice. If someone hears this thing moving, they might wonder why. They might investigate. We need you to be in Val's room, and the pulley at rest, by the time that happens."

She closed her eyes, thinking. "We'll hope for the best."

"Ancestors keep us," he hissed. "Anything else we should discuss before I—"

"No," she said quickly, mindful of her waning courage. "Go."

Aesylt waited, agitated, her thoughts awkwardly fumbling through a series of what-if scenarios. They were all bad, every one. If she was caught, even a trip to the celestial realm wouldn't save her, because she couldn't stay there forever. Her longest stint had been two days, once, and she'd been a dazed mess for a full day after. Skin tingling. Tongue dry. Dizzy as a storm.

Only a staircase separated her from the bustling keep. Her imagination fixated on their bloodlust, how they'd whipped each other into an anti-Wynter frenzy. They were all hoping to be the one to bring in the little pale-haired koldyna who'd sent the village to its knees.

Val. Val is the key. If I can just clear my mind, if I can touch him—

Aesylt jolted when a distant knocking traveled down the chute. She closed her eyes, mouthed a silent prayer, and leaned in to look up. At first all she saw was a man-shaped shadow, but then Niklaus's arms flailed wildly, beckoning, and she released her breath.

She pressed her arms on the platform to judge its stability, but it was pointless. She was getting in no matter what.

Aesylt had started to climb in when she thought of the bulky furs. If they got caught on anything...

She darted into an alcove, shrugged the cloak off, and stuffed it into an empty barrel. Before she could change her mind, she raced for the chute and clambered in. The metal was cold to the touch, and she already missed the fur, but she waved at Niklaus, her heart pounding, and braced for the trip.

Aesylt toppled sideways when the first creak of the pulley jolted the platform. She spread her palms to find balance, but the entire thing listed to the right. One of the four ropes had snapped. *I've had a lot of crazy ideas over the years, but this might just top them all.* She slid to the left to even it out and held her breath, moving her legs and arms akimbo.

The platform moved arduously slow. Niklaus's grunts became more labored with each tug. But at last she heard him sighing in relief, and before she knew it, he was tying the anchor.

Niklaus reached in to help her out, then lifted and lowered her onto the floor. Warmth was the first sensation that greeted her. The next was an eerie silence, nothing like what they'd heard outside or streaming from the keep.

"We need to be very careful," Nik whispered as he ushered her away from the lift. "They know I'm in here, but if they hear *you,* it's over. I told them I just wanted a few minutes with my friend, and they were hesitant even to give me that. I couldn't risk locking the door, or they'd definitely be suspicious."

"Obviously," she said curtly but smiled in apology. "Hvala, Nikky. *Really*, thank you. You're the only one I trusted to help me with this, but I'm not ignorant to the risks either. I promise."

He lowered his stare to the ground. "Just hurry, will you? Anyone could come in here at any time..."

Her hand traced his shoulder. "I know." Aesylt finally looked toward the bed, but her gaze climbed no farther than the rise of blanket over Val's legs. "Is it true they haven't allowed any vedhmas to heal him?"

"I think they want the village to see how he's suffered."

"If they really loved him, they wouldn't let him suffer a moment longer than he had to." Aesylt breathed long and deep. "How bad is it?" She hated how small she sounded.

"Do you want me to describe..."

"No. No, I'm only being..." Her throat caught on the word *ridiculous*. She *was* being ridiculous, sneaking out of Fanghelm and into Hoarfrost in the middle of the worst tensions the village had ever experienced—thinking she could... could somehow learn something and salvage the situation, as if reason had anything at all to do with why the Barynovs were readying to march on their steward.

In a rush, Aesylt spun and faced the bed. She managed not to gasp, but only because she forgot how to breathe. *Oh, Val.* His face was scratched but relatively unharmed, but though the blanket fell right under his breastbone, no inch of skin was exposed. It was all wrapped under layers and layers of bandages. She didn't need to pull the blanket back any farther to know they continued all the way down. *Monsters, all of them, leaving you like this. Leaving you to suffer.*

"I'm here, V," she whispered. Her hands patted along the edge of the bed, but she couldn't sit. Her body wouldn't obey the command. "I'm going to fix this. I know it's what you would want." She breathed deep and rested one knee on the bed. "I haven't done this in years. I told you I never wanted to ever again. Think you might have mentioned you'd one day get dragged out of the forest by a damn wulf, so I could prepare myself?" She reached for the only place she could see exposed flesh, his face. Her palm cupped his cheek. "Tell me how it happened. Tell me how to help you."

Behind her was a creak and then a sharp, startled intake of breath. Aesylt stiffened, her body catching up to what her mind had already registered.

"I *knew* you were up to something. You let this koldyna into our *home*?" A door slammed. Boots smashed against stone, rattling the candelabras.

"Marek, wait. Wait." Niklaus's hurried steps blended with the furious ones of Valerian's older brother. "Listen. Please. You've known Aesylt her whole life. Just listen to what she has to say. Marek!"

Aesylt steadily turned, knowing there was only one chance to say the right words, but a fist around her throat stopped them cold. She gasped for air, kicking her feet as she was lifted off the bed.

"Marek!" Niklaus cried.

"You fucking witch," Marek hissed. He spat in her face, hitting her right between the eyes. It slid down the side of her nose.

Aesylt squeezed hers closed and tried to twist out of his grasp, trying to remember what her brothers had taught her.

"Ota will never believe you just handed yourself over." His chokehold tightened. Rough heat patched her cheeks, her vision hazing. She swatted at his hands, but they may as well have been stone. Distantly, she heard Niklaus's panic, felt Marek's solid form shifting slightly in intermittent recoil.

Aesylt had been visiting the celestial realm for so long, it was almost second nature, but when she attempted to shift, to escape, nothing happened. She tried again, focusing harder and imagining herself sliding from one world to another, but still nothing.

Marek slammed her to the stone wall, squeezing the last of the breath from her. Her legs slowed their kicks and then stopped altogether. Darkness eclipsed the edge of her vision, closing... closing until she could only just make out the jade irises in Marek's crazed glare. Her hands fell away, limp at her sides.

The floor rose to greet her with suddenness. Her head hit the stones, bouncing, and she barely made a sound before she was falling again.

"You'd draw steel on me in *my* home?"

"You lay hands on a woman, Marek, I'll draw steel on you anywhere."

Aesylt gulped inward when something connected with her gut. The pain was immediate, blinding. It stole any air she'd regained in the few merciful seconds since Marek had released her.

In her boot she had a dagger. She always had a dagger. But a hard swoon took hold when she reached for it, and she went sprawling across the stones, wheezing.

Marek started to scream, but he was abruptly cut off.

"If you call your family in here, you may as well say good-bye to half of them. Drazhan will strike before he thinks. He'll raze this entire village before he pauses to consider an alternative. Do you want to be responsible for that?"

"Me? She's the one—"

"Lower your fucking voice."

"Nik..." Aesylt croaked. She lost track of the discussion echoing around her. The next words she heard seemed to be a continuation of a different conversation.

"Tak. That's what I said. And you know it's the right thing to do—the only thing to do, if we don't want blood on our hands." Niklaus.

"You're mad. If my father found out she was here? And I let her go?"

"Your father needs to think rationally. He needs to contemplate his next move. Until Val wakes, we can't know what happened."

"I know what happened. The bitch took him where only the dark witches go."

Niklaus didn't respond for several long seconds. Aesylt had almost enough breath to interject, but he spoke first. "You don't know what you're talking about. And throwing around an accusation like that, without proof? It's dangerous, Marek. For you."

"The place *eats* your soul. It marks you. Only the dark ones survive. She marked him, and the wulves rejected him."

"Aye? Then let a tribunal decide so. You remember what the punishment is for falsely accusing someone of being a koldyna? Your father is already guilty of that crime." Niklaus's boots screeched on the stones. "If something happens to her, I'll tell the whole bloody village how the Barynovs treat unarmed women."

Aesylt dug her fingers against the mortar and tried to pull. Her breath was trapped in her throat with her voice, and a terrible thought struck her. Marek had crushed her windpipe. If she couldn't get more air soon, she was done.

"Ten minutes." Marek pushed the words through a tight jaw. "I'll give you a ten-minute head start before I tell the guards she was spotted on our land. If you can't get her far enough in ten minutes? It's on you." He lowered his voice to a sinister pitch. "And I hope you do tell him, Niklaus. Don't miss a single detail."

Aesylt's head came up off the stones, whipping back. Her arms, her legs, and the rest of her followed. Through slow blinks, she saw Nik adjusting her in his arms.

"Let's hope this hoist can hold two of us, Aes." He released a shaky breath and set her inside before climbing in behind her. She looked up and saw Marek's shadowy form holding the rope. "And that no one follows us. I've never killed a man before, but I don't think I'll hesitate if I need to."

"Clear a path! Clear a path!"

Rahn started to tell Tasmin to stop screaming, until he realized it was himself giving the orders. He was the one racing in the blind dark through a row of trees, with Aesylt bouncing in his arms, his pulse thundering between his ears like a sea of endless waves.

"The barn... The barn is just there," cried Niklaus, panting and pushing his pace. "Tasmin, find a vedhma!"

Tasmin looked at Rahn for direction.

Rahn tightened his hold on Aesylt when she slid from his arms. His gaze flitted between Aesylt's restless stirring and the sincere worry on Tasmin's face. Once Drazhan was involved, there'd be no containing the situation, but he needed to know the Barynovs had attacked his sister. He deserved to decide what happened next. "Go find Drazhan and the first vedhma you see."

Tasmin nodded and disappeared into the night.

Niklaus waved both arms, running sideways toward the barn. Rahn lowered his head to protect against the chill wind and pushed the rest of the way.

One door was already open. Rahn kicked the other one, turning to take the brunt of the backswing, to keep it from hitting Aesylt. He quickly assessed the options available, deciding on a loose stack of hay to the right.

Rahn nestled Aesylt onto the hay. One of her arms was still hooked around his shoulder, her lips moving in wordless murmurs. "Shh, it's all right, Aesylt. I have you. You're all right now. You're safe. Help is coming." Reluctantly, he peeled away and stood with a measured sigh, but he didn't move from the spot. His chest clenched when she whimpered. Tears choked his throat. "I'm not leaving you. I promise."

He turned toward Niklaus, who paced in a semicircle, swaddling himself. "I need you to tell me who did this to her and why."

Niklaus stared at him with a disorganized frown. He looked dazed, lost. "I told you, it was the Barynovs. It was... It was—" He bowled over and breathed in.

"*Specifically* which one?" Rahn inhaled through his nose, digging deep for patience. "Which." *Fucking*. "Barynov."

Niklaus looked up, his expression breaking, a sob bubbling on the end of his words. "Marek. Val's brother."

"Marek." Rahn only knew the man by reputation. He was renowned as a brute, the family muscle. The Barynovs never had to shake down their tenants because none wanted to tangle with their ox of a son.

And that *ox* had put his hands on Aesylt's *neck*.

Rahn pressed a hand to the wall to fend off a white wall of rage. *Breathe,* he reminded himself, but the available air was inadequate to meet his demand.

He released the wall, flexed his hands until he felt the blood return, and knelt by the hay. Aesylt's breathing had steadied, but she was no longer conscious. The deep-purple scores on her neck had him clenching hard enough to scrape his teeth together. There was blood on the back of her head too. *Gods give me strength.* "Niklaus," he said, aware of how *not* calm he sounded. "Walk me through what happened. All of it."

"Shouldn't I... I wait for Drazhan?" Niklaus's teeth clacked.

"You'll only get two words out before he takes over." With a shaky inhale, Rahn smoothed a sticky band of hair from Aesylt's eyes with his thumb. He fought the innate urge to plant a soft kiss on the spot. "Start from the beginning."

EIGHT
THE FLESH REMEMBERS

For the first time in her marriage, Imryll had no idea what her husband was thinking.

The composed calm Drazhan had shown when Niklaus Petrovash had run through everything that had happened at Hoarfrost might have convinced others, but a wife saw things others overlooked. The additional blinks. The cords in his neck, ready to snap. No one else understood the tempest building inside of him, the danger it posed to anyone foolish enough to step in its path.

Drazhan kept the audience small. It was only the two of them, Rahn, and Drazhan's closest advisers, Fezzan Castel and Brita Voronov.

Imryll passed an uneasy glance at Rahn, who wore the pall of a man who'd made peace with the gallows.

Drazhan tented his hands under his chin. His gaze pointed at the fire.

"Drazhan." Brita cleared her throat. Her hands brushed down the sides of her untouched mug of ale. "We await only your word."

Fezzan nodded, his head swinging animatedly. "My men can be armored and ready within the hour. Two at most."

"Mine as well."

Drazhan dipped his chin onto his fingers, over and over, the final one nearly a slam. "And the stewardess? What does she think?" His eyes flicked Imryll's way, but his face was still.

Imryll glanced around the long table. Drazhan valued her counsel, seeing her as a balancing agent to his natural impetuosity. If anyone in the room was expected to advocate against war, it was her. But her heart was too heavy, too uneven, for rationalizing. Aesylt would recover, but the damage was done. There was no longer any question of how far the Barynovs were willing to go. "Ah..." She spread her hands along the deep grooves of the wood. "I've never known war. You all have. So I'll not advise for or against something I cannot understand." She breathed in, but there was no steadying her nerves. Her pure, raw anger. "But if I had a sword in my hand right now, Drazhan, I would run it through the man myself."

He nodded, glancing briefly her way. He was still nodding when he said, low and strained, "I want Esker Barynov here, tonight. Alone."

"You expect the man to accept an invitation to his own execution?" Brita dipped her chin in disbelief.

"I'm not going to execute him," Drazhan drawled, taking his time with each word. He remained fixed on the fire. "I'm going to give him a choice."

"A choice?" Imryll asked, narrowing her eyes as she tried to read him.

"A simple one. He can renounce his words against my sister, publicly, and submit his son for tribunal, or the Barynov name dies with him."

Fezzan dropped forward over the table. "An apology?"

Imryll moved her hands under the table, clenching through her growing unease. "He'll never agree to it, Draz. His *men* are gathered at the bottom of our hill. He's already made his choice."

Drazhan lowered his hands to the table. The daze in his eyes cleared as he turned his attention her way. "He has until dawn to respond." He shoved back from the table, casting a long, broad shadow over the council. "Adrahn, at ease. I know my sister. She was always going to find a way. It's my own fault for forgetting that."

Rahn nodded, but there was no relief in the man's expression. "I don't intend to transfer responsibility from my own shoulders to anyone's." His jaw rippled with tension and something else, something Imryll prayed her husband hadn't also noticed. "I do, however, have a suggestion, but I'm not certain you'll approve."

Drazhan held his hands out, waiting.

"If you want to lock her away, she needs something to do. Her mind is restless. *She* is restless." Rahn's throat jumped. He stared at the table, looking at no one. "She's taken a keen interest in the observatory—"

"Fuck no," Drazhan barked with a snort.

"Draz," Imryll whispered. She reached for one of his hands. "Hear him out."

"She needs something to occupy her, or..." Rahn shook his head. "Send us up there with as many guards as you want. But let her work. Allow her some sense of purpose and control in this unfortunate situation. Otherwise, I think we can expect another night like tonight." His mouth pressed tight. "Or worse."

"Mm." Drazhan glanced at Imryll. "You think this is wise?"

Imryll nodded, knowing she could lay her fears bare with him, that he would treat them with care. "We almost lost her tonight. She's been accused of something untenable, and she's desperate to clear her name, no matter what the cost to herself, so do we really have a choice? Whatever danger there may be in them traveling up the mountain, it cannot be half of what she faced tonight... and will continue to face if Val and the accusations are all her mind has to focus on."

Drazhan's tongue darted across his lips. "Fine. I can spare some of our guard to take them up." He rapped his knuckles against his thigh. "But I reserve the right to recall my choice at any time."

Rahn's eyes closed briefly in relief. "Hvala."

Drazhan turned away. "Brit, you'll carry word to the Barynov scout about my offer?"

Brita shoved back from the table. "Right away."

"Fez, have some of your men come to Fanghelm now. Back road, to the north. Quietly."

"You know it."

"Imryll could barely meet Drazhan's eyes when he leaned in to kiss her goodbye. He didn't bother with reassurances.

She flagged Rahn to stay and waited for the others to leave.

He returned to his seat, watching her. "I wouldn't have suggested it if I had a better idea."

"You're right. She'll do it again unless we can keep her focused on something else. She's desperate to clear her name and help Val, and who could blame her? I'd do the same thing." Imryll met his eyes. Now that Drazhan had given his blessing, she needed her old friend's full focus on Aesylt. The curricula matter was her problem. Hers alone. "I'll find a charming way to communicate the temporary shift in our cohort's focus to the Reliquary. Aesylt's safety is more important than anything we're doing here, and if it means you two have to work on astronomy for a while longer, then that's what it means. They'll still get their reports on time like always."

Rahn nodded. "Thank you, Imryll." He paused. "I *should* have been more alert to what she was planning. Looking back on the night... There were signs."

Imryll scoffed. "Locking her away was never the answer. But Draz harbors an immense amount of guilt. In his self-loathing, he fails to see his sister became a woman in those years he was away, shaped by these experiences. In many ways, for the better. In some ways, for the worse. But she doesn't need him in the way he believes she does, and..." She glanced out the long windows with a sigh. Was she really going to say it? Shame Rahn for caring about Aesylt, after all he'd done? She'd issued the warning once already, but that was before he and Aesylt had become research partners—before she'd seen the violent grind in his jaw when Aesylt's injuries were numerated. The slow smoldering rage he could barely restrain. "Just be mindful, Rahn."

"Mindful?"

Imryll shot him a knowing look. "You're an honorable man. That's not in question. But emotions are running hot. Hers. Yours. Mine. Everyone's. There are few people in this world I trust as much as you. Drazhan sees you as an ally. A friend. That is no light matter. The man is more discerning than a king." She straightened, for a moment seeing the very future she hoped to avoid. Whether it was divination or fear, she couldn't know. Not yet. "Let's not add more trouble to the boiling pot."

"You take that end, Nik." Aesylt made a clicking sound with her tongue. "Niklaus."

Niklaus made a tight shake with his head and turned, his stony expression fading as his daze broke. "Sorry. Take what?"

Aesylt shifted the unwieldy roll of vellum in her arms to keep from dropping it. She spotted Rahn near the glass, setting up the lenses for observation. He'd said nothing on the long ride to the observatory, and his only words since arriving had been him running through the setup, clinical questions and answers. She'd made several searching attempts to snag his gaze, but he'd creatively diverted all of them. "The other end," she said, returning her attention to the matter at hand. "So we can open this map and get to work?"

"Ah." Niklaus cleared his throat and hooked his fingers under both sides of the roll. He walked backward until he could go no farther, and together they spread the sketch over the table.

"Grab those rocks. Just there." Aesylt pointed at the basket. She stole another look at Rahn, but he was still occupied.

Niklaus gathered the stones and waited with a dumb look.

"To hold it down?" she asked, swallowing impatience. He knew what to do. They'd done it dozens of times at the keep, long before they'd had a half-built observatory to play with. "Where are you right now?"

Niklaus quickly placed the stones. He rubbed his eyes. "Tired is all."

Aesylt stepped closer. She'd been working up the courage to ask about Val, about the situation with the Barynovs, but he'd made it clear the subject was uncomfortable for him. "I know what tired looks like on you. This is something more."

He snapped his head up. "Not Val. Last I heard, no change."

She nodded, scraping her teeth along her tongue, weighing whether to push harder. "Is this about the armistice? If you're worried about Esker, he was never going to agree to Drazhan's terms. I'll eat my right arm if the man actually shows up to read his apology tomorrow in the village."

"Your brother is too smart not to expect duplicity," Niklaus replied with a slow, careful drawl. "It's all but guaranteed, I'd say."

Aesylt ran her finger along one of the smooth stones holding down the corners of their celestial map. "Then what is it?"

"Is what happened the other night not enough, Aes? How close that monster came to killing you?"

She searched for the right words. "Nien, Nikky. If it were only that, you'd be clinging to me like an overprotective oma. Just tell me so we can move on."

Niklaus rolled his head with a huff. "I guess I, uh, wanted to tell you something."

Aesylt waited.

"I've been thinking more and more about our research here, and my part in it. Particularly since the armistice."

Aesylt had been expecting it after hearing Fez and her brother whispering in the halls. "It's not your fault your family is breaking tradition to ally with the Barynovs. It can't be helped."

Niklaus twisted his mouth. Frowned. "Nien. That's not it. And folks can stop wagging their cursed tongues because we're... We're *not* aligning with anyone. My father sent word from under the mountain confirming our neutrality. The kyschun can't afford to be seen choosing sides. I don't know... Doesn't matter. It's not that."

Aesylt's hand moved to her neck, a semi-conscious gesture she'd been making in the days since Marek had nearly strangled the life from her. In her quiet moments, she'd stood before her mirror, pondering that night, replaying every grueling moment. The bruises were gone, the dents of Marek's thick thumbs long smoothed, yet the flesh remembered. But fear was an ancestor of death. She had not begged for her life that night, nor the eve of the Nok Mora, and she never would. "What then?"

Niklaus followed her gestures with a dark expression. "I'm staying with the cohort. I've decided... at least until I have to join the rest of the kyschun under the mountain. And... I've thought about what you told me the other night, on the way to... you know, about the curricula. About the participatory nature of it." He cleared his throat, his face blooming with red.

"Tak?" Aesylt's eyes narrowed. "And?"

He brushed his hands down his shirt in nervy passes. "We've known each other our whole lives, Aes. We're practically family. We trust each other. We've seen each other... in vulnerable states."

Aesylt snickered. "You mean naked?"

"Whatever word you want to use." The awkward discourse seemed to cause him physical pain. "I'd like to think we were both, uh, unaffected by this, because of our closeness. And it got me thinking that if there were any two people who could conduct the, uh, experiments in a participatory sense and, uh, *not* be affected by the complexity of the, uh, intimacy, it would be... us."

Aesylt's breath caught. Her gaze traveled again toward Rahn as she tried to find words. His suggestion made some sense, but there was a baffling tightness in her chest, the kind that accompanied loss. "Well—"

"You shouldn't have to... *do* this with the scholar, Aes. Not when you have me."

She swallowed a dry thatch in her throat, but it only made the feeling worse. Across the room, Rahn bent low, angling his face up against the telescope he'd built with his own hands. His head shook in frustration as he adjusted the many knobs, and he dug into his pocket, exasperated, for his spectacles. She should be helping him, but she'd made comfort impossible between them, first with her unfathomable proposition and then with the trouble she'd caused him after. He wasn't just cross with her; he was exhausted *of* her. Probably wishing he'd never asked her to be his disciple that night he'd come to Fanghelm, full of ideas. She was nothing to him anymore but a symbol of regret.

"Aes?"

She blinked away a soft burn in her eyes and looked at Niklaus. "I'll let the scholar know, when we have a moment to discuss."

The palpable relief on Niklaus's face was almost humorous. "I was a little worried you might think... but good. Good." He rolled his lips in and out. "I have to get back to the village. I'll see you tomorrow."

Aesylt nodded, her mind a cyclone of clouded emotion as she watched him leave.

Rahn hadn't intended to spend the day with so much unaddressed awkwardness between them, but the longer he and Aesylt went without addressing what had happened, the harder it was to make space for it.

She was a consummate professional, documenting everything he read back to her as he examined the skies. When it was her turn, she recited her observations the way he'd taught her. Her misery lived only in her hooded eyes.

When midnight fell and the guards appeared, Rahn reflected on the day as a successful one.

For the research, anyway.

They traveled in the middle of a procession of Drazhan's men. Rahn drove the cart with Aesylt slumped at his side, pretending to sleep. It would be the perfect time to assure her he wasn't upset with her, only himself—to return the small, sly smile to her face he'd realized was as much of a comfort as his morning needle tea or the smooth evening fog rolling down from the craggy crests of Icebolt.

Aesylt stirred, her furs sliding atop the wood as she rolled her head his way. "I just wanted you to know, Scholar, you don't have worry about the upcoming curricula. Nik is staying on, long enough..." She tilted her head into her hood and yawned. "Long enough for he and I to satisfy the requirements for practical study within the cohort."

Rahn's hands tensed on the reins. Tightness pinched his sides, forcing him to straighten to draw breath. "You and Niklaus want to handle the curricula yourselves? The two of you? As in..."

Aesylt gave a sleepy nod. "We're comfortable with each other, and it will be nothing. A simple matter." She pulled her hood tighter and turned away in her seat, curling her legs up. "So it's no longer your problem, Scholar."

His response died when a guard rode up beside him. "My lord, we're diverting down the east pike path. May be nothing, but Barynov guards were spotted at the end of the road, and the steward has directed we treat every suspicion as a valid one." The man's eyes traveled toward Aesylt, slumped on the bench. "It will be a rough ride. I would fasten the stewardess's restraints."

Rahn nodded absently, reaching sideways to feel for the unbuckled leather. He watched the guard join the other men, and he grew cold, then hot as he secured Aesylt's straps and commanded the mules toward their new course.

NINE
TROUBLE YOURSELF NO LONGER

Aesylt hesitated in the doorway of her brother's office. It was the same room it had always been, since the days of their father, their grandfather... For nearly a decade, she'd sat in the tall thorny chair of her Wynter ancestors herself, wondering if Drazhan was ever coming back or if fate had consigned her to take his place.

Nothing had changed. Nothing except her.

From the furrowing pass of her brother's stony gaze as she made her way inside, he knew it too.

"You wanted to see me?" She took another step but held close to the door. Outside, four guards waited to escort her back to her apartments—her new, "upgraded" prison. Her own living quarters were bigger than the scholar's, and they wanted her to be comfortable in her confinement, seeing as it wasn't ending anytime soon. So said Imryll, who had only been grudgingly parroting Drazhan's despotic orders, for no one's benefit.

"Come in, cub." Drazhan was seated. He rarely sat at his desk. Even in meetings he was prone to pace, or hover in a corner and scowl.

"You're making me nervous, wulf." Aesylt fingered her mother's sapphire necklace resting against her heart. Val had the matching one... At least, he had when he'd entered the forest. It could be anywhere. It might even have been the symbol his family had needed to condemn her.

"Close the door."

When she planted herself in prideful indignation—sometimes it felt like it was all she had left of herself—he waved a hand, and a guard did it instead.

"Aes, sit. Please."

It was the please that did it. Aesylt flopped onto the chair with a hotheaded slump that instantly made her feel idiotic. Correcting it would have been worse, so she shrugged and waited.

His quick grimace was ripe with disappointment, but he shifted forward, clasping his hands over the desk, and looked straight at her. "Tomorrow is the village apology and Marek's surrender. It—"

"*Won't* be happening. Let me save you a visit to the soothsayers," Aesylt quipped with an unladylike snort.

"Of course not." Drazhan sat back. "It was never going to happen."

Aesylt's smug grin faded. "Then why propose it at all?"

"So all the Vjestik, all the village, can see I have acted fairly and reasonably. Another leader would already have Marek's head greeting visitors as they ride into town."

"No, you're not known for your reasonableness, are you?" The vitriol in her tone cut the pain of his unintentionally thoughtless words. The visualization of heads on pikes brought forth one image and one image only.

Drazhan's expression softened. "I will never be that kind of leader, cub. It's not who I am—who we are. I can *feel* Marek at the end of my bare hands, dying the same death he tried to offer you. I can taste it. I dream of it." His hands clenched at his sides as he forced calm upon himself. "But the Barynovs will not let this go. Whether they truly believe..." He shook his head in disgust.

"Doesn't matter to me what they believe. They'd let our entire world burn to make a point. And I can't let it happen."

Aesylt crossed her arms, thinking. "Why... Drazhan, why do you think they want to blame *me* so badly? I understand the confusion, the not understanding, the shame, but... There has to be a bigger reason. Doesn't there?"

Drazhan pursed his mouth. He glanced to the side. "Before Valerian left, Esker came to see me a few times about a betrothal between you and Valerian." He cleared his throat. "I refused."

Aesylt scoffed. "That's not a secret. And how many betrothals has it been that you've turned down on my behalf?"

"Eight. Maybe nine. None of them even half-fit to share home and hearth with you." Drazhan breathed deep. "But after speaking with Esker last night, I believe I understand their... campaign better."

"You spoke with him again last night?"

"Mm. It's why I had the guards take you home through the forest path. His men were waiting for our meeting to conclude."

Aesylt's pulse raced. Something was wrong. Drazhan never took his time. He said what he needed to say. "Out with it, whatever it is."

Drazhan leaned in again. "Tell me it isn't true that you agreed to wed Valerian before he left for the forest."

She slid her hands onto her lap with a slow inhale. Her brother's stare burned her as he waited for her to either confess or lie. But she had a question of her own first. "How could they possibly know what was or was not said between Val and me before he went into the forest if he has not regained consciousness?"

Drazhan scraped his finger against his stubble. "It seems Marek met him on the path after he left you."

Aesylt had to restrain herself from leaping out of her chair. "Then I was *not* the last person to see Val!"

Drazhan's neck bulged. "Valerian told his brother two things. Two *significant* things. The first was that the two of you would be..." He rolled his hands with an annoyed twist of his lips. "Wed, should he return. The second was that you had taken him..." He opened his mouth wide on exhale. "Into the fucking *celestial realm* before you said good-bye. And *that,* little sostra, is why they've waged this smear against you."

Aesylt's jaw went slack. Her tongue dried upon the back of her speechlessness. "Draz, I—"

His hand came down on the desk as he leaned in. "We don't lie to each other, Aesylt. Don't start now."

She settled on her chair. Her eyes closed. She hadn't planned to lie, just explain herself. But her brother wouldn't care what her reasons were. In his mind, there were none big enough for her to return to a place he believed might one day be the end of her. "Both things are true, wulf. And if you actually care *why*, I will be happy to explain."

His eyes rolled as his hands came up, looping over his head. "Oh, cub. I know why. You thought you were helping. When a man stares death in the eye, he needs a reason to break his gaze. You gave him one."

Aesylt lowered her gaze. To hear her justifications spoken back to her, so lightly, enfeebled them. She wished the earth would rise and swallow her. "I thought I was doing the right thing, wulf."

"Right. Wrong. The Barynovs aren't concerned with either. These accusations, these tensions... They were diversions. For this." He waved at her. "For you."

"The betrothal?"

He nodded. "And now, Esker claims he will accept nothing less than my blessing."

"Or..." Aesylt swallowed. "Or what?"

Drazhan didn't answer. He glanced at the portrait of their father. "I don't want you to worry about this. I only needed to know whether it was true, and you've confirmed it."

"They commit a treasonable act and accuse me of being a *koldyna,* and they think you'd relent? It makes next to no sense, Draz. So does anyone believing me capable of it."

"Oma was a quarter Medvedev. They may be known as peaceful druids, but their magic isn't well understood in the kingdom. Easy to exploit that lack of information, to point to your blood to make their claim. After all, who else among us can starwalk?"

"But no one ever said a foul word against Oma when she was alive."

"Because it's a shite excuse to make their play. They don't need everyone to believe them to start a civil war. A few will do. There have already been pockets of riots. Not everyone is happy with a Wynter in this seat."

Aesylt's mind was racing. Marek had seen *and* spoken with Val after he'd left her, but it didn't make sense. Val had kept her secrets for years, so what could have caused him to tell his brother her biggest one? The betrothal she could almost understand, but to share with Marek that Aesylt had taken him to a place forbidden? When Val and his brother had never been close? It didn't add up. "What now?"

"I'm not selling you to the fucking Barynovs, if that's what you're asking." He rustled through a stack of documents on his desk before shoving it all aside. "And Marek is a dead man already, he just doesn't know it yet. Esker might be right behind him."

"Val may never... may never wake up anyway," she countered. "Maybe we should agree, knowing it won't ever—"

"Never, cub. We don't negotiate with seditionists. We deal with them. Decisively." Drazhan lowered his head with a hard laugh. "Though, Esker has graciously informed me that in the event his youngest son doesn't make it, his eldest will do."

Aesylt's hand shot to her neck. Drazhan followed it with a dark look. "*Marek?* No. No, no, no."

"No," Drazhan stated. "That's what's next. *No.*" He lifted to his feet with a weighty sigh, dropping himself over the desk with a glance at her. "As long as you're behind a locked door when the sun sets, then you're..." He sucked his teeth. "Free to move about the grounds during the day. The grounds *only*, and no wandering off where no guards can't see you. At night, if nothing has gotten worse, I'll approve more trips for you and the scholar to the observatory. Is that a fair compromise?"

Aesylt's heart sank and soared in concert. "Yes."

"Good. Cub... practice restraint. Do your experiments. Try not to kill the poor scholar. And trust me to handle the matters of our house."

Aesylt didn't have a destination in mind when she left her brother's office, but her feet carried her to the rear courtyard and the row of barns. They were all occupied with horses and mules except the last one, used for storing tack that had fallen into disrepair. Others in the kingdom might have discarded such leftovers, but the Vjestik let nothing go to waste. It wasn't uncommon for someone to show up asking if they had any leather scraps or metal tines to spare.

She'd always chosen the end barn because it was quiet. Cobwebs and old board creaks revealed how seldom anyone ventured inside. As a girl, she'd sit on the old saw table, leave the barn doors cracked, and watch the men banter before they rode off to attend to their business. They'd occasionally spot her, but no one minded a precocious girl running around. None foresaw the day when that same precocious girl would take all she'd learned and run the Cross for years in her brother's absence.

It was the one thing she needed to say to Drazhan but couldn't: *I do know how to do this job because I did it. For years. While you were out grinding your jaw and dulling your sword on other men, I kept the fires burning. Neutering me now may assuage your conscience, but it re-opens a very deep wound in me.*

Aesylt sighed and climbed up onto the table, her legs swinging under her heavy woolen gown. The courtyard was empty beyond the guards lining the perimeter with stoic, forward stares. There were no conversations to eavesdrop upon nor swordplay to study—only the enveloping silence of fresh morning snow.

Her hands traveled back to her neck, and the memory of Marek's meaty fists... the rough dig of his thumbs. In a proper fight, she might have stood a chance. He was a large man, but she was quick on her feet and fast with a sharpsword, trained by some of the best warriors in the north. But the moment he got his hands on her, there'd been no recourse. She'd never know if Niklaus had saved her or if Marek would have returned to his senses. She'd never know how close she'd been to death. None of her celestial deaths had prepared her for the confusion of one in her world.

Motion in the barn next to hers disrupted her daze. She stilled to listen, but the yelling was easy enough to make out.

As were, she realized, straightening, the voices.

"You're not listening to me! You always... You've always been like this, looking down at me over your little spectacles like I'm a child."

Tasmin.

Aesylt carefully slid off the table, readying to leave. She shouldn't be hearing what was obviously meant to be a private exchange, but as she angled her body through the small gap in the doors, another voice paused her escape.

"That's simply not true, Tas." Slow, patient delivery. "I love you. And I respect our bond too much to say nothing."

And the scholar.

"And what would you know about love, Adrahn?"

"Enough. Enough to be confident in my words today."

Aesylt froze in the gap. She'd inadvertently intruded on a lover's quarrel. Or the end of one. Whatever they'd been talking about, the conversation hadn't started in the barn.

"I'm leaving either way. You can support me or you can shun me, but if you truly love me, you'll understand why I need to go. Some things are bigger than ourselves." Tasmin's voice was laden with sadness. "Of everyone, Rahn... You know me best in all the world."

"I have tried reason, Tasmin, and it hasn't worked. Begging... I cannot. You will do as you believe is best, but I will not pretend. I will not smile and wave as you ride off to a man who is beneath you."

"Then stand alone. Seems to be the way you like it anyway," Tasmin retorted and stormed from the barn.

Aesylt watched her friend march across the flagstones. A dangerous lump formed in the center of her throat. Waves of pinpricks danced along her skin as her belly turned with angst, unnecessary pain seeping in. It shouldn't hurt. It shouldn't. She'd rationalized her inappropriate feelings for the scholar by reminding herself that love and respect were spokes on the same wheel. That she was simply *confused.* Even her suggestion for them to partner on the illicit curricula had been a challenge, to prove to herself she could leave emotion out of work, like a proper woman of science.

But this... the burn behind her eyes... the twisting ache in her gut... She wanted none of it.

You're a wulf. Act like it.

Aesylt adjusted her furs tighter against her face and left the shelter of the barn. She didn't look back, but the moment she exited, she knew she was being watched, and by whom.

"Ah, Aesylt. I'm so sorry. You heard that?" When she said nothing, he continued in a rush. "I thought the barns would be more private." Rahn sighed, starting after her. "But I was hoping to speak to *you* about something actually."

"Oh?" Aesylt continued her swift march across the stones. She nodded at some of her brother's men, stationed around the perimeter for her protection, which only made her feel worse.

"Any reason you're practically running?"

Aesylt sucked in a bracing breath and slowed near the old yew at the center of the courtyard. "It's rather cold, if you hadn't noticed."

"When is it not?" Rahn caught up and jogged into place beside her. "Is now a good time to talk?"

There was nothing to say but yes. She had no good reason to refuse—no explanation for why she felt the pervading need to put as much distance between her heart and Rahn Tindahl as possible. "Let's... step under the eaves at least," she muttered.

"I thought perhaps inside? Since it's so... cold, as you say."

"This will do fine." Aesylt spun once she was under the covering. Her heart skipped and pattered at the sight of the man, flush-faced and solemn.

"Are you all right?" Rahn came closer, his head tilted and his eyes wide with genuine, maddening concern.

"I've just come from speaking with my brother, and I'm... tired." *There*, she thought. Not a lie.

"Ahh." Rahn cleared his throat and shrugged. "I thought later, since tonight looks to be cloudy, we might stay in the apartments and go over our past charts, search for commonalities as we did with the bowman."

As you did with the bowman, because I was too emotionally bruised to take part. Aesylt nodded. "Sure. Yes." She glanced over her shoulder, toward the nearest entrance.

Rahn noted this with a frown. "Good. We can begin, say, after supper?"

"Yes."

"Splendid." He rubbed his hands together and brought them to his mouth with a shiver.

"Was that all?"

"No, there is one more thing." His brows creased, his hands falling away. "I've given some thought to what you told me last night about the curricula and Niklaus. It would be unprofessional of me to allow it, and it is my duty, my responsibility as the lead of this cohort, to find an alternative that satisfies the requirements without compromising the researchers. Do you understand?"

Aesylt squinted one eye. "And do you have one? An alternative?"

He held out his gloved hands with a sheepish half smile. "I'm working on one."

"Hmm. So you keep saying." A deviant streak rushed across her chest, offering temporary easement to the ache that hadn't left since she'd realized what was happening in the barn next to her. "Well, you needn't worry, Scholar. I'm not interested in an alternative."

"You're..." His brows fused. "Not?"

Aesylt plastered a smile on her face. "No, in fact, the more I've thought about it, the more I'm looking forward to it."

The disappointment in his expression was a hollow victory, but it made the smile on her face turn real.

"We both are. So trouble yourself no longer."

TEN
DRUMS OF WAR

Rahn had been staring at the drafting page for the better part of an hour. He'd focus on one constellation until his eyes blurred the lines into an ink-smeared puddle, then move on to another, making no meaningful progress. Mostly he was trying not to pay mind to the nervous giggles coming from the other room, where Aesylt and Niklaus were reading through the coitus curricula. Niklaus had arrived nearly an hour after Rahn's testy conversation with Aesylt in the courtyard, and he seemed in no hurry to leave.

He mopped his brow and tried again, but the waning sun's glare was blinding. He debated moving his work into another room, but they'd be called to supper soon enough.

A guard opened the door. Rahn looked up and saw Teleria walk in. She closed the door and bolted it behind her.

With a defeated sigh, he set his charting aside and smiled. "Let me guess, you're going a little mad as well?"

"A little?" Teleria made her way over. Her unusually modest skirts were bunched in her hands as though she were wearing a ballgown. She was a striking woman, a decade his senior but as beautiful and youthful as her daughter. She'd taken him under her wing when he was orphaned, but it was more like having an older sister than a mother. Over the years, that bridge shortened, until they became friends and confidants.

"Anything new?" he asked, hopeful.

"Nothing you don't already know." She lowered herself onto the chair opposite him. "Drazhan is still holding them back from the gates, but that doesn't exactly inspire ease, now that we've seen how determined the Barynovs are."

"Any further riots?"

"The same small pockets as before."

Rahn nodded. "And Tas? Has she... Did she depart?"

Teleria's cool expression soured. "About an hour past."

"You're still angry with her for leaving."

Teleria arched a brow. "So were you, as I and half of Fanghelm recall."

He had been angry, but he was also the only person who knew Tasmin's full motivations for traveling to see Lord Marius Quintus in Whitechurch. To those in Imryll's sphere, Quintus was the man whose actions had nearly killed her, and had inadvertently led to King Torian's demise. If Drazhan ever saw the man again, he'd breathe his last. Everyone knew it, including Quintus, who had unsurprisingly made no attempt at a persistent role in Imryll's life.

But to Tasmin, he was a potential ally in a war far bigger than the skirmishes and threats incited by the Barynovs, one that was on hold but far from over.

The trouble was, Quintus was a mercurial, perilous man who was just as threatening when on their side as he was on the opposition. Even if he agreed to hear Tasmin's plea, the price for his aid would be more than anyone should have to pay.

"I said what I felt I needed to say. She didn't take my words well, and I knew she wouldn't, but I had to try." His eyes traveled toward the closed door, but he caught himself before Teleria could note it.

"You know people are talking about it. If you don't want others to think you're courting her, acting like a jealous, spurned lover in the courtyard might not be prudent."

Rahn bristled, shifting in his chair as he again tried to ignore the strange laughter coming from the other room. "I have no control over the thoughts or suppositions of others, nor any presumption of my ability to persuade them from their chin-wagging."

Teleria's eyes narrowed slightly, and she turned in her chair. "Are we going to pretend you're not solely drawn to whatever is going on in that room?"

Rahn conjured a dozen denials in the time it took Teleria to return her gaze to him, but she knew him too well. He settled on a half-truth. "I wish I'd pushed back when Imryll asked me to take over for Jasika. I'm feeling... concerned for Aesylt and her, ahem, eagerness to work on it. She's young, unmarried—"

"She's only a year younger than Imryll, and the Vjestik don't hold court over purity standards like Duncarrow does, but go on."

He frowned in annoyance. "You're missing my point."

Teleria waited with a patient smile, which left him even more disassembled.

"She's a very apt student and takes our research more seriously than anyone else in the cohort, sometimes even more than I do." He continued with more caution, choosing each word knowing Teleria would dismember them for meaning. "And I fear she's going forward with these experiments because she feels accountable for the future of this effort."

Teleria uncrossed and re-crossed her legs. She cast a look at the hearth, one he recognized and had been hoping to avoid. "While she has the stubbornness of her brother, and a touch of his impulsiveness, she is more deliberate in her thoughts and actions. And I can tell you, Adrahn, that there is no affliction women despise more than being thought unable to make choices for themselves. If she and Niklaus are both consenting and in clear understanding of what they're going to embark upon, then your worries will only breed unnecessarily. They may even compromise the work itself."

Rahn sat back. He hadn't considered the matter in quite those terms. It was possible Aesylt *wanted* to explore intimacies with her friend, in a safe and controlled environment, but the prospect left him surprisingly troubled. "I see. Thank you for that perspective."

"Just don't let Drazhan find out. All the man's Vjestik sensibilities take flight when his wife and sister are concerned." Teleria's eyes rolled. "But if the research keeps Aesylt from running off again, I see it as a positive for all involved."

Niklaus's tongue slipped over hers for the seventh time. He wasn't as smooth of a kisser as Val, but the firm tug of his hand at her lower back was oddly arousing. Each kiss had been more demanding, less clinical. She recalled the instructions on some of the more advanced levels in the prospectus, about making sure she was "ready" to receive him. With enough kisses like that, she might be, but that was a problem for another day, because he would need to leave soon.

Niklaus pulled back, swiping the back of his hand across his mouth with a broad grin. "Well, we've conquered the kisses, I'd say."

Aesylt grinned through a hot flush in her face and neck. "Should we work on our notes then? While our thoughts are fresh? This is different than our usual work, when we can revisit it over and over if we forget to note something... Though, I suppose we *could* revisit our research here as well, if we needed to, but we have so many topics to work through, we'll never get to them if we have to keep going back to refresh our notes. I think it's especially important to differentiate between how the first kiss felt and the last, because both are relevant, yes?" Her rambling stopped when she caught him adjusting the bulge in his trousers. She launched into a discomfited search of the room. "Where did you put the notes?"

"We could do that..." He glanced away.

"What?" Aesylt pulled her sleeves over her hands, precipitously more anxious than she'd been before the first kiss of the day.

"I need to get back before supper." His teeth brushed his bottom lip, his stare traveling to her chest and then lifting abruptly. "I think we should make the most of the time we have left."

"What did you..." Aesylt's gaze shot to the window, the setting sun. The tingle between her legs turned to a buzz. But it wasn't Niklaus she was thinking of, nor was it who she'd been imagining for the past hour. "Have in mind?"

He chewed the inside of his mouth. His hands twitched at his side. "According to the rules, we have to start simple and work our way through the more... challenging topics. We've already completed the easiest one, at least once our notes are done, but the next step or two don't seem to require much preparation."

"Tak, and?" Aesylt felt each blink, every prick of heat dancing across her flesh. But kisses were trivial. Everything else on the list would be further than she'd ever gone with anyone.

The thought of Rahn one room over, listening, was the most exhilarating of all—the most damning.

"Lie back, Aes." Gone was the boyish gentleness of her childhood friend. His irises flared, reminding her of a wulf watching from the forest. "And I'll show you. You don't have to do anything except focus on how it feels. We'll do our notes right after, so we don't forget."

She swallowed the dry thatch in her throat with a stilted cough. Suddenly, she understood. He wanted to continue their lesson on kissing, but it wasn't her mouth he had designs on. "Oh. *Oh.* You want to... You want to do that now? Isn't this skipping a step?"

"Do you not?" The fire in his eyes dimmed slightly. He looked embarrassed. "I know we're supposed to try fondling first, but I've heard women enjoy that more when they're already..."

She understood what he was trying to say, but she could find no response.

"We don't have to do anything you don't want to do. I was only thinking of our schedule and trying to work in as much as we can when I'm here."

"Nien, nien, you're right. Of course you're right." Aesylt nervously fumbled with the stays of her dress, her fingers skipping atop the fabric, unable to take hold.

"You can leave it on if you like." His throat jumped as his eyes traveled downward, then back toward hers. "I can... Your gown is simple enough for me to work around."

"All right." Aesylt backed up until she connected with the bed. She looked across the room, stalling, but Niklaus's patience broke her daze. Planting her hands, she hoisted herself up and scooted back until she could lie back against the pillows. Her heart pounded so hard, she felt it when she breathed, when she swallowed. She'd been the one insisting the science could come before everything else. If she let her weakness take over now, they'd never finish. She'd never prove to herself she could be an objective academic.

There were few people she trusted as much as Nik, she reminded herself.

Niklaus climbed up on all fours. His hesitation was short-lived and then he was bunching her dress up and over her waist, exposing her undergarment to the chill in the room. It happened so fast, she'd had no time to reconcile the look in his eyes, the lust burning there, and the understanding he intended to bury his face in her nethers.

He rocked back on his heels and started tugging on her undergarment but paused. "You're sure?"

Aesylt nodded, lying to herself and him. But it was another man's tongue she imagined rolling around her privates. Another man's hands hooked around her thighs as he tugged her taut to his face.

"I… Ancestors, you're so…" He reached a finger forward, barely swiping the fabric, but it was enough to send her ass clenching and her eyes rolling back. The press of his finger to his mouth was almost too much. *Scholar*, she thought, and nearly came.

"What does it… taste like?"

Niklaus shook his head, his eyes cast to the side in deep thought. "I don't know exactly, like nothing I've ever tasted. I'll need more to decide."

Aesylt closed her eyes and drew a shuddery breath, waiting… tensing. Her heart raced, skipping and doubling beats. When Niklaus's hands skated across her flesh, traveling up her thighs, it sent a wicked shiver through her, and she sounded an involuntary shriek.

He went stumbling back with a horrified look. Aesylt started to explain herself, but the door slammed open, silencing her attempt. Teleria's *oh dear* was drowned by Rahn's heavy boots slapping stone.

Aesylt had never moved so fast in her life, scrambling first to pull her legs up, then to smooth down the fabric of her gown, which was embarrassingly difficult, bunched up underneath her in evidence of how quickly they'd transitioned from the innocence of kisses.

"Niklaus. Out." Rahn's voice had the forced evenness of a man struggling to control his pitch. Aesylt could barely register it in her horror, in the knowledge he'd seen her in such a vulnerable position. She felt all her truths were exposed, that he'd somehow know it was *him* she'd fantasized about when her eyes were closed. All she felt was the shame of one who had been so certain she'd known what she was doing but had been woefully wrong.

Niklaus raced out of the room, with one hand on his collar. Teleria's brows shot up as she turned and followed.

The door clicked closed.

Aesylt itched to escape to the celestial realm. Her flesh tingled, readying, but Rahn's tense shoulders, lifting with each hard breath, ripped the air from her lungs. In the silence, she died a dozen mortifying deaths and made twice as many guesses as to what he was thinking, what he would say next. Whether he'd address what he'd seen, and why he'd sent Niklaus away.

Strain lined the edges of his jaw. His mouth opened, but no words followed. His eyes darted everywhere but at her, enough that he couldn't hide the intention of his avoidance.

"We should talk about this," he said. "But I find myself at a loss for words."

"Scholar..." Aesylt slid off the bed and started toward him, but he flinched, so she stopped. "I—"

Rahn held up a hand, as though surrendering to something. "I know you're trying to save this project. And I respect your commitment. But..." His hand traveled to his throat, scratching at stubble. "Even you believing it's your responsibility means I've failed you."

"That's *not* true." Aesylt rushed over, despite the command in his eyes for her to stop, to keep her distance. "Everyone else is gone now. It's up to us. Not you, both of us." Her words tumbled out in a messy gust. "You may not see me as a partner, but that does not change my own feelings on the matter. There is no one else anymore."

"Aesylt."

"There is no one else!" She threw up her hands with a shaky inhale. "Tas is gone. Elara has taken a leave. Val is... I don't know what Val is, but no matter how all this ends, he's never coming back. But Niklaus is still here, and he wants to help. You said we *must* include work done within the cohort, conducted by approved researchers, whose names are on record with the Reliquary."

"Aesylt."

"I'm going mad in here! I'm housebound, fighting everything inside of myself not to rush off again, try to fix this. I had nothing to do with what happened to Val, and yet I am forbidden from seeking the truth and putting this matter to rest. And all the while a war brews, in my name." Her heartbeat soared so high, she felt dizzy, but she couldn't stop the confession from rolling out of her.

"The *only* thing I'm allowed to do is our research, and if the skies are too cloudy for astronomy, that leaves one thing. One thing! And since you're not capable of creating the separation between lust and science, then it is on *me* and on Nik—"

Rahn seized her by the shoulders, stilling the rest of her passionate monologue. "Aesylt. I'll talk to Imryll."

Her turmoil faded to suspicion. "Imryll? And say what exactly?"

"Maybe we can work on a third project on the cloudy days. We could... We could even help Jasika finish coastal patterns."

Aesylt threw her head back and laughed. "How many bandages are we going to slap on this wound?"

"Will you give me until tomorrow?"

"You keep dancing around this issue, when there's really only one way through, isn't there?" Her pulse picked up again, sending blood rushing back to her face.

"Tomorrow. Please?" His eyes burned her, pleading harder than his words. How could he show so much concern for her choices but still fail to see her? To see she was right in front of him, ready to face a world of learning and adventure?

She didn't understand him. Trying only hurt more.

"I don't even know what I'm agreeing to." She twisted out of his grip.

"Take a pause on the research for the night. We'll go down for supper soon and then night will be here before long."

"And who could eat when we are on the brink of war?" Her nose flared, her cheeks on fire. "Fine. Fine! Go."

He exhaled his relief. "Thank you. Tomorrow—"

"Go!" Aesylt yelled, putting her entire chest into it. She didn't think of Teleria, whose suspicions would be undeniably raised, nor the guards, always listening. All she could process was the need for the man in front of her to leave before he turned her to dust.

"Very well." He backed up slowly. Even in his retreat, he wouldn't look at her. "I'm going."

When he was out, she firmly shut and latched the door behind him, waiting until she heard his reluctant footsteps recede. Certain he was gone, she dropped in a crouch, placed her head between her knees, and exhaled the weight of the past minutes.

The drumming began just after dusk. Rahn heard the first roll of the ominous elegy as he escorted an icy Aesylt to the dining hall, her walking two paces ahead with an unnatural pinch in her shoulders. Her head cocked slightly, enough to confirm she'd heard it too, but she didn't miss a step.

Chanting joined the thrumming hymn as the table was set around them. Wearing a stricken expression, Imryll nestled Aleksy at her chest instead of in the infant seat beside her. Drazhan gripped his spoon and knife in opposite hands, staring across the table at nothing, at no one.

"Roast hare, sweetened tubers, and carrot pie." The kitchen maid blurted the words fast enough to break Drazhan's iron gaze and send it her way. She nearly tripped into her curtsy. "Enjoy." The girl rushed back to the kitchen.

"Delicious." Teleria regarded the spread with a slow exhalation. Her hand gently shook as she reached for the spoon to scoop her tubers.

More voices joined the wronged chorus at the bottom of the hill, but Rahn could no longer tell if they were still at the bottom or if they'd climbed closer. He had to put his trust in Drazhan's hardened men, who had orders to treat any encroachment as an act of war. But his mind kept traveling to dark places, where good men turned traitor under the right combination of pressures.

"Shh, shh," Imryll whispered to Aleksy when he broke out in tears. Her mouth brushed his head, her eyes glued on her husband.

"I can take him." Aesylt rose, but Imryll shook her head. "You need a break."

Imryll's refusal the second time was tighter, more harried. Aesylt slowly settled into her seat, but she didn't take her eyes off her sister-in-law.

The drums and chanting escalated, loudening. The windows rattled.

Aesylt's fingers traveled to her neck.

Rahn's hand twitched against his leg. He clenched it into a fist before he did something errant, like allow it to migrate from his leg to hers in an imprudent attempt at comfort.

"Eat," Drazhan commanded, a lower, raspier edge to his tone. He dug deep for a throat clearing. "Duchess, so Tasmin left us a day early?"

It wasn't a question, no matter how he'd posed it. Drazhan had been heavily involved in her protection and transport out of Witchwood Cross.

"Mm? Oh, yes, she..." Teleria glanced across the table at Rahn, then turned toward Imryll. "She felt it best, under the circumstances. Didn't want to be another person for you to waste precious guards on, and—"

Aleksy's sharp wail cut her off.

"Well, she just thought it best."

"It's not a waste," Drazhan replied. "But she's free to do as she pleases."

Imryll's eyes were shot with red as she passed her chin softly along her son's head. Tasmin hadn't said good-bye to anyone except Teleria. And while there might have been some truth to Teleria's excuse, it wasn't the whole truth.

Aesylt's cold treatment of Rahn was related, he suspected, for as little sense as it made. His relationship with Tasmin was his business, and so was their argument earlier that afternoon.

A visceral, violent new song kicked off amid the sonorous humming. Teleria startled in her chair, mumbling an embarrassed apology. "Of course," she replied, nodding at her untouched food. Her spoon hovered above her plate.

Rahn turned only slightly toward Aesylt, but it was enough for her to return the tight, proud lift to her chin. Tension rippled down her lean neck, and he couldn't strike the horrible image from his mind of the purple swell in her flesh that night. The bluish tint to her lips as she'd struggled to stay conscious.

He repressed a sigh and regarded the food on his plate. Earlier he'd been ravenous, but all semblance of appetite had fled with the drumming and chanting. Imryll's plain fear, Teleria's jumpiness, and the unusual crack in Drazhan's steel nerves turned his empty belly.

Aesylt stabbed a tuber with her knife and slid it onto her spoon. She jabbed it into her mouth and chewed. A sour look flashed on her face but she persisted, her nose curling as she forced the food down her throat. Her arm shot out to her mug of ale, but she hesitated before sliding both hands under the table instead.

Rahn's pulse throbbed in time with the menacing beat. Sweat peppered his temples. Was Drazhan really not going to address what was going on outside? Everyone at the table was falling apart with each shift in tempo as it inched unmistakably closer.

Aesylt sucked in a sharp breath when her mug rattled.

Rahn's words caught before he managed them. "Drazhan, are we not going to speak of this?" Rahn pointed a hand toward the windows. "What's happening *out there*?"

"I'm aware." Drazhan's jawline could have chipped diamonds.

Rahn flipped his attention to Aesylt, incredulous, but her stare was as intense as her brother's. She pointed hers at the table's centerpiece, a solitary winter lily already wilting in its modest vase.

Imryll shifted Aleksy to her other shoulder. "Drazhan met with Esker *again* today. It didn't go well."

"Imryll." Drazhan turned toward her with an aggressive blink.

"We don't keep secrets in this house when they belong to everyone," Imryll said smoothly. "And your intimidation has exactly one effect on me, so I suggest saving it for a more suitable occasion than the supper table."

"Disgusting," Aesylt muttered, but she was still studying the dying lily with a glazed look. Rahn couldn't define why that unsettled him the most, even more than the drums and chants, but his sense of danger was tuned specifically for her. Everything inside of him was screaming to get *her* out of the keep, out of the Cross. "Met with Esker... Was that before or after *we* met, Draz?"

Imryll responded when Drazhan didn't. "After, Aes."

Drazhan's mouth curled. "We'll discuss it later—"

Aesylt shot out of her seat. "No, Drazhan, we'll discuss it *now*. It must have involved me for you to be so cagey. Did he bring up the prospect of forcing me into a marriage with Marek again?"

Drazhan's shoulders rose and fell in strained, emphatic breaths. "Can we not enjoy a meal as a family? Is that an impossible ask?"

Rahn squeezed the edge of the table in his hands. "Marek?" He choked on the word but forced himself to say it again, to make Drazhan's revelation real so they could destroy it in the next breath. "*Marek* Barynov? There is no fucking way that's happening."

Everyone at the table turned to look at him.

Rahn dug his tongue against the roof of his mouth, praying the others couldn't see the river of rage within him. He flashed a thin smile and tried again, his voice a more reasonable tempo, but Drazhan's suspicion was back, fused in his brows. "Forgive my heated language. We're all still reeling from that night. I know you aren't giving the matter serious consideration."

Drazhan placed his hands on the table and leaned in. "Do I need to validate that with an answer, or can we move on?" He shifted a withering glance to his sister. "Will you sit down? Please?"

"I know you didn't agree to it because they're sounding the *drums of war* on our land!" Aesylt kicked her chair back. "So what *was* said, wulf? What roar did you leave in the man's ear that he is ready to march upon his own steward?"

"You know, I'll speak to the kitchen, have our meals sent to our rooms..." Teleria said, but Drazhan stayed her with a raise of his hand.

"You want to know what was said, cub? You want to know what *I* said to the man I once regarded as a *father* before he attempted to extort me?" Drazhan shoved his plate across the table. The clatter was the only sound until he spoke again. "I told him the deal was off. I don't accept his apology. I don't accept his meaningless posturing. I don't accept his son should meet justice in the hands of the law. The only fate *I* accept for a man who would put his hands on a woman's neck is for him to meet his end from mine."

Rahn's heart lighted with the same stone resolve, but it also sank in anticipation of what would come next. Drazhan's patience was shorter than springtide in the Cross, and the Barynovs had exhausted it.

Aesylt's lips peeled back. "*Mine*, you mean."

Flecks of red and orange lit up the night sky beyond. Rahn slowly pushed back from the table, but it was Teleria who put voice to the problem.

"Drazhan. Imryll." She flicked a nod toward the windows. "I suggest we calmly and quietly—"

Everyone started at the sound of glass shattering. An echoing thud followed. Drazhan's sword was drawn before the incendiary could bounce once. Imryll screamed and leaped from the table, clutching Aleksy.

Rahn was up and behind Aesylt faster than all of it. She turned toward him, alarm widening her eyes.

"Fire!" someone screamed, from another part of the keep.

Drazhan ripped a tapestry from the wall and threw it over the firebomb. "Adrahn, get them to the gatehouse. Now!"

Rahn gathered Aesylt under one arm and beckoned for Imryll and Teleria with the other. He ushered them all out, set to the increasingly desperate nature of Aleksy's cries, rising in urgency at the same pace as the fevered bloodlust breaching their gates.

Aesylt rushed into the lead. In one fluid motion, she stretched a hand into her boot and withdrew a dagger. When she reached the first turn in the hall, she paused, breathless, and said, "Teleria, you come with us. Imryll, give me Aleksy."

Imryll paled. She crushed a hysterical Aleksy to her shoulder. "What? Why would you say that?"

"I can see it in your eyes. You don't want to leave my brother, I understand. And if he were thinking straight, he wouldn't want his probably pregnant wife and heir in the same place. So give me Aleksy, and we'll meet you both in the gatehouse."

"The gatehouse is just a meeting place," Imryll blurted. She squeezed tears from her eyes with a dazed look. "We're going to Fezzan's. Into hiding."

"Make a choice, sister." Aesylt's voice was clear as fresh ice. "But make it quick."

Imryll kissed her son and turned to look back. "All right." She passed him to Aesylt. "We'll be *right* there. Don't you let—"

"I would never." Aesylt shifted Aleksy to her shoulder and brandished the dagger. "I would die before I let it happen, Imryll."

Imryll wiped her eyes, spared her son one final helpless glance, and ran.

"Give me the dagger," Rahn said evenly. He saw in her steeled gaze that she hadn't pulled it as a precaution. She wanted to hurt someone, and gods, so did he, but he couldn't fathom what might happen if she followed her instinct, as raw and wounded as it was. "Aesylt."

She met his eyes. "Do you even know how to use one, Scholar?"

"Aesylt, give it to him!" Teleria cried. "What if you trip? You're carrying your nephew."

"I know how to use one," Rahn said darkly. He saw the moment Aesylt recorded his unspoken truth, storing it for later. Would she ask him? Would he tell her? "Please."

She handed it over hilt first with an injured grunt.

No one had to say silence was necessary. Their harried pace carried them down one hall, then another. Rahn knew the way and still cursed every step, questioned every turn. The cries outside shifted to the zealous pitch of fresh battle.

Aesylt paused at the courtyard door. She peered carefully outside with a quick look in all directions, then gave Aleksy a kiss and tucked him into her neck as she raced into the night.

Teleria signaled the guards, who weren't surprised to see them. Fezzan Castel marched straight to Aesylt as soon as they were inside.

"Ah, cub," he said, with a crestfallen sigh. His eyes traveled toward Aleksy and then beyond the group. "This isn't everyone, is it?"

"For now," Rahn replied. The gatehouse was filled, shoulder to shoulder, with guards. Some wore the Wynter standard—a snarling wulf—the others the compass of the Castels. "You were expecting us."

"Was hoping not to see you, but I feared I would anyway." Fezzan traced his beard with a finger. "Drazhan and Imryll..."

"Are coming." Rahn verified the door was locked, and of course it was. Bolted. Three men stood before it, forming a drawbridge. "I cannot say when."

Screams filled the courtyard. None of them winced this time. Aesylt's dark, hooded gaze was jarring with the way she was whispering sweet assurances against Aleksy's reddened cheek.

Rahn continued. "We need to get them out of here before this escalates beyond our control."

"And you, Scholar." Fezzan sized him up. "You're going with them." He squinted one eye at Aesylt, who was trying to catch an outside view through the huddled mass of soldiers. "If she tries again what she did the other night, it won't end well, you understand? There's no sneaking about anymore, none that doesn't get her in a world of trouble."

Rahn nodded, his solemn gaze still locked on Aesylt across the room.

"Now Drazhan seems to harbor some inexplicable belief she'll listen to you, even after she slipped out right under your nose."

Fezzan frowned in reproval. "So you're to stay with her at all times. I've arranged for you two to take my sister's apartments, second largest in Castellan. She joined the Ancestors in the sky last year and won't be needing them. You think you can handle her this time?"

"I can hear you, Fez," Aesylt said coolly, casting a look over her shoulder. "And I understand the situation. I don't require the scholar's diligence, or yours, to keep me from running off."

The windows rattled in their frames. Mail and leather shimmered as the guards tightened their formation in response. Rahn caught Teleria's anxious glance drilling him from the dense crowd of guards, but he had nothing to offer her worries. Fezzan and Drazhan might be unnaturally calm in the face of war, but that scared him more than a fevered response would.

"Good. Then I'll say no more." He offered her an apologetic smile and turned back toward Rahn. "I have to go join the steward now. My son, Uli, and our men will take things from here." He checked his sword belt with a grunt. "If the Ancestors are truly with us, this will be over soon."

ELEVEN
WE CAN'T KEEP RUNNING

Aesylt hadn't changed her path in hours. She moved from one end of the hearth to the other, then a quick dip behind the couch, followed by a window pass. Aleksy stayed calm as long as she didn't stop.

Rahn and Teleria watched her like she were made of solid ice, impenetrable against the evening's horrifying developments. She preferred it that way. In fact, she almost enjoyed the concern in their eyes, flickering now and then to fear. For her... of her. The specifics were unimportant. As long as they stayed away. As long as no one *touched* her... because if they did, she might shatter.

Failures were lessons. Gifts. Her father had taught her that, and the wisdom had transcended words. He'd been so hard on Hraz, the eldest, but his toughness came with grace. She remembered little about Ezra Wynter because most of those years had been swallowed by the stunning shock of unresolved grief, but she remembered that. She lived by it.

Until tonight, she'd been the only victim of her ill-fated choice to visit the Barynovs. With Drazhan and Imryll still unaccounted for, and no official reports from the battle they'd left behind at Fanghelm, she couldn't know how far her transgression had rippled. Who it had swallowed in its destructive wake. Whether there'd be any atonement sufficient.

She'd spent enough time at Castellan over the years for it to feel like a second home, but there was nothing familiar about the cold room they'd shrouded in darkness for fear candles might draw attention to the apartments from the outside. No one on the opposing side knew they were there, but it wouldn't take long to figure out the Wynters had fled to the home of Drazhan's top man. If her brother had a plan beyond getting them through the night, he'd better reveal it soon.

"You're being such a good boy," Aesylt whispered into Aleksy's mussed hair. His red curls caught the moonlight as they passed by the window. Imryll was a redhead, but Aesylt's mother had also been one. None of her children had inherited it, only the grandchild she'd not meet. "Oma will be here soon. So will Ota. I can't wait to tell them how brave their little wulfling is."

"Dawn is breaking," Teleria stated. No one responded. The guards stationed near the windows and door didn't react at all.

Aesylt caught Rahn's hard gaze as she approached the hearth. She broke it and kept walking.

Commotion sounded in the hall and then the door flung wide with an echoing thud. Imryll came marching in first, Drazhan right on her heels. Stormbringer was sheathed, but the steel Drazhan had crafted for his wife with his own hands was still swinging from hers.

"Thank the gods. Thank the gods," Imryll cried. She thrust her sword hilt out to Drazhan and rushed across the room.

"Ancestors deliver us," Aesylt whispered, cradling Aleksy tighter. She met Imryll halfway, passing her nephew off with reticence she hoped no one else noticed. Strength was the first thing Aesylt noticed of Imryll, blooming across every inch of her, but there was something deeply unsettling just beneath it.

Imryll crushed her son to her bosom with a long, quivering breath. Aesylt smiled because it felt like the right thing to do, the only thing to do, but her unease followed her as she went toward her brother.

"Don't you even think of making something up to protect me." She spoke before he could, her blood already boiling in anticipation of his coddling. "Hold nothing back, or I swear upon the names of every last Ancestor—"

Drazhan's hand shot out and cupped her cheek. With a tired smile, he brushed his thumb along her jaw. "We drove them back to the gates. Fanghelm is secure. My men have a decisive hold on the perimeter now. But it's not safe for us. For you. No one was killed, but there were a couple dozen wounded. That's all I can tell you, cub. *Thank you* for coming here. For seeing the wisdom in taking Aleksy. You did well."

Aesylt clamped her hand atop his and squeezed. "Good. Good, wulf." Her emotion started as a tingle in her jaw. There was little relief in learning there'd been no mortalities, only a sharp ache of remorse that gripped her from head to toe. "I'm sorry. I'm sorry for starting this. Anything you need from me, I'll do."

Drazhan's grip tightened. He shook her with a stern, commanding look. "Nien, sostra. You are *nienta* to blame. Whatever happened to Valerian is not your doing. The Barynovs have been looking... Hey... Hey, cub, it's all right. Spare no grief for opportunists, and none for a crime that is not yours to bear."

Aesylt peeled his hand from her face and backed slowly away, nodding at the ground. Her brother's absolution washed over her, but there was no reprieve from the guilt. "Everyone is safe. It's what matters."

She felt his eyes on her, waiting, but she couldn't make herself look up again. She hardly had the energy to stand. Handing Aleksy to his mother had made her realize how much tension she'd been holding onto.

Drazhan nodded. "Duchess, Baroness Castel will show you to your apartment. Imryll, Aleks, and I will be two doors down from here. Aes, Adrahn, get some rest. We won't be here at Castellan long—it's no safer than Fanghelm—but I'll have a better plan within a day or two."

Aesylt didn't breathe until she heard the door close. The settee creaked with the shift in weight as Rahn rose. She stilled, tightening with every step he made that brought him closer to her. He stopped about a foot away, but his presence, his heat, was unmistakable.

"Tell me what you need." His voice, low and hoarse, rooted her in place. Chills rippled down her arms, into her fingers.

She shook her head at her feet, her shoulders lifting as she willed her body to turn. "Sleep. That's what I need."

"You struggle with how much to share with your brother. I understand why." Rahn paused. "But everyone needs... needs someone they can be honest with, without fear of wounding or inciting them. You don't have to talk to me, Aesylt, but I want you to know you *can*, if you find holding everything inside is hurting more than helping."

"Talk to you? Draz isn't the only one called to impulsiveness." Aesylt spun to face him. Her pulse turned erratic as she realized what she was about to say. "I wasn't so out of it that I didn't notice how you reacted when Nik brought me home that night."

Rahn's hands moved to his pockets. His expression made her think of a hare facing a hunter's arrow. "I only saw what he did... what that *animal* did to you. I won't make apologies for taking it seriously, nor should you expect me to."

"Hmm." Aesylt's eyes blurred from the weight of the night... from the heaviness of Rahn's confusing comfort. The night at Hoarfrost wasn't the only one on her mind either. There'd been other charged moments, whispers in time she'd tried to forget. She feigned a smile and started toward her bedroom. "I'll be fine. Dobranok, Scholar."

"Wait."

Aesylt paused.

"Did you mean what you said tonight?"

"About not running off again? Acting like an irrational child who does the opposite of what her elders ask her to do?"

"Well, I didn't say it." His chuckle was dry, humorless. He'd said so little throughout the entire evening, and she was understanding why. He was in shock, exhausted, and likely repressing a good deal of fear.

"If I give my word, you can believe it. I never said I *wouldn't* run off before," she said. "But like he said, this reprieve at Castellan won't last long. We can't go home. We can't keep jumping from one keep to another. So what *I* will or won't do is not the issue." She glanced back over her shoulder with a swallowed yawn. "This will all come to a head soon, and Ancestors help us if we're not ready."

Aesylt had been staring at the mysterious letter throughout dusk and into the first throes of true night. How it had even made it to her was a question she could ask no one. Was there a spy at Castellan? Was it as simple as someone accepting an irresistible bribe? It was, after all, only a piece of paper.

But it was evidence their sojourn at Castellan couldn't last.

She'd found it under her stew bowl, folded into a small square and tacked to the bottom with resin. If the bowl hadn't been slightly off balance, threatening to spill sludge all over the copper tray, she'd have never seen it.

It was sitting alone on the tray, refolded. The paper reflected in the muddled copper, evidence it was real.

With a harsh inhale, she peeled the folds back one by one, until it was crinkled but open.

The words, she'd already memorized. They were few but clear.

Your brother will never see reason. You know our terms. Tell no one. If you surrender to us, no one else will meet harm. Our word upon the wings and bones of the Ancestors.

Fire popped and crackled in the hearth. She should burn the letter. Forget she ever saw it. Certainly *complying* was out of the question.

Wasn't it?

I would die before I'd let Marek touch me. But if Val wakes...

As it had been the last time she'd spoken to him, the thought of being his wife was simultaneously thrilling and gutting. He would be the perfect husband. He'd dote upon her... love and desire her. But there was something missing, something she couldn't define. Something she didn't want to define.

It was the very thing that had been eating her alive from the inside out for months and months.

She slithered off the bed and knelt by it. With one hand she lifted the mattress, and with the other, she shoved the wadded paper as far in as her arm could stretch.

TWELVE
THE STAG AND THE BOWMAN

A visit to the observatory was out of the question, but when Asa Castel mentioned the old atelier at the top of the eastern tower of Castellan, even Drazhan couldn't agree fast enough. That was how Rahn knew how truly scared the man was for Aesylt. Even in a crisis, he would ensure her needs were met.

Rahn and Aesylt had marched up the hundred and twenty steps with an entire retinue of guards, who went no further than the door. The studio was small, but the walls and ceiling were all windows. Unfortunately, the night was ill-suited for star-watching, but he sensed it wouldn't matter soon. A new plan was imminent.

"Scholar, you've been staring at the same spot for a half tick of the moon. Do you believe you can will those clouds to clear?"

Rahn grinned to himself, his head shaking as he angled it slightly toward Aesylt. "All clouds eventually clear, do they not?"

Aesylt screwed her upper lip into a frown that made her seem young and impertinent. "Is that supposed to be a pithy metaphor?"

"If so, it was clearly wasted on you, wasn't it?" His smile slowly faded as he returned his gaze to the hazy, cloudy sky. "This isn't the night for this." He waited for some fresh jibe from her, but she simply stared through the thick-paned glass with a thoughtful expression. "Nothing clever to say to that?"

Her brows fused as she stared harder. "Whatever happens next, we won't get more nights like this, will we?"

Rahn nodded at the cloudy night sky. "I don't get that impression, no."

"What happens if we don't have more notes to submit to the Reliquary soon?"

He sucked his teeth. "Well... We're beholden to how quickly other matters resolve themselves, but... nothing good."

"So if we cannot produce more observations on astronomy, our only option then would be for me to continue my work with Nik?"

Rahn prickled, heat rising within him, hard and fast. "No, Aesylt, that's not what I—"

"Relax." She choked out a dry laugh. "I'm only trying to understand the situation for what it is. Fair to say we need to make the most of our time tonight?"

"More fair to say," Rahn replied testily, "that it isn't up to us."

"What if it was?"

"It's not."

Aesylt tapped the sides of her chair, staring at the fire. "The celestial realm is a mirror of our world. There are no terrestrial variances. The land is our land. The sky is our sky. The only notable difference is no one else is there, unless I bring them with me." She stretched an arm in front of her, pointing it upward. "What I did not tell you, Scholar, is I can influence that world, in some ways. Limited ways. If we were to go there, we'd see the same clouds, but I believe I could clear them. I think the world adapts to what I need from it, while the fundamentals stay the same."

Rahn turned in his chair. He couldn't deny his curiosity, but his rational mind was all too aware of the dangers involved in blind exploration. Even Aesylt knew little about the world she'd been visiting her entire life. A place without rules was a place anything could happen. Even something as innocuous as watching the sky could be hazardous.

He briefly weighed the risks and fears against the alternative. One good night of charting could keep them both busy with documentation for days, no matter where Drazhan sent them. Aesylt would stay occupied with something useful, and it would keep her from feeling obligated to compromise herself with Niklaus.

And if Rahn was there with her in the celestial realm, he would know if something went amiss. He would have, at the very least, an opportunity to help her.

"Scholar?"

"If we do this..." Rahn tented his hands under his chin, thinking. "What will happen if the guards come in looking for us?"

"They agreed not to bother us," she said.

"It doesn't mean they won't."

"If they come in, then they'll find an abandoned post, but if we transition, say, behind that wall over there... then we can just say they didn't see us. They certainly wouldn't see us come back if we were hidden."

"The plan seems thin, Aesylt."

"Then we..." Aesylt breathed deep, tilting her head toward the sky again. Her pale hair fell behind her like a silken wave, and he had to look away again. "We come back, once an hour. If we're gone only an hour at a time, and they come in between those times, we can simply say we climbed outside for a better look. We'd have plausible deniability."

"Plausible deniability? Are you a lawman?" Rahn chuckled, to cover the fact that he'd already decided the moment she'd proposed it. His protectiveness of her had been no more than a confine she was determined to squeeze through, but embracing her way of thinking was the one thing he hadn't tried. "If we do this..."

Aesylt rolled her eyes. She didn't even know what he was going to say. He smiled inside.

"Then we agree if either one of us wants to come back, we both come back. No questions. No arguments. Same outcome if we sense even a hint of trouble."

"Seems fair to me." A soft smile split her face. "Gather everything we need now, because the only things we can be sure will come with us are the ones we're holding onto."

"No, no, no. The stag and the bowman are the *same,* Scholar. Look. Look closer."

Rahn shot her a skeptical, sidelong look before approaching the dusty lens. Asa's old telescope was more decorative than serviceable, but it was all they had.

He leaned down, squinting until he found the right spot again. "Aesylt, how many stags do you know that have a man's head affixed to their back?"

"I'm not friends with any stags, but do you not think that head is a cloud? Look closer. No, don't look at me, look at the *lens.*"

"Thought you cleared the clouds," he muttered, fully expecting an elbow and feeling almost disappointed when it didn't come. They'd been in the celestial realm for several hours, carefully returning to their world every tick of the moon. But the guards had kept to their post. The only thing working against them was time and exhaustion.

He'd almost gotten used to the strange shimmer in the air and the foreboding otherness about the place.

"The worst of them. Are you even looking?"

The first hour or so had been a flurry of talking over each other, rediscovering new facets of constellations they'd already mapped and revealing a brand new one—the pheasant—that they'd only seen brief flashes of in the past. "I *am.* And respectfully, I think your eyes may be tired." He backed away and gestured at the telescope, blinking his own exhaustion away. "Not a cloud. I would suggest you look again, but you're swaying on your feet. Maybe it's best we call it a night."

Aesylt tilted her head back and locked her hands in her hair with a frustrated grunt. "We may only have tonight."

Rahn's hands lifted briefly in an urge to offer physical reassurance. "For now. But the trouble won't last forever."

"I just need..." Her mouth opened into a wide sigh. Her mouth snapped closed as an intense expression passed across her tired face. "I just need to close my eyes a moment. Clear my mind." She glanced behind her and rushed to the blanket she'd brought with them. She snapped it and spread it on the ground before plopping down with another sigh. "There's no reason we can't go all night if we pace ourselves."

Rahn looked at the clear sky, fighting a yawn. "I'll take the first shift, but you still need to bring us back every hour."

"No need for shifts. I won't fall asleep," she said, curling into a ball on the soft blanket. She slithered around with a soft sigh, stretching her limbs before returning to her comfort. "I have something I need to say, before I lose my nerve." She bowed her head toward her hands, which she fidgeted in her lap. The movement drew his attention. "I'm sorry I've been so obstinate, that I've given you so much cause to worry since Val came back. We're supposed to be partners, but I haven't acted like one. I don't feel right about any of it, and you should not have to go to such lengths to manage me."

Rahn's breathing slowed to a near stop. He left the comfort of the telescope, approaching the blanket. "Manage you? That's not what's happening here, Aesylt. Your restlessness is understandable to me. I'm only trying to help you."

Her eyes fluttered closed with a soft laugh. "You're always so politic, Scholar. Is there a playful side of you?"

Rahn scoffed and lowered to a crouch. He scraped his hands along the unruly stubble he'd need to address soon. "You've seen my playful side."

"Glimpses only." She nuzzled her flushed cheek against the blanket. "You don't have to be so serious around me."

Oh, but he did. Every lapse in the stoic mantle he wore around her seceded ground to a darker side of himself. There were some lines that, once crossed, could not be walked back. "You say serious; I say professional."

"Pfft. You aren't like this around Tasmin."

"I've known Tasmin all her life. She's family."

"Family?" Aesylt's voice gained a hard edge. "Not... lovers?"

"Lovers?" Rahn was so taken aback, he dropped onto the blanket next to her. "Is this about what you overheard in the barn?"

Aesylt rolled her face against the underside of her arm. "Ah, Ancestors. Forget I said anything. It's neither my place nor my business."

"No. Don't be ashamed of your curiosity. It's what makes you an excellent researcher." He reached out and brushed back the hair that had fallen over her buried face. "Tasmin is like a sister to me. It's why I couldn't even entertain the idea of partnering with her on the experiments." And why he couldn't understand how Aesylt could so easily partner with Niklaus.

Aesylt peeked one eye over her arm. "Why were you so angry with her in the courtyard before she left?"

Rahn grimaced, sighing. "That I cannot tell you, because it's not for me to tell. I'm sorry."

"Presently feeling like a right fool," she replied.

When she tried to bury her face again, he clamped a hand onto her arm, startling her into looking directly at him. "You may be many things, Aesylt Wynter, but I would not lump you in with the fools."

Her head lolled back. She stared up at him. "Is this why you're against partnering with me then? Am I as a sister to you?"

How I wish it were so simple. But he couldn't find words that were close enough to the truth to be worthy of speaking.

"And you're just feeling... protective, is that it? You don't want your little sister compromised by the darker side of learning?" Her words sounded petulant, but her tone was warm, almost solicitous. She was inviting discussion, not provoking an argument.

"That's..." Rahn studied the serious expression staring back at him. "There's a difference between choosing intimacy because you truly want it and giving into it because you feel you have no other choice."

Aesylt considered that for a moment. "How does that make it different from anything else we study?" She shook her head. "If the matter comes down to free will and agency, then is it not on the same level as everything we do? My commitment to studying the stars is a choice, so why can I not make an equivalent one about this?"

"You make a reasonable point," Rahn conceded. He rolled onto his back. Overhead, the auroras danced in ribbons of violet and turquoise, a phenomenon he never would have believed if he hadn't seen it with his own eyes. So much about the White Kingdom was a wonder to him, particularly when he had no memory of his own homeland of Ilynglass. "Is that really how you see it? That the matter comes down to the simplicity of choice? Nothing more?"

"Only if you see choice as a simple matter," she replied. He felt her watching him, reading him. "If you really want to know, Scholar, I view the assignment as a challenge. If I want this life, then I *must* be able to separate feeling from fact. What subject offers such a test as this one? As the one thing in all the world people *cannot* be rational about? If I can do this, then I can do anything else the Reliquary sends our way. And then I'll know, without question, that I am made for this life."

Rahn was lost for response. He'd spent most of his life teaching others, but every day with Aesylt was an unexpected lesson. No one else had made him question his way of thinking. If the assignment was her personal challenge, perhaps she was his. And if she could apply such pragmatism to the matter, he should be capable of the same rationality. "I hadn't thought of it that way. Perhaps we understand each other better than I realized."

Aesylt's sleepy laugh pierced the air. "What a revelation. Been telling you that for months. Maybe..." She buried her face in the blanket and yawned. "Maybe you could even look at me one day and see a reflection, rather than a precious vase one foul wind away from shattering."

Rahn's long exhale shuddered out of him. He rolled his head toward her. "I don't see you that way at all. I never have. Not for a moment."

"You're a confusing man, Rahn Tindahl." Her hand inched across the blanket and settled close enough to his for him to feel her warmth. "But I'm glad you came to Witchwood Cross."

For the rest of the night, and the ones to follow, he would wonder what in the stars had compelled him to climb his hand closer. What the gods he'd been thinking when his pinky tickled hers and linked with it. He could have stopped her when she slithered closer... should have said something when she hesitated, as though waiting for him to object, and then nuzzled her face to the side of his shoulder.

Aesylt's thigh half draped over his was the end of him, he knew it even then. All that remained was to determine the haste of his decline.

Her leg slid up his as she adjusted, coming dangerously close to brushing the rock-hard betrayal he was failing to will away. Her breath against the exposed hollow of his neck was enough to make him turn, but they were locked together in a suspended moment, neither able to speak or move.

Rahn's cock throbbed in aching rebellion. If he could just shift her, even slightly... but he didn't. Couldn't. He measured each breath, no longer thinking about the stars, the stag, the sky, or any of it. Perhaps the problem was entirely him; Aesylt might be able to throw up a wall, but she'd been crumbling his stone by stone since the day he'd met her. There was no victory ahead no matter what he did. He would either suffer through watching her with another man or suffer by agreeing to her challenge.

Aesylt adjusted again, wrapping her leg further over his, locking her groin to his thigh. Her very *damp* groin that moistened his trousers. He was certain she'd withdraw then, embarrassed, but the only thing to follow was the soft shift in breathing indicating she'd drifted off. Their hands were still linked on the blanket, an awkward joining with the way she was lying but one he couldn't make himself sever.

Light drool trailed from her mouth, coating his shoulder. How it was *that*, and not the sensuality coursing through her and into him, that made his toes clench was confounding, but it was also the start of the end. Stars of another kind exploded behind his eyes, his body lurching through his weak attempt at control as an orgasm involuntarily ripped through him. Cum coated his trousers, spreading evidence he'd never be able to hide if she woke.

Rahn rolled his head back in a silent, desperate pant.

Gods help me, he thought, as he realized the depth of the decision he'd made without being fully aware of it. The future awaiting them both. The restraint he'd failed to preserve and would no longer need to. Even if he changed his mind in the few hours left to them, it would not alter the course of his thoughts, forever reformed. He'd been silently fighting his entire life, but never harder than he'd battled to evade the temptation of the most enchanting, gifted, and beguiling woman he'd ever known.

Rahn breathed deep and fixed his gaze on the magical auroras, searching for the calm that could only be found after resolve. He'd need to wake her soon to return to the real world—and the even more real danger still brewing just beyond their walls.

He had until then to find the right words to tell Aesylt he would be her new partner.

THIRTEEN

PRINCIPALS OF NEUTRALITY

Apprehension followed Aesylt through the morning. It began as she helped Rahn pack up their scrolls and charts, attempting to catch his eye but equally hoping to avoid it. The hand he'd held was still warm with the memory. She still felt the strength of his thigh pinned under hers and the way their breathing had matched, uneven and inadequate.

He'd nearly run into her when carrying a trunk back to the door, forcing them into an awkward dance of shifting and flattening against the nearest surface. He'd squeezed past, his hip brushing hers, and she stopped breathing until he was clear.

The farther she moved from him, the more she felt as though someone had taken a scooper to her chest.

Once back in their quarters, he seemed more relaxed, even glancing her way a couple of times. She turned, locking his gaze, and caught him smiling.

"What?" Aesylt feared the answer. The past week had felt like pressure gradually building under a geyser, but that morning was different.

Rahn shook his head and returned his gaze to the window, folding his hands around a mug of cider. "The others always worked hard at whatever we assigned them, but you... I see now, it was always personal to you. Your concern for the work is more than a question of ethics."

Aesylt's flesh burned hot. "You're only now coming to this realization?"

"I never doubted your commitment or your passion. But the way you spoke of marriage... I suppose I presumed, perhaps wrongly, that you would move on from this and start a family." He must have sensed the indignance rising in her because he quickly continued. "And *yet,* I feel all the more the fool for assuming the two lives must be exclusive of each other."

Aesylt sat back and breathed in air not yet warmed by the hearth. The burn was a constant reminder life was not guaranteed. "I don't want children, so a family looks different for me. What I want is a partner in this life, one who will stand beside me, not four steps ahead of me." She grinned to herself as that very future streamed through her mind, her eyes on her gloved hands. "Maybe I want both. I want it all. Who's to stop me?"

"I pity the person who tries," Rahn quipped. "And wish them a swift demise."

Aesylt laughed, tilting her head his way. "I only deal in absolutes, Scholar. Nothing worth doing is worth doing halfway."

"You're more like your brother than you think."

"Or he's more like me." Aesylt pulled her collar higher on her neck, woefully conscious of the heat rising to her cheeks. "I'm the one who stayed. Who held—" She abruptly halted. Even the edges of the thought were enough to spoil the light mood, and she regretted speaking at all.

Rahn's eyes found hers and held her gaze. "Drazhan's vengeance was mighty... and in the end, he was eviscerated by it. All those years he gave to training were nothing compared to what he gave up in doing so. What *you* did took an immense amount of courage. To stay and lead your people through their darkest days and face the darkness with them. I have a great deal of respect for your brother, but if the end came today, Aesylt, my coin would be wagered on you leading us into the unknown future."

Aesylt tried to speak but realized she was trembling. It was her hands, mainly, but the buzz spread quickly to her limbs, then to her ears, until it was all she could feel or hear. She finally understood what had drawn her to the duke from the start. It was the way he saw her, even when, in her frustration, she believed otherwise. She could try to blend into a room, but he would find her. Would know her, as she had always wanted to be known.

"We don't have to talk about it."

"I've tried to talk about it," Aesylt answered, hoarse, "but Drazhan cannot... He cannot. And there's no one else. Oma, Ota, Hraz, they're all gone. It's why Nik and Val sometimes feel like all I have."

"In my experience, family is a choice. Teleria, she took me in because she wanted to. Over the years, our relationship became many different things, but it was then, and always will be, one of family. A bond that transcends blood." He released her gaze. "But they're not all you have, Aesylt."

Aesylt moved her hands under her dressing coat, twisting them. The urge to cry was almost too much to fight, but no tears would fall. At most, her eyes would gloss over, a gentle pool under her lids. "If I could spend the rest of my life studying at your side, Scholar, I would need nothing else."

Rahn said nothing more until they approached the gates at Fanghelm. "You will always have a place at my side." He cleared his throat, readying to say more, but something caught his eyes, causing him to rise off the settee.

"What is it?" she asked, standing to follow where he looked out the window, at a throng of people. Hundreds. "Something's happened."

"If something had happened, Drazhan would have sent for us." Rahn didn't seem convinced.

"He will soon enough," Aesylt said before leaping up and charging toward the apartment door. Her heart comprehended the situation well ahead of her head, beating in urgent, wild thumps. She heard Rahn shouting behind her, the damning letter from the Barynovs burning more than just her pocket.

Valerian was awake. Aesylt seemed to have known it before Drazhan had delivered the official news, but it had been a shock to Rahn. His instincts told him the Barynovs had only kept him alive because they were in denial. No one had been talking about the boy with the future in mind, only the past. His fate had already been decided in the minds of the village.

Rahn's questions were answered before he had a chance to ask. No, Drazhan was not agreeing to their extortionate wedding demand, not even for Val. No, no one from Fanghelm had actually seen Val, but the Barynovs had paraded him around the village square to make their point, and plenty of villagers had seen him. He was convalescing under intense guard.

All of that was not surprising.

Drazhan's solution was.

"Lord Dereham has sent a response to my plea."

"Lord..." Aesylt cocked her head. "You never mentioned any plea."

"He will play host to you until it's safe to return." Drazhan's stoic delivery was jarring compared to the chorus of objections that rose after.

"Who is *you*?" Aesylt demanded. Her hands were splayed atop the table, but Rahn, beside her, could see how she'd lifted out of her seat... how she was barely sitting at all.

"You, cub," Drazhan said, gritting, "and your scholar."

"And the others?" Aesylt's fingers twitched on the wood.

"Teleria will go to Eastport to wait, in case Tasmin returns early. We can't send a raven that might be intercepted."

"But Tasmin isn't expected back for *months*."

Imryll cradled Aleksy with an avoidant glare at the table. Rahn caught her eyes briefly, but she wasn't sharing her feelings this time.

"And your wife, wulf?" Aesylt gaped between the two. "Are you banishing her as well?"

Drazhan didn't answer.

"Imryll, you *know* this isn't right," Aesylt pleaded. "You don't have to leave your own home."

"We're already not in our own home, Aes." Imryll sounded exhausted. "And I have to think of more than my wishes."

"Wynters don't *run*. We didn't run when the king's men came for us, and we will not run when one of our own is the trouble."

Drazhan slammed his hands onto the table, shooting to his feet. "And look how that ended, Aesylt. Ota, Hraz, *dead*. Our friends' allies, way too fucking many of them, bleeding in the streets, on pikes, discarded like trash. Is that what you want to see? Is that what staying means to you?"

Aesylt's face darkened several shades. Her eyes narrowed, glossing in fury. "And what would you know about it, wulf? You weren't even here." Wood shrieked on stone as she shoved back from the table and stormed from the room.

Drazhan retreated to his chair slowly, breathing out as he lowered himself, clearly rattled by her words. "I hope I do not have to explain to the rest of you why this is necessary."

Rahn was still watching the archway Aesylt had fled through. Her anger had incited his, but he had no choice but to temper it to stay and hear the rest of Drazhan's proclamation. "If you feel it is, then it is. But she'll need—"

"Aesylt will have anything she needs. You can..." Drazhan flapped his hand. "Continue your research in Wulfsgate. I only care that she's safe."

Rahn turned toward Imryll, whose silence seemed intentional. "And you? Where will you go?"

"We discussed the options available," she said quietly, "and Wulfsgate offers both the best protection for Aleksy and me..

and the best resources for an expecting mother. So I'll be coming with you."

"Imryll." Rahn tried to smile, but it turned out half-formed from the weight of the revelations. "Blessings to you both."

Imryll mouthed a halfhearted thank-you.

Drazhan's lips twitched. "I'll celebrate when she's safe. When they all are."

"Their son is *alive.* Awake. Why would they still be pushing for war?" Rahn asked.

"My husband likes his secrets, but I do not." Imryll transferred Aleksy to her other shoulder. "They were on Draz's father about a union long before the Nok Mora. They say Ezra Wynter promised Aesylt to Valerian, but there's nothing in writing and no witness to any of it. But they believe they're entitled to her, and the situation with Val seems to have accelerated their urgency."

"Why do they want her so badly that they're willing to risk war?"

"They want my seat," Drazhan said, answering for Imryll. "They want Fanghelm. They think a union between the two oldest families will win support to their cause, and their effort is already gaining support."

"And then how does it end? Not with Aesylt married." Rahn scoffed.

One of Imryll's eyes squinted. "Aesylt will wed no one she hasn't chosen for herself."

"She'll never wed a Barynov," Drazhan muttered. His eyes closed as he inhaled. "Even if she chooses one." He rapped the table with his knuckles and whipped his gaze Rahn's way, his eyes hard and narrow. "You want to know how this ends? They either renounce their false claim on my sister, both on her hand and their smear against her reputation, and turn Marek over for justice, or they see firsthand how much less merciful I am than the king. I don't fear war, and neither do they. My sister is your charge now, Rahn. You do anything it takes to keep her from putting herself in danger. *Whatever* it takes. And when this is over—and it *will* end—I'll be indebted to you. Anything you want from me is yours. I couldn't refuse."

They departed Witchwood Cross at nightfall. Aesylt kept to her side of the plush carriage, opting for silence. She was practically swimming in the layered teal gown Imryll had given her for the journey, chosen for presentation to the lord of the Northerlands, who Rahn doubted would care at all about what they were wearing when they showed up in the middle of the night as refugees.

He'd been working up to the words all afternoon. Once said, they could not be taken back, and though he didn't expect to regret them, the *way* in which they were said—the precise nature of the message—mattered. What he said would set the tone for their entire partnership going forward. It would be the difference between sealing their bond and sundering it.

Rahn pulled the thin curtain back and peered into the night. There was nothing to see but dark, tall trees and snow. So much snow. The South Compass Road was serviceable, even in the winter seasons, but there were no other safe paths. It would take them several more hours to reach Wulfsgate than it would in springtide, when the hunter's trails were clear.

Behind them was a carriage carrying Imryll and Aleksy, and beyond, a caravan of Drazhan's men. A few would stay behind with them, the rest returning as soon as the group was settled. There were more than they needed on a good day, less than required on a bad one, and a road ambush had crossed Rahn's mind more than once. But if their litter was too large, it would draw the very eyes they needed to avoid while traveling under night's cover.

"I have something to say," Rahn ventured aloud. His choice of words, the same ones she'd used to issue her apology, were intentional. He saw from the sharp slant of her curious eyes, subtly turned his way, that she knew it. "About our research."

"They don't have an observatory. Even the Wintergarden is... The village is too busy. Wulfsgate is not the best place to watch the stars. We'd need to travel up Torrin's Pass, and there's no chance of it being approved," she said, turning her face back to the plush cushion.

"I wasn't talking about astronomy."

Aesylt sat up straight. Her chin tucked down in soft alarm.

"Coitus." He nearly spat the word trying to avoid it. But if he could not even say it around her, he had no business making the proposal. In the end, the word would be the easiest part of it all. "You and I. Partners."

"You..." Aesylt's red lips turned to a confused pout. "You want *us...*"

"It's a matter of practicality, not want." Perhaps if he repeated the lie enough, he'd believe it and be set free of his torture. "The war with the Barynovs has set us back, and we either move forward with a plan or accept that we never will."

She bristled. "This is *our* work, and I will not let the Reliquary take it from us."

"Nor will I." Rahn dug his hands to the pleats of the bench. "And I see no other way forward than for us to proceed with your idea of the two of us handling the curricula ourselves. But only if you are still fully, and I mean *fully,* prepared for what that means."

Aesylt's eyes flitted around as a series of emotions played out across her tired, peaked face. "You're serious? You're no longer concerned for my chastity or honor or whatever it was holding you back?"

"I didn't say I wasn't concerned," Rahn stated firmly. "But you made a point I can't refute. If this is your way of challenging yourself, of embracing not just a passion but a life in science, then standing in your way would be to betray my own principles of neutrality in research. And... If I believe I have more authority to choose for you than you do for yourself, then it betrays my values as a man."

Her mouth parted in a slow grin. "I see. And you're prepared to go through everything on the list? With me?"

Rahn swallowed. "Yes," he croaked.

"This time without your voice breaking."

"*Yes,* Aesylt. I'm prepared to go through everything on the list with you." He wasn't, not even a little, but it was his challenge to overcome, not hers.

"And it will change nothing between us?"

It would change everything, and she knew it. They both did. "We will have rules, of course. To protect us both and the research. The most important being we perform these acts only in the celestial realm, where our actions have less consequence." He almost said *no consequence*, but that would have been untrue. Their memories followed them across worlds. He would know her, feel her, in both. "I won't rely on your vedhma's grimizhna tea to keep us out of trouble."

Aesylt's face flushed deep red. "Ahh. Yes, fair... fair point. And how will we... How will we take credit for the work? Drazhan can *never* find out." Her laugh was dark. "But neither can Imryll. I won't put her in that position."

"I've thought about that," Rahn said. He wanted to peel back the curtain once more, take another glimpse outside to cut the tension in the small carriage. "Elara and Niklaus have not officially been removed from the cohort, not in the Reliquary's records. We can put their names on the work when we submit it. I'll... offer to submit the work to the Reliquary myself, and if it comes down to it, I'll find a way to explain things to Imryll."

Aesylt nodded to herself. "The Reliquary won't be the problem. Imryll is going to want to know exactly who conducted these experiments."

"We'll figure it out."

"And us?"

Rahn cocked his head.

"Can we agree that... no matter how, ah, *intense* our studies get, we'll still be friends when it's done?"

Rahn's heart fluttered. "Aesylt, it would break my heart if this resulted in the end of our friendship. It's the very thing I hope to avoid."

"I want us to shake on it." She sat forward, the ruffles of her dress sliding along the bench in a soft chorus. "I want us to swear on it."

He leaned forward, stretching his hand toward her. "I promise."

She slipped hers into his with a firm shake. "As do I. If things *ever* get too difficult..."

"We stop."

Aesylt nodded. "We stop."

Rahn released her with a hidden sigh of relief. It was done. It was said. It was over. The only thing left to do was begin. "We'll start as soon as we're settled."

FUCKING
FOR SCIENCE

FOURTEEN

SOMEWHERE SHE CAN SEE THE STARS

Aesylt had been to Wulfsgate many times as a child. She'd always looked forward to spending time with Lord Dereham's children, Pieter and Nyssa, and running through the magical Wintergarden, with its radiant year-round blooms. It, like all the world, had been different then.

The last time she'd gone had been almost a decade ago, to offer solemn testimony to Lord Dereham of all she'd seen the night of the Nok Mora. Drazhan had already begun his slow retreat into himself, so Fezzan had escorted her, and that had been just as well. The Derehams had taken such good care of her, just like Fezzan had, but their pity was all she'd seen. It had driven her heart straight into the ground, and part of it was still there, waiting for the thaw.

The broad stone walls encompassing the great city were the same as she remembered. So was the sense of the world ripping open as the colossal gates sluggishly parted, powered by a dozen straining men on each side. The moon was nearly full, as it had been upon the night of her last arrival, and a low fog cut the village down the middle, like a tear in the sky.

She'd lost track of the time, but the capital of the Northerlands never slept. As their retinue made a slow advance through the town center, only half of the shops were boarded for the night. Smoke billowed from every other chimney, warm lights flickering behind panes. Laughter and conversation drifted toward them on the road, blurring with the night.

It wasn't as glamorous as the gleaming spires of Whitechurch, where Tasmin had gone—or so Aesylt had been told, as she'd never been beyond the north's borders—but laying eyes upon the visage of the towering stone fortress on the hill stole no less of her breath.

"We passed a couple of nights here on our way to Witchwood Cross," Rahn muttered, peering out his window. "But I never saw the keep from the village at night. It's forbidding, isn't it?"

"That impression is intentional," she said as she watched more of the stone towers come into view. "The Northerlands once had enemies and opportunists all over the kingdom. There are so many untapped mines in these mountains, *our* mountains. So many resources for others to ravage. There's nothing a Northerlander loves more than land and home... That's one important thing they have in common with the Vjestik. It's why we settled here. Our needs are simple. Our passions are simple. But they're not for sale." She realized how much she was rambling. Self-conscious, she cleared her throat and finished her point. "Then a new keep was raised, the great walls constructed. Who needs diplomacy when you have such a powerful deterrent as *this*?" She tapped her chest. "The most effective fear is the one that thrives in the absence of words."

Rahn's intense stare was like standing too close to the hearth. He held it through the strange silence that followed.

The slow climb uphill took another half tick of the moon, but soon the ground leveled, and they pulled to a stop.

Voices manifested outside and then the carriage doors were flung open. A man about Rahn's age with a dazzling grin turned it on her and held out his hand. He seemed familiar, but her vision was all but a blur in her exhaustion. "You are a dream, Lady Wynter. Welcome back."

Aesylt wrinkled her mouth in amusement as she took his hand. "I'm no lady, but thank you for the warm welcome."

"Far too cold to offer otherwise. You're much changed from the last time I saw you," he said, gently guiding her down from the carriage. It was unnecessary, and she almost said so, but a chill gale wrapped her tight. It might be colder in Witchwood Cross, but she'd forgotten that Wulfsgate Keep sat atop an exposed crop of land that offered no reprieve from the wind.

She shook her head, smiling through her fatigue. "Forgive me, but my mind is a jumbled mess right now."

He was a full foot taller than her, so she had to look up to see the comically wounded look he wore. "Is your favorite childhood friend so easy to forget?"

Aesylt clapped her hands to her mouth. "Pieter! Oh, I'm so... Forgive me." How could she have not recognized him? "It's been a long, long night."

Pieter was seven, perhaps eight years older than her, but the difference hadn't kept him from joining in when Aesylt and Nyssa had played in the Wintergarden. Tall, striking, with a boyish but serious face, all those things had become *more.* She wondered how Nyssa had changed with the years.

Pieter's smile trailed away as he looked to her left. "And you must be Duke Tindahl."

"Rahn. Or Scholar, if you have a penchant for titles." Rahn stepped forward, his eyes skimming her briefly before he took Pieter's hand. "You're Lord Dereham's son?"

"Couldn't guess what he'd say if you asked him that question." At Rahn's confused look, he clarified. "His failed heir. Yes." Pieter's broad grin didn't falter. He swept an arm toward the carriages in front of them. "My father is greeting Stewardess Wynter and her son, but he'll offer proper welcome in the morning, after you've had a chance at some rest."

"You weren't here when I passed through a year ago with the Farrestells."

"I was not, Scholar," Pieter agreed. "Shall we?" He turned and started down the long path toward the entrance. "Your trunks will meet you in your apartment. I'd offer you a tour, but Aesylt knows the place well, and you've had one before, I suspect," he called. "Have you broken fast since Witchwood Cross?"

"Not hungry, thank you," Aesylt and Rahn said at the same time. He offered a sheepish glance from the side, his eyes drowsy and lidded from the long ride. She gave him a lighthearted nudge and hastened to catch up with Pieter.

"I always knew you had an affinity for older men," Pieter teased. Aesylt would have rankled at the implication, but there'd always been a playful side to him that brought out the same in others.

She grinned, already feeling bits of the weight around her heart melting away. A familiar, friendly face was exactly what she needed amid so much uncertainty. "My vedhma says it's the lack of strong male influence in my life."

"Does she? And what does your brother think of that?"

Aesylt laughed, her eyes on the massive looming doors ahead. There were more armed guards in the courtyard than there'd been in all of Witchwood Cross. "Best no one mention it to him."

Pieter smiled. "It's good to see you."

"And you. But where have you been?" She felt Rahn close behind. "The Scholar said you weren't here a year ago?"

"I actually left about eight years ago." His hand rested at the small of her back when she started climbing. She usually rejected such empty chivalry, but the familiarity was an unexpected comfort. "Wanted something more than this."

"More than being the future lord of the Northerlands?"

"You never struck me as someone particularly fussed about titles."

"I'm not," she said as they stepped inside. The main hall of Wulfsgate Keep was cavernous, broken up only by a series of tapestries for warming. A central staircase ran down the center, with further halls to the left and right. An entire line of staff waited at the bottom. "But I understand duty."

The doors whooshed closed behind them. "Of course you do. I haven't forgotten." His hand twitched against her back and fell away. "We'll be going just to the back here."

"The back?" Aesylt checked to make sure Rahn was still close, but he seemed distracted. "Where are Imryll and Aleksy?"

"My father has already taken them to their apartment. Your brother wrote ahead, asking if you could be provided, ah, how did he word it... special privileges? For your research, is that right? You're working on something important?"

Rahn cleared his throat. "We have a research endeavor we'd love to continue, if possible. But special privileges will not be necessary, my lord."

"If you're not a duke, then I'm not a lord," Pieter said amiably. "And Steward Wynter specifically said, 'Somewhere she can see the stars.' I suppose that applies to all of the grounds, but there's one very particular place we've fixed up for you that should work well, should the clouds clear."

Regret tickled the back of Aesylt's eyes. She hadn't left her brother on the greatest terms, but he'd been thinking about her happiness when he'd made the request. "Wherever it is, I'm sure it will be fine."

"Now, it hasn't been used much. We have three bell towers at the keep, as you might recall, but we only actively man two of them. The third made itself obsolete when we expanded the residences further into the foothills. No one wants to hear bells going off in the middle of the night outside their window, eh?" Pieter winked and exited through the back of the keep, which opened into another courtyard. The mysterious Wintergarden lay just beyond, to the west, and to the east was the Northerland

Range. "The stairway is daunting, but you're both young. At the top... Well, I'll just show you. Come."

Rahn stepped in beside Aesylt as Pieter jogged ahead. "A childhood friend of yours?"

"Yes," she said as everyone in the courtyard stopped to watch them. "You'll like him."

"He's my age."

Aesylt grinned. "That an admonishment, Scholar, or an observation?"

Rahn tried not to grin back. "When have I ever admonished you, Squish?"

She cocked a brow. "So you're back to calling me a squirrel?"

"A *resourceful* squirrel."

"Just up here, Aesylt, Scholar."

Pieter took them through a series of short, tight alleyways, which opened into a small garden, surrounded by the walls of other structures. On the north end of the garden was a tower. It stretched about six stories high, the outer walls cracked but solid. Moss burst from the mortar, crumbling off in chunks. The bell at the top was rusted, but just beneath the platform was a series of windows. The bellman's apartment. Aesylt had never seen one so didn't know what to expect. There were no bellmen in Witchwood Cross, just guards in sparse stone monoliths.

"This is Halifax, but you can call him Hal, or even Billiards if you're feeling cheeky. Maybe he'll even tell you why," Pieter said, pointing out a congenial guard with golden hair cascading down his back from a leather ribbon. Hal glared at the disgraced heir in a mix of playfulness and annoyance. "One of the best guards we have, and certainly the one you'd want playing your money in a game room." He grinned. "He'll be in charge of your tower protection while you're here. Anything you need, any concerns... He's your first line of defense at night. His brother, Kezza, takes over in the daytime and is equally experienced. You're in capable hands."

"A pleasure to meet you, Hal, and thank you for looking after us," Aesylt said amiably. Rahn echoed her words. The man flushed and bowed.

"Your trunks are already up there. Our men are fast," Pieter said, holding the door for them and tipping a nod at Hal. He grabbed a torch from a basket on the wall. "We brought two eternal flames here, one at the top and one at the bottom, for when you need to climb the stairs after dark. But there are far more candles than you'll ever need once you step inside."

Rahn held his arm out for Aesylt to go first. He joined right behind, close enough she could feel his warmth and inhale the not-unpleasant musk of hours on the road. She wondered how she smelled, if he was thinking about her the same way. Every few steps his hand would brush her back.

Yes, he is.

On they climbed, up and up. In her head, Aesylt counted the stories, but her math was woefully off, as Pieter confirmed when he called out *we're halfway* when she was certain they were about to reach the top. Exhaustion beckoned, but she was sharply aware of everything happening around her. The spiders crawling along the dark walls, dancing in and out of the light of Pieter's flame. Pieter's long legs disappearing around every winding turn. Rahn's prevailing presence at her back.

Pieter slowed when they reached a small platform and a door. "Privy. It's a half story below the main apartment, which may seem inconvenient to you now, but given the lack of proper air circulation in the structure, you'll be grateful for it."

Rahn chuckled. Aesylt frowned at the door and followed Pieter up the last flight.

Pieter set the torch in a sconce and unlocked the door and handed the ring, key dangling, to Aesylt. "After you, love."

Aesylt stepped inside. The room was larger than she'd imagined, and surprisingly well furnished. A living area, a dining area, and a bathtub were the first things she saw, followed by two sizable desks, each holding a stack of books. But then she noted the beds, separated by thin curtains, and it hit her. One room. It would not be like her prior confinement, where they'd each had their own space. Any privacy in the bell tower would be an illusion, as wispy as the curtains. "We're staying here? Both of us?"

Pieter chuckled. "Wherever you are at night is where you must stay until morning, for your safety. As your astronomy work can only be done at night, staying in the keep would have kept you from it. My father was assured it would not be a problem."

She gestured at the two beds. "Drazhan knows we're sharing a room?"

"He informed us in his correspondence that you'd been staying in close quarters with your scholar since the troubles started. This is no different."

Yet it was. Whether in Rahn's apartments or hers, they'd never shared a bedchamber.

"Have we misunderstood?" Pieter asked. "I can call for the porters—"

"No," she said quickly, wondering where Rahn's head was, why he'd said nothing. "You're right. This is no different."

Pieter ran down all of the accoutrements, but she was hardly listening. She snuck a glance at Rahn, but his attention was on their host.

"I left some books on your desks I thought might be of interest. We have quite a library here at Wulfsgate Keep, which you're welcome to make use of. But, ah, the reason I prepared *this* place for you... Come, come." Pieter ushered them to what she thought must be the north side of the room, to a series of three windows. He unlatched one, and it swung open. "Look."

Aesylt stepped closer and craned her neck out. The cloud cover was too low to see anything, but the views were otherwise unobstructed. He couldn't know their astronomy days were on hold—or why—so she smiled and said, "This will be perfect. Thank you so much."

Pieter watched her reaction closely enough to make her question her performance, until he gave her shoulder a squeeze and stretched his hands above his head. "It's late. You're both exhausted. We break our fast at the eighth hour in the Great Hall. Aes, do you remember the way, or shall I come meet you?"

"I know the way."

"Splendid. When you want warm water, just notify the kitchen staff, through the guard duty, and they'll have it sent to the ground level, where it can be hoisted via pulley." He pointed at the corner the tub was in. "And I'll cease running my mouth so you can both enjoy some needed rest. Dobranok." He bowed. "Did I say it right? That means good night in Vjestikaan, yes?"

Aesylt, smiling, nodded. "Tak. You did. Dobranok, Pieter."

"Dobranok," Rahn said, his eyes following Pieter all the way to the door. He didn't move even when the man's steps faded down the stairs.

"It's... cozy," Aesylt ventured, stepping slowly around the room. "We'll have the seclusion we need. Just don't tell poor Pieter his astronomy tower won't be rising to its intended purpose."

"Hmm." Rahn was still watching the door.

"Are you here with me or somewhere else?"

Rahn puffed out a breath and turned. "Sorry. Of course I am. It's late. Shall we turn in?"

It shouldn't have felt like a rejection, but it did. She had extended no invitation with her words, but the lack of acknowledgment left her more insecure than she'd felt in a long while. Perhaps he'd changed his mind. Maybe he already regretted the offer before the partnership had even begun.

Or maybe your imagination is a wild garden you should remember to prune from time to time.

Aesylt rushed to her trunk before he saw any of that written on her face. A shadow fell over her, and she looked up just as Rahn was leaning past her. He grabbed the latches and lifted with a grunt.

"This should be near your bed," he said and disappeared behind the curtain. "Actually, I should have asked first. Which one do you prefer?"

"They seem the same to me," Aesylt said, dazed. She was tired too, far more than she'd realized. "Thank you, Scholar."

He popped back out with a stern look that he aimed not at her but past her. "You may as well start calling me Rahn." Then, dusting his hands down his torso, he made a strange face and headed toward his own bed.

"Not a chance, Scholar."

A faint laugh echoed from behind the curtain. "Dobranok then."

He was both the most transparent man she'd ever known and also impossible to read. But the next however many days, weeks, would be untenable if they were tiptoeing around each other, around their arrangement.

Aesylt didn't return his good-night because her mind wouldn't rest until she knew for sure where his head was.

Once he disappeared behind his side of the curtain, her heart a racing, unconfident mess, Aesylt started to undress.

Rahn shed his layers meticulously, in the same order as always. By the time he finished removing his vest, he was on fire. Sweat trickled down his temple. His hands felt ready to explode into flames.

The belltower was meant for workers, not lords, and aside from a few tapestries, a bearskin rug, and the modest hearth, there wasn't much to heat it. If he were to accidentally leave a window open, they'd likely freeze to death in their sleep.

But it wasn't the room sending the heat through him in lashes, it was *her*.

He was down to his blouse and trousers when he poured himself a mug of whatever was in the pitcher he'd seen on the desk. He slammed down one round of the watery drink and was debating pouring another when he heard Aesylt's light steps trickle in behind him and stop. From limb to limb, his body seized. He was suspended between the decision to pour or abort, waiting for her to return to her bed, but she didn't. She didn't move at all.

Rahn slid his finger along the rough wooden edge of the mug. He trapped a breath and turned, but whatever pleasantry he'd planned flew straight from his mind at the sight of her in a thin night slip. The gauzy fabric clung to her lean curves. Her erect nipples—gods how he tried not to look—sat atop perfectly arced breasts that he'd noticed before but had not seen like this.

He took a single step, his pulse screaming between his ears. It was all he could manage.

"And another with me," she said, hoarse and raspy, and the world shifted. The room was the same, same fire roaring in the hearth, and she was just as breathtaking in the celestial realm as the real one.

One of Rahn's hands reached for her, a command dredged from a part of himself not fully in his control. It brushed her warm skin, causing her to lift onto her toes with a shiver, and traveled to the wisp of a strap keeping her nightgown from meeting the floor. Both of their breaths hitched when it slid down her shoulder and rested on the edge of the muscle of her upper arm. The lace covering her breasts fell away on one side, revealing raised flesh along the cut of her cleavage.

Aesylt's shoulders rose in a charged shudder, but her eyes... She kept her crystal irises fixed on his in challenge, in permission. For what... Ah, he should ask. He should break the spell and remind them both that whatever current was flowing between them was for the good of the research.

His hand traveled along the stretch of her milky neck. She craned her head to the side and his fingers skimmed the underside of her chin, lifting it. Her eyes never closed, and her gaze never faltered, but a single flit of her tongue on her lips was all it took.

Rahn was still drowning in her gaze when he leaned in and swept his lips against hers. She lifted again to her toes with a soft moan that made his stomach wind into knots. Her arms folded behind his head as she stretched higher. He dragged his hands down the fabric, skirting one of her breasts, and let it rest against her hip.

His tongue found hers and something inside of him snapped. He reached around her hip to her ass and cupped it, lifting, and she leaped up, wrapping her legs around his waist. With his thumb caressing the edge of her mouth, he tugged, opening it to drive his tongue deeper, memorizing the warmth, the soft, sweet taste of her, and the clench of her thighs against his hips.

She slid against him, against his cock, which didn't belong in his trousers. It belonged in *her*, in her soft mouth, her delicious pussy, her tight ass, her...

Rahn lowered her and took a faltering step back. He wiped his mouth on the back of his hand, panting and turning his startled gaze to the fire.

"Scholar?" she asked, small and anxious, her arms wrapped around herself.

He shook his head, trying to speak, but nothing came out. He coughed to clear the clog in his throat, but it was no better.

"Have I done something to upset you?"

"No," he rasped, turning his attention back to her. There was hurt in her wide eyes, caused by him. But he'd agreed to this, had even been the one who had proposed it the second time. The mixed messages weren't fair. He had to do better, for her. "I was only... thinking, we're both very tired, and if we don't stop now, we'll need to do this again in the morning, so our thoughts are fresh for our notes."

A shy grin pulled at her mouth. "Would that be so bad?"

Rahn wasn't quick enough to bury his own smile. "I wouldn't be devastated."

A fuller smile appeared. She closed her eyes and whispered, and they were again in their own world. She was already moving away from him, returning to her bed. The moment ended as quickly as it had commenced.

Rahn went to his own bed. He sat on the edge, removed his trousers, deciding at the last minute to leave the shirt. Nude was his sleeping preference, but the chill air aside, it was for her benefit he stayed clothed.

It was only when his head hit the pillow that he realized neither of them had gone for their notes.

He closed his eyes but was no longer tired. Heat pounded the backs of his lids, his flesh a minefield. He shifted, trying to get comfortable, but all he could think about, all he could *feel,* was the soft fold of her arms behind his neck, her eager lifting. They'd kissed once before, but not... not like that. Not with intent. Not with enough longing to burn all of Wulfsgate to the ground.

A muted whimper drew his notice. He stilled, listening, but it was another few moments before he heard it again. A sharp inhalation followed, set to the rustling of blankets.

Gods, she's pleasuring herself. Rahn gripped the sheets, his toes curling toward the pads of his feet. All he had to do was slip out of his bed and into hers. Perhaps she wanted him to. Quiet as she was, she could have been quieter. Unable to say the words, she'd sent him another kind of message.

But there was an order to their curricula. To move ahead was to admit none of it was for science at all, but to satisfy some dark, feral longing for someone he could never have in any meaningful way, and shouldn't want.

Rahn's hand moved between his legs. The gentle squeeze sent his eyes rolling back and nearly pushed him over the edge, but he went slow, listening to her breathy pants intensify. He matched her pace, ignited by her unashamed knowledge of her body and its desires. When he imagined her fingers dipping lower to drive her wetness higher, he had to bite down to keep from finishing.

At last he heard her open-mouthed gasp, the torsion of flesh against fabric, and he gave his cock several rough strokes, angling his face against his arm as he came so hard, he nearly yelped.

"Dobranok, Scholar," Aesylt whispered. In her tone was all she didn't say. That she'd heard. She'd been right there with him for all of it.

"Dobranok, Aesylt," he responded, and soon after, sleep offered its warm embrace.

FIFTEEN
FOR THE NOTES

They dressed in silence, stealing charged glances in place of words. Aesylt was desperate to talk about what had happened after they'd retreated to their own beds, but every time she got a bolt of courage, the moment seemed off. Either his back was turned or he was washing his face, or it was some other excuse her mind invoked to let her off easy.

The little splintered grunt he'd made when he had come played over and over and over.

An exhilarated thrill tore across her chest. The way he'd kissed her... It certainly hadn't felt very clinical. Very *scientific*. How he'd snapped her close... a small shard of his reserve disintegrating. When she completed her notes after morning meal, she'd spend additional time describing those fractional moments. If she were brave enough, she'd write about how they'd made her feel.

In the celestial realm, he was another man, less inhibited and more himself. She couldn't wait to learn more.

Rahn mouthed the words *after you* as he waited at the open door leading to the stairs. She flicked her eyes toward his, then demurely averted them, slipping past with a racing heart. He was close behind her all the way down, his steps echoing alongside hers in perfect concert. When they reached the bottom and the open arch leading to the small courtyard garden, she turned, once again seized by a moment of courageousness, but a gregarious greeting stopped her.

"Dobryzen, Aesylt, Rahn." Pieter took a crunchy bite of a mostly eaten apple and tossed it into a bush. His hood was pulled low and taut, and Aesylt soon realized why. It was pouring rain. She'd been so preoccupied getting ready, she hadn't even noticed the weather. "I trust you both slept well?"

Aesylt tried not to look at Rahn when she answered. "Yes, thank you. You were right. It's the perfect location to see the stars." She tugged her hood into place with a shiver. A man who looked like Hal, but was taller, nodded at her and she nodded back. Kezza, she presumed.

He made a *hunh* sound. "Not last night, I reckon. Another storm coming in."

"Yes, well, we didn't do any stargazing last night, with how tired we both were. You know, we both went to sleep almost immediately, hardly even spoke if I'm being honest, but I'm sure it will..." She looked to Rahn for help.

"Stunning views," Rahn agreed, patting his vest like he'd forgotten something.

Pieter slowly nodded as he regarded them both. "Good. I trust you'll pass many productive nights here." He turned and started toward the keep.

"Many," Aesylt replied, then shrugged and winced at Rahn when he gave her an incredulous look.

They jogged behind Pieter, racing to get out of the rain. Her head was down when her boots hit dry stone, so she didn't see the towering man until she smacked into him. "Lord Dereham," she said, looking up. "Forgive me, I—"

Rustan Dereham smooshed her in a bighearted hug. "Our resilient little wulf cub has returned" were his first words, in a singsong voice that sounded peculiar with his deep, booming tone. He released her, holding her at arm's length. "It has been far too long, Aesylt. You needn't wait for tragedy for an excuse to visit. Tell your brother as much."

Aesylt bowed and smiled gratefully. "You're right, my lord. And I will pass the message to Drazhan as well."

"And you are not just the first duke to grace our halls, but twice now!" Rustan tipped a respectful nod at Rahn. "Though I seem to recall you telling us you prefer no deference?"

"Duke is a title I happily left behind in Duncarrow when I came to the Northerlands," Rahn said graciously. "I've always preferred Rahn."

"Scholar Tindahl," Pieter said, chiming in. "Is what he goes by now."

"A man of many names is a man who has lived." Rustan sized Rahn up once more. "Duke or scholar, though, I trust our Aesylt is safe in your hands and that no oversight of your studies will be necessary."

Aesylt read the threat, and from the look on Rahn's face, so had he.

"Steward Wynter was fine with your arrangement in the tower, but you both understand that after nightfall, you're to stay put. No wandering. The courtyard is teeming with guards. Hal and Kez are the best you could ask for. You needn't worry about being safe," he said. "But I'm asking *you,* Scholar, from one honorable man to another, if the arrangement works for *you.*"

"I would never let harm reach her. We're comfortable with one another and will not require alternate arrangements," Rahn answered, his cheeks tightening. "We thank you for your hospitality while Steward Wynter works to resolve matters at home."

"The Barynovs won't be put down so easily. Weak men seek validation, not resolution. Your steward has his work ahead of him, dealing with that unruly baron. All Drazhan has to do is say the word, and we'll send men, end the whole ordeal. Ezra Wynter wouldn't have been too ashamed to call upon the generosity of his lord." Rustan tapped his chest with a cough. "Felice and Nyssa are already in the Great Hall and are beside themselves to see you, Aesylt. Stewardess Wynter should be there by now as well. Shall we?"

Rustan went ahead of Aesylt and Rahn, with Pieter falling behind. Aesylt was bursting to say something to the scholar, but the Dereham sandwich limited her options. "Quite the rain we're having. I'd guess it'll freeze over later," she remarked.

"Treacherous, isn't it?" Rahn scratched his fingers down his neck and tugged on his collar. "We'll need to be mindful on the walk back."

"Our men take the salt from the mines and lay it down on all surfaces the moment rain falls," Pieter said from behind. "You needn't worry about safety in your lord's domain."

Rustan stiffened when his son spoke.

No one else said anything until they entered the Great Hall. Aesylt spotted Imryll in the center of the endless table and broke away, rushing toward her. Imryll stood and wrapped Aesylt in a fierce embrace and whispered, "We'll talk after."

Aesylt kissed her cheek. "Where's Aleksy?"

"In the nursery with Hadden."

"Hadden?" Aesylt frowned in confusion.

"Much has changed since we last broke bread, Aesylt." Felice, Rustan's wife, rose and brushed kisses along both of Aesylt's cheeks. Her golden curls were piled high and tight against her narrow, comely face. "Hadden is my son. He's two."

"You have another son, my lady?" Aesylt asked as she dipped into a perfunctory bow. Had she been so wrapped up in her own world that she'd missed the announcement?

Felice shot an icy look at Pieter, still smiling at Aesylt. "Needs must," she said tersely. "Shall we break our fast?"

Aesylt caught Nyssa smiling at her from the other side of the table as they all took their seats, and she smiled back, stunned to see how much her childhood playmate had matured. She had been around six or seven when Aesylt had seen her last, and now was staring down womanhood. Her cheeks bloomed with radiance, her dress cut less modestly now that she was on the marriage market. Even her buoyant blonde waves had been styled with drawing attention in mind. There was no negotiation prize with more bargaining power in the north than a Dereham bride.

Aesylt waited as the table was laden with several generous trays of bread, jam, and fruit. A heady aroma arrived with a smaller tray, comprised of meat shaped into small disks. *Swine*, she thought, breathing deep, trying to remember the last time they'd eaten meat during morning meal in the Cross.

"Lady Dereham, Lady Nyssa, it's lovely to see you both again," Rahn said as he spooned steaming food onto his plate. "We will try not to be an imposition while we're here."

"Most of our guests want something material from us. Money. Land." Felice smiled at the attendant who poured her port wine. "Your only requirement is a safe place to conduct research, which makes you a far more intriguing visitor than we've had in some time."

"I'm not surprised, Aesylt, not at all," Nyssa said, her hands flitting about in exuberant passes. "You were always so curious about everything. Just like Pieter." Her smile faded.

Rustan cleared his throat and dug into his pork. "Tell us about this research. Steward Wynter said you're working on a compendium for the realm?"

Aesylt exchanged a glance with Rahn. He started to speak but then stopped himself when he saw she was. She did the same, until they both sputtered into awkward laughs. "It's Imryll's passion," she said, smiling in Imryll's direction. "She's been kind enough to invite us into it."

"Ah, yes, she's told us all about it. How as soon as the Reliquary caught wind of it, they stepped in and took charge. How unsurprising that the crown darlings would take without restraint," Felice said. She tapped her spoon against the air. "You're charting the stars, Pieter said?"

"That's right," Aesylt said carefully. "We've been working on it for months, and once the observatory in the Cross is ready, we'll be able to do so much more. We believe that understanding the stars in our sky will answer many other questions about our world, previously unknown to us."

"Fascinating," Pieter said, leaning in and dropping an elbow onto the table. "For once, I agree with Nyssa. I'm not surprised at all to see you walk this path."

"Well, what else is she supposed to do, with her brother being so obstinate about betrothing her?" Nyssa quipped. "A woman must pass her hours in some usefulness. Thank the Guardians the scholar came along."

"Aesylt is an excellent scholar in her own right." Rahn fingered his mug of ale. "I don't know that I could do this without her."

Aesylt felt herself flush. "Scholar Tindahl came to the Cross with years of instructive experience. We're fortunate to have him."

"Well surely, anyone could stare at stars and write what they see," Nyssa said, suddenly dour. Aesylt had been watching her watch Rahn for the past few minutes.

"With all the two of you seem to have in common, it's a wonder Steward Wynter has not made a more formal match," Rustan said through a mouthful of food. His next words were unintelligible.

"Perhaps because she'd be marrying up more levels than is acceptable," Nyssa muttered with an impudent lift of her brows.

Aesylt lowered her fork and stared at her old friend in disbelief. Nyssa's eyes were the same, her face more mature and angular, but she'd aged into a person who was only a shadow of the sweet girl Aesylt had played with and shared childish secrets with.

"He's considerably older, dear," Felice stated. "Though, I suppose that was true of us, wasn't it, Rustan? But your father was relentless."

"Mine?" Rustan directed a skeptical look at his plate. "This is your second trip here, and this time you must tell us about Duncarrow, Scholar. Is it as debaucherous and bloody as the rumors say? And you must be old enough to remember where you came from before that, yes?"

Aesylt tensed on Rahn's behalf. She answered for him without thinking. "Rumors are far less interesting than reality, my lord. This is why I'm so curious about what Pieter has been up to these years."

Pieter dabbed his face with his napkin. His nostrils flared, but it was the only evidence he was disturbed by the question. "I've been away studying. It began as a short expedition with my childhood scholar, and over time, I decided I rather liked it."

"More than us," Nyssa said with a pout. She slid her spoon across her plate without collecting anything.

"Never." Pieter grinned.

"Were that true, you'd have bothered to visit us more than twice." Felice sipped her port. "And I would not, at the ripe age of fifty, have an almost-two-year-old son I now have to groom to take his father's place. Pray your father does not spend his promise early, or I'll be ruling the Northerlands myself until Hadden comes of age. Guardians deliver us all."

"Fel," Rustan cautioned with a tight head shake.

The years since Aesylt had last been to Wulfsgate came into sharp relief. Pieter had defected in favor of his studies, Felice had birthed a replacement heir, and the weight of both loomed impossibly heavy over a family that had once been so close, even loving. "Well, perhaps we can... discuss the nature of your studies another time," Aesylt said.

Pieter nodded. "Another time."

"Stewardess Wynter, perhaps *you'd* like to tell us about Duncarrow then." Rustan slumped back in his chair with a thoughtful look at nothing.

"Oh. I..." Imryll furrowed her brow. "What would you like to know, my lord?"

"Why you would give up such a distinguished title as princess, for one."

"It may be you find the title distinguished because you've never had to wear it." Small titters echoed down the table. "I never wanted it and was told I was not fit for it. They only gave it to be me because they were persuaded by my perceived easiness to control. They were wrong. King Torian was my dearest friend. His dying made the keep unlivable for me." She sighed deep and tried to smile. "Witchwood Cross is home for me in a way Duncarrow never could be. I may not have met my husband in the most traditional way, but fate put him in my path for a reason. And I thank fate for it every day."

"My bodyguards are all ugly old men," Nyssa complained. "Is this why, Mother? You're worried I'll run off to some far-flung village and elope with one?"

"You are uncouth and will be lucky to marry the woodcutter's son with that mouth," Felice snapped. "Stewardess Wynter, by all accounts, you have made the steward an honest, settled man, and there were years we were not certain it was possible. Ignore my daughter, who has only learned to receive respect, not give it."

Nyssa *hmphed* at her plate.

"It's quite all right, my lady. I would be a fool to expect others not to be curious about the princess who defected with her guard." Imryll set her napkin on the table. Aesylt caught her eyes, witnessing a darker pain than her words would allow. "Would it be rude for me to excuse myself to check on Aleksy? He didn't sleep well last night."

Felice waved a hand. "Being a mother must come first."

Imryll lifted from the table, bowed, and left in a rush.

"Is talking about Duncarrow so undesirable that Aesylt would change topics and Imryll would flee the room?" Rustan asked with a wry grin. The question was loaded though. Few men in the realm hated the crown as much as Rustan Dereham.

Aesylt tried to answer, but Rahn stayed her with a quick nod and a smile that didn't fully form.

"I have few memories before Duncarrow, my lord, and I spent my years on the island teaching others. There's little to tell that would not bore you," Rahn explained. "Like Imryll, I've found a greater sense of purpose in Witchwood Cross and am grateful for the opportunity provided by the steward and his generosity. And to you, for allowing us to continue while we wait." He dabbed his mouth and pushed back. "If I recall, there's a section of the Wintergarden covered by a canopy of branches that protects you from the elements. If you don't mind, I'll indulge myself in a stroll before the ice sets in. Thank you for the excellent meal."

Aesylt rose, but he shook his head and left without her.

Felice was next, declaring she had an appointment with her seamstress, and then Rustan, who had business in the village.

"The scholar really has no wife?" Nyssa asked, frowning at the door everyone had exited through. Her face was half-lit by the roaring hearth, the other side steeped in shadow.

"Correct," Aesylt said. She watched the door, slighted by Rahn's gentle rejection. "And has no desire for one."

"Do the two of you talk about your desires often?" Nyssa's tone was impish, with a matching grin. "And does your brother know?"

"The scholar is a treasured friend of the Wynters," Aesylt replied testily. "And Drazhan encourages my passion for science."

"Passion for science or for the beautiful man who could bring a village to his knees with that soft voice of his?"

"Our relationship is purely professional, Nyssa."

"And what does professional mean to you, Aesylt?"

Aesylt glanced at Pieter for help, but he seemed amused by the fraught exchange. She could only wonder, bewildered, where the beautiful coquette goading her had come from and where she'd put her old friend. "Nyssa, what you're implying is, frankly, dangerous and could lead to unnecessary trouble for him. I'm not the only researcher in his cohort."

"Just the one he couldn't bear to be parted from." Nyssa stood, lifting her skirts with a soft bow. "I must join Mother with the seamstress. Only the best for the ball."

"Ball?" Aesylt asked, but Nyssa lifted her head high and took her answer with her.

"More of a cozy soiree now, a coming out of sorts for her marriageability, which is just a formality," Pieter explained when she was gone. He leaned over and grabbed Nyssa's half-drunk wine, finishing it. "Mother still wants to open the ballroom, which is absurd. There won't be more than a couple dozen people in attendance, now that the village is on lockdown."

"Because of us."

He shrugged. "No one else will say it, but they're all a little relieved not to have to put on the full show."

"Well, thank you so much for your help back there," Aesylt muttered and stood. "What did you do with the Nyssa I remember?"

"She's grown up." He laughed.

"She hates me, and for no reason."

"She's *jealous,*" Pieter said, standing with her. "She sees how he looks at you and wonders why no man has ever looked at her like that."

Aesylt crossed her arms. "And how's that, when Nyssa can clearly turn the head of any man in a room?"

"Turn his head, yes," Pieter said. He quaffed down the rest of his mother's port and Imryll's wine as he moved around the table toward Aesylt. "But his mind? Hmm. Nyssa will never fail to arouse desire in a man, but how many would look deeper? And should they decide to, what even would they find worth exploring?"

She was appalled. "You speak of your own sister with such scorn."

"Ah, no. You're a woman of science, Aesylt, and I do not have to remind you that explaining something as it is, and not as it should be, is the *only* way."

She scoffed. "You never said where you've been all these years."

He sidled up beside her, balking at her involuntary cringe. "We've only just reunited, and already I've put you off."

"You and your sister have both changed." She lifted her head. "But so have I."

Pieter lowered his head. "I never meant to upset you. Forgive me." He bowed. "I hope you'll enjoy the books I've left for you and the scholar in the tower. Most are about the village or the grounds, which could be of interest to a couple of curious scholars. May they enhance your stay here."

Aesylt found Imryll in the nursery. She was rocking Aleksy and Hadden both in her arms, the boys fast asleep on each shoulder.

I can come back, she mouthed, but Imryll waved her in.

"The governess will be along soon," she said softly. "How are you settling in?"

Aesylt breathed deep and plopped onto a bench across from Imryll. "They put us in one of the bell towers."

"Draz told me. I worried it might be an awkward arrangement for the two of you, but they don't want you wandering about at night, so there we have it."

"He said he wanted me to see the stars."

"Can you?"

"Not with these clouds," Aesylt replied, shrugging. Badly, she wanted to reveal the truth—to offer Imryll reassurance of her and Rahn having the research well in hand, that the Reliquary's bullying wouldn't work because the cohort had two fearless scholars willing to do whatever the science demanded. But Imryll would immediately want to protect her. "But we'll do everything we can. You can be sure of it."

Imryll brushed her lips across the heads of both babes with a tired smile. "Whatever you can accomplish will be enough. It has to be." She sighed. "I know you want answers, and I wish I had some. But I'll tell you what I do know."

Aesylt nodded, lowering her eyes in respect. "Thank you."

"Val is apparently speaking now. What he has said, no one will tell us. They're still pushing, harder than ever, for a betrothal, and now there are rumors they've secreted Marek out of the

Cross. Your brother isn't opposed to war, but he needs Barynov to draw the first sword, and there's no indication of how soon it will happen." Imryll ceased rocking. "Draz has forbidden messenger ravens between the Cross and Wulfsgate, and we're to pass communications through his scouts, who can only travel as fast as the weather and roads allow. We could be here days. Weeks. I don't know."

None of it was good, but now she knew. "How far along are you?"

"Oh..." Imryll glanced downward. "A season, at most. It was Draz who noticed the changes in me before I did."

Aesylt smiled. "He's a different man with you. He worships you. Of course he noticed."

Imryll resumed rocking with a wistful smile. "One will come along who sees you. *All* of you. Whether you want that... Ah, that's another thing besides. But you should settle for nothing less. You deserve happiness."

It was Imryll's way of telling her Val wasn't the right man, though it was Rahn's face making appearances in Aesylt's mind during the brief speech. "Happiness to me is having the freedom to make the same choices a man would. Drazhan would love to see me studying for the rest of my life, if it keeps me from frolicking with the menfolk."

"It's not up to him, in the end."

Aesylt knew that; it never had been. But she allowed Drazhan's thin authority on the matter to warm the distance still thawing over the lost years. If she ever actually found someone worth fighting for, Drazhan's obstinance would mean little.

Imryll broke the silence. "Speak to him as an equal and *tell* him what you want. Never ask, because then you're subject to the man's unpredictable whims."

Aesylt nodded, her thoughts drifting to the recent past. "Imryll, I did something I really should not have. I told Val—"

"I know what you told him. I once did something similar, for someone I cared about." Her gaze drifted. "What the Barynovs are doing now has nothing to do with private words exchanged between old friends. They've been angling for you since you were a little girl. You're twenty now, and they see your childbearing years ticking away."

"Oh, an old maid now, am I?"

Imryll didn't smile. "To those who would deal with women as commodities, yes."

"If I were already married, they'd have to drop the matter."

Imryll gripped the babies and pitched forward.

"I wasn't suggesting I *do* that." But what *was* she suggesting? Why had she said it at all? Why had it even come into her head? "Only pointing out it is one way to end the matter."

Imryll was appalled. "The Barynovs would view it as an act of war, and that's to say nothing of how your own life would be turned upside down."

Aesylt stood. "Forget I said anything. Sometimes I think aloud, to my detriment." She went to Imryll and kissed her cheek, then peppered kisses atop Aleksy's sleeping head. "I should find Scholar Tindahl. He seemed upset by the lord's questions."

Imryll watched her over the children's heads. "You're very perceptive, Aesylt. Not everyone wants their past dredged, even to satisfy the curiosity of a lord."

Rahn stood over the desk, his hands gripping each end, the three pages of instruction notes for the curricula spread over its smooth surface. He'd been reading for the past hour, working up to how to position things to Aesylt. Striking the right balance between engaged and indifferent would become more challenging as they moved through the full suite of requisites.

The door whipped open, and Aesylt came storming in, huffing. "Of *course*, the very last place I look. For the love of the bloody Ancestors."

Imagining the frustrated flush in her cheeks put a smile on his face. He turned and was rewarded with exactly that. "I can't imagine why the homebase for our research would be the *last* place you'd look, Squish, but your persistence was rewarded."

Aesylt whipped off her cloak and tossed it over the stand. "Why? Because you said you were going for a walk in the Wintergarden. With that in mind, I spent the past hour—"

"You searched for me for an hour?" Rahn removed his spectacles.

Aesylt's indignant glower transformed into a light pout. Her rain-soaked hair clung around her face. "I was worried about you. After Lord Dereham... Well, the man isn't well acquainted with subtlety, is he?"

Rahn smiled to show her he was all right, wondering if he might convince himself in the doing. The questions had sent him on a tortured walk in the garden, which had made him realize what he needed most was to engross himself in something meaningful. "Every person I meet wants to know about Duncarrow. Dereham tried it on me a year ago, and I suppose he thought he might have a different outcome this time."

"But—"

"The only stories he's interested in aren't mine to tell." A half lie. Not a half-truth, for Rahn didn't believe half-truths were anything more than tempered deceptions. "And if he wants to know about Ilynglass, well..." He shrugged.

Aesylt nodded slowly, squinting as she assessed him... the situation. "What's on the desk?"

"The guidelines for our curricula." He nodded behind him. "I had some thoughts on how we might proceed."

She brightened and came toward him. "The day is yet young."

What Rahn needed to do was learn to control the rate of his heart when she was close, but it always caught him delightfully unawares, like a breeze on a warm day. She sidled up next to him and leaned over his shoulder, near enough for him to catch the soft cherry blossom petals she must have walked through in her search for him.

He cleared his throat and tapped the first page. "There are three graduating segments, each more advanced than the last, and the rules specify we must move through one segment to reach the next."

"I've read it." Aesylt leaned closer. "We may need to revisit kissing, since we both failed at our notes last night." She mercifully mentioned nothing about what had happened after. She stepped around him and knelt instead, reading. "The crotchety old men writing these curricula may lack in many things, but certainly not creativity," she muttered. "I missed the part before, where there are four dozen couples doing this. That certainly makes more sense than just us."

"Does beg the question, who are these other couples, if we're not the ones seeking them out?" Rahn traced his finger down the page, starting at the top.

<u>Coitus Curriculum: General Instructions</u>

The team is expected to answer all questions about physical and emotional response, and to give especial consideration to how these answers change as they advance through each segment and sub-segment.

Each segment has specific instructions and requisites that must be met for the research to be accepted and logged into the final record.

For additional instructions and clarifications, please refer to addendum 78.

These instructions are written with partners of opposite genders in mind. For other variants, please write for different instruction.

Segment One: Coitus as a Ladder

In this first segment, the designated team will perform each of the four "rungs" at least once, before advancing to the Ballroom Segment. They are encouraged to meticulously practice each rung in order to be fully prepared for the next phase, and to ensure completeness of notes.

• Rung One: Kissing (closed mouth, open mouth, short duration, long duration)

• Rung Two: Oral coitus (must be performed both female to male and male to female)

• Rung Three: Digital penetration (male to female)

• Rung Four: Vaginal penetration with male completion

Segment Two: Coitus as a Ballroom

In the former segment, the team "climbed" a ladder of natural advancement to reach this point. They may think of this as the experimental segment. Similar to a grand ball, the couple can explore different variations on what they have already done, to learn whether these activities enhance or degrade the overall experience.

Acceptable activities include coitus at different phases of the female's moon cycle, delayed or denied release, increased frequency, adjustments in diet (to monitor for changes in taste or sensation), variable locations, introducing outside stimuli, tandem self-pleasure, coitus while under the influence of inebriation, and anal penetration.

Segment Three: Coitus as a Battlefield

Not all teams will advance to the Battlefield Segment. No formal documentation exists on any of these activities, so any provided by the team will be appreciated, and their efforts lauded and rewarded accordingly.

Acceptable activities include coitus while bound and in submission, questionable consent, paraphilia, and multiple sexual partners in the same act. Should the researchers have additional ideas for this segment, please proceed and include the details and results with your notes.

We unintentionally skipped ahead to the ballroom last night, Rahn thought, wondering if she was thinking it too. If she remembered the creaks coming from his bed… the sounds he'd tried to strangle in his throat. He couldn't stop thinking about hers.

Aesylt finished reading and straightened. "Can I ask you something, Scholar?"

"Of course."

"Have you kissed many women?"

The question surprised him enough to look up. "Many would be an overstatement."

Aesylt nodded, processing. "This isn't a scientific question. I'm only curious, as I've never thought to ask Val or Nik. You can be honest. In fact, I would be hurt if you weren't."

"What was the question?"

"Would you say I'm a competent kisser?"

Rahn sputtered through his first attempt at a response. He didn't know what qualified someone as a competent kisser, but the few he'd had with her were certainly the most memorable. "I wouldn't change anything in your technique."

Aesylt nibbled at her lip. "I have a technique?"

"My turn to ask a question."

She stepped behind him and leaned over his shoulder again, but this time, her arms dropped over his chest, her face resting against his. "Go on."

"For the record, and also because I care about you, I would like to know the extent of your experience in these matters before we go further."

Aesylt hesitated before answering. "Kissing. Might have been more had Nik and I... But everything we do from here will be new for me."

Rahn swallowed the dueling waves of illicit desire and guilt. "And this is still what you want? Still the way you want to experience these things for the first time, as an experiment?"

Aesylt withdrew slightly. "What better way to experience something so intimate than with someone you trust implicitly? I'm fortunate to have someone in my life who fits that description perfectly, though I have a feeling he's going to ask me this question every day, isn't he?"

He grinned at the desk, shaking his head. "You know me well."

"I would be stunned if you behaved any differently." She laughed. "And, uh, we have a few hours before anyone will expect us anywhere, so..."

"So, Squish."

"So, Scholar."

It felt so natural to crane his head back and kiss her. To reach up and cup her face to deepen the connection. She wilted, yielding, as she slid around to the front of him and climbed onto his lap.

Rahn spread his hands against her face, smoothing her hair back. He breathed out, taking her in. *All for the notes.* Dipping forward, he took her lower lip between his teeth for a gentle nip, and the sound that followed told him it was the right move.

"I'm ready to climb a bit higher, if you are," she whispered, tracing the words along his lower lip. She lifted in his lap, her arms draped about his neck, kissing him as perfectly as if she'd been kissing him all their lives.

But kissing was... simple. Once they ascended the next rung, there was no returning to the way things were. No pretending it was even possible.

Even amid the inescapable truth, Rahn answered her invitation by hoisting her onto the desk, sending the instructions scattering.

"Wait, wait," she croaked.

He faltered, frozen by the sinking fear he'd misread her signals.

Until she said, "And another with me," and he realized they were both already lost.

The way Rahn watched her from above, painting his shadow across her, invoked how she imagined it would have felt had she been caught by her wulf on the night of the Dyvareh.

But he had been her wulf all along, and she wasn't running anymore.

He came in for another hard kiss, then broke away to look at her. Aesylt curled her hands into his dark waves, bringing him closer with an aggressive tug. She opened her mouth wider to drive his tongue deeper, her toes curling as the hard bulge in his trousers ground against her.

She arced her head back when his mouth brushed the hollow of her neck, his lips dragging down across her flesh and over her collarbone. His breath awakened her, his warmth assuming a clear path of intent, skating along the soft curves of her breasts and burning through her dress as he dipped lower, inhaling her through the front stays of her gown.

One of her legs caught his forearm as she struggled for where to put it. He lifted his arm, and, with it, her thigh and rested it over his shoulder. She pulled the other one up to join it, and he shrugged them both into place, raising her before he lowered to a crouch.

Rahn's eyes locked onto hers from between her legs. His hands traveled her thighs, edging her dress higher, until it bunched at her waist. She'd never been so grateful to have worn something simple, for anything thicker would have meant she'd have missed seeing the predator lying in wait behind his gaze. The one she'd been waiting for.

She memorized it, for her notes, for... later.

Still watching her, he traced his lips along the soft flesh of her inner thighs, back and forth between one and the other, drawing closer and closer to her undergarment. Chills ripped through her, causing her to clamp onto his head. His response rumbled against her skin.

Rahn peeled back slightly and hooked his fingers beneath her undergarment. "You know I have to ask—"

"Yes." Aesylt panted, her chest rising and falling hard. "Yes, dammit."

His expression darkened with lust. Strong hands brushed down her thighs as he pulled away the last thing holding them back, gliding the fabric down her legs, and released it, where it fell to the floor.

Rahn gave her thighs a tug, adjusting them over his shoulders, and lifted her to his face. She felt the heat of his hesitancy, brushing her just enough to send her climbing out of her skin. Aesylt had harbored fantasies of moments like it for years, afraid to speak of them, to tell anyone how, when the candles were extinguished each night, she found the only release that had ever felt close to freedom.

But she'd always managed her own needs, and this man, whom she respected and cared for, was one flick of his tongue away from fulfilling the crushing desire born of so many nights alone in the darkness.

With a gentle exhale, Rahn parted her with his thumbs and spread his tongue along the length of her in one long, delicate lap. The room exploded with color. Aesylt held her breath, afraid to tarnish the moment she'd waited so long for. He did it again, erupting the stars behind her eyes by starting over at the bottom and climbing toward the spot she knew by heart and wanted him to as well.

He lingered there, swirling his tongue in perfect, spine-chilling rhythm that surpassed even her wildest imaginings. She shuddered all over, an orgasm building far too fast, her body ignoring every command she was giving it to slow down, to ease off.

Rahn abruptly stopped. He looked up. "I don't know... I can't tell... Does it feel as you'd want it to?"

Aesylt was suddenly conscious of her vulnerable position on the table, her legs spread wide for a man she knew primarily as Scholar, a man her brother had trusted to keep her safe. She'd been soaked before he'd even touched her, a mortifying consequence of even being *near* the man. And somehow, she was failing, not performing in some critical way that would show him with her body what she'd already said with her words. "I... Yes, it's..." It was what? Why couldn't she answer?

He glanced behind them, as if to be sure. "No one can hear us. If you're holding back for me, don't. If I'm going to be the first man you share this experience with, I want it to be one you remember fondly, no matter what the reason." His lips sheened with remnants of her. "Close your eyes and give yourself to the way it feels. Memorize every rise and fall of your body in response."

She managed a breathy nod. "For the notes."

"And for yourself," Rahn said, his eyes lingering a moment longer before his head disappeared between her legs.

He wasted no time, finding his place again with ease. He took her swollen flesh between his teeth, and she whimpered in pleasure. His soft laugh against her core told her she'd done well, that there was no shame in adding voice to what her body was feeling... that he *wanted* to hear her. So when he did it again, Aesylt dug her hands to the wooden desk, lifted her hips against his face, and moaned into the cool air.

His hands massaged her outer thighs as he held them in place, his mouth focused solely on what sent all the light in the sky into sharp relief. *We're studying the stars after all.* Her nails slid between the lines in the wood, digging new grooves.

Her thighs trembled. She bared down, grating her heels down his back with short, stunted breaths as her body began the transition to the end. She was on fire, from the inside out and the outside in, and there was only one way to quench it.

It hit her like a moving wall. Aesylt threw her head back with a silent, wide-mouthed cry, no longer thinking about her shaking legs or anything except the way he'd latched on, riding out her climax with her.

Aesylt slid back down against the table. Her legs sagged down his arms, but he gently lifted them and settled them on the desk. She glanced up just as he licked his lips, the briefest, sexiest indulgence before he wiped his face on his sleeve.

Rahn helped her to her feet. He had to steady her another moment when her knees buckled, but she smiled weakly to show him she was fine. "Was it..."

She lifted onto her toes to kiss him, the only way she knew to answer his question. His exhale passed into her as she skated her tongue along his, tasting herself. It was sweeter than she'd imagined, and she wondered how it would compare to his seed, a thought that had her ready to push him up onto the desk and mount him like a stallion. Ladder be damned.

Rahn broke the kiss with a reluctant grin, tucking stray hair behind her ears with both hands before turning and taking a deep breath. "Good."

Rahn closed his eyes. He flexed his hands. He rolled his shoulders. He silently recited the words to one of the tedious old litanies of the Rhiagains, word by word.

Nothing restored his focus.

He stared out the circular window revealing rain so thick, he couldn't see the mountains. It was loud enough to overcome any sounds from behind him. Aesylt was at her desk making her own notes, he could only assume, but he couldn't turn to verify. He might never be able to look her in the eyes again. Definitely not when he was nursing an erection so swollen, it filled his thoughts with alarming images of perfectly ripe tomatoes bursting.

He licked his lips but that, too, was a mistake.

First evidence of physical response was raised flesh on the female's upper thighs. Male notes this elicited a physical response of his own. Rahn tapped the feather of the quill against his head. Adjusted his spectacles higher on his nose.

Gather yourself, Adrahn.

His eyes shifted back toward the rainstorm. He could just make out the hazy outlines of the conifers and, maybe, if he watched long enough, the distant traces of the Northerland Range. What he'd never see in those conditions was the sky. But—

Rahn's chair slid. It screeched across stone, the culprit a red-cheeked Aesylt who stole his gaze and held it as she crawled under the desk.

"Aesylt, what are you doing?" He held his hands up and out, unsure what to do with them.

Grinning, she tugged on one leg of his chair, straining as she tried to pull him into place. He didn't know what else to do, so he helped her.

Rahn stared at her, resting on her heels between his parted legs, with a devious look. His head shook—and kept shaking, as he realized her intention.

"I finished my notes." She twisted her hair from the front and let it fall down her back. "I've never done this before either, but with a little guidance from you, I believe I can manage."

"I haven't..." Rahn swallowed. He shifted in the chair, but there was no hiding the bulge. She was staring right at it. "Finished mine."

She waved a hand. "Go on then."

Rahn stared at her, bewildered. It had been in the back of his mind that they couldn't climb the next rung without finishing the one they were on, but he wasn't in a hurry either. The longer he delayed the inevitable, the longer he could convince himself he hadn't gone too far.

Aesylt drew a deep breath, held it, stretched a tentative hand out, and rested it on his buckle. She started to unhook it but struggled, and Rahn found himself leaning down and gently taking her other hand, joining it to the one on his belt. She gazed up at him, wide-eyed and eager, and he had to look away.

She wrenched his belt free and slowly unbuttoned his trousers, yanking until he lifted off the chair to let her slide them the rest of the way off. She went for his shorts next, and then those were off, and his cock sprung free, turning her eyes to saucers again. The slide of his tongue over her came crashing forward in his mind. How wet she'd been, how perfectly ready for the next rung. A bead of precum rolled down his shaft.

"And another with me," she whispered as she exhaled.

Rahn clamped his hands to the chair arms when Aesylt took him in her hand. Both hands, wrapping around him to form a knot. She breathed out, tendrils of it passing over his sensitive head. It occurred to him he should stop her, but the time for that had been before he'd helped his favorite researcher come all over his face.

Aesylt's tongue flitted against his head, sending Rahn jerking upward, one of his knees banging the wood. He gripped the chair tighter, burrowing his feet to the tips of his boots when her mouth spread wider, her tongue traveling down from his head and her lips dragging his shaft. Breath shuddering, he chanced a look down to see her mouth was spread so wide, it was nearly cracking at the corners.

She withdrew with a light *pop*. "You don't have to stop writing."

"There's not a chance I could continue." Rahn panted, his hands squeezed against the wooden arms so tight, they were shaking.

"Am I satisfactory, Scholar?" She swirled her thumb over the head of his cock, fisting it with the other hand.

"Ah..." Rahn's belly caved. His eyes rolled back as he nodded profusely. His thighs were clenched into rocks as he strained for control.

Aesylt slid him back into her mouth until his cock hit resistance. Her lips were still an inch or more from the base, and the thought of driving himself down her throat to finish made him gulp.

She was a natural, in a way practice could never improve upon. It was not the first time a woman had taken him into her mouth, but as he looked down at her, working him like a prodigy, he realized nothing that had come before mattered at all.

"Aesylt, I..." Rahn's knuckles turned to peaks as he bore down. "You need to stop before I..."

"I know..." Aesylt spoke between slurps. She tried to grin, but her mouth couldn't do more than twitch. "For the notes."

Rahn released the chair and locked his hands into her hair, knotting it behind her head as his body lifted, his seed coursing into her mouth, every muscle in his body clenching and releasing with her enthusiastic suction.

She waited until he'd ceased moving before pulling away. Her mouth was closed, but he saw her throat moving. Her eyes glistened from how deep she'd taken him.

"How was my technique in this area?" she asked. Gone was the flirtation, and she was his favorite researcher again. It gave him no pleasure to realize it was *that* look he'd see in his fantasies. Brimming with curiosity and keen for his guidance.

"You... You were..." Rahn exhaled slowly, returning to himself. A delicious shiver tore through him. "Perfect."

Aesylt beamed. She wiped her mouth and dropped back into a crawl, shuffling out from under the desk, and shot to her feet. Rahn held his breath. He heard the scrape of her chair and then, "*Now* let's finish those notes."

SIXTEEN

MERCY

Aesylt hadn't expected the scholar to be so... *carefree* the morning after they'd crossed such a significant boundary.

He was a man who held tight to his shame, so she feared he would regret everything they'd done in their little tower apartment, the freezing rain their only witness. Or that he'd announce a swift end of their research, and an overblown concern for her precious chastity.

But he'd actually been *playful* as they readied for the day, ribbing her about silly things. He'd been a totally different man than the one who had been going out of his way to keep her at arm's length for weeks. When he'd suggested they get out of the keep for an hour or so and explore the great walled city, she hadn't known what to make of his unusual enthusiasm.

He laughed as they walked the path of stalls along Wulfsgate's Mercantile Row, Kezza and a few other guards holding a friendly distance. The freshly fallen snow was powdery and welcoming, perfect for the children playing in the banks while their mothers and fathers finished their weekly commerce. Even as an adult, she recognized good playing snow. She couldn't wait until Aleksy was old enough to pack onto a slab of wood and slide down the foothills with her.

"Watch this woman's face," Rahn whispered, leaning close. His warm breath sent a shiver down her spine, but she spotted the person he was talking about. "This isn't the first time she's tried to steer her husband away from the blacksmith, is it?"

Aesylt's face erupted in a slow grin. The poor woman wasn't even trying to hide her annoyance with her excited husband, who was perusing a display of gleaming knives like he'd not seen one before. "She should find something she enjoys. I would."

"And what would you choose?" Rahn asked. She felt his eyes on her.

"Hmm." She debated how to answer. She'd always loved the markets in Wulfsgate. They had a liveliness that was missing in Witchwood Cross, remote and uninviting for anyone but those already there. "I would go find the inksmith. He makes ink of all colors, not just black, and also mixes the most luxurious paints. You won't find any like them in the rest of the Northerlands."

"Do you paint?"

"I used to." *In the before times.*

He must have heard the reticence in her voice because he didn't push.

"And you? What would your favorite stall be, Scholar?"

Rahn tilted his head with a thoughtful look ahead. "Anywhere I can get fresh ink for my notes is—"

She tsk-tsked her tongue. "Nope. Too easy. There's more to you than learning, and I'd like to know what it is."

"You fancy me a mysterious man?" He balked in surprise. "I hate to disappoint you."

Her eyes narrowed playfully as she waited for him to explain.

"Our world on Duncarrow was small. No markets." He gestured around at the bustling commerce. "No fresh wonders to discover, just a weekly ship delivering the necessities. The *only* thing I was given as a child was a quill, ink, and a modest stack of vellum I was told never to squander, for there might not be more tomorrow. And *then* I was told, we don't speak of Ilynglass, so when you teach these children, Adrahn, though you are but a child yourself, you must pretend as if it never existed. As if the White Kingdom is all there is and ever was."

None of this was a surprise to Aesylt, but him speaking of it so openly certainly was. She searched for the expected signs of tension or hesitance, but despite the acrimony in some of his words, he seemed at ease. "What did you teach them then?"

"More than I was allowed to. Less than I wanted." He angled his mouth sideways in a mischievous grin. His eyes traveled toward the sky. "Imryll will tell you, I was not quite the rule follower everyone believed me to be. When I was a little older, I befriended some of the merchants who made deliveries and got my hands on a few books from the mainland."

"You were the one who slipped Imryll the vellum, even though it would have gotten you thrown in the Sky Dungeon if anyone had found out." That had been one of Aesylt's favorite stories Imryll had shared from her Duncarrow years.

"She had so much curiosity. It had to go somewhere. The biggest mistake the crown made with her was trying to stifle her." He nudged Aesylt with a soft smile. "You two are very much alike, actually."

"You're not the first to say so." She sidestepped when a group of children went tearing by. Rich, gamey meats wafted on the winter breeze, and she was suddenly famished. "What other rules do you like to bend?"

"Only the ones which serve no good purpose," he said with a whimsical look at a stall teeming with furs. He'd been acting differently all morning, and it wasn't just his unusually upbeat temperament. When they'd entered the gates of the market, he'd made a strange detour to an unknown stall without her. *Wait for me right here*, he'd said and then hadn't bothered explaining himself when he'd returned empty-handed. "Squish, I can see you eyeing those rabbit skewers like you haven't eaten in days. Shall we put you out of your misery?"

"I'll take two," she responded, and he squeezed her arm with a laugh before jogging off to the stall. By the time she reached him, he was already handing over the coin.

"One for you, one for your lovely wife," the man said.

Aesylt almost told the merchant she wasn't his wife, but waited to see if Rahn would do it first. He didn't, so she let it slide too.

"Thank you, sir," she said distantly, watching Rahn, trying to figure him out. She was still studying him when he walked away, handing her the second skewer with a conspiratorial wink. "Didn't want one?"

"I'm not the one who skipped breakfast," he teased. "Though that does smell good..."

She yanked hers away with a smirk. "Should have bought one for yourself then."

"Woeful regret is my lifelong companion."

Aesylt abruptly stopped and slid a knot of steaming meat from the stick, then lifted it to Rahn's mouth before she realized how careless she was being. Kezza and the others, they were watching, and while she didn't believe they had orders to spy on them, how could she ever be sure?

But Rahn accepted her offer, his eyes fluttering back as he worked the bite in his mouth.

A smudge of food at the corner of his mouth had her leaning up to clear it with her thumb. She brushed it against the edge of his lips, glancing away when his gaze was too much. He licked the spot when she was done, and she had to fight the desire to stretch up onto her toes and kiss him.

But they were not in the celestial realm, and this was not research.

The market had been Pieter's suggestion, after Rahn had told him their intention to get out for a few hours. *Nowhere safer in the realm than Wulfsgate,* he'd said. It was the most fortified town in the kingdom, with walls taller than any man could scale on his own. The gate guards searched everyone going in or out, allowing only those in who were confirmed residents or approved visitors of the Derehams.

"If you're not going to eat that..."

Aesylt shoved half the meat from one stick in her mouth. His brows furrowed in amusement as she struggled to chew so much at once. She grinned, her cheeks puffed, and he threw his head back with a laugh that made her heart sing. He leaned in and tidied the edges of her mouth, still laughing.

She swallowed the half-chewed food with a hard gulp and handed him the second stick.

"I was only teasing. Eat up." He grinned and started walking again, then paused when they passed a stall of furs. "These are much more colorful than the ones they sell in the Cross."

"Vjestik like our furs like we like our hearts, Scholar. Rough and dark." Her heart slowly returned to normal.

Rahn shook his head and pointed. "You asked me what interests me. Cultures. How different they are. Why these differences exist. I can read a thousand stories about a thousand villages, but there's no replacement for experience."

"So the Vjestik are specimens to you?"

"They're fascinating to me, as all peoples are." He lifted his arms under his cloak. "When you visit other villages, do you not note the differences?"

Aesylt discarded her empty stick on a nearby burn pile and started in on the second one. "Of course I do. But I'm not as well traveled as you. I've never even been beyond the Northerlands."

"If you want a contest of who's been more sheltered, I promise I'll win." He smiled. "And I've only seen the realm in passing, on my way to you. Not much time to assess it."

On my way to *you*. Not *Witchwood Cross*. Not *your family*. *I'm reading way too much into a single word.* She sighed. "Is this something you want to do? Travel the realm?"

"One day." He took her last empty stick and tossed it in another burn pile. "With the right companion."

"I would happily travel with you."

Rahn smiled, but his eyes were on the path behind them. "They'll be expecting us back at the keep soon, but there's somewhere we need to stop first."

Aesylt held fast to the small keepsake under her robe, beaming as she marched in through the east entrance of Wulfsgate Keep. She wanted to take it straight to their tower apartment, where she could get a closer look, but she'd promised to visit Imryll after the market.

Rahn had already gone on without her. He said he wanted to read more of the books Pieter had left. She'd nearly swooned at the idea of it, and she'd never swooned in her life. Val and Nik would rather play than do just about anything else. They'd only joined the cohort for her. They never understood why she found her greatest solace when her nose was tipped toward a book.

The scholar's little gift was evidence he *did* think of her beyond the research, but his mind was still a quagmirical mystery... How any man could claim her the way he had the day before and then speak in clear sentences about the weather and other pleasantries defied logic. She needed to study his separation tactics, or she'd never survive the rest of their experimenting.

Assuming he even wanted to continue.

The present in her pocket did nothing to clear anything up.

She turned down the hall toward the guest quarters, still grinning when she ran straight into Lord Dereham.

"Ahh, Aesylt!" He chuckled and held her at arm's length with a fatherly sweep of his gaze. "Pieter tells me you spent the morning in the market with our enigmatic duke."

She straightened, swiftly restructuring her thoughts. "It was just as colorful and fragrant as I remember."

"That it is," he agreed, watching her closely. "Do you have all you need in the tower?"

"Oh, yes. Thank you again."

"And... Are you still comfortable sharing quarters with the duke?"

Aesylt's nod was fast and desperate as she thought of them being separated, stuck in quarters where they'd lack the privacy and seclusion they needed. She was still stunned Drazhan had endorsed the notion of her sharing the tower with Rahn, but he probably believed the man valued his life too much to overstep. "It's exactly what we needed, my lord. Now if the skies would only clear..."

Lord Dereham laughed. "All citizens are wishing for the same thing right now, albeit for different reasons." He released her. "Have you had the chance to catch up with Nyssa?"

"I hope to soon." She hoped no such thing, after her chilly reception, but nonetheless wanted to resolve whatever had prompted it.

"As does she, I imagine. She's never taken to many of the girls her age here, but she was always fond of you." He breathed deep, looking past her. "You're looking for the stewardess?"

Aesylt nodded.

"You'll find her in the study, going over her notes." He shook his head. "There aren't many women scholars in the realm."

"Imryll is brilliant and deserves far more acclaim than the Reliquary will ever concede to."

"Don't mistake my truthfulness for criticism, cub," Lord Dereham said. He clapped her on the shoulder and started to move again. "I respect what she's doing. What you and the scholar are doing. But the Reliquary is already powerful, and even in their infancy, their reach is long. The crown has funneled more gold into their efforts than anything else since they arrived on our shores. The Reliquary ministers aim to be the foremost authority in all things knowledge and spiritualism in the realm, and the crown would use them to regulate both. The best the stewardess and you can hope for is their allowance of this work to continue, but there will never be credit given. There will be no glory for the researchers in the north. You'll be fortunate if anything you submit even makes it into their precious annals, for neither the Reliquary nor the crown are concerned with facts that impede the ones they create for us."

Aesylt hadn't been expecting such candor from him, nor words that bordered on treason. The Northerlands had been the only Reach to rise against the installation of the usurper kings from Beyond, but they'd paid a heavy price for it—though nothing like what the Cross was still experiencing, years later. "You're right, my lord, and trust we know so as well."

"Good. Carry on then." He squeezed her shoulder and walked on.

When she reached the study, her mood was instantly restored at the sight of Aleksy scampering across the room, chasing after one of the Derehams' tomcats.

Imryll grinned and rolled her eyes playfully when she looked up. "Do you not miss the days when simple things could occupy your attention for hours on end?"

"I certainly miss simpler days," Aesylt answered, shutting the doors behind her. She knelt and hoisted Aleksy into her arms, spinning and kissing him. "How is my sweet wulfling?"

"Ace!" he cried, one of the few words he knew.

"That's right," she said, laughing in delight.

"Ready for a nap, I hope." Imryll stood, but Aesylt shook her head.

"No, don't get up." She kissed Aleksy once more and released him for more fun with the striped cat. "I'll come to you."

"I'm barely pregnant, Aesylt, I don't need—"

"And it isn't what I meant." Aesylt held up her hands as she slid onto the chair across from Imryll. The table was positioned in front of a curved window full of colored glass, which bathed the snow outside in prismatic hues. "Anything from Draz since yesterday?"

Imryll's hands slid away from the stack of papers she was holding. Her eyes flicked toward Aleksy with a sigh. "This morning, yes."

Aesylt waited.

"Nothing new." She folded her hands and bowed her head. Her red waves fell over her shoulders. "Except I'm told it is no longer safe for me to send dispatches to the Reliquary, as protecting our location is top priority."

"What?" Aesylt leaned in. "What does that mean?"

"I don't know." Imryll turned toward the kaleidoscopic window. "The Reliquary has been waiting for this. For us to miss a deadline, submit errors in our work. And I sit here, pondering how they've played us, how they must be *laughing* at us, and wonder if my dream was the wrong one all along."

"Imryll." Aesylt slid both hands across the table and grabbed hers. "Look at me."

Imryll's chin dimpled. She turned to face Aesylt.

"Power knows no dreams." She shook her head. "Whatever the Reliquary is becoming, it is not what it was conceived to be. But if those of us who know this don't keep fighting, keep trying, that *is* the path it will take. What we are doing here matters. It *matters*. I *promise* you it does. Your dream is the one this realm needs, and we cannot give up."

Imryll smiled tightly and withdrew one of her hands to wipe her eyes. "The last time the north crossed the Rhiagains, they paid dearly. There's only so far I'm willing to go to protect this dream, Aes. And it starts and ends with the safety of our people."

Aesylt lowered her gaze. "We'll solve it. I promise."

"I didn't expect to miss my council, but I do. Anton and Jasika are both so different, and I value that."

"I may not be on your council, but I wouldn't encourage you to continue if I didn't believe it was the right thing to do." Aesylt pulled her hands back and into her lap. If she was going down a treacherous path, she had to be quick about it. "I was there when the Rhiagains retaliated, and I know one thing, Imryll. And it's an important one. Conceding to bullies, to tyrants, only empowers them. More than anything, I want to pretend that never happened, to keep our people safe in a bubble of warmth and love.

But the Rhiagains must answer for what they did, and if we cannot best them in war, there are other ways. Better ways. And we're doing them."

The study doors opened, and Pieter walked in. "Ah. Forgive my interruption."

"Not at all." Imryll sniffled and stood with a politic nod. "Please, come in, my lord."

"My father is a lord. I am most decidedly not." Pieter's smile spread across his face. "I came to inform you both of a weather shift coming, and soon. The winds have turned off the range, and a blizzard is expected before nightfall. Our elemental diviners predict it will be over before we know it, but we should all be safe inside when it happens." He nodded at Aesylt. "So I came to escort you to the tower."

Aesylt understood the weather in a way most did not—the science of it, what caused the snow levels to drop, the pressure to change, and the temperature differentials required in the creation of storms. It was all knowledge the Reliquary would hold onto and parcel at their leisure, if allowed. Knowledge everyone in the realm had a right to. "Very well. Thank you, Pieter."

He nodded and waited for Aesylt to offer her good-byes.

She leaned in close as she embraced Imryll, whispering, "Don't lose hope. Don't give up. The scholar and I are conspiring our own ways to make this work. Trust in us, as we trust in you." She kissed her cheek and backed away.

Imryll's look was unreadable as she nodded, her eyes shifting into a slight squint.

Aesylt squeezed Aleksy and followed Pieter.

"And how are you finding the tower for your research?" he asked, gesturing for her to go ahead when they turned down the hall.

"It will be perfect once the skies open up for us," she said carefully, thinking of the lord's words, of Imryll's. Aesylt's nerves frayed in anticipation of the troubles closing in on all sides.

Guards opened the rear doors for them, and they stepped out into the wintry afternoon. The wind had already picked up, and snow swirled around them. "And I trust you and the scholar are getting on?"

"We always have."

"Quite well, it seems."

Aesylt's boot caught on a flagstone. "Pardon?"

"Have you looked through the books I left?"

She pulled her furs tight, puzzling over his earlier question. "Scholar Tindahl has, and I hope to soon. Tonight, perhaps, since we'll be sequestered and starved for the rest of the day and evening."

"Starve? Never. The kitchen will bring your meals up early," Pieter said. His gait slowed. "I know you must feel very isolated right now, but I *am* your friend. Before, now, always."

Aesylt smiled, her eyes locked on the tower ahead. The candles were burning in the topmost windows. "I know, Pieter. Thank you."

He held the door open, his eyes following her as she stepped inside. "Anything you need, ask." His eyes held hers with enough intensity to make her glance up the stairs for a moment of relief. "Stay warm tonight. Both of you."

Aesylt breathed deep and forced a smile through her sudden discomfort. "I'll see you tomorrow?"

Pieter bowed as he backed away, closing the door.

For the past hour, Rahn had been poring over the stack of books Pieter had left. They were all about the Wintergarden. But it was the tome on top, *The Aphrodisiacal Flora of the Wintergarden*, that had him the most perplexed about the man's intentions.

He'd sifted through the entire book page by page, all of which featured a different plant in the garden and how it could be used for enhanced sexual pleasure. Citrus, when consumed, was purported to make his semen taste more agreeable. There were several fruits listed that were said to change the physiology of a woman's privates as well. He wondered if anything written had also been considered for the compendium, or if they should include it in their own submission.

By most standards, the book was not appropriate as a gift, but it was especially peculiar under the circumstances. Pieter Dereham hadn't left it accidentally, but his true intention was hard to guess. Perhaps the man was just indulging his devious, playful side?

The door flew open, and Aesylt marched through. He heard her cloak snap when she tossed it over the rack, and he turned and found her flushed and serious. She passed him the briefest unconvincing smile before disappearing behind her curtain. The bedframe creaked as she dropped onto it.

Rahn pushed back from his desk and walked to their sleeping area. He paused, listening for any sign she was changing, but there was nothing, so he carefully stepped around the curtain and found her lying on her side, the wooden squirrel he'd commissioned for her cradled in her hands. The one that said *Squish* on the bottom... the one he'd talked himself out of buying a dozen times before he'd finally handed over the coin. The one so like the hawk statuette someone—he couldn't remember who—had gifted him in kindness before his life had upended.

What's a squish? The merchant had asked when he'd jotted down Rahn's request.

A reminder for someone dear to me. That strength is like branches in a tree, some harder than others but all part of surviving.

Right. Give me a full tick of the sun.

"Aesylt?"

She scrambled, pulling her legs up as she quickly sat. "Scholar."

He gestured toward the end of the bed, seeking permission. She nodded without looking up. He couldn't read whether it was solitude she craved or company. "Did you see Imryll?"

She nodded and shoved her hands, and the squirrel, under the folds of her gown. "Drazhan is afraid that sending dispatches to the Reliquary puts our location at risk and has asked us to hold off for now."

"Ah." He wasn't surprised Drazhan had made the request, only that he hadn't made it sooner. "How does Imryll feel about it?"

"I'm sure you can guess." Her tongue passed along her lips and then she closed her mouth tight.

"How do you feel about it?"

"She sees a defeat; I see a challenge." Aesylt's shoulders lifted with her breath. "Then, I am radically disobedient at times."

"*No*. You?"

Her mouth twisted into an almost grin. "Not everyone agrees with me that we should never hide from our fears but confront them, even if it leaves us quaking with the promise of the unknown." She shrugged. "How are the books?"

"Illuminating… and confounding." He told her what he'd found, watching her eyebrows slowly rise and then fuse. "Do you suppose he's being cute?"

Aesylt blew out. "I… Perhaps? He wasn't so mischievous as a boy, but I haven't seen him in years." She seemed to be holding something back. "But did you learn anything?"

Rahn blurted a laugh. "Oh, plenty." He had the urge to grab the stack and join her in bed so they could read them together. But there was something in her expression he couldn't ignore. "What's really going on, Aesylt?"

"Nothing. I'm just tired."

"We promised to be open with each other."

Her hands moved around in the velvet of her skirt. She withdrew the squirrel and put it on her nightstand, her gaze lingering on it a moment before she spoke. "If I ask you an honest question, will you give me an honest answer?"

"I will."

"Because I cannot read you, Scholar." She lifted her gaze to meet his. "And, oh, I've tried, but you're a confounding man."

Rahn chuckled softly. "Then my efforts have not been in vain."

"Do you have many regrets in life?"

He wasn't prepared for the question. And the answer... If he said yes, would she leave it alone? "All men do, if they live long enough."

"But do *you*?"

With a threaded inhale, he nodded slowly. "Yes, I do. What's this about, Aesylt?"

Her hands twisted in her lap, but her eyes stayed locked on his. "Do you regret agreeing to partner with me? Please... Think about this before you answer. Really consider it."

"I don't need to think about it," he said, though he had been thinking about it, all morning, all afternoon. Between every word he'd offered the woodcrafter who made her the squirrel, something he'd done on a whim but not without careful consideration. Every time he'd made her laugh in the market. When she'd brushed her thumb to the corner of his mouth to clear the smudges, and when he'd done the same for her—how easy and natural it had all felt. It had been his way of saying *nothing has changed. We're still friends, still partners.* "The only thing that would give me regret would be if I saw it in you. If I thought what we'd done—what we are yet to do—was harming you. And I trust you to tell me if that were to happen. Or if it already had."

Aesylt looked at her hands. "It has not." She glanced up again, fire dancing in her crystal eyes. "And you should know I will do every last thing on the Reliquary's list if that's what it takes. Battlefield and all. There's nothing out of bounds for me because I trust you. So please don't... look at me and see the girl you invited to be a disciple a year ago. See me as a woman who is more than ready to rise to the challenge after a year of your tutelage."

Rahn's flesh tingled from the force of her intensity, the depth of her stare as she waited for his response. The temptation to read her notes from the day before was so compelling, he'd nearly caved, but it would have grossly violated her trust. She'd told him they were private, for now, and he needed to respect that. "And it's your choice to continue our efforts, even though we're bound from sending any of our notes to the Reliquary for now?"

Aesylt pushed up onto her knees and slowly crawled toward him. "When we finally send these notes, I want those stodgy old relics to be in awe of our commitment."

Rahn lifted his hand to her chin, tilting it. His mouth parted in anticipation of the kiss he hadn't decided if he should give. "They'll be expecting us at dinner."

"No they won't." She grinned and rocked back on her heels. "There's a blizzard coming, and we're to stay safe... and locked away..." She pitched forward and danced her lips against his. He swallowed a soft moan. "Until morning. So, we can watch the snow fall and wait it out, or we can climb the ladder a little higher and find our own warmth on what looks to be a very, very cold night."

Rahn cupped her face in his palms and delivered his response as a kiss that had her whispering, "And another with me, and another with me, for the love of the bloody Ancestors."

Aesylt lay back on the bed as Rahn slowly climbed over her. His erection brushed between her legs, sending blood straight to her head, but that wasn't the rung they were on. They had to go in order, or it could compromise the entire experiment.

"We go as slow as you need." Rahn traced his words along her jaw. The way he studied for her hesitation, reading her at every step, almost tricked her into believing it was all real. "If you're not ready, it may hurt more than it should."

"You'll soon see how ready I am," she purred, feeling recklessly bold as she squirmed to lift her dress. She wished they'd taken it off altogether, for his clothes to be scattered around the celestial room as well, but there was intimacy and there was science.

Her legs fell to the sides, inviting him to direct the next phase.

"Gods," he whispered, so low she almost didn't hear him at all. His chest rose and fell, hard and fast, as he first stared and then dipped down to kiss between her legs. Her head rolled back with a silent scream of pleasure as he dragged his tongue along the length of her. "You are ready, aren't you?"

Aesylt nodded, but he couldn't see her because he was still nestled betwixt her thighs. Her throat rasped under the skill of his gentle but demanding tongue, her heels digging into the hard mattress as her ass tightened and lifted when an orgasm ripped through her, quick and thunderous. Her scream echoed across the celestial stones, heightening to a shrill whine as he held on.

Finally she pushed on the top of his head, unable to take another moment. Panting, he peeled back and wiped his mouth, watching her. "I thought you might... enjoy beginning with that," he said between breaths.

"You do know..." She caught her breath, her eyes fluttering briefly closed. "That this means I'll be returning the favor before the night is ended."

A grin played at his mouth, one he was visibly attempting to restrain. "Does it?"

Aesylt bit down on her lip, nodding, her breaths still ragged. *Maybe we can even climb to the very tippy top of this ladder.* "But first..."

His lips screwed together, still trying not to smile. "For the science."

"Of course, if you don't get enough information for your notes..."

"We can always do it again..."

"And again." Aesylt smoothed her hands along her inner thighs. His eyes followed her movements. She brought them to rest where his face had just been, sliding a finger down herself, knowing exactly what it would do to him despite her inexperience in the matter. "I'm not afraid of a little pain, Scholar."

He blinked hard in visible restraint. "I'll start with one finger."

Aesylt traced her tongue along her bottom lip.

His cheeks flexed to contain himself, but Ancestors, how she prayed he wouldn't. In some of her wildest fantasies, she imagined his entire fist delivering her across the delicate line between pleasure and pain.

Rahn came down over her again. He seemed reluctant to kiss her, so she kissed him first, showing him it was okay.

She guided his hand between her legs, relishing the abrupt groan that escaped him when his finger traced the outside of her mound. Even with Val, it had not been prudence keeping her chaste. Before the scholar had stormed into her life, waking her soul all the way up after so many dormant years, she'd not known true desire. Had never understood that pleasure started as an ignition within the soul before it became a physical need.

His middle finger traced the length of her once, twice, and dipped down, teasing her. She pressed on his hand, and in his finger slid, causing her breath to catch and hold as she waited for him to push all the way in.

"Is this all right?"

"I'm ready for more," she cried, squeezing onto his finger.

"Already?"

"I'm not a delicate flower, Scholar."

"We'll see about that," he whispered, withdrawing long enough to add a second finger. But that wouldn't be enough either; she knew it before he re-entered her, even as the first murmur of pain had her clenching down.

She spread her legs wider and closed her eyes, her breathing riding the gentle rhythm of his two fingers working in, out. She locked her hand atop his wrist and guided him to go faster, and this time he didn't ask her if it was all right. His teeth latched onto her bottom lip as he pumped, panting in tune with her soft cries.

"More," she commanded, guiding him out so he could fulfill her demand. He peeled back to catch her eyes, and whatever he saw must have given him the confirmation required. A third finger joined the mix, and this time the pain was utterly exquisite. She squirmed, but never relented on her guidance, both hands on his arm as he impaled her with his hand.

"I'm hurting you," he said, even as she shook her head to the contrary.

"Not nearly enough," she cried, yanking on his arm until he speared her hard enough to send stars shooting into her eyes.

"You like pain, Aesylt?" It was not the same man who asked the question. He was different now, a primal, feral creature like herself, ascended beyond the realm of right and wrong and whatever rules governed how their trysts were supposed to go.

"Oh, yes," she moaned. "Do you, Scholar?"

"Mm, yes, I do," he croaked. "But even more..."

"You enjoy giving it," she said, finishing for him. Her eyes flashed open. Her urgent command of his arm never lost pace. "Don't you?"

Rahn's mouth parted against hers. His eyes rolled back as he nodded.

"Will you put that in your notes?"

"Not a chance."

"Just for us then?" Her hips lifted higher as a new pleasure took hold. She felt like she was climbing another mountain, her feet practically folding down the middle.

Rahn's other hand traveled to his trousers, his cock straining against the fabric.

"I invite you to hurt me. I give you full permission to act out your darkest fantasies with me, whatever they may be. It will never be too much. I will never regret saying yes," she said, using her other hand to cup his cheek, forcing him to look at her. Her chest fluttered as the force of his hand sent her hurtling toward release. "You'll find my limitations are not the same as others."

"You don't know regret. Not yet." His mouth turned up in a sinister grin she wanted more of. "You don't have any idea what you're asking."

"If I say I do?"

"With a flick of my hand, I could turn you inside out." He parted her mouth with his thumb and tugged it wide. "Make you forget your own name."

"Oh, please." Aesylt moaned, her head rolling back and her jaw still in his hold. "Do that."

"Fuck," Rahn mumbled, and she looked down and saw the dark stain spreading across his pants. The sight of it was too much, and she shuddered around his hand as an utterly different orgasm hurtled through her. She held fast to his arm, pinning herself under him, riding the waves until there was nothing but their heavy, labored breathing.

He fell onto the bed beside her. It was several moments later when he said, "I don't think I need to ask if you enjoyed that."

She turned to her side to cuddle into his shoulder. "Nor I you."

"That part was unfortunate," he muttered with an annoyed look down.

"It was sexy." She slithered against him. "I feel as though I know you a bit better now."

"Do you?" He raked a hand through her hair and locked it behind her head.

"Don't be ashamed. I'm not." She kissed him. "It's yet early. We could continue to collect observations for our notes... and I have designs on giving you a more proper finish."

He licked the tops of his teeth. "How could I refuse?"

Aesylt climbed atop of him. All it would take was a quick reach between his legs, but no matter how much of his resistance she'd broken down, there was yet some remaining. As long as he could convince himself he was doing it for the research, he could live with it. But she knew better. She knew what he was refusing to acknowledge. She might understand little about sex, but what had happened the past two days was far beyond clinical.

He slid his hands along her ass and then pulled one to the front, dipping it between her legs and working his fingers into place. "You sure you don't need a rest first?" His eyes narrowed in mischief. "I went easy on you, Aesylt. I won't be so gentle next time."

"I'm far from crying mercy." She grinned and urged him on by riding his hand. "So you have work to do."

Rahn's head was a spinning mess by the time he sat to do his notes for the evening. Aesylt bathed behind a curtain, the gift of hot water left by the kitchen staff and brought up by pulley. How he'd wanted to stay with her... to sponge her back when she was too tired... to see with his own eyes the bruises along her inner thighs that she'd urged him to inflict—and then tend to them. But she'd smiled sleepily and insisted she welcomed the time alone with her thoughts, and that was just as well. Things were already confusing enough.

He squinted, wiping more sweat from his brow as his quill struck the page. *Male researcher continues to be intrigued how female is always physically ready for his advances. Not just ready but in a state of total desire, as though there had been hours of foreplay preceding the activity.*

He tapped the feather of his quill, his head tilted back to catch his breath. What else could he write? And how could he possibly write it without bringing in the illicit, consuming power of the past few hours, the barriers they'd broken between them, and the closeness that had been present before but had become all he could think about.

Rahn's eyes traveled toward her desk. She'd done her notes swiftly, hovering over her chair when it had been too painful to sit. Even the thought made him hard, because gods, how she'd wanted it. She'd begged for the fist, but he had to draw the line somewhere, even if she couldn't.

But if she could take three fingers, she could take him.

Not that his cock could offer anything more to the evening. She'd taken him into her mouth twice, which was to say nothing of the mortifying premature release he'd made in his pants when she had asked for more pain. Not his first time around her. Probably not his last.

Rahn adjusted in his seat, his gaze still on her desk. The locked drawer. "You still all right in there?" he asked, clearing his throat.

"Enjoying the warmth, Scholar. Care to join me?"

"We're not in the celestial realm, Aesylt."

"And?"

Oh, she was a crafty one. Perhaps she even meant the invitation. But the celestial realm was all that stood between him and the last vestiges of a belief that he was a good and decent man. "You finished your notes quickly."

"I had lots of thoughts desperate to escape." She laughed. The delightful sound echoed across the stones.

"I think we should compare ours soon, so we know if we need to backtrack, collect more experience."

"You just want to read mine."

He grinned to himself. Of course she'd seen through him. "I confess I do. But calibrating our findings is an important part of research. It's how we assess whether we're aligned on everything."

Her tone was heavier when she responded. "I know. I just need a little more time with mine before they're ready for anyone else's eyes. This isn't quite the same as watching the sky and reading the stars, is it?"

He closed his eyes to center himself. There was a reason she didn't want him to see her notes. He just didn't know what it was yet. "If you need anything, just call out."

"You can go on to bed. I think I'll stay here a while, watch the snow and soak my limbs a bit longer."

SEVENTEEN
A PERFECT PREAMBLE

Rahn was up before the sun. He had slept little, his mind working around what Aesylt could be keeping from him. And she *was* keeping something from him. He was certain.

Betraying her wasn't an option, so he grabbed the book on aphrodisiacal flora and wandered to the garden at the edge of the courtyard for some fresh air.

The snow hadn't yet been cleared. The world was still, like he was the first to greet it after the storm. He pulled his furs taut around his mouth, hunkered down, and trudged toward the Wintergarden.

The garden floor was green and inviting, untouched by the tempest of the night before. It was a place where seasons didn't exist at all, where colors that didn't belong anywhere near the frozen north proliferated without resistance. The cherry blossoms were renowned across the kingdom for being the most beautiful a person could lay eyes on, and every time he stepped through their soft carpet, he understood.

Rahn passed a generous magnolia in full bloom, beneath which were the largest, most ornate toadstools he'd ever seen. Farther down was another row of cherry trees, their roots covered in vibrant orange moss, and a grove of citrus trees, a mix of citron, grapefruit, and some sort of dark orange. Nearby was a bench, and he decided it was as good of a place as any to sit and read.

He thumbed to his bookmark and opened the book. *The mix of acidic and sweet make the citron a perfect preamble to copulatory activities. Equal benefit can be realized whether it be the man or woman who consumes the fruit, making it a versatile choice for bed-chamber delight.*

Rahn looked up, suddenly self-conscious. He could pretend he was reading it for intellectual reasons if anyone came upon him, but the truth most likely lived on his panicked face.

"Duke Tindahl, you are a brave soul, venturing out after a Wulfsgate blizzard!" The dainty trill of Nyssa Dereham was nearly lost in the menagerie of exotic trees and plants, but so on edge was Rahn that he'd heard her as if she were standing right on top of him. "And all by yourself? What happened to your partner? Has she abandoned you already?"

"Good morning, Lady Dereham." He startled and closed the book, then thought better of it when he noticed the title, big and bold. He had a good enough read on her to appreciate she wasn't one to miss much. "Aesylt is still resting, as I imagine most of the keep to be."

"Wrong," Nyssa said, appearing from between two cherry trees with a flushed face and a vibrant grin. Her gown seemed to be giving her trouble, so full and layered it was. "Wulves rise before the sun."

"Not the wulf in the tower," he said, and they both laughed. If Nyssa knew *why* Aesylt had been so tired that morning, they'd be having a different conversation. "And you? What has you wandering alone?"

Nyssa made her way closer, her eyes traveling the wonders as if she hadn't seen them a thousand times before. Every movement she made seemed fully intentional. The sweep of her gaze, her chin tilted downward, was precisely choreographed. Her forefinger and thumb pinched the layers of her skirts, leaving her pinkies uplifted. With her eyelids fluttering, she at last fixed her gaze on him with a demure smile. "I was in my father's study, and I saw you walking across the courtyard. Curiosity prevailed."

"Ah." Rahn smiled politely, hoping it was just friendly enough not to offend but with enough coolness to indicate he wasn't looking for company. "I'll see you at morning meal then?"

Nyssa's eyes narrowed in interest as she stepped closer. "And what are you reading, Duke Tindahl, that has you so engrossed?" She daintily lowered herself onto the bench beside him and reached for the book without asking, flipped it. Her eyes widened to saucers. "Indeed. I imagine this is entirely helpful for you in your... astronomy research."

Rahn cleared his throat, but he could do nothing about the mortifying heat flooding his face and neck. "Your brother curated some books for us. It was quite the assortment."

"My brother, you say." Nyssa licked her lips. "He's been a deviant ever since he ran off." Her words died there, and she gestured into the cool air instead, as if they both know where Pieter Dereham had been for years. "But really, don't feel obligated to indulge his utterly bizarre behavior. I hardly think he expected you to read them. He simply wanted to get a reaction." Her smile formed again. "Unless you believe the contents might be useful to you?"

"Purely intellectual," Rahn assured her, tensing to keep from adjusting his itchy, cloying collar.

"Of course." Nyssa nodded like she were indulging a child's fantasy. She leaned in, close enough he wondered if she was going to rest her head on his shoulder next. "I came to ask if you might be kind enough to save me a dance at my soiree?"

"What soiree?" Aesylt appeared, rescuing him from whatever awkwardness Nyssa had planned for him, but the irritated scowl on her face kept his relief at bay. It was at Nyssa her gaze was aimed.

"Oh, Aesylt! The little wulf in the tower awakens." She curtsied from the bench but stayed firmly in place beside Rahn, winking at their private joke. "I was just explaining to your dear scholar that my father has decided to go forward with my invocation. You do remember me telling you about it?"

Aesylt rolled her tongue around in her mouth with a sour look. She hadn't acknowledged Rahn at all. "And what *is* an invocation?"

"A woman's invocation into society? A coming out event? Do you not... No, of course not. The Vjestik are a bit arcane, aren't they?"

"Your brother said it wasn't going to be a big event," Aesylt replied.

"And what would Pieter know of a woman's business?" Nyssa dusted herself off like she needed to be rid of the thoughts themselves. "Well, of course I want you to come as well! I even have the perfect dress for you! It might need to be taken out a bit, of course, to fit you properly."

Rahn could see clearly what was happening. Nyssa was preening, poking Aesylt to get a reaction, just as Pieter seemed to be doing with the books. And it was working.

Red-faced and disgusted, Aesylt flashed a comically ineffective smile. "I have my own gowns, but thank you."

"Not for an invocation, you don't." Nyssa laughed as though they all understood what was funny.

He decided to put an end to it by standing and creating distance between himself and the debutante. "Lady Nyssa, it was lovely to see you this morning, but Aesylt and I—"

"Did you forget your citron, Scholar?"

"What citron?" Aesylt eyed them both in baffling suspicion.

Rahn tensed his jaw, watching Aesylt come unraveled before his eyes. "As I said, Lady Nyssa. Purely intellectual."

Nyssa winked at Aesylt. She held out her hand toward Rahn, who took the hint but ignored it. She waved it again, and he pecked it with a kiss that had her blushing and touching her cheek. "A gentleman, you are. So few of them around. Are you *sure* you're not on the marriage market?"

"He's sure," Aesylt groused.

"As for that dance?"

"I..." Rahn tried to catch Aesylt's eyes, but she'd turned her annoyance on the grove of citrons. "It would be impolite to refuse."

"Splendid." Nyssa curtsied and backed away. "We should meet like this every morning, Duke Tindahl. A girl could get used to it."

Rahn said nothing, and after a beat, she turned and left.

Aesylt followed, but Rahn rushed forward and grabbed her arm. "Squish."

The look she turned on his hand was scorching. "You could have told me you were coming to the Wintergarden to see her."

"I didn't tell you because I wasn't," Rahn replied, his words quick and harried like he'd done something wrong. "I came to read. Alone."

"The book about the fucking sexual lemons? I read it too." Aesylt snatched her arm away and grabbed the book. "No wonder she thinks you're ready to ask for her hand."

Rahn balked in surprise. "You read it? When?"

"When I couldn't sleep last night." She readjusted her furs and sniffled from the cold air. "She's lovely. But if you're going to court her, then we should stop what we're doing."

"Aesylt, that is *not*—" Rahn exhaled through his dawning understanding of the situation. "You're jealous."

"What?" Aesylt's face crumpled in annoyance. She reached up to wipe her red nose. "That's ludicrous. Of what?"

Rahn's mouth fell open in astonishment. "What's ludicrous is you thinking I have intentions on courting Nyssa Dereham."

She crossed her arms and lifted her chin. "Yet you haven't denied it."

"I should not need to issue a denial when we both know I have no such intentions, toward her or any woman." The book fell from his hands, and she reached down to grab it at the same time he did, but she was quicker.

"Hm." She pursed her mouth and turned the book over. "Pick a citron. Or not. I need some air."

"But you're already outside!" Rahn was dumbfounded. He didn't know what to make of her behavior—how to address it or if he even should. It was entirely nonsensical and utterly unlike her.

"*Different* air."

"Do you realize how you're acting? You are not yourself."

"Maybe I'm not." She smiled thinly, still glaring at the tome in her hands. "But I'd really like to be anywhere but here right now. Enjoy your book, and..." She waved her hand around.

Aesylt handed the book back without looking at him. Incredulous, he watched her march across the fallen cherry blossoms until she disappeared into the distance.

Oh what a fool she'd been! An absolute and complete fool. She knew it through every painful, pulsing second of the encounter, and worse, so did Rahn and Nyssa. She had no idea how she was going to face them at morning meal and decided it was probably best she not go at all.

What the bloody devil is wrong with me? she thought as she climbed the stairs of the tower in shame. She'd never been one to leave things unsaid, and not making time to speak with Nyssa, to understand the abrupt shift in who had once been a treasured friend, was a personal failing. Letting her get under her skin, when that had been her obvious intent, was another.

With luck, Rahn would go straight to the keep, and she'd have an hour or two of quiet admonishment. She couldn't even muster an apology when he'd rightfully called her on her conduct, because she was too far mired in her own irrational feelings to do anything but sulk.

She climbed higher, already winded. Of course Rahn wasn't trying to *court* Nyssa. Nyssa had fixed her gaze on the scholar from the moment she'd met him, and she had probably followed him, hoping to catch him alone. Goading Aesylt had just been a delightful bonus.

Sighing, she stopped to gather her breath. Jealous. Yes, she was jealous, and she detested herself for it. There was no damn reason to be. He was not her beau, nor even her lover, but her partner—a point *she* had hammered home in defense of them working together. Every bit of intimacy between them was for one reason and one reason alone. He'd made it excruciatingly clear he'd never see her as anything but his favorite disciple, no matter how ardently he'd worked her last night. No matter how dark and heavy his gaze had been as he'd watched her ride his hand like he'd not seen anything like it.

Maybe she should feel ashamed for that too, but she didn't.

Aesylt sighed again and finished the last leg of the climb. She owed him an apology. More so, she needed to pull herself together and remember why they were doing what they were doing—and disabuse herself of any other illusion.

She dug in her pocket for the key, but the door was cracked. Except she knew she'd closed it.

Going for her dagger occurred to her, but it was a silly notion. She was safe in Wulfsgate, safer than anywhere else. It was likely a member of the kitchen staff cleaning up their supper remnants or leaving more fruit in the bowl.

Except the staff always left and collected their food outside the door.

There was only one way to find out.

Straightening, Aesylt entered and found Pieter sitting in her chair, hunched over, a piece of vellum in his hand.

She knew right away what it was.

Unanticipated fire exploded within her. She launched herself across the room, practically flinging herself through the air, as he looked up in shock, in disbelief. He had just enough time to cover his face before she was clawing for the letter.

"That's mine!" she screamed, reaching for the paper he held high above his head, higher than she could reach. "You had no right!"

"Aesylt, calm the—"

She leaped for the paper and went crashing onto the desk when she missed. "Give it fucking back!"

Pieter shot to his feet, his hand still stretched above his head like a challenge. But he was remarkably tall, and there was no chance of besting him in a game of height, so she sucked in a hard breath and hurtled herself at him as hard as she could, knocking them both to the floor.

She growled and climbed him, but he held her back with an arm at her neck. When she started gasping and choking, he relented but asked, "Will you calm down?"

"You have no—" She coughed and spat in his face. "That is not yours. You cannot—"

Pieter bolted upward and licked her face, catching her so off guard, she momentarily relented. He used the opportunity to shake her off of him. "Guardians, Aes, I don't remember you being so damned feisty. Will you *calm down*? Please?"

"I will *calm down*," she said through gritted teeth, panting as she pushed back to her feet, "when you *return my property*."

"I wanted to tell you that I can *help* the two of you, with your Reliquary conundrum."

Aesylt went for her dagger. She unsheathed it and held it out, drawing a stunned look from Pieter. "Give. It. Back."

"I'll give it back," he said calmly, unruffled by her brandished weapon, "when you cool down."

Aesylt sucked in through her nose, her entire body aflame. He'd read the letter from Val's family. The one *no one* else knew about—and could never know about. "That letter, Pieter, is none of your business."

"Oh, I disagree." Pieter shook his hand in the air. "This letter is why you're here, in my home. So it is my business."

"You mean the home you turned your back on?" She narrowed her eyes, her nose flaring. "Where were you anyway? What did you do that your own family won't even speak of it?"

He tossed a casual glance up at the letter. "I don't recommend complying with the Barynovs' extortion. It won't end with marriage. They'll use you to push your brother out and take his place, and I would not expect it to be bloodless."

Aesylt closed her eyes momentarily to center herself. The letter was one problem, but why he was in her room, rooting around, was the real issue. "Tell me what you were doing in my room when you thought I wasn't here."

"Looking for this," he said coolly. "I knew there was more you weren't saying. I have to know what trouble might find its way to our steps."

"Do you even care? The heir who turned his back on his birthright?"

"I care about my family." He cocked his head. "I care about you."

Aesylt's fury returned in an instant. "You've been *playing* me."

"Untrue."

"What is it you expected to find in here?" Another thought, this one far more terrible, occurred to her. Her notes... But the drawer was still locked. Unless he had a copy of the key?

Rahn's notes, however, were stacked on his desk in a neat pile. It was impossible to tell if they'd been disturbed.

"I didn't know what to expect." He rolled the shoulder of his outstretched arm, clearly straining. "You didn't even hear me when I said I can help you. I can get your correspondence to the Reliquary without your foes being the wiser."

Her eyes traveled to the letter. She couldn't let him leave with it, even if they both ended up a tangled, bloody mess. If Drazhan found out... "And why would I trust you with something so important when you clearly *cannot* be trusted?"

Pieter wilted with a wounded look. "Your inability to be forthright is not my shortcoming. Now I know, and we can move on."

"We can move on when you give me my letter back."

"Ah, but you seem to be growing angry again, and I—"

The growl started deep within her, born of something primal and long neglected. A deep, painful rage bubbled up, one unlike any she'd felt for years. It was wholly incongruous to the moment, but she wasn't thinking about that at all as she leaped up, grabbed his shoulders, and scaled him like a tree.

Pieter yelped in surprise and they went stumbling, tripping, and falling onto Rahn's bed. The force caused her to lose hold of her dagger, and it went flying, then clattered somewhere. She clambered up and over him, but his hands shot to her hips where he held her, pinning her from going any farther. Aesylt screamed in his face.

"You're like an animal, listen to yourself!"

"What's going on?" The door slammed. Heavy, hard boots on stone followed. "Aesylt?"

Pieter lifted his head to look, and Aesylt quickly stretched forward and grabbed the letter. It tore at the corner, and she shoved it into her dress with haste, just as she toppled over.

"You want to tell him, Aesylt?" Pieter asked.

She attempted a graceful return to her feet, but her hair and dress were a frightful mess. "What, that you were snooping around in our room when we weren't here?"

"Ah, so you don't." Pieter sprang up.

"Tell me *what* exactly?" Rahn asked, dividing his attention between them. Each word sounded like he was straining them through his teeth.

"Morning meal awaits. I'll... have them send yours up instead." Pieter clapped Rahn on the shoulder. Rahn flinched, his nose curling in anger, but Pieter was already gone.

Chest heaving, Aesylt plopped onto the bed and leaned over her knees.

"Squish. Look at me. What happened?" Rahn dropped to his knees before her and lifted her face, studying it. "Did he hurt you?"

"I came back and he... He was rifling through our things. I may have lost my temper," she breathed.

Rahn's expression clouded. "What was he looking for?"

The last thing she wanted to do was lie to Rahn, but she couldn't tell him about the letter. "He said he thought I was keeping something from him, and he wanted to know what it was."

"What does it matter what you keep from him? You don't owe him your secrets." He ground his jaw. "Did he find our notes?"

Aesylt hung her head and shrugged. "Not mine because the drawer is still locked. Whether he found yours... I don't know. I don't know, Scholar, I don't know why..."

Rahn stretched up and gathered her in his arms. "It's all right, Aesylt. I'll talk to Lord Dereham, let him know how grossly inappropriate his son behaved toward you."

"No." She pulled back, shaking her head furiously. "Please, say nothing. Please."

"Pieter *cannot*—"

"Please." Her eyes burned with tears that wouldn't fall. "We need this place to work for us. We have nowhere else to go."

Rahn watched her, reading her for several terse moments. His mouth drew tight, his head shaking. "If he comes near you again like that, I won't even do him the courtesy of going to his father. I'll handle it myself."

Aesylt nodded, trying to stand and put the horrible episode behind her. But Rahn stopped her with a hand on her shoulder.

"You're bleeding," he said, hollow and distant, and went to the basket of bandages and balms in the corner.

"I am?" Aesylt patted her face all over. It was her temple. She withdrew her hand, surprised at how much blood came back. "I don't even know how..." The room swam. Her words slurred. Darkness encroached the edges of her vision.

When she came to, she was lying in the same bed. Rahn's bed. "You scared me, Squish."

"I didn't mean to." She tried to sit, but wooziness prevented her. "It doesn't hurt. It's nothing to fuss over."

"You lost consciousness. That isn't nothing." Rahn returned with a rag and a bowl, along with some cloth bandages. "I have half a mind to march into that savage's bedchamber and do the same to him."

"Except... It's my fault. I'm the one who charged him like a raging bull and engaged him in a ridiculous battle that I'm frankly embarrassed by, now that I'm calmer."

"Good one of us is calm," he muttered, dipping the rag in the water.

Aesylt, finally, really looked at him and what she saw sent her heart into tatters. He was *truly* angry, his face a barely disguised tableau of hot rage. The flush in his cheeks didn't fade when his eyes softened, when he dabbed the rag gently against her wound.

She lifted her hand to his, stilling his movement. "I'm really all right, Rahn."

His entire expression shifted at the sound of his name. Tension rippled along his jaw. His hand went rigid under hers. "You may have persuaded me not to confront him, but you cannot stop me from looking after you."

"I can dress my own wound."

"And yet I'm doing it for you anyway."

"In the celestial realm, I can actually heal myself. I have all sorts of magic I can't use here in our world." She angled her face inward, toward his outstretched arm. On a whim, she pressed her lips to the soft underside of his forearm and left them there, breathing in.

Rahn stilled again. The only sound between them was their unmatched breaths. "I need you to say the words please."

"What words?"

"And another... another with me."

"You want to go to the celestial realm? For me to heal myself?"

"Just say them." He sucked his teeth with a tight inward groan. "Please."

"And..." Her voice trembled against his skin. "Another with me."

The world shifted. She barely had time to adjust before Rahn's lips were on hers in a crushing kiss. A soft sob escaped him and he pulled back, just enough to wrap her in his arms.

She let him hold her like that for what seemed like minutes, during which her wound slowly closed and the pain dulled, but she could no longer restrain the question. "You wanted to come here to kiss me?"

"I just realized... I realized..." He swallowed, his eyes traveling toward her healed wound before continuing. "How many things in our world are actively trying to destroy you right now. And I needed to take you somewhere that couldn't happen. Just for a little while. Can we stay? A moment?"

Aesylt bit her lip, nodding. Something had changed, but as usual, she couldn't read him. She couldn't discern his intention at all.

He could have kissed her in the real world. He could have bolted the door, locking them away if he wanted to keep her safe.

Rahn wanted something else. He just didn't know how to say it.

Aesylt sat up so she was beside him. She flattened a palm against his chest and let it slide down to his belly. "I want to apologize for how I acted in the Wintergarden."

"No." He shook his head. "You don't need to."

Aesylt closed her eyes and breathed deep. "I do. It was out of line, and you didn't deserve that side of me. I hardly recognized myself out there."

"I didn't know Nyssa would be there," Rahn replied.

"I know."

"I would have waited for you, Aesylt, but I felt you needed your rest after... the night we had."

"What I'm saying is there's no need to explain anything." She lowered her eyes, then lifted them with a nervous squint. "I came looking for you because... I was working up to a way to tell you

I was ready to climb the final rung of the ladder with you. That I'd… I'd *been* ready last night, but I feared scaring you if we moved too fast."

"Scaring me?" Rahn repeated her words, but his eyes had traveled away from her. "I look to you for how we pace this. Your comfort."

"If it were up to me, Scholar…" Aesylt lifted onto her knees so she was looking down at him. She didn't finish.

Rahn tilted his head up to look at her. "What? If it were up to you, what?"

Aesylt's words caught. *If it were up to me, we'd be making love instead of talking.*

"When I saw you and Pieter in here, I thought, at first…" He pursed his lips. "And then I saw what he did to you, and I was furious, like I haven't been in years."

Aesylt ran her hands down his face and kissed him firm on the lips. "There's no reason we can't start this day over. No reason we can't climb a little higher and put the past hour behind us."

He seemed more surprised than he should. "You know what the next rung is?"

She nodded, looking up at him.

"Aesylt." Rahn tucked his chin when she nipped up for another kiss. "Are you sure? Are you sure *I'm* the man you want to share this memory with, and not someone you love?"

She let the word *love* roll over her. "I'm sure that if you ask me the question again, I'll shove you onto your back and take advantage of your vulnerable position, corrupting us both forevermore."

Rahn's calm demeanor disappeared. He licked his lips. "Promise?" A soft smile appeared and then dissolved. "We don't have to do this now. I can see you healed yourself, but—"

"Healing is a curious magic, Scholar. More complicated injuries linger, requiring multiple sessions, but simple wounds can be erased in an instant, like they never happened." Aesylt wrapped her arms around his neck, letting her hands fall down his back as she leaned in. "I need you to lead. Can you do that for me?"

He nodded, the edges of his cheeks tightening. With a grunt, he lifted her onto his lap. His eyes traveled her face, then moved down her neck. She started ripping at the stays of her dress, offering him a slow reveal.

Soon he was helping, sliding the gown off her shoulders before bunching it and lifting it over her head. He'd seen her nude before, but not so vulnerable and exposed. His shaky inhale told her he was just as nervous.

"You're truly exceptional, Aesylt. Never settle for anyone who doesn't remind you of this every damn day." He dipped in to kiss the hollow of her neck, saving her from a response to the second most wonderful thing anyone had ever said to her. *You are as imitable as the stars in our interminable sky.* Her skin raised as his warmth traveled lower, across her breasts, and stopped at one of her nipples, which he took into his mouth.

Rahn lifted his hand to her chin, tilting it."Oh," she moaned, her eyes burning with more tears that would never form. *You're truly exceptional, Aesylt. Never settle for anyone who doesn't remind you of this every damn day.* "That feels lovely."

Rahn whispered something unintelligible as he suckled her, then moved to the other breast. She knotted her hands in his hair and tilted her head back, ready to be lost with him.

His hands moved down her sides, sliding along the curve of her hips, and tightened when his fingers dug into her ass. She tore at the buttons on his shirt, frustrated when they wouldn't open fast enough, but then she had it off, pressing it over his shoulders and strong arms.

Rahn released her nipple and kissed her mouth again before gently laying her back on the bed. She pulled her legs up tight, conscious of her exposure, but something in his eyes made her relax them again. He moved off the bed and unbuckled his trousers, letting them fall to the floor before climbing back up, the throb lifting the bottom edge of his shirt.

He brushed her hair off her face and kissed her. His cock rested on her mound, sending her whole body into a solid clench of anticipation. She almost hoped he didn't fit, that he would plunge inside and tear her open until the pain was replaced by something new and beautiful.

And then the sensation was gone, because he was sliding down her body, spelling it with kisses in places she never knew could be sensual. Her collarbone. Her shoulder. The underside of her arm.

Rahn sighed along her flesh, trailing the tip of his tongue. Her skin pebbled, the hair standing up in response to his passing through. Aesylt closed her eyes and relinquished herself to the raw openness, to the trust she felt for the first man who'd made intimacy seem not only desirable but safe.

He exhaled down the center of her torso and moved to her thigh, which he hooked over his shoulder, peppering more gentle kisses all the way to her knee. Aesylt sighed in capitulation, her legs falling wider as she let go of her awareness of her exposure.

Rahn nibbled the edge of her foot and kissed the underside, drawing a surprised giggle from her. He grinned against her flesh and did it again before moving to the other leg and repeating every tender ministration, moving back between her legs for another gentle graze.

He made a soft, rumbling sound when his tongue met her readiness. She used to think she'd be mortified if he ever knew she was *always* ready for him, but not anymore. He enjoyed seeing what he did to her. He was proud of it.

His head raised, his eyes full of hunger. For *her.* Science or no, he wanted this. She would make sure he knew how much she wanted it too.

Rahn came down over her, spinning her pulse faster and faster. "You decide the pace, Squish." He locked his mouth to hers and lingered. "You decide, at any time, if it ends."

She nodded, knowing full well she would push him all day and night if he allowed it.

With his forehead pressed to hers, balancing himself on one arm, Rahn reached down and circled his cock in his hand. He pumped it twice, his eyes rolling back. Aesylt tightened in expectation. Then he met her eyes once more, settling his head at her opening. He seemed to be waiting for one final confirmation.

"Yes, Scholar," she said, breathless.

Rahn's push was gentle, but the pain was immediate, the new incursion mingling with the last one. Her hands tangled in the blanket, tensing. *Relax.* His eyes widened in alarm at her response, but she brought her hands around to his ass with an encouraging squeeze, to show him she was fine. His mouth fell open as he pushed in farther, and this time she did everything she could not to let him see how much it hurt, how overcome she was by the wild sensation of being stretched and filled. She channeled the pain through the curling of her toes, locking her feet behind the back of his thighs as he slid past the last of her body's resistance and sank himself deep inside her.

Rahn paused for her reaction.

She looped her arms around his neck and lifted to kiss him, whispering, "You're the perfect fit, Scholar."

Something changed in him. It began with a shadowing of his expression, the feral rigidity to his limbs reminding her of a predator zeroing in on prey. "The *only* fit, Aesylt." He dragged himself all the way out and back in, repeating until her eyes rolled back and her mouth could no longer close. "Like my cock was made for you."

"I was made for you," she answered, delirious from the shift in his demeanor, the side of himself he'd held back for so long. Only in the celestial realm would he ever show her, but she'd cherish every cursed moment while she could.

Rahn groaned through every thrust, his back dipping and arcing with each fluid movement. She climbed her legs higher to lock them around his back, and he went faster, plunging even deeper than before, a move that made her vision skip.

"This is so... much... better than I imagined," she cried, lifting her hips to match his rhythm, remembering how important it had been to him that she articulate her experience. "More."

"You've been such a good girl," he panted, sliding his tongue along hers in the deepest kiss he'd given her yet. "How could I deny you?"

She moaned into his mouth, whimpering when his pace slowed and howling when he withdrew and then slammed into her with enough force to leave her wondering if she'd be walking when they were done.

"Tell me," she whispered between ragged breaths. "Tell me what... what you would do if there was nothing stopping you."

"I would..." Rahn pulled out and slammed in again, drawing gasps from both of them. "Fuck my favorite little researcher until the stars wink from the sky and the ocean replaces the land."

Aesylt traced her tongue along her lips, then rolled them into her mouth. "More."

Rahn slowed as he considered her question. His lips peeled back. "I would stretch her until she begged me to stop."

"But you wouldn't stop."

"No force exists capable." He rocked her so thoroughly, her feet slid away, and she couldn't re-fasten them. He reached behind to lock them in place and fucked her harder, then slipped his hand between her legs.

"When you close your eyes at night, it's me I want you to see," she purred into his ear, dangerously close to coming. "Every. Night."

"You're too late for that," he mumbled, his head falling back with a soft, eyes-closed moan.

His confession was a truth for the celestial realm only, one he'd never acknowledge in the real world, but then, there, Adrahn Tindahl was hers and she was his.

Suddenly she was clenching, coming all over his cock as her body pitched up and off the bed.

"Come for me, Aesylt." He moaned. "Come for me until you can't find your breath."

"Come *in* me," she panted before she was crashing again.

"Try to stop me."

"Do everything to me here that you can't do to me out there," Aesylt whined, digging her hands to the soft mattress.

His response was lost to a grunt, which had him tensing, sending a flood of delectable warmth into her. He held his position until the last of it left him, and he fell beside her and landed on his back. Panting, he rolled his face her way and asked, "Please say something, Aesylt."

She'd still been woefully sore from the finger session the day before, so she had become so raw, she was afraid to move at all, but *something* else had changed. It was not only the loss of her virginity, which she'd never held onto for any honorable reason anyway. It wasn't even that she and the scholar had actually had sex, a fact that would need time to settle. It was knowing that Rahn *could* be an open man, a readable man, when he wasn't afraid.

She answered by climbing over him and grinding against his tender but still-hard cock, suppressing a wince. "I like this side of you. I want more of it. How's that for 'something'?" Remembering how he'd used his hand to guide himself, she reached down to do the same, stroked him until he was ready, and nestled him against her tender entrance.

He stared up at her, flushed and wordless, a brief flick of his tongue dancing across his lip.

"I know this means nothing in the real world, Scholar, but I wouldn't have wanted my first time to be any other way. Or with any other man."

"Aesylt..." he whispered, but she had no intention of letting him finish his sentence.

She lifted to take him in, and they moaned together. From pleasure. From pain. From the freedom of consequence.

"Ah," he said, half under his breath. His next words were meant for her to hear. "You are as imitable as the stars in our interminable sky."

Her breath shuddered to hear him repeat the words she'd wondered, in her most raw and helpless moments, if he'd forgotten saying it at all. But he hadn't. And this time, they'd been the confession of a lover.

Rahn clamped his firm hands to her hips and guided her, showing her how he wanted it, which turned out to be exactly how she liked it too. She shed the last of her innocence, the last of her silly fears she wasn't pretty enough... wasn't as sexy as the glamorous, infamous women he'd been with on Duncarrow.

It didn't matter.

He'd chosen her.

Perhaps not forever.

Perhaps not even tomorrow.

But in the celestial realm, Rahn Tindahl belonged to her the way she belonged to him everywhere, always.

They stayed in the celestial realm all day and into dusk, returning to the real world occasionally as a precaution. But all they found were trays of food left outside their door.

Aesylt slept on his bed in the real world. She'd earned her sleep, as insatiable as she'd been. Three times they'd had sex, though Rahn had only finished twice.

She'd fallen asleep in his arms, but after an hour of staring at the rafters, he gently extricated himself from her tangle of limbs and walked to the courtyard for some air.

He passed a nod at Hal, wondering if the guard—if any of them—could read the truth in his anxious gaze.

There was no longer any going back. His relationship with Aesylt was irrevocably changed, and only time would reveal whether it was for the better. His greatest fear all along had been losing her. As his friend, his partner... from the moment he'd met Aesylt Wynter, he'd felt a chasm in him close, one he'd assumed would always remain open, a wound incapable of healing. A wound he couldn't even think about without losing himself.

Sex complicated even the strongest bonds, and no matter why they were doing it, it would complicate theirs.

Still, it wasn't regret he felt. It was the muted shame of knowing he'd gotten exactly what he wanted—and he wanted more. Of all the women... No, there had been none before her, because the memory of every peak and valley of Aesylt Wynter's body was emblazoned in his mind, replacing everything that had come before, just as it had the night he'd brought her to climax with his mouth. Her fingers digging into his back... her soft heels bouncing along his spine. The way her nose curled up whenever she whimpered from overwhelm.

There wasn't a chance he could come again that night, but everything inside of him was screaming to prove that wrong.

Gods, he was a lost man.

When he returned to the tower room, she was awake, staring at the spot where he'd lain. She looked up with a soft smile, but it faded to apprehension. "What's wrong?"

Rahn chuffed and shook his head. "Nothing at all." He sat beside her and smiled. "How do you feel?"

"Like if I have to go ask the kitchen for ice, and they make me explain why, I'll be sent to a monastery for wayward women."

Rahn laughed. "Do you need ice?"

"Will you put it on for me?"

Why, *why* was even that sensual? "If you need me to."

"Hmm." She slithered under the blanket with a yawn and a stretch. "I feel alive, Scholar. That's how I feel."

As do I. For the first time since I washed up on the shores of Duncarrow with horror in my heart. "Then no ice?"

"Oh, I definitely need some ice." She winced and made a playful *oof* sound. "But I told you, I'm not afraid of pain. If I was, I could just return to the celestial realm and heal myself. It's... Well, I suppose I should save this for my notes, yes?"

"If you prefer," Rahn said carefully. He didn't just want to know how she was feeling; he needed to know. As the ranking member of their cohort—

Just stop. Just fucking stop. You desired her. You had her. You want more. If you're going to lie, at least don't lie to yourself.

"But you can also tell me," he said, finishing the thought.

"You won't look at me the same," she said with a sideways glance.

"After everything we've done, it's a few words that worry you?"

Aesylt shrugged against the pillow and turned her eyes toward the ceiling. "I don't have the experience to know why the pain brings me even more pleasure... why it heightens it." She rolled her head to face him, her brows fused in earnest, endearing concern. "Am I broken? I am, aren't I? I'm constructed all wrong. Maybe I was born in the wrong part of the moon cycle. I know you think it's superstitious nonsense, but I'm telling you, there's something to it."

"Broken?" Rahn lay next to her with a reproaching scowl. "Aesylt, don't be ashamed of what brings you pleasure. Ever. If it's receiving pain, so be it." He was hard again.

"And if it's inflicting pain..." She drilled him with a knowing look.

Rahn averted his eyes with a soft laugh. "I gave that away, didn't I?"

"I felt you reading me. I read you too."

"So now I'm readable?"

"Only when your guard is down. Only in the celestial realm." She laughed. "And you did actually confess it, so..."

Rahn didn't know how he felt about any of that.

"But would you not say that makes us the perfect pairing for these experiments?" Aesylt propped herself up on one arm, wincing. "There's nothing I can imagine you doing that I wouldn't welcome."

"We should eat. The food is already cold." He bounced out of the bed, his heart messy at the turn in the conversation.

"You don't think I know what you're doing? Do I need to whisk us away to another world so you can face me again?"

Rahn's hands hovered above the tray. He closed his eyes, stilling. "I don't know where the boundaries are, Squish. All I know is there aren't any in the celestial realm. But here... I just don't know. I'm sorry."

He heard her slip from his bed, followed by the soft patter of her feet as she went to hers. His chest caved in failure. He'd said the wrong thing, though it had been the full and honest truth.

"Then we'll speak of it again when we're in the land of no consequence," she said, her voice soft and groggy. His heart eased. She wasn't upset after all. "Good night, Scholar. And thank you. We should misunderstand one another more often if it ends like that."

EIGHTEEN

LETTING THE DARK IN

Six Weeks Later

As she passed the curtain on her way to the rack, Rahn grabbed Aesylt, drawing a delightful shriek he swiftly sealed with a kiss. An adorable moan rolled up from her throat. She smiled against his mouth before pecking him and sliding away.

"Wouldn't want to be late for morning meal. First thaw hunt is a taxing day," she said, then squealed when he palmed her ass from behind to give her one last kiss on the back of her neck. Her stiffness eased off, as her words drifted into a sigh. "Or... We could not eat."

"I cast my vote for starvation," Rahn murmured, snapping her back against him.

"With me, you'll never go hungry, Scholar." Aesylt winked with an impetuous and utterly calculated drag of her teeth against her bottom lip. The sultry dusk in her eyes lingered a moment longer. She'd never exactly been shy with her desires, but over the past six weeks of exploration, she'd shed every last bit of self-consciousness. She was clever, intoxicating, and insatiable.

He wondered if it were possible to be in a state of longing for enough duration to actually die from the effect, but if so, he'd already be in the ground.

Say the words, he nearly demanded, but it was Pieter he was thinking of when he straightened, kissed the corner of her mouth, and said instead, "The gods are testing me today. But you're right. We still need to visit the blacksmith to seal our notes for the scout as well."

Pieter had been their "ally" for weeks now, secreting their notes out through his personal scout, who then hand delivered them to the Reliquary in the Easterlands. Helpful Pieter, always ready with a solution to every problem. Rahn had been vehemently against his involvement in any way, until Aesylt showed him the exact method they used to carry messages that required extra safeguard. A metal tube, sealed by fire on each end, that could only be opened once without destroying the container. If tampered with, the Reliquary would know.

It still made Rahn nervous, but Aesylt had insisted she and Pieter had made peace after what had happened that day in the tower. She was smart enough to decide for herself, but he still didn't trust the man's helpfulness. It wasn't jealousy—not anymore. He didn't think Pieter was interested in Aesylt that way, but the man *was* interested in her work, more than he had any reason to be, and it was worrisome.

If Pieter ever found out what they were actually doing, there'd be war of another kind.

Rahn had lost mental count of how many times he and Aesylt had consummated their work under the hazy light of the celestial skies. Only in his notes, most of which had already been sent off to the Reliquary, did the numbers live. All he knew was the beautiful blur of frozen time and perfect symmetry. Losing himself in the work... in her... watching the soft snow paint the land through the last throes of wintertide, he'd let go of his guilt and embraced every beautiful, torturous moment with her in the land of no consequence.

They'd experimented plenty within the bounds of the final rung, slipping into the ballroom level of their research: mutual release, sex while inebriated, tracking the changes in stimuli during the different phases of the moon, and trialing positions he'd not realized were possible. There were other variables to test, but there was nothing keeping them from ascending to the battlefield level either. She'd made it clear from the beginning that nothing was off-limits, but there were things on the list that seemed dredged from his darkest, most forbidden fantasies. Things he'd never done with any woman.

Rahn would happily drown in the abyss with Aesylt, which was the problem.

"Meet you at the stables, Scholar." Aesylt snatched the roll of paper with a silly grin and skipped on ahead of him, her pale hair swaying with her hips as she disappeared out the door and down the long steps.

His smile faded when she was out of sight. The light of her presence was replaced by the dark memories of hearing her call out for her brother, Hraz, in her sleep, a mournful cry that had no answer. On some nights, it was for her father. But it had started a few days after they'd consummated their relationship. His own nightmares had begun around the same time, and he didn't yet know what to make of them or what might connect their research to the memories.

Aesylt's Nok Mora was his version of the Passage. Better left unaddressed. Un-remembered. But he wondered what happened to the unaddressed, un-remembered pieces. They hadn't died with the past.

He couldn't ask, because questions about the past were impossible for him too. He couldn't bear to do that to her. The only power he had against the darkness were the nights under the stars when they made their own light.

And once Drazhan concluded the business with the Barynovs in the Cross, it would all end.

Aesylt had the business of the research notes well in hand, so Rahn grabbed his cloak and prepared to head to the keep. But as he shrugged the furs over his shoulders, he noticed a stray scrap of paper under her desk. He quickly leaned to reach for it, worrying she'd forgotten a page, and skimmed the words.

I lack the words to describe what's been happening to me. I have never felt more myself than I do with him. I remember what it is to know strength now. To know it can come from so many other places than trauma and war and strife. But the closer he brings me back to myself, the more the past returns, mocking me, as though there's work to be done and I'm failing to do it. Work I don't have the faintest idea how to begin. Memories I can't quite access and truthfully don't want to. Everything comes with a cost, it seems. Everything—

Hands shaking, Rahn dropped the paper. Aesylt's private notes. He doubted she'd meant to include something so personal in the Reliquary package, so the page must have slipped out when she'd compiled the roll.

He almost tore the paper trying to feed it through the small gap between the drawer and the top of her desk.

Aesylt rode beside Pieter, several paces behind Rahn and Lord Dereham. They all pulled their heads low as sharp bands of sunlight reflected off the melting snow. All around them, by the dozens—hundreds, she thought, watching them stationed every ten yards—were guards. Mostly for her protection, she'd been told by Lord Dereham. As their host, he refused to leave his treasured guests at the keep when he had the means to safeguard them. They were surely homesick by now, he'd said, and it was important to keep their minds busy.

Other hunters streamed behind them, townsmen fortunate enough to be invited to one of the most important days of the year for Wulfsgate.

Aesylt wasn't the only woman on the hunt, but there weren't many. Neither Nyssa nor Lady Dereham had come. Only the women on the lord's council had been invited to participate.

There was a fleeting period every year in the far north that belonged to no season. Some called it the "in between," others "the deep breath." It was the portend of what was to come. If the ground thawed, there was hope for a few weeks more of relief. If not, they hung their heads and prayed for a better next year.

With Wulfsgate being farther south than the Cross, their springtide was often more than a whisper, and they actually celebrated the passage of autumnwhile. But both micro-seasons were treasured and never taken for granted. The first thaw meant a greater variety of beasts emerged, harkening an urgent hunt to restock the meat stores for all the village. The Derehams had a long-standing tradition of involvement in the many traditions that kept life moving in the capital.

"You're unusually quiet this morning," Pieter remarked. She hardly heard him over the prattle of conversations ahead and behind. She'd been perfectly happy riding in silence.

"Am I?" Aesylt's breaths slowed by will alone. Her heart had been a cataclysmic mess ever since she'd handed the last notes to the scout, though she didn't know why.

"Your first hunt?"

That prompted a snorting laugh from her. "No."

"Your first potential kill then?"

A hard fist gripped her heart, but it was gone just as fast. "Not my first kill either. We do learn to hunt in the Cross. We just have to travel far beyond our own woods, and it comes with its own host of challenges."

"Do the Vjestik have an annual tradition like this one?"

She almost couldn't believe he'd asked the question, and when she turned toward him in disbelief, she saw a flash of regret in his eyes. "You mean the one where we send our boys into the forest, praying they'll return, so we can finally hunt our *own* forests again? And since they almost never do, we then pay twice as much as the meat is worth to Wulfsgate so we don't starve?"

"I'm sorry," he said, shaking his head with a tortured look upward. "I was trying to make conversation, and I wasn't thinking. We can talk about something else."

"I'm fine not speaking at all," she muttered, training her eyes on Rahn several paces ahead.

"I really am sorry, Aesylt. You pick the topic. Anything you want. I won't refuse."

She started to roll her eyes when an opportunity formed in her mind. Rahn thought she was naïve in her trust of Pieter, but he was their only path to the Reliquary for the time being—and for who knew how long, as the news from Witchwood Cross had been the same for weeks... more riots but no move from the Barynovs that would turn tensions into outright war—and his guard had slowly lowered around her in return. Her show of trust in him was as much a matter of needing his help as wanting him to believe *she* believed his aid was purely altruistic. Men had been underestimating her for years.

"If you want a conversation so badly, tell me where you've been for the past eight years," she said with a haughty smirk, indicating she knew exactly how his answer would go.

Pieter straightened in his saddle, and she thought that would be the end of it. "You really want to know why my family won't look me in the eyes and often pretend I'm not even in the room?"

"I've only asked a dozen times."

His face scrunched in thought, his gloved hands readjusting on his reins. "How much, if anything, have you read about the villages scattered among the foothills of the Seven Sisters of the West?"

She'd actually read little about the seven-peaked range in the Westerlands, but it was purely because she'd not gotten her hands on any books or pamphlets. Back when Imryll was the sole architect of the concept of *The Book of All Things*, her original vision had included travel across the kingdom, but once the Reliquary took over, and co-opted the project as their own, the institution had limited their scope to the Northerlands. "Not much."

"Ah." Pieter grinned. "My boyhood tutor, Gillibrand, first introduced me to the old stories about the women and their magic there. I was fascinated from the start. I may have a book you can take with you, though it's fraught with more fiction than fact, I'm afraid. Most of what's been written about these villages has been lost or destroyed, which, of course, only fascinated me more."

Aesylt flicked a glance his way to show she was listening, hoping he couldn't read how interested she was.

"There are dozens of these villages. Not all are matriarchal, but many are. The ones with rare magic anyway. Magic that most in the kingdom assume is fantasy, or prefer it be. Gillibrand, though, he believed in all of it. Wholly. He'd been to several of the villages himself and had seen, with his own eyes, women who could transmute water into liquid gold or create an entire garden of blooms with a pass of their hands. More, he'd claimed to be present for more than one instance of anastasis."

Aesylt's blood froze. "Resurrection?"

Pieter nodded. "I didn't believe it either. Not then anyway. Magic has been a part of our kingdom for thousands of years, as long as we have memories to pass down the generations. Now, the Medvedev... No one knows what they can do. They don't live under our kingdom's purview, so I'm not including them in this. But among our own, there are some deeds that have always been beyond what we know of magic. Anastasis is only one example, Aesylt, of what the cunning women of the Seven Sisters are capable of."

The Vjestik were a nomadic people who had called many places home, but according to the kyschun, they'd originated from one of those small villages in the foothills of the Seven Sisters. Something within Aesylt warned her against mentioning it, in the same way she never volunteered the fact that she had Medvedev blood from her mother's side. "I assume you're going to tell me you went there."

"Gillibrand and I went together." Pieter reached up to scratch his neck. The din of conversation had softened. Pieter's voice lowered as well. "I never intended to stay so long, but what I saw there turned me from a scholar by hobby to one by profession. I knew I'd never be happy playing politician, and I had a decision to make. Then Gillibrand died suddenly."

"How?"

"Slipped and fell from a mountain path one day when he was collecting different species of plants."

"But you were surrounded by women who could raise the dead."

"There can be no resurrection without a body." Pieter's mouth quirked.

Aesylt frowned and looked again at Rahn ahead. For some reason, she thought of her notes—not the official ones sent to the Reliquary but the ones just for her. The ones she still wasn't sure why she'd written at all, except she'd felt oddly compelled, almost against her will. *Even when the light is brightest, the darkness calls. There can be no light if one cannot recognize the absence of it. I've been living in the gray for so long without ever knowing it.* She cleared her throat. "And you stayed to continue his work?"

"Silence, friends!" Lord Dereham called from ahead, turning to repeat himself several more times. "In half a tick of the sun, we'll reach the staging area. Turn your thoughts inward and your prayers to the Guardians, who alone decide how much bounty we return to our village with this afternoon."

Aesylt glanced at Pieter, who seemed relieved to be done with the conversation.

He'd said more in those few minutes than in the entire month they'd been in Wulfsgate. But it still didn't explain the enmity with his family or what led to him to forsake his birthright... what had made Lady Dereham so convinced he was never coming back that she had another child in her middle age to protect the ascendancy.

Somehow, she'd get him to tell her the rest of his story.

But it moved to the back of her mind as she mentally steeled for the moment she'd been quietly dreading for days.

Rahn helped the men set up the camp. It consisted of two long assembled tables, one housing a row of weapons, and the other, longer and broader, for dressing the meat of the beasts they felled that day.

He counted fourteen hunters, besides Rustan, Pieter, Aesylt, and himself. He didn't know if that was a lot, but it felt excessive, especially with the obscene number of guards stationed around the forest perimeter. There were also a dozen young men who were there solely to retrieve the felled animals and dress them while the hunters worked. Lord Dereham had explained that while there were always regular hunters bringing in game for fresh meals, the eighteen hunters gathered would restock the meat stores at Wulfsgate Keep, as well as the emergency reserves for the city.

Rustan rubbed his gloved hands together with a tight look at his son. He then turned toward Rahn with a smile. "Your first hunt?" He nodded. "Of course it is. Nothing to hunt in Duncarrow, and the Cross only hunts when the boys win. Or if they can weather the capricious forests between their town and ours."

Rahn glanced Aesylt's way to gauge her response to the almost callously casual way they spoke of the Cross's deepest wound, but she was busy perusing the weapons table. She'd only been eight the year Drazhan had won the Vuk od Varem—and Rahn hadn't asked, but he couldn't imagine much celebratory hunting had occurred after Drazhan had returned to a village in rubble—and before that there hadn't been a victor in years. Hunters violating the agreement between the wulves and Vjestik, thinking themselves clever or above the law, didn't return home with breath in their lungs. The only animals the Vjestik were sanctioned to kill were those unfortunate enough to wander out of the forests and too near to town, or, as Lord Dereham had said, in the forests beyond their borders, and those were more perilous than their own.

The only explanation Rahn could muster was that she'd learned to hunt in the celestial realm with her brothers, same as she'd learned to fight and die.

"And that is their way," Rustan said. "However..." He tapped another man on the shoulder, who then raised a stick, painted in dark green, into the air. Everyone went silent and gathered close, drawing a tight circle around the lord. "This year, half of what we kill belongs to our friends in Witchwood Cross." He glanced at a stunned Aesylt. "Gold-free, and no taxes due. They've had a troubling year, and we're going to make it a little less so. So, lads, ladies, bring your best today, for we'll need to take enough game to make up the difference."

The hunters nodded and dispersed, each heading to the table to choose their weapon. Aesylt approached with a dazed, faraway look. "Lord Dereham, your kindness is... greatly appreciated. But the Cross will pay for what is ours."

"You will pay when I accept your gold. And today, I do not." He smiled and clapped a hand onto her shoulder. "Don't feel you have to take part, cub. Sit and watch, breathe in the warmest air we've had in months, and enjoy some time away from your tiny tower. You're perfectly safe here."

"Respectfully, my lord, I will do my part like all the others. I came to help, not to watch."

Rustan's brows knit. Soft concern speckled his eyes. "Then might I suggest the crossbow? It's the quickest to learn, the simplest to maneuver—"

"I'm comfortable with traditional bows and spears."

"The spears are only for the boar, which we rarely see, and only a few of my men have the skill to use them humanely. Most will carry bows or crossbows because we're mainly after deer, elk-kind, and grouse. And land fowl if they're foolish enough to wander through while we're here."

"I know, my lord."

Rustan glanced at Pieter, who could only shrug. Rahn's sense of danger had spiked considerably during the brief exchange. His concern for Aesylt was so irrational, it had him envisioning the feasibility of swaddling her in his cloak, tossing her over his shoulder, and riding her back to the keep, where she'd be safe from whatever unidentified danger seemed to be waiting for her in the forest.

But he had no basis for his concern. Only a feeling.

"We have one new hunter with us today, our once-duke, Scholar Tindahl. He has better odds of walking away without a kill than with, but we wish him good fortune," Rustan announced to whoever was still listening. "Rahn, I hope you're not afraid of a little blooding."

"Blooding?"

Aesylt found a bow she liked, wrapping her fingers in the grip and pulling back the string in several quick tests. She nodded at it and grabbed a full quiver, which she strapped to her shoulders. Her expression was lined with cool confidence, but there was a darkness in her eyes that left him with the same, paralyzing fear that something terrible was about to happen.

Rahn stepped in beside her. "I suppose I should start with the crossbow then, from what Lord Dereham said?"

She stretched her arm past him and slid the metal contraption his way. "Here's how you load the bolt. You want the metal ones, not the arrows we use with the bows. Make sure it's lined up right down this scoring here, along the stock, or you'll misfire." She secured it, lifted the weapon, and aimed it away from everyone. "This hook here is called a trigger. But you won't pull it until you have your target perfectly in your sights, which you can do by aligning it... Like this, see? If shooting in the sky, pull a half-second earlier than you believe you should. If shooting on land, aim for the heart as much as you can. Never the gut, if you can help it."

"Why?"

"They take longer to die, and that's not how we honor the beasts that keep us fed. If we cannot offer a swift death, we shouldn't take the shot," Aesylt answered. "And, whatever is still in the stomach and intestines of the beast can sometimes contaminate the meat around it and make part or all of it inedible, which is not only a waste of food but of the life taken." She sighed and glanced back at the table. "Don't be one of those men who thinks because he has a good arm he'd be deft with a spear. You'll either maim the beast or yourself, so just... do not."

Rahn was impressed, though her sureness did little toward easing his growing dread. "You really do know what you're doing. Mind if I come along with you?"

Aesylt shrugged, but quickly shook her head. "Stealth is key to a successful hunt. We need to stay as quiet as we can while we wait for our moment. I'm already at a disadvantage with all these guards pretending to be shrubs." She slung the bow over her shoulder and reached for one of the remaining spears. She tossed the shaft, caught it with a strange smile, and lowered the sharp end toward the ground. "My advice is to stay as close to camp as you can, in case you need help. There will always be one or two men here at all times, refreshing their cache, and the dressing boys will be on quiet patrol throughout the afternoon."

"You'll be fine out there alone?" His sense of danger intensified with the suspicion she had other reasons for wanting to be alone.

"Would you ask any of these men the same question?"

He sighed in capitulation. "As always, you remind me to check my sensibilities." He fought the urge to kiss her. It had become so natural—too natural. He was terrified they'd slip in front of the wrong person and that what they'd been doing in the cool tower room would become obvious to everyone.

"See you at dusk," she said as she walked away.

Aesylt marched through the melting forest with purposeful breaths that matched her full stride. She passed several men she only recognized from the ride to the woods. They weren't spaced out nearly enough for her liking, and a couple seemed to even be partnering up. There was a reward at the end for the hunter who brought in the greatest weight. A gold cache, if she recalled, but she hadn't really been listening, any more than she'd listened to the men whisper-prattle as they'd set up their blinds.

She adjusted her spear higher in hand when she reached a thicker patch of brush. The bow was small, like one given to a child, but it was the same kind she'd learned on. Killed with.

Tell them, girl. Tell them all how the king sends his love.

Aesylt staggered a step at the unexpected recollection, her vision flickering. She choked back the soldier's cruel words, returning them to their safe compartment, where also lived the sensation of the monster's spit running down her face and the horror of his trailing laughter as she rocked, shaking, on her father's bloody bedroom floor.

Aesylt blinked hard and pushed on. She hadn't seen a hunter in a while, and all she could hear was the occasional crunch of an animal and the heartbeat drumming between her ears. Her breathing labored, involuntarily allowing more holes to open in her mind, releasing what was inside.

She climbed to her feet, slipping twice on her father's blood. Sobs shook her; tears blinded her. The competing stenches, every one of them unthinkable, had her fading. Father and Hraz were gone. Drazhan was still in the forest, if he was even alive. The celestial realm called, and it would be so easy, so easy...

"Nien," she hissed under her breath. "This can't happen if you don't allow it." She slung the bow tighter over her shoulder and grunted as she climbed a small embankment overlooking a modest valley.

She didn't remember the walk from her father's apartment to the gates of Fanghelm, but suddenly she was standing on the road. Smoke and flame burned to the east... the west. She headed south, toward the village, where most of the screams were floating from.

Aesylt closed her eyes tight and lengthened her limbs, focusing on being present, on leaving the past behind her. Lord Dereham's offer was beyond generous, and her people desperately needed the meat, now more than ever with the town under siege and another failed Vuk od Varem behind them. She could actually *help* her village if she pushed through her discomfort, a win she desperately needed after being at the center of their present troubles.

The main road was littered with bodies. Bloodied. Charred. Some seemed to have died while running away from something, others while facing it head-on. There were hands, feet, and heads strewn about in a way that was so surreal, her mind convinced her a dream was the only explanation.

She screamed when she saw Niklaus's mother clinging to a hitching post, her mouth frozen in the horror of death. Beside her were both of her dead brothers-in-law, kyschun who were only in the village one week a year, the week of the Vuk od Varem.

Smoke blinded Aesylt as she wondered who would replace them under the mountain, if there was anyone left to replace them.

Wheezing, she opened her mouth wide to take in more air, but it sent a billow of smoke straight into her lungs. She collapsed, but something caught her. She looked up and obscured through tears was the sobbing face of Nik.

Aesylt, shaking her head to clear the ash, wiped her face on her arm and spread her tools out across a tan blanket in a methodical line, cataloging and counting them. Last of them was the flare she was supposed to fire off when she was done, to signal to the dressing boys where to collect the carcasses.

She glanced into the tree she'd leaned both weapons against. She could climb it, but she and trees weren't on the best terms after the Dyvareh. But the spot she'd chosen had plenty of brush cover, and she'd still have clear sight into the valley below, where several animals had already emerged to enjoy the thaw.

Aesylt counted her arrows. Forty. Her bow might be designed for a child, but she'd taken one of the larger quivers, sharing a glare with a hulking redheaded man who'd looked at her like she was being wasteful and ignorant. He didn't know though. None of them did. Not even Rahn. He was perhaps the one person she *might* be able to talk to, but he was the last one she wanted knowing every smirk and sneer of the demons within her.

"Aes. Aes! It's you. It's you. Ancestors help us, it's the end of the world." Nik panted and sobbed, bowling over before standing, his hands tugging his hair in a silent scream.

"Nikky, look at me. Look at me." She didn't know why she'd said it. "Where are the men who did this?"

"Did you hear? Drazhan has returned with a heart." Niklaus clawed at his sooty neck, his tears cutting trails down his blackened cheeks. "Praise the Ancestors."

"What? What?" Aesylt reached for both of his hands, batting at them. "Is that true? Is he back? Did he truly win? Where is he?"

"I saw him. I don't know. I don't know where anyone is." Niklaus shook his head, his eyes traveling the remnants of their once-great village. His lower lip curled into his mouth. "My mother, Aes. My...."

Aesylt threw herself into his arms. "Ota and Hraz too, Nikky. They took their heads. I saw..." She couldn't finish.

They held each other, sobbing, until Val's cracked voice cut through the haze. "Most of the king's men have gone, but there are three at the north end of town." He sniffled and turned back the way he'd come.

"V!" Aesylt cried and folded him into their embrace. Everyone else was gone, but two of her friends were there, and they'd avenge their people. They'd crawl on their hands and knees to Duncarrow if they

had to, but they'd do it together. "Oh, thank the Ancestors you're all right. You're both..."

"Both of my sostras, Aessy. Both of them." Val cleared his throat, coughed, and spat black phlegm onto the snowy road. "Those men aren't leaving this village."

Aesylt wiped her filthy face with blood-stained hands. She dabbed her tears on the sleeve of her nightgown and looked toward Fanghelm. "My father has a private armory."

Aesylt blinked harder. She had an arrow ready. She brought the magnifiers back to her face and scanned the valley, shrugging her shoulder to remove the weighted ache. Her chest was so tight, she had to sit tall to take deep breaths. *This is not that day. This is the day I help my people. Leave the past in the past.*

There were too many young beasts milling about, and though the men loved their tender meat, she refused to hunt anything but the mature ones. She spotted a buck grazing near a small spring and nocked her arrow slowly. It was almost too big for the bow, the size difference causing her hand to shake, but she closed one eye, steadied, and took aim, then waited for the buck to look her way, to expose himself so she could offer a respectful, painless death.

Heart shot. Instant.

The buck collapsed to the half-melted ground.

Aesylt exhaled. She set the bow aside and cradled her hands together to stop the tremors.

The boys both picked swords, too heavy for their growing hands, but Aesylt went for her father's hickory bow. She'd trained on something much smaller, but she wasn't hunting hare.

"None of the king's men leave this village today," Aesylt said to them both, echoing Val's earlier message of resolve. "And when we've sorted it, we need to feed what's left of our people."

"With what? They burned our meat stores. They torched our gardens." The weight of the sword Val had chosen made his left side sag.

"My brother has returned with the heart of the wulf." Aesylt hoisted the heavy quiver until the straps were secure over both of her shoulders. "The forests belong to us now."

"Then we should find him, Aessy! He's the steward now. We need a leader."

"Tak, well until he shows up to do so, it falls to me. The last Wynter of Witchwood Cross," Aesylt said, locking eyes with Val and then Nik. "I don't know how many are left of our people, but there will be even less if don't stop these terrible men. We protect. We defend. We feed. All right?"

The boys wore identical looks as they examined her, reading her words. Reading her. There was an ocean of sadness behind their eyes, but at the edges was fear—not of the men who had taken everything from them, but of her.

She was afraid too, but if she stopped to think about it, about anything, she'd shrivel into a wraith of grief and never again rise.

"All right?"

Val glanced at Nik, who raised his brows back. Finally, they both nodded.

On their way out, Val grabbed a spear.

One grouse. Then another. Aesylt nocked, aimed, fired, nocked, aimed, fired.

Both fell to the earth.

The three of them crouched along the inner wall of the north battlement. Val and Nik recited names as they spotted people they knew, those still among the living. Every name was a bolt of warmth on the coldest day of her life. Not all had been lost.

Aesylt clutched the bow, stringing the icy air through her teeth and into her lungs, where she held it. Movement caught her eye, so she rose onto her knees, peering through the gaps in the wall to see two of the king's men laughing as they inspected their loot bag.

Saying nothing to the boys, she rose, drawing an arrow in a slow slide. She nocked it, her hands unsteady as she took aim.

One of the men spotted her, and they both startled. It was too late. Aesylt loosed the arrow, and it sliced through the first man's neck. The second man bolted, leaving his spoils behind. Val and Nik scrambled to their feet, heading for the stairs, but by the time they reached the ground, the remaining man would already be gone.

Panting and desperate, Aesylt grabbed the spear propped against the wall and returned to the spot where she'd fired her arrow. She saw her father's panicked eyes—scared for her, knowing he'd never learn her fate because his was already sealed—as his head was taken from his body. She saw Hraz screaming, his arms out for her as the sword plunged into his chest from behind. The entire, torturous day bubbled up from within, a dangerous brew that had her backing up and charging the wall, her arm releasing the spear with enough force to send her flagging over the stones. The air stilled, allowing space for the ghastly whisper of the weapon hurtling from the battlement. The man looked up in surprise, and that was what killed him. The hesitation. It was the last expression he made as the spear struck him in the gut.

"Ancestors keep us," Niklaus whispered as he pulled her back over the wall to safety. "Val, she's fading."

"Our people need to eat," Aesylt murmured and drifted away.

Aesylt swooned, the tree catching her before she could fall. She registered pain in her hands and saw they were already blistering from the force of her grip. Rain had set in, but the bowing needles were sheltering her from most of it. The sun was already past the center of the sky, so she'd been out there for hours—except that wasn't possible. She'd only just set up her station.

Yet her quiver was half-empty.

She grabbed the magnifiers to scan the valley. Her breathing stopped.

Nock. Aim. Release.
Nock. Aim. Release.
Nock. Aim. Release.

"Aesylt, it's past dusk. We need to get back, find shelter." One of the boys. She wasn't sure which.

Nock. Aim. Release.

Nock. Aim. Release.

"Aessy, we have more than enough for now. We can come back tomorrow. We have all season."

Nock. Aim. Release.

Nock. Aim. Release.

Nock. Aim. She fell to her knees and tried to stand, but the ground wobbled.

Arms folded around her from behind. She screamed, but then hands were peeling away the bow. Both boys held her as she thrashed and sobbed, and they were crying right along with her. Though her face was buried in Nik's shoulder, she saw a pile of carcasses as tall as Val. Deer, elk-kind, air fowl. So many. They'd taken down so many. How, how had...

No, not they. She.

"You've done enough," Nik whispered.

Aesylt woke with her face on the wet ground. She sputtered through the melting snow and sat up, finding it was dark. Her quiver was empty.

And she wasn't alone.

Down in the valley, four or five dressing boys were working to pile the results of her hunt. She reached for the magnifier, but boots drew her gaze upward, where she found Lord Dereham peering down at her in distress.

"I found her!" he cried, lowering to a crouch. The world upended as she left the ground. She saw Pieter collecting her bow and empty quiver. Another man rolled her instruments up and took them away. "Aesylt, what *happened*? Why didn't you signal us?"

She shook her head because she didn't know. A powerful swell of nausea rolled up from within, and she closed her mouth tight to fend it off. Light from a torch swung across her vision.

"We have a count, sir." Why did the man sound so concerned? "Three bucks, two hares, six grouse, and..." He hesitated. "We found a sizable boar with a spear through him."

"That cannot be right," Rustan said. He shifted Aesylt in his arms. "Twelve kills? She was out here alone?"

"All day and evening," said someone else. "Nearest post was Baron Silver, a half mile to the east."

"It's not possible." Pieter. "That's double what anyone else brought in. And a boar? Really? Count again."

"Aesylt!" Rahn's voice cut through the confusion. She heard thrashing in the bushes, desperate crunches of boots in slush. "Is she... Lord Dereham, what *happened*?"

"Too soon to say." Rustan sighed through his teeth. "Can you stand, cub?"

Aesylt nodded and he set her down, but Rahn was straightaway at her side, one arm around her waist. Her head rolled back, her eyes fluttering as she met his troubled gaze. "Told you I could hunt, Scholar."

Rahn's face was frozen in worry. "I never should have let you go off by yourself." He steadied her tighter against him. "We need to get her back. Now. She's freezing."

"I'm fine," she murmured, and her eyes rolled closed.

She watched her friends tell the gathered crowd where to find the meat. There was no joy in the village square, but there was hope. They wouldn't starve. Whatever was left of them anyway. Vaguely, she realized their losses would actually mean more food to go around.

Bonfires raged with the fuel of over a thousand bodies. Someone had counted, but she couldn't remember who. Her father and brother were in there somewhere, their bodies at least. Their heads were on pikes greeting visitors to the Cross. She needed to get them down. There was so much to do.

Drazhan had left the wulf's heart on the steps of Fanghelm, but no one knew where he'd gone. Aesylt only knew he wasn't dead, because she could still feel him. If she had the energy, she could even find him, using the private, secret channel in their minds they'd discovered when she had still been in nursery.

Fezzan Castel came to where she was huddled on the steps of a tavern. He sat beside her and, for a long time, said nothing.

"I had my men take down your father and Hraz, cub. They've been secreted away somewhere safe, until we can honor them." He waited for her to say something, but there was nothing to say. It was just another task completed and a million more to go. "We've replaced them with the men you killed. Any still foolish enough to linger will carry that message back to the king."

"The two I killed are nowhere near what they've taken from us," Aesylt stated, shivering.

"Two?" Fezzan cocked his head. "Aesylt, you killed ten of the king's men today."

"What?" Those were the words that finally made her look up. "No. That was someone else."

"It's all right, cub. Val and Nik told me everything. You're a hero to our people. Who knows how many others would have died if you hadn't—"

"They're wrong." Aesylt shook.

He steadied a hand on her shoulder. "You really don't remember?"

"I said it wasn't me, Fezzan!" Her entire body convulsed, but it abruptly stopped when a woman's arms gathered her from behind with a gentle shushing sound. Asa Castel, Fezzan's wife. She was Aesylt's late mother's cousin, who had always felt more like her teta, just as Fezzan was like an onkel.

Aesylt relaxed some. The haze of fires blurred into a line of orange and smoke.

Fezzan nodded to himself, squinting at the row of fires. His voice broke. "The wife and I will take you with us tonight. Maybe for a longer spell even. Get you cleaned up. Hopefully some rest. It will be all right, cub. I promise it will be all right."

Rahn sat on one side of the bed, Imryll the other. Aesylt hadn't regained consciousness since the forest. They'd taken her straight to Imryll's bedchamber, upon Rahn's insistence. He couldn't know if Aesylt was injured until Imryll laid hands on her, and Rahn wasn't letting the Dereham healer anywhere near Aesylt with her so unstable.

Physically, she was fine. Just some blisters on her hands and a thin scratch where her face had been resting against the ground. They'd had to wash blood off of her, but none of it had been hers.

Rahn had wanted her to ride back with him, where he could keep a close eye on whatever was happening to her, but Lord Dereham had insisted they clear out one of the wagons and use the pelts to keep her comfortable. The man's face was pallid when he'd said, *You don't seem nearly as surprised as the rest of us, Scholar.*

He'd been stunned, actually, but even in his shock, his first thought had been how he was going to protect her.

Still, he'd ridden close to the wagon, and it was a good thing, because if anyone else had been staring into the back at the young cub lying in a pile of furs, they might have noticed her blinking in and out of existence.

"Rustan is going to want answers, Rahn." Imryll stroked Aesylt's brow with the back of her hand, sighing. "Truthfully, I do too."

"If I had answers..." Rahn squeezed one of Aesylt's hands in both of his. He didn't need to note Imryll's soft disapproval. "I'm so worried about her, Imryll."

"That much is quite clear."

Rahn closed his eyes and turned his face toward the warm hearth. "She's been dreaming recently... I hear her call for Ezra and Hraz. She sounds so small and afraid, so unlike herself." He pursed his mouth. "But she won't talk about it with me. Maybe you'll find more luck than I have."

"Even with me, there are things she can't bring herself to say," Imryll said softly, still passing her hand along her sister-in-law's brow. "If Drazhan had only let her talk of that night when they were younger... if he hadn't fled just as the village was rebuilding and families were moving on. He cannot see that, for all her strength, she is using thin gauze to heal decaying wounds. As long as she had purpose, she could keep moving. But when he came back after years away and her purpose disappeared, even the gauze was no longer effective."

"You can't force someone to address their trauma."

"I suppose you would know." She smiled thinly. "But she's different with you, since you came to the Cross. She has purpose again. Even when we're all so worried about matters back home, she's come alive. So why is this resurfacing for her now? Is it the situation with Val?"

Aesylt disappeared again. Imryll made a frustrated sound.

Rahn stared at the empty spot, the shape of Aesylt still embossed in the dent of the pillows, the wrinkles of the sheets. "I suppose that in order to peel back the curtains wide enough to allow yourself to experience the light, you risk letting the dark in too."

Imryll frowned, considering his words. "Tell me again what happened when you found her."

"I was... several paces behind Lord Dereham when he spotted her, and by the time I got there, he already had her in his arms, where she was shaking and... speaking nonsense, fragments of words or thoughts." Rahn shook his head at the empty bed. "She said something about bonfires, soldiers. She'd wake up long enough to be confused about all of it and then slip away again. Thank the gods she didn't starwalk when all those men were watching." He'd had no choice but to let Imryll in on Aesylt's secret after the first time she'd disappeared right in front of them. "But, Imryll, it was the stack of carcasses." Rahn breathed deep to recall just the facts, not the way they'd made him feel. "She insisted it wasn't her who had done it, but the animals were already in a neat pile in the valley when the dressing boys found her. They looked sincerely scared when they told Lord Dereham about it. About the boar, her spear still stuck in his throat. Now the birds, of course, those are easy to move. Even the deer, perhaps, if you balance your weight properly. But the rest? There's a reason they put those boys in pairs when they go out to retrieve the carcasses. For some game, they even send three."

"So it's impossible."

"I know."

"But you're not proposing a more reasonable explanation either. So what are you suggesting, that she has beyond-human strength?"

"Do you remember what I taught you about how people are capable of impossible feats in certain heightened scenarios? How something within us kicks in to protect us or others. It's how mothers can lift fallen carts off their injured children when under ordinary circumstances, they could barely tilt it. We don't have a name for it yet, but there are instances of this happening everywhere, all throughout history. No one yet knows why, but we will one day."

Imryll squinted, then nodded. "What I remember is that the other students didn't believe you."

He almost grinned. "Few appreciated my lessons as you did."

"But Aesylt wasn't in danger out there, was she?"

"You should have seen the size of Dereham's guard." Rahn startled when Aesylt reappeared. He again took her hand, tighter this time, as though it would do anything to keep her from leaving. "But there's more than one way to be in peril."

"Don't I know it," she muttered, standing. With a stretch, she glanced out the window, where the thaw had ended as quickly as it had begun. Fresh snow had already carpeted the ground in the few short hours they'd been back. "We had a scout from Eastport today. Tasmin sent a letter to Teleria that she may extend her visit in Whitechurch."

"Why?" Rahn shook his head.

"She didn't say. But it worries me. Marius is a skilled manipulator. He handled me like a marionette, and I fear..." She sighed. "Tasmin is wise though. I have to trust she knows what she's doing. Anyway, whatever my fears about her situation thousands of miles away, we have a bigger problem closer to home."

"Which is?"

"No one has seen Marek since they reported him having disappeared."

"Even if he did come here..." He gestured around with his hand. "He'd get no more than a step before he was cut down. You've seen the amount of guards Dereham has."

"If he came in sword swinging, yes." Imryll turned toward him. "But you don't know the reason the Barynovs felt so comfortable tossing around the word koldyna."

"Weak men only know how to engage in weak reasoning."

She laughed. "It's because they have a koldyna in their own employ." She ground out the last word. "And before you ask why Drazhan has done nothing about it, he's tried. They deny it. We can't prove it, and if we can't prove it, we cannot make a public accusation without subjecting ourselves to the same laws he's trying to hold them to now. But we know it's true."

Rahn warmed Aesylt's hand between his. Every time she'd returned from starwalking that evening, her hands were like ice. "And what could a koldyna do... that a sword could not?" He asked slowly, uncertain if he wanted the answer.

"Koldynas don't respect any rule of law. They answer to the demon realm. We cannot know what their limits are. We don't even know *what* they are, other than they come from some remote hovel in the Seven Sisters. Presumably." Imryll crossed her arms with a look down at the bed. "She'll stay with me tonight. Tomorrow, we'll talk more."

Rahn braced even before saying the words. "I'm not leaving her side until whatever this is passes."

Imryll closed her eyes, tilted her head back, and laughed. "You're not even trying to hide it anymore, Adrahn. I hope for both your sakes you know what you're doing. You think because we're not in the Cross, word won't reach my husband? That the walls here talk any less than the walls of Fanghelm?"

"If you want me to deny that I care about her, I won't. But you're making more of it than there is, Imryll, and I would expect more nuance from you, given how many nontraditional friendships with men you've had in your own life," Rahn said, watching her eyes widen with each word. He sighed, easing off on the unintended chastisement. She'd asked him a question, and she had her answer. He stood. "Drazhan looked me in the eye and made me promise I would keep his sister safe. Aesylt wanted to hunt alone today, and I should have pushed harder to stay together. I could have... I might have prevented this—whatever *this* is. When she wakes, I need to be here, not a thousand yards away in a tower. If she needs me, and I'm not here... Well, it can't happen."

"If she needs you, and you're not... Rahn, I mean this as your friend, but are you listening to yourself? The words you choose when you speak of her?"

He scoffed in indignance. "I choose to speak of her as someone who respects her and who has promised not to let her down."

"Unlike her brother, you mean?" Imryll's eyes clouded.

Rahn's fingers tightened at his sides. "Aesylt's relationship with her brother is hers to define. I can only speak to the man I aim to be."

"One who talks in circles and says nothing of use," she said, disgust curling the edges of her mouth. "Unless it's about your treasured research."

"*Our* treasured research, Imryll. This was your passion. I'm just here to help."

She snorted and pivoted, glancing at him sideways. "For a man embroiled in a lifelong love affair with truth and facts, it astounds me how easily you can avoid your own when its inconvenient."

It wasn't inconvenient. It was inefficient. Long ago, he'd learned to store such inefficient feelings where they couldn't destabilize the parts of his life that gave him purpose. Some people found comfort in processing their emotions, but that was not his experience. He stubbornly pointed at a chaise on the other side of the room. "I'll sleep there."

"So it's not enough to have chins wagging about you and Aes. Now you want them to talk about us too?" She lifted her shoulders in exhausted defeat. "Fine. Stay. We'll just tell the truth, say you were worried about her. No one needs to know you're in love with her."

Rahn threw up his hands, heat flooding his neck. "I'm not in *love* with her, Imryll, for gods' sake!"

Her eyes narrowed. "But in return, you promise me you'll leave me out of whatever is going on between the two of you. Because I would lie for you, and I would lie for Aesylt, but I will not lie *to* my husband. Ever." She reached for a quilt lying on the back of a tall chair and tossed it at him. "You're both adults. You don't need me to remind you of the consequences. Just don't look surprised when the fates come to collect their due."

NINETEEN
THE SURPRISE

Aesylt answered Rustan's and Pieter's questions as best she could. She said nothing of the blending of past and present, the way the visions had usurped her sense of time and place until she could no longer be sure whether she was eight-year-old Aesylt or twenty-year-old Aesylt.

But she was telling the complete truth when she'd said she had no idea how she'd hunted so many animals nor how they'd come to be stacked so neatly before the dressing boys had arrived.

It was the same line of questioning she'd sat through ten years ago with Lord Dereham, giving her testimony of that horrible night. Back then, it had been Fezzan Castel at her side for gentle encouragement. This time, it was the scholar.

No, Lord Dereham, I don't recall killing so many of the king's soldiers. I can only remember two.

No, Lord Dereham, I don't recall hunting so many animals yesterday. I can only recall two.

Rustan exchanged frequent, troubled looks with his son, whom he seemed to be getting along with again. "Aesylt, I want you to understand that no one is accusing you of anything," he said after a long breath out.

"I should hope not." She straightened at even the hint she'd done something wrong. He wouldn't have felt the need to use those words if he wasn't at least thinking them. "Women are skilled hunters in the Cross, as good as men, even if the occasion to use the skill is less than we'd like. I was trained by three of the best, and even if... Even if those years are long behind me, when I picked up the bow, it was like no time had passed at all."

"And the spear?" Pieter leaned in, his eyes soft, like he was afraid she'd combust if he pushed too hard.

"What is the question?" Aesylt retorted.

"I think she's answered enough." Rahn settled her cloak over her and stood. "She needs more rest."

"She won the competition," Pieter said, looking at Rahn. "It's customary for her to accept the gold in front of all the hunters who participated."

"I won't be accepting any gold," Aesylt said. She pinned her cloak at her neck, offering Rahn a grateful smile. He'd been there when she'd woken from the terrible nightmare, and he was determined not to leave her side for any reason. She'd never needed a man to make her feel safe, but he did, just the same. "I understand Wulfsgate is one of the few cities who still has a healing monastery for the indigent to receive care."

"That's right," Rustan said slowly. "But they are already well-funded from my coffers. As well as any profitable infirmary."

Aesylt thought about it. "Then distribute it evenly amongst the rest of the hunting party, including the dressing boys, with my gratitude for bringing in enough game that the half you've offered my people will be life-changing."

She'd reached the courtyard before Rahn matched her pace, instead of walking behind her. "I need to think about something other than what happened yesterday." She paused at the garden and turned toward him. A bolt of sadness struck her at how much she wanted to kiss him, in the open where anyone could see, and how it could never, ever happen. "I know what you're thinking, and no, I don't want to starwalk today." *Maybe not for a while,* she thought, remembering how little control she'd had over her entrances and exits throughout the night.

Rahn's head tilted sideways—in disappointment or concern, it was hard to tell. "I wasn't thinking anything of the sort. My only concern is you at present."

Aesylt wanted to reassure him she wasn't insinuating what he seemed to think she was, but it was nice to feel wanted. To be someone's priority. Not since before the Nok Mora had anyone treated her with such warmth and concern as Rahn Tindahl. "Lord Dereham said the skies might clear tonight. I know I could clear them myself in the celestial realm, but I don't... have the heart to go there right now. Can we make it an astronomy night?"

He brightened. "I'll pull the charts out and get the ink ready."

"Looking forward to it." She grinned to mask the pain she was desperate to be rid of. "Actually, I do want something else. But without starwalking, we cannot... There are things we shouldn't do if we're not there." She twisted out an awkward chuckle. "I really don't know what I'm suggesting or asking. For you to come up with a way around the rule? To surprise me, I suppose?"

"Surprise?" The confusion in his face was adorable. "What sort of surprise?"

"Do you not know how surprises work?"

One of his hands traveled to his chin. "You want to experiment in *our* world but not in a way that compromises the work or the promise we made when we started?"

Aesylt nodded, exhaustion creeping in. "That makes more sense than the way I said it."

Rahn placed a hand on her back and guided her into the small garden. "I have been casually making a list of activities we might add to our list. Thinking, of course, that if we submit additional work, it would be well received and lead to other opportunities for us. The cohort, that is. Some of these ideas might fit what you're... proposing."

"Uh-huh." Aesylt narrowed her eyes impishly. "So you've been looking for more ways for us to play, in the name of science?"

"To *study.*" Rahn shook his head, but his lips hid a smile. "You seem better today."

I've gotten very good at convincing others of this very thing. "So, a distraction?"

"And you want to be surprised?"

"Yes."

"But how will that work? I'd never do anything without your consent."

"I'm giving it to you now." Aesylt shrugged. "Whatever you come up with, I'm fine with it. I trust you."

Rahn shook his head emphatically. "No. Your permission is not an open-ended arrangement, Aesylt, not now, not ever." He leaned his head back to look up at the tower, his eyes moving in thought. "I might have an idea of something that could be done here, in our world, and I could wait until the last minute to share the plan, to leave you in *some* sort of suspense..."

Aesylt brightened with hope. "Sounds promising."

"I'd dismissed it as outside the scope of our work, but it would fall within the rules—mostly. The important ones anyway."

A yawn bubbled up from her throat, but she swallowed it down. She *was* tired, but sleeping meant dreaming, and she couldn't trust her dreams anymore. Closing her eyes for a spell, however... "I'll take a brief nap while you figure this out. And then I still want that astronomy night, Scholar."

She could see the ideas churning behind his eyes. His deliberations came to a halt when he lifted his gaze to hers. "Aesylt, *are* you all right?"

"Sorry?"

"I know you left things out that, for whatever reason, you didn't want Lord Dereham and his son to know. If it were me, I'd keep my truths close as well."

Aesylt stiffened but made no denials. Weeks ago, she might have, but before her stood a man who knew her as she wanted to be known. Wounding the bond with a lie would have been unconscionable.

"I'm *here* is all I wanted to say." He traced his palms down her fur-covered shoulders. "Not just to ply you with distractions to steer your mind away from the dark places either."

Oh, the ache this sent to her chest. He was offering friendship, but her heart was stubbornly confusing it for the deeper companionship she'd craved her whole life. She forged a smile. "Thank you, Scholar. I know."

Rahn nodded, reading her with a light squint. "And this surprise, it's what will clear the clouds for you?"

Aesylt sucked in her bottom lip and nodded.

"Then you need a nap and I need to plan, so let's get climbing."

Rahn never actually intended to tell Aesylt about his discovery. He'd found the idea on a dog-eared page of the erotic plant manifesto Pieter had left for them, and on a walk through the Wintergarden the prior week, Rahn had tested it.

On his hand first. He'd experienced the exact sensations described in the book: an intermittent but intense tingling to the applied area.

His conscience wouldn't allow him to test anything on Aesylt that he hadn't first tried on himself, so he'd smeared some of the concoction—mint leaves and nettle made up most of the paste, but there were three indigenous plants, with names he could barely pronounce, responsible for the effect—on the tip of his cock just before bed the night before the hunt. The suggested science behind the inconsistency of the effect had to do with the way their minds managed information and signals to the body. As the sensation was foreign, the body sought to identify and subdue it. The writer of the book seemed to believe the time between reactions was the time it took for the body to return to normal. Over time, the author believed, the reactions would come more frequently, until the mind eventually came to recognize them not as a foreign invader but as a welcome and pleasurable experience.

Apprehension rarely had a place in his research, but he'd been a bundle of nerves waiting for the balm to activate before his test. He hadn't waited long. Every minute, roughly, a delicious bolt of pleasure surged through him. It would pass just as quickly, but each subsequent wave, each arriving faster and faster, drove him further out of his skin, and before long, he'd come without even touching himself.

All this he explained to a blank-faced Aesylt as he sat on the edge of her bed, holding a bowl.

"So you want to watch me writhe in pleasure until I go mad," she said with a bland grin. Her eyes sparkled with mischief. "So you can listen from your bed and touch yourself without breaking any rules about what's allowed in this world?"

Rahn hung his head in mock shame. "Alas, my plan unravels."

She sat up straight, pulling the blankets around her waist. "I don't think that will work for me, Scholar. I'm sorry."

Rahn was more relieved than anything. It was an absurd idea, and there was simply no way of knowing what the long-term effects might be, nor whether she might be allergic to any of the ingredients, a fact which would be unpleasant to discover after the fact, though he would have tested it first on her hand—

"Scholar? You still with me?"

He snapped his gaze to hers. "I have other ideas for suitable distractions, not to worry." He withdrew the bowl, but she snaked her hand out and pulled it back.

"You misunderstand me." She dipped one finger in the mix, regarded it with a squint, and then spread it over the top of her hand. He watched her in perplexed, breathless anticipation. "Ahh!" she squealed, her eyes widening in delighted surprise as she turned them his way. "I knew something was coming, but it was still so unexpected. Every minute, you say?"

"From what I gathered from reading, one's physiology affects how the body responds, and how frequently. For some, the stimulations have only seconds between. For others, minutes. For me, it was between fifty-four and sixty-nine seconds."

Aesylt grinned. "You timed your self-pleasure?"

Rahn balked. "Are we not scientists, Aesylt?"

She laughed and yelped again. "I should have been timing it."

"Forty-seven."

"You were counting? Of course you were counting." She rolled her eyes, tilting the bowl in her hands. "How many nights have we listened to each other pleasure ourselves?"

Heat flooded his cheeks. "Plenty."

"There's a suggestion in the ballroom section of the curricula that proposes—in the addendum, where they go into more detail on the hypotheses and expected outcomes for each test—that scenarios in which the researchers engage, in *public* fornication, may produce such a unique series of stimuli that it cannot be replaced or replicated with any other activity. The thrill of being caught in the act engages a part of our brain akin to committing a heinous crime or attempting to escape mortal danger."

Rahn had read that part as well, but he wasn't following her point. "Fornicating in front of the Derehams is out of the question."

"I wasn't suggesting we rut like wild animals on the table, though that *would* be something," Aesylt replied. She twisted her mouth back and forth, staring at the bowl. "We have just enough time to get dressed and make our way to the keep before supper is served."

He began to see where she was taking him. "No... no. The effects could last an hour or more. We cannot know how you'll respond."

Aesylt dipped a finger into the bowl and lifted her skirt with the other hand. Rahn's breath faltered as he watched her work the paste between her legs, her eyes turning upward before she extracted her hand. "There we are. This should solve two problems for me."

Rahn tried to swallow before speaking, but his mouth and his throat were dry as a desert. He opened his mouth, but nothing came out. She actually intended to sit at a table full of Derehams—not to mention a hawk-eyed Imryll—while... overstimulated.

In none of his considerations had he accounted for *that*.

A cloudy look passed over her eyes. "I don't want to talk about it again, beyond what I'm about to say. Yesterday I lost control, in a way that has not happened to me in many years. I'd like to prove to myself it was a chance slip and not a sign of a bigger problem. If I can will myself into compliance while my body is actively working against me, then I'll know I'm not..." He heard the start of the word *broken,* but she cut herself off and smiled instead. "Oh, I really need to get used to this *before* I ask someone to pass the bread."

Rahn cleared his throat. She was serious. She was actually going to do it, because she felt she had something to prove to herself, and even if it wasn't too late, even if she hadn't already spread the paste, he could see the single-minded determination burning in her eyes. "I think it may be best to have our meal sent up tonight," he said, one last attempt.

She grinned. "Have some faith in me, Scholar. You know I've never met a challenge I wasn't ready to destroy."

They were late for supper on account of Aesylt's struggles. Several times she'd stopped along the way, but by the time they reached the keep, she was feeling considerably better about her ability to normalize her body's reactions.

Everyone else was already seated when they took their places at the table. Aesylt missed a step when a tingle hit her, but only Nyssa seemed to notice, with a slight narrowing of her eyes.

"We were discussing my invocation," Nyssa said testily, a saccharine smile plastered across her face. "You remember, Aesylt, my coming-out ball?"

"Your soiree, you mean?" Pieter asked, mocking her between slurps of his soup.

"I said what I meant, brother."

"And unless Mother has radically expanded the guest list, you're still wrong."

"Not my fault we had to change all our plans at the last minute."

"Or maybe no one *cares* like you do?"

Nyssa stuck out her tongue, glaring.

"Oh, yes, the coming out," Aesylt muttered as she carefully settled between Imryll and Rahn. Her sister-in-law's gaze lingered upon her for an extra moment. "Soon, isn't it?"

She squeezed her legs tight when a fresh tingle lit her up. Rahn cleared his throat and made a show of folding his napkin.

And so it begins.

"Not to worry, cub. Everyone in attendance will be searched thoroughly before entering the keep," Rustan said and slurped from his bowl. "We've cut the list down considerably, just to those closest to us."

"You haven't forgotten our fitting is tomorrow." Nyssa's spoon hovered midair, matching the offense in her expression.

Aesylt had absolutely forgotten. "I'll be there." She winced in delicious agony.

"Is something the matter, dear?" Lady Dereham asked without looking up. "You seem restless. Is it the nasty hunting business my husband won't stop talking about?"

"Felice." Rustan grumbled. He glanced at Aesylt. "Were you able to rest?"

"Yes, I am much more rested now, my lord. I appreciate everyone's patience with me as I—" She bowled forward from the latest bolt of pleasure. Imryll touched her leg, and Aesylt jumped in her seat.

"Aes?" Imryll's tone was all concern.

Rahn made a small but guttural sound and plastered on a polite smile. "We see no point in lingering on what happened now that she's better." He seemed to be doing his best not to look her way. "What is this, boar?" He waved his fork. "It's quite good."

"The very one your disciple took down." Rustan was looking directly at Aesylt, but so was everyone else. All except Rahn.

She squeezed her legs tighter, but the result had her nearly scaling out of her chair from the force of the building pleasure. But she could not—*not*—let it go that far at the table. The whole reason she'd done it was to prove she *hadn't* lost her self-control.

"Your face is as red as an apple, Aesylt," Nyssa declared. "Are you coming down with something?"

Aesylt shook her head, biting down so hard on her tongue, she drew blood. In their weeks of experimentation, she still hadn't learned to temper her fulfillment, to draw it out. Even when Rahn had insisted on a delayed gratification exercise, her body had had other ideas. "Fine," she squeaked.

"You are not fine," Imryll whispered from the side of her mouth. She passed a hand over Aesylt's leg, transferring calm to her.

Aesylt breathed deep in relief. It wouldn't last. "I just woke from a deep rest. Forgive my rudeness, my lord, my lady."

"Think nothing of it," Felice said. "We're only worried about you. The tales of yesterday have already grown quite tall, enough that it's hard to know *what* the truth is."

Aesylt caught Pieter wearing an oversized, knowing grin, which unsettled her. She quickly looked away, catching Nyssa's suspicious stare as she returned her attention to Lord and Lady Dereham.

"Mother, I don't just *want* loads of lace; I *need* loads of lace. At least twice as much as any other woman in attendance," Nyssa said with a pointed glance at Aesylt. "Please tell me you invited the laceworker and not just the velveteer?"

"You'll outshine every woman in the Great Hall, regardless of whether you're wearing lace or a flour sack." Felice sipped her wine, watching Aesylt battle another wave. "It would not hurt, Aesylt dear, for you to see our healer. Just to be certain."

"I appreciate the offer, my lady, but Imryll already helped. I promise I'm fine."

The next jolt sent her straight out of her chair, with an awkward gulp full of regret and shame. How had she not seen how terrible an idea it had been? No amount of control could outsmart her own biology.

Rahn focused his fractured breaths through his nose. Everyone else watched in bewilderment.

"You do not seem fine, dear," Felice remarked. "At all."

"She seems perfectly fine to me, Mother," Pieter said, with the same smarmy grin.

Rahn's hand subtly brushed the outside edge of Aesylt's leg through her dress, grounding her momentarily.

"I might need more sleep after all," Aesylt said, praying her explanation covered both past and future behavior.

"Perhaps you should come stay with me again this evening," Imryll said, her tone suspicious.

Even the idea of storing her pent-up release until morning rattled her. "I..." She swallowed hard, fighting a wince as the pressure continued to build. "Sincerely appreciate your concern." She made herself glance around the table while she was still coherent, to show them what her words were insisting. "All of you. But I swear, I'm fine."

"We'll add more guards to the courtyard, at the very least," Rustan said before stuffing his mouth full of meat.

"Why?" Aesylt asked, looking around. "We have more than enough."

Imryll sighed with a hard look at Rustan, who had, apparently, said more than he should have. "A scout came today while you were resting. One of Lord Dereham's. Marek has *potentially* been spotted in the forests just north of Wulfsgate. I say potentially because there's no way to verify the veracity of the claim, and when there's a significant bounty on a man's head, he's liable to be seen just about everywhere."

Rahn leaned forward until he could see Imryll. "Please tell me there are men in these forests searching for him."

"There are always men in the forests. It's how we received word of the sighting," Rustan said evenly. "But it's easier to get lost in them than it is to be found."

Rahn bristled, straightening, just as Aesylt twisted again. "You don't seem concerned."

"Forests... roads... doesn't matter." Rustan downed his ale. "He'll never breach our walls."

"Your confidence is inspiring, my lord," Rahn said drily. He flicked a sidelong glance at Aesylt. The veins in his neck looked ready to snap. "But what if you're wrong?"

Aesylt had to get out of there. Between the absolute agony between her legs and the terrible revelation about Marek, she'd lost any hope of control.

"Aes, how I wish I could read your thoughts," Nyssa mused.

"I did say she was acting oddly," Felice replied. To Aesylt, she said, "Dear, you've gone from flushed to peaked."

"I promise, I'm fine." Aesylt gripped the chair with both hands, but it was no good. The end was coming, and there'd be no hiding it if it happened at the table. She was going to be rude or become a scandal, and while she didn't much care what people said or thought of her, they'd tie it all back to the scholar, and he'd be ruined.

"I'm not," Rustan answered with a belch. He regarded his empty plate with an almost-forlorn look.

"Not *what* dear?" Felice asked, exasperated.

"Wrong." Rustan wiped his face on his sleeve and stood. "The traitor in our forest is only a minor problem on my list. We have a border skirmish down near Salthill, and my men are awaiting direction. I bid you all a good evening," he said and marched out.

Felice sighed and shook her head, returning to her meal.

"Aesylt, I was hoping we might speak after... this?" Pieter's bemused words trailed Aesylt as she shoved back from the table and fled.

Rahn thought he'd lost her until he spotted her entering the Wintergarden between two bowing oaks. He checked to make sure no one had followed, and he followed her inside.

She was on her knees in front of a cherry tree. Rahn approached slowly, but she whipped her head up and leaped to her feet. "Help me end this." She moaned.

Rahn bowed down and lifted her face with his hands. He kissed her until she'd calmed some. "It only lasts about an hour, so it's almost over." He wanted to feel bad; he *should* have felt bad. But gods, if the sight of her becoming a puddle of desire for him was wrong, he'd forsake the righteous path forever. "Say the words, Squish."

Aesylt, scrunching her face in agony, did as he asked.

Rahn lifted and pinned her to the tree before the world had even settled. One hand cupped her ass to hold her aloft while the other ripped her dress up and around her waist. Her legs folded around him, squeezing as she electrified him with feverish kisses.

His buckle snapped and cracked the back of his hand in his rush to free himself. He flinched but didn't slow until his trousers were pooled at his ankles and his cock was buried inside her.

"Ahh," Aesylt cried, her head lolling sideways against the smooth bark as he thrusted. She slipped her hand between her legs, but he pushed it away, replacing it with his.

Rahn squeezed her ass as he plunged deeper, tracing the faintest passes along her very swollen bud.

"Please," she moaned, bucking her hips. "Don't tease me. I can't..."

"I'm not teasing you, Aesylt," he said, low and warm against her ear. "I just need you to feel my release deep within you as yours rips through you."

"Rahn." She panted, and his knees buckled at the sound of his name on her tongue, clouded with the torturous delirium he'd caused. Her fingers dug into his ass, coaxing him to go faster, harder, but faster and harder were the only commands his body would abide.

"Do you see me fucking you on the table while they all watch?" Rahn asserted, despite the cold sweat rolling down his cheeks. No matter how hard he pushed, it wasn't enough. It wouldn't be enough until he'd consumed her entirely. "Me filling you as they all stare, horrified?"

"As they watch me come for you." She sucked in her lower lip.

"Until there's nothing left of you." His eyes rolled back. "Until they all know who you belong to. Who you answer to." He slammed her against the tree. "Though it might be hard for you to tell them anything with my cock stuffed down your throat."

"And if I disobey?" Her mouth parted with every thrust.

"You know what will happen." He angled her hips to drive himself deeper. "But you like being disobedient. You like to be punished."

"Almost as much as you like to punish me," she cried. "Make it hurt."

When he was close, he increased the firmness of his hand between her legs. She lifted, contracting, her mouth peeled open in a silent cry. She was all tremors, head to toe, clenching around his cock, her whimpers buried in his neck as she rode out her well-earned release, freeing him from his own torment as his body joined hers.

Rahn froze when a terrible revelation came over him. He verified it with a glance at the sky and another all around him, finding the muted colors of their own world.

Aesylt slid down the tree with a shaky exhale and gently twisted out of his grasp. Her flushed face peered back at him over her shoulder as she smoothed her dress, but the look on his had her asking, "What?"

"How..." His pulse rocketed as he quickly shimmied his trousers back into place. He and Aesylt were so close to the entrance to the garden—close enough anyone walking by could have seen. He was afraid to turn toward the arch of oaks. "How are we in our world, Aesylt? How long have we been back?"

"What do you mean?" Her mouth remained open, her eyes widening as she came to the same understanding. "I... I don't *know* how. You heard me say the words to get us there, but I never commanded our return, I didn't—" Her hands flew to her mouth. Her attention was on the entrance.

Rahn spun around in time to see the edge of a cloak disappear. His heart plummeted toward the cold ground. He didn't know how or when he and Aesylt had slipped back into their own world, but it didn't matter. They'd grown careless, ignoring their own rules. "Who, Aesylt? Who was it?"

When Aesylt finally responded, her voice trembled. "Pieter."

True to his word, Lord Dereham added more security. Aesylt worried it would draw more suspicion to the half-forgotten tower, but there were more at the gates as well, as well as spread throughout the keep and village.

Aesylt and Rahn hadn't spoken about the incident with Pieter, but that didn't mean it had left her mind. His haunted look suggested it hadn't left his either.

They worked on their notes that night together in silence, him at his desk, she at hers. Her thoughts drifted to several nights earlier, when they'd done their notes in the celestial realm, her in his lap, him buried deep inside of her. *If you move, I'll punish you,* he'd warned, and so of course she'd moved as much as possible. The way he'd tackled her to the floor, pinning her hands above her head, commands burning his tongue...

But he hadn't so much as kissed her since the Wintergarden. The dark thoughts in her head threatened to take over, but he was worried, same as her. That was all.

I've never felt more exposed. More alive. More afraid, she wrote. She tapped her quill, considering the answer to her unformed question. *Would I do it again? Yes, in a heartbeat. But I fear*—Aesylt stopped short of writing anything about Pieter. They were supposed to be Elara and Niklaus. *I fear being caught, and the resulting fallout. Though what I feel most of all is that it wasn't enough. What if nothing is?*

That was all she had the heart for, so she unlocked her drawer, slid the vellum inside, and locked it again. She stood with a long stretch and murmured a good night to Rahn, who was lost to his own journaling.

After she'd changed into her nightgown, she climbed into bed. Pieter discovering their secret was an enormous problem that couldn't wait, but all she'd been able to think about was Marek's thick hands at her neck, throttling her life away. If he *was* in the forest north of Wulfsgate, it was because he knew she was there. No matter why he'd come, if he succeeded, only death awaited her.

Between the Marek and Pieter situations, her sanity was being torn down the center.

A shadow appeared behind her curtain, and Rahn stepped around it. He sat on the side of her bed and nudged her over.

"What are you doing?" she asked as he climbed in beside her.

"I know you're thinking about the man in the forest," Rahn said. "So am I." He brushed stray hair out of her eyes. "Sleep, Squish. Or try to. I'll be right here."

TWENTY
CAREFUL, YOUR DESIRE IS SHOWING

Pieter had waited for her in the tower garden.

She'd slipped out ahead of Rahn for her fitting with the Dereham seamstress. Nyssa had been building her own gown for months, and all that was left was to stitch even more lace into the design. Aesylt had no idea what Nyssa had picked out for her, and she was about as eager to discover that as she was to attend the soiree at all.

Socializing was the last thing she felt like doing.

No, she thought, watching Pieter's breath cloud in the cold air, his eyes regarding her like a hawk sizing up prey. *This is.*

Aesylt tried to push past him, but he sidestepped, blocking her.

"Aesylt, please. I'm the last person you'd get judgment from."

"I'm going to be late." Her jaw clenched harder with each word. Pieter had worn many hats since Aesylt and Rahn had arrived. Old friend. Spy. Co-conspirator. Rahn had been right; she shouldn't have been so quick to let him back in, even if she had been cautious. He was as shifty as a snake.

"The scholar is a catch. I can't say I blame you," he said, moving to let her pass. Unsurprisingly, he followed. "If you're worried I'll tell my father or the stewardess—"

Aesylt spun on him, full of fire. "I know you won't, because I'd kill you in your sleep."

Pieter's eyes widened, his hands moving up and out in submission. "I followed you yesterday because you were acting so strangely at evening meal. I wasn't trying to collect damning information on you."

"You don't even know what you saw," Aesylt countered, lifting her chin. "And I don't owe you an explanation. I'm going to walk away, and you're not going to follow me. If you do, I'll know your intentions were not the wholesome ones you're trying to sell me now."

"I won't follow you," Pieter said slowly. "And I'll keep your secret. But it didn't take a diviner, or me stumbling upon the two of you, to know what's been going on in the tower."

He stepped aside, and Aesylt marched past without responding.

By the time she reached the sitting room, Nyssa was already being poked and prodded by a handful of young women. Her emerald gown had so many layers, she took up the width of four grown men. The cost of the amount of velvet it had taken to produce such a dress would have fed a Vjestik family for a year. The lace only made the entire ensemble more garish.

"Was wondering when you might decide to join us," Nyssa said, smiling at herself in the long mirror.

"Apologies," Aesylt muttered as she threw her furs over the back of a chair. "I'm here now."

"Well I know you're not particularly fond of dressing up, so I've taken the liberty of finding you a more... subtle piece." Nyssa shooed the women away and waved an arm at a tall armoire in the corner. "Fetch it already, one of you. Guardians."

One of the young women scurried to the armoire and returned with a dark-brown frock that had almost no detailing whatsoever. Instead of broad, sweeping skirts like Nyssa's dress, the piece was slim fitting, like the way a nightgown wrapped around a woman's curves, but it was at least twice as thick. The neckline was so high and tight, she could already feel herself suffocate in it.

"Nyssa, did you steal this from one of the old monasteries?" Aesylt asked with a short laugh.

"I might have come up with something more appealing, had you told us you were coming months ago," Nyssa said with a dainty shrug. "But you're taller than me, and my other gowns are simply hemmed too high for you. It's not as if we'll be dancing in *streams*, for Guardians' sake. This one will suffice."

"You said this was yours? *Where* would you even have worn such a thing?" Aesylt fingered the ungainly fabric.

"I wore it on a diplomatic trip to Darkwood Run. The Arranden women are less, well, showy, and Mother thought a more modest cut would be the respectful way to go. And it was springtide, so perfectly in season. We didn't have time to get it to the seamstress, so I just had to carry my hem around all afternoon."

Aesylt laughed and shook her head. "Modest is really underselling this smock, Nyssa."

Nyssa grinned from her reflection. "It's not the dress, Aesylt. It's the woman within it."

Aesylt released the dress with a cordial nod at the seamstress maiden holding it. "I'll find something in my own trunks."

Nyssa flipped around so fast, she teetered, and the women had to scramble to keep her from toppling off the chair. "You will *not,* Aesylt Wynter. The Vjestik simply have no sense of... No. Your gowns are drab and lacking life. If you want to traipse about your lord's halls in them, I can't stop you. But you're not wearing anything of your own to *my* ball. I won't have it."

"Nyssa, nothing I own comes close to as drab and life-lacking as this."

"You're being difficult. This evening isn't about you, and I'm not asking for much."

Aesylt sighed. "I'll be happy to spend the evening in the tower, working on my notes. Honestly, I've never been one for celebrations, and I'd only pull the mood down."

"You should thank me, Aesylt. If you're wearing *this,* your darling man of science won't be so likely to make a fool of himself in front of others." She flitted her wrist with a disgusted look. "You know, you're twenty... and cavorting with a man old enough to be your... much older brother. If you don't secure a betrothal soon, one will not come."

Aesylt snorted. "And would the reason you're helping me have anything to do with the way you've been eyeing him for yourself since we arrived?"

"A duke would please my father. There's only a handful in this entire kingdom, and most are married already." Nyssa twirled side to side on the chair, admiring herself. "But as he is no longer in favor with the queen consort, it would create a political nightmare for us that even I can appreciate."

"Rahn isn't out of favor with Queen Adamina." She started toward Nyssa and the chair, growing even hotter than she'd been after her encounter with Pieter. "He left because he wanted to."

"Rahn? Careful, Aesylt. Your desire is showing." Nyssa huffed and slowly toddled around so she was facing Aesylt. "We were once friends. I *am* trying to help you, whether you believe me or not."

"We were," Aesylt agreed. "And then I arrived to find my once friend acting cold and strange toward me, for reasons she never bothered to explain."

Nyssa dodged the accusation. "Or you *could* wear something colorful and flattering and then word would reach your brother of what a perfect match you are. He'll have no choice but to allow it."

"You don't remember Drazhan very well if you think that would do anything but incite his anger."

"Who could forget the way he trained like a gladiator for years so he could kill two kings and steal a bride?"

"You know that is *not* what happened in Duncarrow, Nyssa."

Nyssa held out her hands, indicating the women should help her down. She waddled toward Aesylt. "No, he failed to kill them, didn't he? Fate intervened and finished it for him. But he walked away with King Torian's prize. And for that, if nothing else, he should understand the heart makes its own choices." She brushed a hand atop Aesylt's shoulder, making her flinch. "He abandoned you and followed his own whims, and now he gets to decide what life *you* lead. It's not right, and you know it isn't."

Aesylt backed away. Nyssa was wrong about Drazhan. It was easy for outsiders to look back and see an heir abandoning his duties, but they hadn't been there to witness the guilt that hung heavy in every haunted look he wore, every tortured step he took. He'd stalked the halls for months, aimless and wound with fury, until it had come to a boil. *I love you, Aes, but I can't lead our people with such a crime unanswered for. I've tried and tried and tried, and I cannot even see, even breathe, without imagining my hands about the coward king's neck.*

You're leaving us?

Volemthe, sostra had come his answer, and he'd crushed her against him with a hug that felt far more like good-bye than his words had. *But the Cross will not recover until vengeance has been had.*

The Cross is already recovering. We've been rebuilding for months! You're their steward, Draz. Do you not want to be part of it?

One day, Aes, they will awaken from this renewed sense of purpose and recall how the usurper king took everything from them. I leave the Cross with you and Fezzan and Brita, and I know you can manage the task. When I return, it will be with an answer for the blood and ash. Only then can we move on.

Her vision wavered as her painful memories returned to the past. "You know nothing about what happened to us in the Cross. Not a damn thing."

Nyssa visibly softened. "I know you were the true leader of Witchwood Cross for almost a decade. You were *eight* when he left, Aesylt. A child! A child who had witnessed horrific, terrible things no one should ever have to see and then led her people because retribution was more important to her brother than the family he had left." Her arrogance returned with a toss of her head. "Of *course* I'm sweet on your scholar. He's devilishly handsome, sensitive, intelligent... and he looks at *you* the way every woman wants a man to look at her. And I will dance with him and laugh with him and flirt with him, and perhaps it will pique your jealousy, as it did in the garden, but it will not be Nyssa Dereham he's wishing was in his arms. I'll pretend it is..." She laughed. "And everyone there will wonder if my father is readying an announcement about me and the mysterious duke. But I'll know. And if you're honest with yourself, so will you." A broad smile returned to her face. "You'll wear the dress, because if you don't, you'll cause a scene when the man follows your every move, and I won't have it. But we both know that when the two of you disappear into your little tower bedroom, it won't matter."

Aesylt closed her eyes, bracing for strength. She sighed and started toward the chair in front of the second mirror when Nyssa brightened suddenly.

"I almost forgot! The stewardess brought by a letter for you. The scout delivered it."

"A letter?" Aesylt turned in confusion. "From whom? Drazhan?"

"Niklaus." Nyssa pranced to a table and rifled through a stack of papers. "He signed it Nikky, but Imryll said Niklaus." She shrugged.

"How would you know how he signs his letters unless you read it?" Aesylt demanded, but she was already thinking about what the letter might say—and why Drazhan had even allowed it to be sent with the scout. The only letters Drazhan had been approving were the private ones he sent to Imryll.

"All correspondence that comes into our halls is read." She handed the letter over and waited with impatient blinks. "Well, aren't you going to look at it?"

"You already know what it says." Aesylt refolded the letter and squeezed it in her fist. "And you have nothing in response to what I said about how you've been treating me?"

Nyssa tugged at her curls. "Maybe I've just grown up, and you're not used to how I am now. Or... Perhaps you're imagining a problem that doesn't exist."

"If you say so." Aesylt shoved the letter into her gown and made the submissive trek to the chair. "Let's get this over with then."

Rahn had intended to spend the day in the Wulfsgate library while Aesylt was busy surviving her poking and prodding with Nyssa, but he'd just cracked open a tome about the effect of coastal patterns on mountain flooding when Rustan Dereham walked in and shut both doors behind him, then bolted them.

His heart plummeted, wondering if Pieter *had* told his father what he'd seen. But Rustan smiled civilly and nodded at a tray that Rahn hadn't noticed earlier. Two mugs and a pitcher of ale sat atop it, along with a basket of bread and cheese.

"What's all this?" Rahn closed the book but held onto it.

"I thought you and I might have a palaver," Rustan said. He was watching Rahn as he lifted the tray and carried it to a cozy sitting area. He set it upon the table and poured both mugs. "Aye?"

Rahn tapped the book in his hands, sighed inward, and set it on the bench so he wouldn't forget it later. Rustan handed him an ale before he'd even fully sat. "Thank you, my lord," he said, mug raised.

"Don't thank me just yet, Tindahl. I'm only plying you with ale and bread because I need something from you."

Rahn's brows perked. "Oh?"

"Information."

"I'm not sure I can be much help, but I'm happy to try."

"You have the trust and ear of Steward Wynter." Rustan drew a sip. Foam lingered on his red beard.

"Not half of what I imagine he has for his own lord."

Rustan swatted the air. He snatched a chunk of bread from the basket and offered one to Rahn, who politely refused. "This isn't the Easterlands, Tindahl. I'm not a lord who commands what should be given freely, and this is a rather delicate matter. I don't believe it would suit anyone for me to turn it into a mandate."

Rahn gripped the mug in his hand with budding apprehension. "I'll admit, you have my curiosity. And a touch of my concern as to where this is heading."

"My wife would say I'm not much for suspense, so we'll get on with it." He tossed his bread back in the basket untouched. "I've been giving some thought to the matter of our Aesylt's lack of prospects. Lack of prospects isn't the problem though, is it? It's her brother turning away perfectly acceptable suitors."

"I can't offer much perspective there, I'm afraid," Rahn said carefully. He had a hunch where the conversation was headed but hoped he was wrong. It was odd enough that Dereham was involving himself in the civil matters of one of his stewards. "Drazhan has his own reasons for everything. Ones he does not see fit to share, many times."

"But he is not seriously entertaining any offers?"

Rahn shook his head. "Not that I'm aware of. Imryll may know more."

"So he has not sent you along to Wulfsgate as a test of sorts? A worthiness challenge?"

"Sorry?"

"He's not evaluating you for the role of her husband and protector?"

Rahn's breath caught in the middle of an uncomfortable laugh. "No... no. That is not... on the table."

Rustan rapped his knuckles on the chair's arms. "He could do no better than a duke for her. Perhaps it's your age, which is shortsighted, considering the years between him and the stewardess. Good for me but not for thee." He frowned in thought, and Rahn's uneasiness sank deeper. "If you're certain it would not impede on any plans you have with Aesylt, then I'll aim to move forward with proposing a match between her and Pieter."

Rahn sputtered his ale back into the cup and frantically wiped his mouth before shoving the mug rudely onto the table.

"You all right, Tindahl?"

"Went down wrong," Rahn screeched. He should have seen it coming. He *had* seen it coming, long before the gentle library ambush, and had convinced himself he had been reading more into things than was there. As Rustan no doubt saw things, Aesylt needed a husband, and Rustan needed a more malleable—and settled—son.

Rustan waited for him to stop coughing. "Pieter has not always been a source of pride for us, but he's home now, and I believe with the right match, he'll be ready to take his place at my side. He's taken an interest in Aesylt—purely academic, as I understand, but most matches begin with less, wouldn't you say?"

"Mm." Rahn nodded to hold back his distaste.

"If Wynter refuses *this* match, the best anyone in the Cross has ever been offered, we'll know he has no intention of betrothing poor Aesylt, and at that point..." Rustan sighed. "Intervention on her behalf, by me, may be necessary. It is her right to marry. Her life should not be sidelined by an overprotective brother. As her liege lord, I won't allow her to suffer needlessly."

"I agree; it is her right," Rahn said, clawing at his neck like it would help the itch there. "But would it not be sensible to ask Aesylt what she thinks before moving forward with a formal proposal?"

Rustan snorted with a look that said, *huh*? "Why?"

"Should her own wishes have no part in this?"

"Our cub has already expressed her wishes, and they have been ignored and denied by Steward Wynter." Rustan's cheeks swelled red with the start of anger. "Pieter has been her friend since childhood. They're very fond of one another. Guardians, they even share interests. Pieter won't crush her excitement for learning, like many men would. What highborn woman is so fortunate?

My own daughter will probably not be half as lucky in the man we've chosen for her."

Impartially, Rustan wasn't wrong. Pieter would be a fine match for Aesylt, at least at the surface. But Rahn didn't trust him a whit, and he certainly didn't trust him to be honorable with Aesylt. He'd already shown he wasn't above violating her privacy. If he did keep their secret, it would be a matter of judiciousness, nothing more. When it served him, he'd weaponize it.

"Furthermore," Rustan said, "it would put to bed this foul matter of the Barynovs and their untenable claim on her. They might not fear a war with another Vjestik, but it would be self-annihilation to go up against the might of Wulfsgate."

Rahn could refute none of the man's points. There was nothing he could say that would not sound thin and weak. Nothing that wouldn't plainly reveal his own confusing feelings. He reached again for the ale to bury his expression.

"Good." Rustan slapped the arms of the chair and rocked to his feet. "You've confirmed for me there are no pending betrothals and that you are not a candidate, so I feel confident we can move forward with this. Your counsel is appreciated, Tindahl."

Rahn managed to wave when Rustan opened the doors to leave.

It was another hour before he moved from the chair.

Aesylt waited until she was curled in her bed before reading the letter. She wavered between excitement and dread. Nyssa had given no sign one way or another what to expect, just smug satisfaction.

The letter had gone soft after spending the day within her cleavage, but it unfolded easily enough, and the ink was unblurred. She considered waiting for Rahn but realized the contents would determine whether she told him about it at all. He still didn't know about the Barynov letter. No one did.

Except Pieter.

Aesylt closed her eyes, pulled a deep breath, and focused her eyes on Nik's familiar scrawl.

Dearest Aesylt,

I was surprised your brother agreed to let me send a letter. I still don't know where you are, but I know you must be safer than you would be here. I know he's reading every word, but nothing herein should be a surprise for him.

I spoke with Val. He asked for you first, then for me. He got half of what he wanted anyway. But his family wouldn't leave us alone, so there was no chance to ask all you and I both want to know. You'll be relieved to hear they finally allowed a vedhma to properly heal him. He's even been out and about in the village. Always with a full escort, of course.

By now you must know Marek is gone. The Barynovs claim ignorance to his whereabouts, but in my bones I feel they've been planning this from the start. A third of the village has turned on the Wynters, the other two-thirds ready to strike them down for going against their leader. Many believe this will all subside soon and everything will return to normal, but it won't. I'd stake my life on it. The Barynovs will not give up until they've won... or lost everything. Your brother will see Marek punished, or die trying.

Wherever you are, no matter how frustrated you must be, you are safe. Trust that your brother wouldn't keep you from your own home if it wasn't necessary. Marek is out there, looking for you. What he would do if he found you is beyond my imagining.

So much would have been different had you just married Valerian from the start. His family might still have been grasping for power, but Val would have aligned with the Wynters. I won't be surprised if your brother strikes that from the letter, but I had to say it. Our vedhmas always say the look back is so much more satisfying than the look forward, and coming from a family of history keepers, I have to agree.

I know you're frustrated. I can feel it from here, as though you are right beside me! But I write, of my accord and my love for you, to tell you that your brother is doing his best. He's trying to protect you from a terrible fate and to keep the village from full-on war. We've already lost too much.

Wherever you are, Aesylt, please don't do anything foolish. Stay safe.

My hope is that if you hear the words from me, you'll know they're worth heeding.

I hope to see you sooner than later, though I would rather never see you again if it put you in danger.

Volemthe,
Nikky

She read the letter a second time. Then a third. The line her eyes kept traveling back to was *so much would have been different had you just married Valerian from the start.* He had a point. The Barynovs may have settled for a seat at the table before, but now they wanted it all.

The door to the tower room opened.

"Squish? You in here?"

She balled the letter in her fist, searching for a suitable place to put it. Grunting, she leaned over the bed and slid it between the mattress and the wood frame.

"I can hear you."

She sat up in bed, straightening her hair and gown. "I was just about to nod off."

"Won't be far behind you there," Rahn said lightly. The sound of him shedding clothes made her long for a foray into the celestial realm, but her heart wasn't in it. She still didn't know how they'd transitioned back in the Wintergarden or why she'd winked there and back after the hunting incident.

"Eventful day for you then?" she called, watching his silhouette through the curtain.

"Not really. You?"

"No, not especially."

Rahn appeared in his night shirt with a tired grin. "Your cheeks are flushed."

"Are they?" Aesylt's hands flew to her face.

"A touch." He nodded for her to move over, and she realized he was joining her—again. Like it were the most natural thing in the world. "You get your dress all sorted for tomorrow?"

"It's more of a sack," Aesylt groused, making room for him. Her heart raced at his nearness, but it wasn't born of desire. What she most wanted was to collapse in his arms, her head on his heart, and drift off to the sound of his gentle breathing. "Did you find what you were looking for in the library?"

"No," he said as he rotated, facing her. "I hate to even ask, but has there been any further news on Marek?"

Aesylt shook her head. She prayed she'd stuck the letter far enough under the mattress.

He turned his hand over and ran the back of it against her forehead. "You really do seem warm. Feeling all right?"

She made herself smile. "Just tired, Scholar."

"How tired are you, Squish?"

Aesylt cocked her head.

"We never got our astronomy night." He tilted his head toward the ceiling. "And I seem to recall we have a talented little witch in this room capable of clearing clouds at will."

Her smile reappeared slowly. "You want to work, Scholar?"

"I pulled all our notes out the day you suggested it."

Aesylt sat up with a glance out the window, at the darkness beyond. Some healthy astronomy felt like exactly what she needed, even if she was hesitant about starwalking. She screwed her mouth into happy mischief. "Well, better go get them then."

Rahn sat on one side of the windowsill, Aesylt the other. They'd started their adventure bundled, but she'd not only cleared the obstructions; she'd also eased the cold. A light rain fell, another sign she couldn't control everything in the celestial realm, a reminder they really knew next to nothing about the place, no matter how often they escaped there.

Both of their notebooks were balanced on their knees as they independently counted the constellations they recognized, and recorded their brightness and clarity. They were limited without their telescope, but just sitting there with her, working on something healthy and innocuous, wrapped him in so much warmth. For all he looked forward to during their starwalking trysts, he'd missed the simplicity of just *being* with her—learning alongside her, volleying excitement between them as more and more of their research came to life.

"Ah, our friend the bowman. How I'd missed him," she said softly, her quill whistling on the vellum.

"I imagine he's even more elusive here, with all the smoke from the Wulfsgate commerce," Rahn replied.

"How fortuitous we're not bound to the real world's limitations." She squinted at the sky before making another note. "Everything happening in the Cross makes me so sad. And though it's nowhere near the top of our priorities, I'm mourning the observatory. It might never be finished now."

"All terrible things have a beginning and an end." He lifted his spectacles and let them fall to his chest. "The madness there won't last forever, and life will continue. Everything in our history points to these same cycles."

"If I'd just married Val..." Aesylt sighed with a pained look at the sky. "Oh, and there's the siren. You see her?"

Rahn pressed his notebook to his chest in alarm and leaned forward. "You're just going to drop that sensational suggestion and move on?"

"What? Oh... only thinking out loud. You can't deny I'm right though."

"Do you love him?" Rahn nearly choked on the words. "Is marrying him what *you* want?"

"No one seems to trouble themselves over what I want." Her quill made furious swirls.

"That was a crafty way around the answer."

Aesylt looked up but not at him. "Could I be his wife? Of course I could. He's my dearest friend, and I trust him with my life... with everything. Does he make my soul..." She shuddered inward. "Light with the stars and sky itself? Do I feel like I've finally come home when I'm in his arms?" Her head shook. "But not everyone can be Draz and Imryll, can they?"

Rahn grew solemn. He tilted his head back against the window frame and set aside his notebook. "You wear the burden of this civil war, but I will remind you that you've done nothing wrong. You love Val and tried to make his final moments as pleasant as possible. You then tried to help him when he came back and were..." He could hardly say it, even now. "Strangled by his brother for your kindness. You may be the focus of this conflict, but you are not the cause. If there was ever a wrong reason to marry anyone, it would be this. You would do both of you a great disservice."

"Perhaps the problem is me," she breathed. "For how could I not love a man as devoted as he is to me?"

"Love doesn't work in such terms."

"Have you ever been in love, Scholar?"

Rahn shook his head, though there was a shade of untruth he left withering in the unsaid.

"Then how can you know?" She crossed her notebook over her chest, fully invested in his answer.

"We are possessed of nothing more invaluable than our instincts," Rahn said, with a bracing look at the sky. She'd done a phenomenal job of clearing the clouds and haze. All their old friends danced and glittered against the darkness, lit only by the fading, distant auroras.

In its own way, it felt like coming home.

"Beautiful, isn't it?" she asked, following his gaze. "Even here, watching from a window that could crumble and fall out of its frame at any moment. We get to be a part of something so much bigger than us, and I never want to lose this feeling. Ever."

Rahn slid one foot across the frame until it was touching hers.

She glanced his way.

"Whatever else happens, Aesylt, no one can take that from you. From us."

"Then why..." She closed her eyes and shook her head. "Why does it feel like there's some force working against us, even now? No, I don't mean the Reliquary. It's something else. I can almost grab it, but I can't *see* it."

He didn't have the answer, but he understood the foreboding, because it had been creeping over him for weeks. At first he'd attributed the sensation to guilt or shame over their nocturnal adventures, but it was at its strongest when he was with the Derehams or alone. "I promise you, there is no force capable of extinguishing the spark within you. You don't need *anyone's* approval to take part in the unlimited curiosities of this world. You're Aesylt Wynter, as imitable as the stars in our interminable sky, and that's simply a fact as universal as the tides and the weather."

She leaned in. "You've said this to me more than once. And each time, I think I know exactly what it means, until the next time and then I'm lost again."

"It means," Rahn said, reaching for one of her hands and taking it into his, "that there is only one you, and you are incomparable. Never forget it. And let no one into your life who would try to persuade you otherwise."

"You see me. You always have," she whispered, her eyes traveling downward. "Hvala."

He brought her hand to his mouth with a gentle, enduring kiss, riding out the drumming patter of a heart that shouldn't be racing. "Thank *you*, Aesylt, for seeing *me*. Until you did, I hadn't realized how lonely it could be to blend in with the world."

Aesylt leaned down and kissed their joined hands. "I'm getting sleepy, so let's finish our charting another night."

Rahn nodded and gathered his things. "I'd feel better if you let me stay with you again tonight, under the circumstances."

She leaped onto the floor, grinning back at him. "You can stay with me whenever you want."

TWENTY-ONE
THE SORDID NETHERWORLD OF SEX CLUBS

Thank the Ancestors for Imryll, Aesylt thought as she and her sister-in-law stood, stone-faced, watching the Derehams and roughly forty of their carefully chosen subjects spin and twirl around the elaborately festooned parlor. Nyssa might be upset that her event had been downsized because of security concerns, but she was still the belle of the ball, fielding so many requests for dances, she had to turn half of them down.

"I'm rather jealous of Aleksy, sitting in the quiet nursery with his toys," Aesylt muttered, sipping her mulled wine, one arm crossed over the thick fabric of her dress. She'd had a few offers herself, despite being garbed like a sack of tubers, but she wasn't in the spirits for dancing.

"You're telling me." Imryll was drinking goat's milk, something Felice had suggested would help with fetal growth. Aesylt understood the benefits of a nutrient-rich milk for newborns, but she had a feeling Felice's suggestion was less rooted in science and more in old fishwife tales. "Nyssa is truly glowing tonight. It's admirable how she gives each suitor her full attention. She would have made a far better princess than I was."

Aesylt eyed the yards of gold garland strewn about the rafters, wound around pillars, and even lining the dark stone walls. Her dress was a close enough match that she'd been fantasizing about slinking against the wall and using it as camouflage until the night was over. "Surely Lord Dereham has already narrowed it down to one or two potentials."

"He's already decided on one, and a contract is in the works." Imryll shook her head. Her red curls bounced with her humor. "He can't be seen as weak by not throwing a fete for his own daughter, so this is the compromise."

"Nyssa isn't happy with me about this compromise."

"Nyssa is fortunate to have never known the fear and trauma you have. Pray she never does."

"Imryll, I know why..." Aesylt hesitated to speak of Imryll's birth father, the sorcerer Mortain who had been the architect of the Nok Mora. There was still so much Aesylt didn't know, and she had always been too nervous to ask. "I know Mortain is why Witchwood Cross was the example King Carrow made. I know he put my brother on the path of vengeance that led him to you. That sometimes fate is an individual, not a force of nature. I *know* all these things, but..." She paused to be sure her words hadn't gone too far.

"You're going to ask me if I think the Derehams colluded with the king to save themselves at our expense?" Imryll eyed her from the side. "No, I don't think so. Mortain sees long and far, and he had no qualms making an entire village suffer endlessly to get what he wanted. Lord Dereham only bent his knee for Carrow after he saw what the king was capable of, to spare not only Wulfsgate but the rest of the Northerlands from the same fate. I can't imagine how much it burned his heart to do so. There is no love for the crown in these lands."

"Maybe things will be better now that Carrow is gone and his grandson is being raised and counseled by a woman."

"You've not met Adamina." They both laughed. "She was devastated when King Torian was murdered, but her blind obedience died with him. She'll do her best by young King Farian, and we can only hope it's enough."

"Are you not afraid Mortain will come back?"

"He already has what he wants, Aesylt. His line continues, through me, through Aleksy. Whatever his true plan, it won't be realized in our lifetime. Time for an immortal means nothing." Imryll finished her milk with a sour look. "Ah, Rahn *is* here. He's speaking with Lord Dereham. I assumed you two would come together."

Aesylt followed where Imryll was looking. Rahn was watching back, and their gazes connected briefly before he returned to his conversation. "He's been acting strangely since yesterday. He denies it, but something is off."

"The two of you have really bonded here." Imryll's even delivery made it impossible to read her meaning.

"Our interests are highly compatible," Aesylt said carefully, stepping back when a handful of drunken men stumbled past, howling in laughter. "But the more time I spend with him, the more aware I am of how little I know of who he really is."

"How so?"

"He has never spoken of what happened to him as a boy on Duncarrow, not to me anyway."

"Not to anyone, as far as I know." Imryll smiled and curtsied at Felice as she strode past in her sweeping violet gown, followed by her attendants.

Aesylt absentmindedly did the same, more interested in Imryll's response.

"He lost everyone he knew and loved when he was only eight years old, and was forced to grow up very fast... like you did."

"But how can you really know someone if they keep such a big part of themselves hidden?"

Imryll turned to look directly at her. "Have you told him everything that happened to you the night of the Nok Mora?"

Aesylt felt the blood drain from her face. "Well..."

"Have you told *anyone*?"

Nik, Val, and the Castels each had pieces of that night, but no one had the complete picture. "What's done is done. Vjestik trust in our Ancestors to guide us. Only the kyschun see the need to look into the past."

"Then consider he may feel the same about what happened to him." Imryll squeezed Aesylt's arm. "I know you're cross about the gown, but you're beautiful no matter what you wear. You might ponder accepting at least *one* of the offers you've been rejecting. If you have to suffer through this, you may as well find some enjoyment."

"Don't feel much like dancing," Aesylt said, right as Rahn was pulled onto the dance floor by a giddy Nyssa. She watched them, glowering silently, until she felt Imryll's eyes on her. "What? You're not dancing either."

"The last man I danced with who was not my husband regretted asking." Imryll grinned, her eyes toward the side in remembrance. "I know your heart is heavy, and tonight feels like an unnecessary distraction from what matters. But when things are darkest is when we need the light the most. We need our strength to face our trials. And, ah, don't look now, but I believe Pieter is coming to ask you for a dance."

Aesylt dug deep for a whisper of patience and braced. She mustered a mannerly smile right as he walked up. "Pieter."

He gave an exaggerated low bow. "Stewardess. Lady Wynter."

Aesylt wrinkled her nose. She delicately searched for Rahn and Nyssa and straightaway regretted it when he didn't exactly look miserable. "Enjoying yourself tonight?"

"No more than you two." He swept his gaze over both women with a sly grin. "You haven't been with your scholar all evening."

"And?"

"Aesylt and I have been enjoying some sister time." Imryll looped her arm through Aesylt's with an affectionate tug. "We've hardly seen each other." She pecked a kiss on her cheek. "But I'm missing my son and think I'll retire early, if it isn't too impolite."

Aesylt squinted at her in alarm.

"Not at all," Pieter said. He reached for Imryll's hand and brought it to his mouth. "If no one else has told you this tonight, Stewardess, you are a vision. Your husband is a fortunate man."

"We both thank the fates for each other every night," Imryll said. She squeezed Aesylt's arm once more, ignoring her silent plea to stay. "Good night then."

When she was gone, Pieter turned toward Aesylt. "I believe you owe me a dance."

"I'd remember if I owed you anything. I never neglect a debt." Aesylt cocked her head. She forced her eyes to blur against the distance when her gaze landed on Rahn and Nyssa again, who were enjoying a *second* dance. *She's trying to turn heads. There's nothing more to it.*

"It's an expression, Aesylt." He held out his hand. "But if you prefer me to ask formally, then may I please have the pleasure of a dance with you?"

She didn't have the energy for a refusal, and as soon as she put herself in motion, hand in hand with the forsaken heir, the heaviness she'd been wearing all evening surprisingly lifted. Rahn's eyes twitched slightly when she passed with Pieter, and that, too, felt good, even though it was childish.

If nothing else, it would take her mind off her newest fear, fresh off a bout of sickness and a moon cycle that hadn't arrived. That the most logical explanation was impossible, given their careful use of the celestial realm, wasn't the comfort it should have been.

The music was a beautiful but mournful melody Aesylt recognized as an ode to the time before the Rhiagains, when the Derehams had still been kings. Of all the realm, only the north had ever had kings and queens.

She settled into formation with Pieter, who placed one hand against the middle of her back, the other still fixed to hers.

"I know what my sister was doing, having you wear this dress. But she underestimated just how well it would suit you. Others are noticing as well."

Aesylt rolled her eyes. "I have no need of their kind of notice."

"What kind are you interested in then?" Pieter asked as he guided them through the steps.

She was already exasperated. "One who judges on appearance is a fool. And it's hard to be happy about dancing and laughing and drinking when my village is struggling and my research is always one bad submission away from being pulled altogether."

"That..." Pieter leaned down so his mouth was beside her ear. "Is why I wanted to dance with you tonight. I have a confession to make."

Aesylt reared back. "I don't have the belly for another one of your games."

"It's been weighing on me, this dishonesty. The day in the garden... It wasn't..." His eyes briefly widened as he shifted his head back and forth. "My first exposure to what's been going on in the tower."

Aesylt's rebuttal disappeared with her shock. "You said you'd suspected."

"Hypotheses are founded in educated guesses, but I didn't need to guess." Pieter eased her back into a dancing position when others turned their attention their way. "I *knew* because your letter wasn't the only thing I read that day in the tower. Your scholar's notes weren't locked up, as they should have been."

The room gathered a hazy quality, a soft blur of light and sound that seemed to belong to another time.

"Aesylt, did you hear me?"

"I heard you." Her mind and heart raced faster than the music. He'd read Rahn's notes. He didn't just know they had been intimate; he knew why, which was far more dangerous. "What do you want, Pieter? Money?"

"Money?" He sounded genuinely affronted. "If I wanted money, I wouldn't have run from the most lucrative post in the Northerlands, would I?"

"What then?" She lowered her voice. "Sex?"

"You think I have trouble getting what I need?"

"You're so mysterious, how would I know?"

"Aesylt," he whispered. "I want to *help* you."

Sweat beaded under her hairline. "Oh, this again."

"Have I not helped you thus far? Despite that you've been lying to all of us about the fun with *astronomy* the two of you've been having?" He guided them farther from the other dancers. "I know the Reliquary leadership is testing you, to see how far you'll go. And you've risen to the challenge, haven't you? Valiantly." He snickered. "But you also know, at any moment, they could pull you from this project. This project *Imryll* envisioned, created, and championed."

She could hardly feel the hand he was holding anymore, and the other was tingling so violently, she had to drop it from his waist. Pieter had known, for weeks, and had been hoarding the information for the right time. "What *do* you want? You haven't stored this revelation for nothing."

"It's not what I want, Aesylt. It's what I can do for you. You've done everything the Reliquary has asked, but you need to do more if you want to hold onto this. And I know just the thing."

As they spun around, she saw Nyssa, but Rahn wasn't with her anymore. She searched for him, but she could hardly keep herself anchored to the conversation. She blinked when her vision doubled. The bonfires of the Nok Mora flickered behind her eyes.

"I know a thing or two about the men running the Reliquary myself," Pieter said, "and men like them will keep pushing and testing until you break. You have to be ahead of them if you want to win."

Aesylt heard him and even understood him, but she couldn't fight the sense she was drifting away from him, from the oppressive soiree... from the very keep itself. She responded to ground herself. "And what grand gesture did you have in mind?" The heat left her in a rush, substituted by chills that left her skin peppered in gooseflesh.

"There's a club in the village that meets when the moon is at its fullest. Most of us call it Revelry, but it has many other names as well, none of which matter." Pieter leaned in close once more. "It's very exclusive, invitation only, and I could secure two, for you and your scholar, with no trouble at all."

She desperately needed to wipe the sweat rolling down her temples. "Are you going to say what it is, or am I expected to guess?"

"Hedonists." He paused for her reaction, but she was too taken aback to offer one. "You can experiment all you want, collect all the experiences you can manage, and every last bit of it will win you the goodwill you deserve with the Reliquary."

Everything he was describing was vague enough that he could have been talking about a social club for people with similar interests, but that was obviously not what he was whispering about. She breathed deep. "Speak plainly, Pieter."

"It's an orgy, Aesylt."

Aesylt stopped dancing. She untangled herself from him in disbelief, dropping her voice into a hissing whisper. "You want to take me to an *orgy*?"

"Two nights from now, yes."

She squeezed her eyes closed to control the competing emotions and sensations. The sweat, the stench, the din of laughter, and the pitch of the music. Pieter's presence, close, constant, and waiting. An orgy. Multiple partners was on the battlefield level, but she and Rahn had dismissed it out of hand because there was no one they could trust enough to bring in. And the thought of her scholar touching another woman was unreasonably painful. But it was, of everything on the list, the most forbidden. The least expected. And Pieter was not wrong; the Reliquary would be astounded the cohort was willing to go so far.

How many ways did she imagine telling him to fuck off in those precious seconds? And why did none of them make it to her lips? "You attend these Revelries yourself?"

"I attended the last one here in Wulfsgate, and I've been to others across the realm. They're not unique, but they are uniquely private. Only an existing member can invite new initiates, though don't let that word upset you too much. This would be one night... one night of experimentation in a safe setting, where you could do *anything* you desire, with as many men or women as you desire to be with."

"The scholar would... He'd never agree." She closed her eyes when the room started spinning from the opposing forces of past and present. Where *had* Rahn gone? Nyssa was giggling in a huddle of young women her age.

"Then come alone. Or with me." He chuckled. "Now, I'm not suggesting the two of us engage in anything illicit together. We're practically family. But I'm happy to be your safe and experienced guide into the sordid netherworld of sex clubs." He tilted his head and regarded her with an unsettlingly gentle look. "I wouldn't let anything happen to you, Aes. And I would not make this offer at all if I believed it was dangerous for you. There are few true rules of Revelry and they are this: respect the levels, respect the individual, and consent is given freely or not at all. You don't want to know what happens to those who overstep, but they are enough to prevent anyone from daring to. This particular club hasn't had an incident in over three years. Before that, seven."

Aesylt glanced behind her, causing the floor to rise. "I'm tired of dancing" was all she got out before she stumbled across the stones, aiming for the refreshment table. She planted her hands on its smooth cloth, breathing through her nose, and moved sideways until she was at the end, where she could hide behind a pillar to gather her bearings.

She poured herself a mug of mead. Her hands shook as she cupped it in both hands and lifted it to her mouth. Some of it spilled out the side and trailed down her chin, but the more she drank, the better she felt. The competing voices, sounds, and scents blended into the background, her only awareness her pounding heart, which was finally beginning to slow.

An orgy. Pieter had probably been building to this offer all along, and she'd walked right into it. But as much as it burned her to realize that she'd been such an easy mark, his offer had awakened something in her—a certain competitiveness, a call to rise to any challenge and emerge victorious. It was the same perseverance that had made her so determined to embark on the curricula with Rahn to begin with, and she'd proven to herself she *could* handle it. Perhaps sometimes her heart got in the way, but it was nothing she couldn't manage. She had her notes to work such complications out.

She brought the mug back to her mouth and finished the drink. The world normalized again. Voices filtered in. The music returned. She closed her eyes and told herself, *One more minute and then you must go back out there. You must be a gracious guest.*

Shrill giggles appeared from the other side of the pillar. "Nyssa, you are a devil, making her wear that dress!"

Aesylt froze. She didn't recognize the voice, but the young woman was clearly talking about her.

"I heard some men saying they weren't aware Lord Dereham was bringing the kitchen maids to the ball." Another unfamiliar voice.

"I think she looks lovely in it," Nyssa quipped.

The other girls burst into laughter. "You do not! What a rascal you are, Nyssa."

"You're doing her a kindness, even inviting her. I wouldn't let that feral wulf near my family."

"She's not *feral*," Nyssa retorted.

"She's a *murderer*, Nyssa. She slaughtered the king's men."

"Cooked and ate them too, so I hear."

Nyssa groaned. "Only fools repeat foolish rumors."

"Then lost her damn mind. I heard her brother sent her here because he was afraid of what she might do. That she might... you know."

Aesylt clapped both hands over her mouth to keep from screaming. Every inch of progress she'd made in calming herself was immediately undone. She was ripped back to the Nok Mora, the heft of the spear leaving her hand in a hurl of rage. The cries she sounded to the heavens after she took down two men with the bow. There were more, Fezzan had said, so many more, but it was a mercy to not remember them. The kyschun had offered to help her restore what had been lost, but she could think of nothing worse than being forced to relive every detail of that night, over and over and over.

"What, Katlyn? That she might *what*?" Nyssa demanded, exasperated. "I advise you to tread carefully with what you say next. Aesylt is a guest of my family, and her brother is one of my father's greatest allies."

"Guardians, Nyssa, we meant no offense."

"And I'll mean no offense when I cut off your tongue for wagging it too hard, Asa." Nyssa made a shuddery *harrumph*. "Where did my beautiful scholar run off to anyway?"

Aesylt, head between her legs, panted and braced until she heard their giggles trail away.

With her eyes stinging, she climbed to her feet and slinked toward the east exit, praying no one stopped her before she'd made it somewhere safe to collapse.

Rahn had been subtly watching Aesylt all night. He'd seen her shying away from the festivities with Imryll on the far side of the room, as well as when Pieter led her onto the ballroom floor. And he'd certainly noticed when she'd rushed away in distress.

He strode down hall after hall before he finally spotted her, right as she turned to exit through the staff door. The tight cross of her arms and downturned head suggested a desire for solitude, but everything he'd come to know about Aesylt Wynter over the past year told him that being alone was a sentence she'd imposed on herself.

He understood a sentence like that. He'd been serving his own for over twenty years.

A gust of wind and snow assaulted him the moment his boots hit the flagstones. He hadn't left with a cloak, but neither had she, and that was more concerning. Hypothermia was common even among the hardened locals. Death wasn't unusual either, because people were prone to underestimating the thing they respected most.

Ahead, Aesylt's dark dress flashed through the white squall, winking in and out. Wet flakes caught in his lashes, and he lost her again.

But he'd seen the direction she was headed, and it wasn't to the tower.

With one arm raised to shield his eyes from the gale, he shifted into a careful jog. The flagstones, cleared earlier to prepare for the event, were freshly slick, but his singular concern was finding her before her distress put her in real danger.

The courtyard narrowed to a choice of paths. He weighed his options but then noticed small footprints on the leftmost one and started down it. It wasn't long before he had his bearings again and realized where he was.

Artisan Row.

Although the city of Wulfsgate had some of the best artisans in the realm, the Derehams had their own blacksmith, silversmith, coppersmith, arrowsmith, bladesmith, and more, handpicked for the honor of serving their lord and his family exclusively. Rahn sometimes watched them from the tower when his thoughts wandered, stuck on the right word or description for his notes. He often wished he'd learned a useful trade himself, seeing how satisfied the men seemed after a long day of crafting.

The row of stone buildings was peaceful. Storm shutters were closed and locked on every one, blocking any interior view from the path. Crates of rubbish were stacked outside, awaiting porter pickup at dawn.

Her footsteps led into the clothier's building, where the seamstresses did most of their work. The door was only partially closed, snow dusting over the threshold.

Rahn gently nudged the door open with his palm. "Aesylt?"

No response came, but a grunt and then a series of cataclysmic crashes from the back room revealed her location soon enough. He rushed in and found her sprawled among a series of fallen clothing racks, thrashing, shrieking, and—

Disappearing.

She was there and then she wasn't. When she re-emerged moments later, she was screaming and soaking wet.

"Squish!" Rahn scrambled to where she was tangled in garments. Her face was splotched with varying shades of red, her eyes a tortured match. Water streamed from her hair and down her cheeks, like she'd been in a massive rainstorm. She gaped up at him, panting, and disappeared again.

When she returned, Rahn tried to grab her, but all he caught was air.

He waited almost ten excruciating minutes for her to return. When at last she came back, drenched and shaking, he threw himself on top of her.

The shock of it was enough to pause her. Her eyes were wide and brimming with fright, like a cornered animal. It was hard to tell with how drenched she was, but she seemed to be crying.

"Breathe," he pleaded, spreading one hand to her face to clear the hair matted everywhere. Her panting turned to hyperventilation. She twitched beneath him. "Aesylt, *breathe*."

"I can't." She moaned, and he saw it in her eyes; she meant to shift, so he grabbed hold of her chin and forced her to meet his gaze.

"You *can*. And if you insist on disappearing again, I'm coming with you."

"You don't want to go there, Scholar." Her chin trembled. She tore it out of his grip and turned her head to the side. "I think I've flooded it."

"You created a storm?"

Aesylt nodded almost imperceptibly. Her breathing slowed, shallowing. "Of course I would destroy that too. I'm an abomination. I... I'm..."

"Slow down. Breathe."

"Why? Why? Why would I, when I *killed* those men and felt *nothing*?" She whimpered. Her eyes darted in all directions. "I should have died that day with my people. I shouldn't even be here, pretending, acting like..."

Rahn had no choice but to ignore the crushing weight her words had fixed around his heart. "Show me."

She shook her head in confusion, squeezing her eyes tight.

"The storm. *Show me*, Aesylt. I'm not asking."

The command in his voice was enough to shift her gaze back to his. Her lower lip rolled inward, then out again. "And... And another with me."

Rahn was immediately assaulted with a downpour of rain and hail. He whipped his attention up in alarm and saw the roof had been torn away. Wind thrashed trees, bowing them, making the sky whistle. The sky lit up in a pattern of bright zigs and zags, followed by a clap of thunder that shook the earth. He ducked when a tree came crashing through the window.

Aesylt lay on the strewn gowns, convulsing. Tears streamed down her cheeks as rain peppered her body. She no longer seemed in control of what was happening.

Rahn at last understood why starwalking was a danger to her.

He crawled back to her and straddled her to steady her shakes. He grabbed hold of her face. "Aesylt. Aesylt!" He grunted in desperate frustration when she was unresponsive. "Listen to me. I *know* you're there, and I know you can hear me. I'm not letting go, and I'm not leaving. Aesylt." Agony clogged his throat. His thoughts were split between her crisis and the one that had shaped his own life. The crash of the stormy waves upon the Duncarrow rocks echoed in his head as the faces of Carrow's sons, evil and pleading, peered up at him from the inky sea. "I know your pain, Squish. Please don't go where I can't follow."

Lightning split the sky. Crashing thunder shattered a window. He covered her when he felt glass blow against the back of him. "You are not an abomination. Look at me. Look at me!"

"I'm a *coward*! I don't want to remember any of it!" She screamed the words, arching up off the pile of gowns like she were possessed by a foreign entity. "None of it! I *don't want to*. I don't want to face what I am... that I'm... that I'm... just like them."

Rahn replayed her words, *I killed those men and felt nothing*. She was speaking of the Nok Mora, of something she'd done in self-defense. He'd heard Nik and Val whispering about it one day. *She still believes that day ended when she stumbled from the keep and found us in the road,* Nik had said. *And if we love her, we'll let it be* had been Val's response. "You're a leader of people, people who were horribly and terribly wronged. Whatever you did, you did because you had to. There can be no remorse in acts of self-defense."

"Self-defense? No, not even one of them—" Her shaking stopped. Both of her eyes narrowed as she turned them on him. "I..." Rain splattered her face, running down the sides. "I hunted them down like dogs. I *wanted* them dead, Rahn. I wanted to see the light in their eyes wink out when they realized... when they knew. They'd already surrendered. They were..." Her head tilted back as she gulped a breath. "We had them lined up." She scrunched her face in a wince and screamed a sob. Her head whipped back and forth. "I don't know how many. Five. Ten. More. Fez told me, but I... I should know the number, the exact number, but that's how little their lives meant to me. They were on their knees, begging for mercy, crying... talking about their families back home, and... one by one I... took my father's sword and I—"

Another clap of thunder collapsed the back wall. Rahn stared at it, reeling from her words. He bowed his head to find his control again. For her. "We need to go back."

"*You* wanted to come here." Aesylt pushed up on her hands, stretching up. "Now you know. Now you know the monster I am, the monster you've been sharing a bed with and—"

He gripped her face in one hand and crushed his mouth to hers, then whispered, "I'm not leaving you, Squish, but it's not safe here. Please?"

With fresh tears pooling in her eyes, she nodded.

The rain, thunder, lightning and mayhem disappeared. The safety of the clothier's workshop allowed him to exhale, but Aesylt was no less distraught. Soaked to the bone, she released a heart-rending wail. Her fingers moved to her throat, clawing.

Rahn grabbed her hands in his, pinned them above her head, and kissed her again, locking them together until she stopped shaking. She cried against his mouth, gradually relenting until all that was left was wearied grief raining from her eyes. "You are not a monster, Aesylt."

Aesylt's head shook. "I am." She squirmed underneath him. "Only a monster could take life without remorse and then be a coward enough to forget it."

"You were *brave* enough to continue living when most of your world stopped," Rahn pressed.

"Please, I just want—"

"To wallow in pain, and I won't allow it." His grip on her hands tightened. "You're going to talk to me. Nothing you say will drive me away."

"Liar."

"I haven't lied to you yet."

"I've lied to you." Her throat moved in a rough swallow. The flesh was red and angry from the way she'd torn at it. "I can't be trusted."

"Trust is a thing given, and I give you my trust." Rahn noted the defiance in her eyes, the unspoken dare to agree with her and walk away. "What happened tonight?"

Her reddened eyes rolled to the side as she groaned. "These girls... It doesn't matter. Nyssa's friends, they were only saying what I already knew to be true, deep down. I just couldn't face it. I don't know why it's all coming back now. That day in the woods..." Fat tears slid down her cheeks and onto the gowns. "I've cried three times since the Nok Mora. Once when my brother finally came home. The second time, in that tree, wondering if I was going to die. And tonight."

Rahn was beginning to see the degree of deception Aesylt had created within herself in order to survive. She'd convinced herself she was worse than the men who had murdered, raped, and defiled the people of the Cross, and then she'd buried her shame, somewhere it had quietly bred and flourished until she could no longer run from it. "There's nothing wrong with crying. Science tells us it actually has a cathartic, therapeutic benefit."

She wriggled under his grasp with a scornful scoff. "Even now, you're thinking of the research."

He leaned in, pinning her with more of his body. "I'm not thinking of anything except you right now."

She sniffled and drew a jerky breath. "Why are you even here?"

"I was worried. *Am* worried."

"So you followed me, watched me tear the celestial world apart, and now..."

She wanted him to finish the thought, but he couldn't. Even trying was paralyzing. "I just..." *See your pain, because it's mine too. Except I can't reach mine, and like you, that was intentional.* "I don't know, Aesylt."

One of her hands slid up his arm until it reached his face. "Then maybe you should leave."

"Is that really what you want?"

"What I want..." She laughed bitterly. "You're the smartest man I have ever known, Adrahn, but you are utterly unable to communicate about whatever is going on inside of you."

He couldn't deny it, but all his life he'd been surrounded by emotionally stunted highborns, half of whom were oblivious to anything beyond themselves, the other half actively embroiled in the subjugation of a kingdom they had no right to. "What can I do to ease your mind?"

"Nothing." Her hand fell away. Her sad smile lifted her reddened cheeks.

Rahn made a split-second decision, one of the few he'd made in a long while that had not begun with careful deliberations. He slid his hands until one pinned both of her wrists, and the other traveled south, down her arms, her side. She shivered, confused, but he continued on until he came to the soft, warm flesh of her thigh, exposed from where the ungainly dress had lifted. "I've known monsters. I may even be one myself. But I have never seen a heart as true as yours." He dipped down and kissed her as his hand moved higher. She gasped with a slight tilt of encouragement. "Research or no—science or no—I would never share the intimacy I've shared with you if I believed that about you. If I have to prove it to you, I'll do so. Fervently."

Aesylt's mouth parted in bewilderment. "We're not in the celestial realm."

"I don't care." Rahn cupped his hand between her legs. "Do you?"

"I never did." Her eyes rolled back as his hand slid beneath her undergarment.

Rahn traced the length of his finger down her until she was flushed and panting. He paused, holding back an inappropriate chuckle at her wide-eyed offense. "Here's what's going to happen, Aesylt. If you want me to continue, you're going to do exactly as I say."

"What? What are you—"

He pinched between her legs until she whimpered. "Repeat. After. Me. 'I am not a monster.'"

"Rahn, I'm not—"

"Say it."

Fresh tears rolled down her cheeks. "Why?"

"Say it." His finger twitched.

"I am not... I'm not a..." Her face crumpled in pain, melting in pleasure. "A monster."

"Good girl." It was mere seconds before she was writhing beneath him as her release took hold. She slowly relaxed, her cheeks darkened with yet another shade of red.

Rahn removed his hand and unbuckled himself from his trousers. She watched him, clearly doubtful he would have the courage to take her right there, in their world, but he was beyond the confines of cowardice, or even bravery. She needed him, and he needed her, and there was nothing else to be said or done about it.

Entirely bound to the moment, he hooked one of her legs under his arm and lined himself up against her. She dragged her teeth against her lip and lifted, the final bit of encouragement he needed to take himself over the precipice between thought and action.

With a protracted groan, Rahn felt the last of his inhibitions disintegrate, replaced by a tight warmth that was even more delicious and perfect in their world. He pulled out and thrust into her, pushing a stilted exhale out of her that had him doing it over and over again just to hear the sound. His grip on her wrists tightened as he moved within her, but he forced himself to stop because there was more she needed to hear and to say.

"Repeat after me," he said again. "'I am imperfect, but I am brave. I did what needed to be done to protect what was left of my village. And I would do it again.'"

Her hands shifted under his hold, a fresh look of discomfort washing over her expression. "I know what you're trying to do."

"If you want me to fuck you, Aesylt, then you're going to say it."

Her eyes flashed wide. "I need to know this isn't pity."

Rahn offered a soft, humorless chuckle. "It's not pity, Squish. Say the words, and I'll do whatever you want me to do to you, and I'll relish every damn minute of it."

"I'm imperfect but brave. I did what I needed to do, to protect my people. And I would..." Her chest rose in a hard breath. "Do it again."

Rahn released her hands and lifted her hips off the dresses. He dipped his thumbs between her legs. "You've earned it. Whatever you want."

"This," she whispered. "I've only ever wanted this."

He'd been expecting her to make some bold suggestion, when all she really needed was intimacy. And Rahn realized, as he moved with her—as they broke the most important rule they'd ever made—that he'd been craving that very thing his entire life.

"Aesylt."

She watched him through languid blinks. "Yes?"

He kissed her and spread his hands along her face, sighing. "I wish you could see yourself as I do."

She came again, squeezing him, and the effect was dizzying. He pulled out, but she locked her legs behind him and shook her head.

Rahn threw his head back with a cry. He bowed over her, riding it out and slowing as he finished.

Breathless, he pulled out and settled beside her on the thick pile of dresses. The reality hit him immediately, what they'd done, but instead of regret, he felt relief. Peace.

"Am I breaking some rule when I say I prefer it this way?" she asked.

He glanced over and saw her dress still hiked up, her legs spread, and his cum spilling onto the gown she lay on. The need to take her again was all-consuming. To be inside of her, moving together as one... their pasts forgotten, their futures secure. "We've broken every other rule," he said, his voice cracked. "Why not this one?"

"Do you regret it?"

I should. "No."

"Does this change anything between us?"

I don't know. "Of course not." He rolled onto his side, facing her. "Do you feel better?"

She gave a drowsy nod. "I could sleep for days."

And I could hold you for days. "I need you to believe the words. You did what you had to, and your people are better for it. They know what you did for them."

"I don't know if I can ever believe them, but..." She exhaled slowly. "You're the first person I've ever told anything about that night. I expected it to feel so much worse, but I feel lighter."

"You do?"

"A little." She turned to face him. "And you? After what we did, how do you feel?"

Rahn swallowed and looked up at the dark ceiling. "I *should* feel remorse. I should wonder whether I've lost my mind."

"But you don't?"

"No." He rolled his head toward her again. "I don't. Not even slightly."

"And if I kissed you right now... if I crawled over you and said I wanted more?" Aesylt blinked away the last of her tears.

He twined a hand through one of hers. "Ask me, and I'll give you anything you want."

"Do you want to know what Pieter said to me tonight?"

"Pieter?" Rahn startled at the sudden shift in topic. "When you were dancing?"

"Mhm."

"All right," he said, growing nervous.

Aesylt told him.

He was genuinely speechless.

"He claims to want to help. I don't know if I trust that, but... I don't believe he's wrong either. About the Reliquary. What if there *was* something we could do to elevate our research, to remove all doubt that we can handle even the most provocative subjects with the utmost professionalism?"

Rahn could hardly make sense of it. Pieter's offer. Aesylt actually considering it. "An *orgy*?"

She rubbed her eyes with a shuddery yawn. "Ancestors, I can hardly speak anymore; I'm so tired. What an exhausting evening."

"Aesylt, you're seriously... You *want* to do this?"

"Want?" She scoffed. "I *need* to be a researcher, and I'm willing to do whatever it takes to achieve it. Want has nothing to do with it."

"This is beyond the pale." Rahn shook his head, too astounded to form the words he needed to. "This is madness. Even if... No, no."

"Why not?" she asked through languid blinks. "Why would this be out of bounds when nothing else has been?"

"Because... because it involves other people," he sputtered. Why were words so hard? Why could he not find voice for all his objections? "Because..."

"You don't have to come." She rolled onto her back and smoothed her dress. "One of us should be enough."

"No."

"No, what?"

Rahn bolted upright. "Aesylt, this is serious. With you and me there's trust and understanding. We bring outsiders into this, and there's no telling how it will change the variables, how it will affect the outcomes."

She stood, wobbling for balance atop the mountain of fallen dresses. "I need to clean this up. The clothiers begin their day at dawn."

The world seemed to whirl out of control, and he was left with nothing to right it. "We don't have to decide anything now," he said, looking to slow the spin somehow. "We can talk about this some more, weigh the advantages and risks—"

"I've already decided," Aesylt said. "And I don't expect you to come with me, Scholar. If you change your mind, it's happening the evening after tomorrow."

The spell had broken. She was back to calling him Scholar. "So *soon*?"

"It happens once a moon cycle." She leaped onto an open spot of floor and tugged at one of the racks, casually straightening things up like she hadn't just told him she planned to attend an orgy in two days' time. "I'll need you to get up."

Dazed, Rahn scooted off the pile and found his footing. "You cannot know all the ways this could go wrong."

"In fairness, Scholar, neither can you."

"There has to be something else... something on the list you've been wanting to try but are maybe afraid to ask?"

Aesylt paused. The gown in her hands drooped to her side. "There is something, but it's not on the list. And it has nothing to do with the Reliquary or our research."

He held out his hands. "All right, what is it?"

"It won't change my decision."

Rahn sighed. "Tell me anyway."

"The Dyvareh." She set the dress aside. "I'd like to recreate it, except... This time, I want to be caught. By you."

For the second time that night, Aesylt had left him without the ability to speak.

"And when you catch me, there are no rules. No limits. No... safety."

"You..." Rahn pulled his hands down his face. The stability of their strange interlude was slipping away, faster than he could grab it. "Why?"

She shrugged, turning away, but not fast enough for him to miss the little smile she tried to hide. "I realized it was a fantasy of mine. And you're the only one I trust to try it with."

Gods, if she knew how many times he'd fallen asleep dreaming of that very thing—hand on his shaft, his shame deeper than the sea. He'd discovered early in his life that while he was a mostly reticent man, there were times when the only thing he wanted was to dominate someone. To have total control over their pleasures... their pain. Aesylt had given him an outlet for it, but he wanted more. So much more. More than he felt safe acting on with her.

Because the fear of losing himself was suffocating.

"Can I think about it?"

"Of course you can." She hesitated while facing a window, a new gown in hand.

"Did something else happen?"

She shook her head without turning.

"Would you tell me?"

"Ancestors, what a mess. Help me get this rack up. It wouldn't be good for either of us if someone came in here."

"Would you tell me?"

Aesylt's shoulders rose and fell. "*Nothing* else happened. I just need time with my thoughts. The pain and guilt doesn't just disappear because we wish it so."

Rahn came up behind her and folded her into a hug. He pressed his mouth to the top of her head, to show her the support his words seemed inadequate for. "You now have someone who knows your darkest secret, and I only adore you more, Aes. I will always be your friend. I will *always* be a safe place for you."

She tilted her head back with a smile, but the tears had returned. "I know."

Rahn fell asleep to the gentle snores of Aesylt passed out against his chest and the whistle of wind beyond their tower windows.

For the first time since he'd left the only home he remembered, he dreamed of Duncarrow.

TWENTY-TWO

RED IS FOR THE ADVENTUROUS

Revelry was held in the middle of the woods, in a renovated abbey. It was an interesting use for the derelict structure, Rahn had to admit. One of Carrow's first orders upon seizing control of the kingdom had been to close the monasteries in favor of a new structure of faith, united under the Reliquary. Hundreds, perhaps thousands, of buildings had been abandoned in a rush, only to be looted or burned. He often wondered how long the order would last before the people rose to reclaim their old ways. Fear was only a powerful motivator in the short term.

Pieter walked ahead of Rahn and Aesylt. Two of his personal guards pulled up the rear. There were others stationed throughout the forest, but wherever they were, they were apt at discretion.

Rahn and Aesylt had departed Wulfsgate under discreet cover, wearing servants' clothing and masks. Before they'd left the carriage, Pieter's men had confirmed no one had followed them. They were there to evaluate the safety throughout the evening and act quickly if anything changed.

Most importantly, Rahn and Aesylt had to be back before Hal realized they weren't in the tower at bedtime and alerted Rustan.

An elegant, graceful series of notes poured from the well-illuminated building. As they drew nearer, Rahn saw the string musicians playing under a tent just outside the doors.

"Welcome to Revelry, Lord Dereham." A rouge-cheeked man in a crimson robe held a silver tray with three goblets. "And your two beautiful initiates."

Pieter took one, downed it, and handed it back. "Salutations, Proctor. Let me introduce Ella and Gerald. They're visiting from the Easterlands and have long been pondering membership in their own local Revelry. I thought I'd show them what they've been missing."

"Oh, indeed!" Proctor waggled his brows, then turned his scrutiny on Rahn and Aesylt. "Ooh, you know how to choose them, don't you? Mind your jealousy tonight, my lord. You may not want to see *either* of them in the laps of others."

"It's my voracious hope they both enjoy as many laps as they can handle."

The two men laughed. Rahn glanced at Aesylt, to see how she was managing, but she didn't seem half as nervous as he was. She was staring intensely at the door, her expression obscured by her gold filigree mask. Since she'd mentioned her intention to attend the secret orgy, she'd said almost nothing else about it, other than a simple *good* when Rahn had finally told her—because what choice did he have?—he would join her. Even after he'd given her the confirmation, the distance between them only seemed to widen. She'd conjured excuses to beg off of the research. Had hardly looked him in the eye at all.

There was no chance in the heavens he would let her walk into a den of libidinous tigers alone.

"Ah, well, it's quite biting tonight, isn't it? Come, come." Proctor raised a jeweled hand as he turned and headed for the double doors.

When Pieter looked back, his face was lit by the row of torches, which flickered over his features in a way that made him angelic, then demonic. "No one here will recognize you. Stick to the names you were given, wear your masks, and you can indulge to your heart's content." He grinned and followed Proctor.

On a whim, Rahn slipped his hand into Aesylt's. She offered no resistance, but neither did she seem to even notice.

They mounted some stairs, and Proctor gestured toward a small alcove to the left of the doors. Pieter stepped in behind him, and Rahn and Aesylt followed.

"Have you explained the rules to our Ella and Gerald?" Proctor asked. "Even so, we're duty bound to impart them before anyone enters. Before we go a moment further, I must ask. Ella, Gerald, are you both of sound mind and enthusiastic harmony this evening?"

"Yes," Aesylt said briskly.

"I suppose—yes," Rahn said, watching her.

"Splendid. Just splendid." Proctor turned toward a table, wiggling his fingers, and pivoted back to show he was holding three strings, each a different color. Green, yellow, and red. "There are three rules at Revelry. Have fun, mind your tongue when you leave, and respect the colors when you're here. You will each choose a color to wear tonight on your wrists. The color will signal to all others here what you have come in search of. It will inform the nature of your visit and your enjoyment thereof. It does not, however, supersede consent, and you may change your color and your mind at any time. Just be aware, however, that should you choose to wear a red string tonight, checking for consent is not a requirement of the partners who may proposition you. If you change your mind, you must remove your bracelet to signal your consent has been withdrawn. Simply saying *no* is often part of the game for our red bracelets and would not be enough to show you were no longer interested."

Rahn frowned, sighing deeply. "Right. So. The colors. They mean—"

"I shall explain them now." Proctor flicked the green string. "Green is the color of searching. Most who come to Revelry for their first time choose it because they don't know what to expect once they step foot inside our menagerie of pleasure." He laughed to himself. "Green is the color of watchers. Curiosity. As a green bracelet, you may partake in any of the main room festivities—food, drink, conversation. And you may wander to the edges of that room for something a little more colorful. However, you are *not* to leave the main room, what we often call the green room, unless you switch your bracelet to yellow or red, as the side rooms are for the seeking revelers."

Pieter leaned in. "Green is no fun. No one really means to choose it."

Green it is, Rahn thought.

Proctor rolled his eyes. "Do not listen to our good lord here. *Choice* is the only thing that brings us here, no?" He flicked the yellow string. "Yellow is the color of interest. Wearing yellow tells others you are open for most activities, but they must still obtain consent before engaging. There are no limits to what you can take part in if you wear yellow, or to what rooms you may enter, and you may set your own boundaries prior to any encounter. Yellow is the most common color of our revelers, for there is no risk and infinite reward."

"Yellow allows for multiple partners?" Aesylt asked, her first words of the evening.

"Of course, dear."

"Hmm." Her hand slipped from Rahn's.

"I assume we don't even need to ask about red then," Rahn said with a nervous chuckle.

"I want to know about red," Aesylt stated.

"*Red,*" Proctor said, grinning, "is for the adventurous. Red is everything yellow is, but more. Wearing red signals to others you want to be taken—liberally. Taken *everywhere*. Taken without being asked! You may be walking down the hall, and a man comes up behind you, bends you over a chair, and does as he pleases. Red tells him you're open to it. Nay, *inviting* it. Red says, ignore what I say and do as you please." He eyed the string with a strange look. "Unless you remove the bracelet, that is. That tells your partners to cease immediately. And should they decide they're disinclined to do so, we have guards stationed all throughout the abbey to monitor compliance. Also, as Lord Dereham has likely already explained to you, you will enter Revelry without your clothing but with a silk robe you can choose to wear, or not. When you're wearing the robe, it's quite a simple thing to hide your wrist, and if your string is not visible, others are forbidden from bothering you. Many use this tactic for temporary breaks in their evening interludes." He sighed, smiling. "So you see, it really is quite safe."

Rahn's internal gale was building to a squall. *Lord Dereham* had explained none of it.

Pieter held out his wrist. "You know my preference, Proctor."

Pleased, Proctor reached for a red string from the table and secured it around his wrist. "I predict another satisfying evening for you, my lord. Some of your favorites are already inside."

"Music to my ears." Pieter adjusted the string on his wrist and turned toward Rahn and Aesylt. "And the two of you?"

"Green," Rahn said at the same time Aesylt said, "Red."

Rahn turned all the way to face her. "No." He looked back at Proctor, then Pieter. "No, she's not wearing red. That's ludicrous. She'd never done anything like this before. Surely there are rules around a person's first time."

"No such rules, actually," Proctor said amiably.

"It's not your choice, *Gerald*," Aesylt said and held out her wrist.

Pieter lifted his brows. "She's right, Gerald. Only she can decide the experience ahead of her. Are you sure green is your choice? You won't be able to follow her when she ventures beyond the main room... and let's be blunt, she wouldn't be wearing red if she was only interested in the main room, would she?"

"Ella," Rahn pleaded, but Aesylt stared determinedly ahead as Proctor tied the string. "Fine, yellow then. Gods."

"Gods?" Proctor scrunched his face. "What are you, a Ravenwood, Gerald? We've had one or two here before, pretending to be one of us."

"He's just an odd man who says odd things," Pieter explained, with a light look of warning. "Yellow then?"

Rahn internalized his building anxiety and nodded. He barely stood still as Proctor tied the string. It was loose enough to be removed quickly but secure enough for the type of activities occurring right that moment inside the doors. He swallowed with a sweeping look up the stone wall, at the cloudy windows that revealed nothing from the outside. But there were enough whoops and cries and moans to show there was no shortage of pleasures for the eager and willing.

He was neither.

Aesylt was, inexplicably, both.

Worst of all, the whole thing, the road they'd taken to get there—all of it—was on him. He'd told Aesylt that she held all the power, but that hadn't always been true. *He* was the one in a position of authority. There was an expression he'd learned from the dowager Queen Godivah, perhaps the only piece of actual wisdom the insufferable woman had ever doled out: *When you resolve to take something out of a box, be sure you know how it got there in the first place, or you'll never know precisely how to get it back in.*

He'd opened a box without realizing Aesylt was the only one who could close it.

Rahn had no idea how he was going to protect someone who had no interest in being saved, but he had to try.

He muttered a thank-you to Proctor and followed the men into the changing area.

Aesylt clutched the pink robe at her chest and waist as she moved down the long aisle of what had once been a place of worship. The benches had been removed, and there were tables there instead, filled with people laughing and drinking and eating. Although most were in robes with their wrists covered, she spotted strings of mostly green, a few yellows. *The reds must go straight to the good stuff.*

The thought sent a chill tearing through her. She'd made her choice with a clear mind, and as much as she wanted to share the experience with Rahn, she was frustrated with the way he'd been acting, like she needed strict supervision. She was weary of his push and pull of being her superior, her lover, and her friend, but never at the same time, a role dictated entirely by his own whims and moods. It would have been better if he hadn't come at all.

In fact, she wished she'd not told him.

It's not only for the science, what I intend to take part in tonight, she'd written in her notes, with full plans of scribbling the words out later, or even burning them. *It's so I can replace these experiences for his and mine, and my heart can move on. The more men I've known, the less potent he becomes, until this is all just a distant memory of two scholars working on an assignment together.*

Their lovemaking two nights ago—she could think of it as nothing else, for what else explained his gentle kisses, his complete abandonment of the most sacred rule of all?—had been the final fall of the hammer for her. She had overcome her own denial about the potent feelings between them, but he never would. Rahn would never open up, never meet her where she deserved. Of all the gifts he'd given her, it by far the most bittersweet, but also the most important.

I wish you could see yourself as I do.

Aesylt had plenty of desires, and she understood them better because of him. She wasn't afraid of them or what they said about her. Her only real fear was being forced to deny herself.

Revelry was made for someone like her, and if Rahn Tindahl couldn't see that, couldn't respect that, then it was his burden to carry.

She sensed she was being watched and glanced to the left corner of the room, where two attractive men were looking her way. One wore a robe, the other had his draped over an arm. Both were displaying their red strings openly.

With a shaky breath, she nodded and lifted her wrist, unsure if it was the right way to send the message—wondering if she was a fool for sending one at all. The heavy, pitched song from the string musicians drove her nerves to a higher ledge as she awaited their reaction.

They exchanged looks, grinning, and nodded back.

It was on.

Whatever that meant.

"I'll fetch us drinks," Pieter said and disappeared into the crowd.

"Ae—Ella," Rahn said the moment Pieter was gone. He reached for her shoulders, but she ripped away with an affronted scowl.

"Let us get one thing quite clear... Gerald." She took a step back. The ferocity in her eyes was startling. "I came here for the full experience. I was not coerced. I have nothing to prove. This will of course benefit our research immensely, but the truth is..." She lowered her voice to a whisper. "*Rahn,* I *want* this. I want to taste the world of the forbidden, as freely as men do and without shame. If that bothers you, then you can leave. You *should* leave. Because I do not need you nor want you to intervene on my behalf. I don't even..." Aesylt's expression softened into distress. "I wish you hadn't come."

Her confession left him reeling. She'd said *none* of that when she'd told him about Pieter's proposal, so either she'd lied about her intention then or she was lying tonight. Once more, he faced the cost of all he'd allowed to happen. All he'd enthusiastically participated in with her. Everything had spun from his control so fast, he didn't know how to bring it all back together.

"Left you speechless again, did I?" Aesylt's eyes glossed, her lip turning up at the corner. She seemed equally on the verge of bursting into tears as flying into a rage.

"I would never want you to feel shame for who you are or what you want," Rahn said, painfully mindful he was losing her, word by word, and whatever he said next would either solidify that or buy him a little more time. "I worry only for your safety."

"Is that all you worry for? My safety?" She blinked slowly. "Hvala, Ota."

"We don't *know* any of these men, Ae–Ella!"

Her mouth turned in a cheeky grin. "That's the whole appeal, isn't it? I never have to see any of them again."

Rahn tugged one hand down his face and squeezed his chin. "I feel as though I've missed something critical in our interactions that would explain your behavior." He pulled his face into a tight wince. The moment his admission was out, he knew it had been the wrong one.

"My..." Aesylt laughed, her mouth wide in astonishment. "And there it is, aye? I'm still just a disciple to you, fresh-faced about the world, despairing of a knight to protect me from all things dark and dangerous. Even the other night was nothing more than—" All humor in her expression dissolved. "You don't know me at all, and I see now... You never wanted to, did you? Not if it meant seeing me for who I really am."

She loosed the robe from her hands. It opened, revealing the inner arcs of her breasts, her pubic mound. One sleeve, she pushed up, then the other. She lifted her red-stringed wrist with a bold, challenging look.

Mine. The thought came on so fast, so sudden, it was dizzying.

"You don't have to do this," he pleaded weakly, aware the moment was already lost, that she was already lost, to him. Everything he said was only making it worse, but he couldn't stop. "You have nothing to prove to anyone."

"And again, you aren't listening to me." She shook her head in disappointment, dragging her gaze over him. "I can't... I'm done. I came here to enjoy myself, not be lectured or be made to feel my judgment is impaired."

Rahn crossed both of his hands over his racing heart. Every second pulled her further away from him, from the magic they'd made in the tower. What had taken over a year to build was disassembling right before his eyes. "I *promise* you, that was not my intention."

"Then prove it," she said, "and leave me to experience the evening my way."

He drew upon all his self-control to watch her move away.

Walking away from Rahn was unspeakably difficult, no matter how nonchalant she'd appeared in the final moments of their charged confrontation. Her heart had been his from the moment he'd walked into Fanghelm, but his had never been hers, and only more senseless pain lay ahead if she stayed the course she was on. Knowing when to leave and when to stay was a lesson Drazhan had taught her. He'd seen that guiding his people was impossible until he'd experienced his own journey of growth. He'd forsaken his comforts and his relationship with his sister for something bigger than himself.

She wasn't just leaving Rahn; she was leaving a version of herself behind as well.

Her past slipped away with each confident step, like a moth molting into a butterfly. Thinking of herself in that way gave her courage and conviction, and she lifted her head higher, pinching her shoulders back.

The men she'd exchanged nods with were no longer in the corner, but she had a feeling she knew where to find them.

Aesylt felt Rahn watching her.

She passed under the archways without looking back.

Rahn accepted the drink from Pieter without even looking at it to see what it was, downed it, and shoved the cup back into the man's hands. "From the very first, you have had your eyes on her. You planned this."

"Why did you come, eh? You're clearly miserable." Pieter clapped him on the shoulder and sipped his own drink slowly. "You're wrong anyway. I have no interest in her, at least not sexually." He grinned into another sip. "I prefer my women more... mature." He swallowed. "And sometimes I prefer them not to be women at all."

"Then *what* is your intention with her?" Rahn divided his frenzied attention between Pieter and the arch under which Aesylt had disappeared. She might not want him around, but he wasn't leaving without her. "What do you get out of all this 'helpfulness'?"

"The satisfaction of aiding a friend?"

"Horseshit."

Pieter's mouth arched in amusement. "You're far more interesting when you're less reserved... Gerald. Another drink?"

Rahn clenched his hands into fists at his sides when they lost feeling. *I'm not losing it, not here.* "If *anything* happens to her tonight, I won't bother going to Drazhan. I'll kill you myself. And then I'll walk myself into the lawman's office, confess what I've done and why, so the appropriate legacy is the one that follows you into the afterlife, not whatever fairytale your family wants to spin to cover who you really are." He snorted in disgust. "Stay away from her, or you'll see a side of me you would not have thought possible."

"The night is hers to enjoy as she pleases. I have my own ahead of me." Pieter raised his glass, unruffled by the threats.

"Fuck you, Pieter," Rahn spat and charged toward the arch.

Aesylt had been visiting another world her whole life, but the one beyond the wispy curtains was another universe altogether.

The carpeted passageway stretched on forever. Along the west side were a series of doorless rooms, within which people moaned and laughed in delight. The string musicians could scarcely be heard anymore, their song having lost the competition with the symphony of unabashed debauchery rippling down the long hall.

The hall was full of revelers, even more than the main room. Most had already disrobed, displaying a mix of yellow and red strings. She saw a man with another man's cock in one hand, and with the other, he was gesturing wildly toward the woman he was conversing with. Nearby, two women were trading off giving oral pleasure to a satisfied-looking older gentleman.

A sensuous, feminine voice purred in her ear, "You should take that off, love," but when Aesylt turned to see who had said it, no one was there. Another someone placed a drink in her hand with a broad grin and moved on. Aesylt eyed the cup in suspicion, but she was there for the full experience, so she tossed it back and handed the empty glass to the next server she saw.

Incense made the air hazy, but the scent was one she'd not experienced before, warm and oaky and disorienting.

Her gaze traveled to each open room as she passed. They were all accoutred with luxurious cushions, settees, and refreshment carts. But it wasn't the furnishings that kept her eyes from wandering back to the safety of the hall. Twists of sweaty limbs, moving in perfect rhythm together. Women slithering against women, and men penetrating while being penetrated. Their moans wrapped in the sweetness of pure abandonment.

"I dare not assume your color, but how I would love to enjoy you in the darning room."

Aesylt turned and saw a tall, robeless, masked man holding a drink as he grinned at her. His wrist was adorned with a red string. "The darning room?"

"First time, love?"

She felt her first shame of the evening when she nodded.

"Ah, and your host failed to explain things to you. Tsk, tsk." The man draped an arm over her shoulder and gestured around with his drink. "Every one of these rooms has a theme. That one nearest us is the magi room, reserved for those who enjoy adding a little magic to their play. This one here is called the domestic staircase, because it's where highborns and servants come to switch roles. The highborns are whipped and dominated by the servants, and the servants are lavished with pleasure beyond their imagining. Ah, and that one there is the accounting room. Men and women there charge for their services, and they are all too eager to part with their money. And *this* one..." He trailed off. "It's more fun to explore on your own. The darning room, though, you asked. In there, I would dress you in a thick, ungainly woolen garment. To earn your body, I would need to unravel you thread by thread, until there was nothing left but my unslakable lust for you."

"Oh, that... That all sounds intriguing," Aesylt said, trying not to let her eyes wander downward. "I'm flattered by your offer, but I'm still trying to decide how I want to spend the evening." Unsure why, she lifted her wrist to show him she was red. She felt a stab of pride, like it was proof she wasn't afraid. "But I'm here to do more than learn."

The man's eyes widened approvingly as his head tilted. "A first timer *and* going all in? I'm impressed. And a little afraid for you." He threw his head back with a deep laugh. "Do be careful, love. It's so very rare to have someone who is both new *and* willing to do anything anyone wants. The wrong man or woman hears about you, you'll be in for quite the night."

Aesylt curled her mouth defiantly. "Maybe that's what I'm here for."

"Then off goes the robe, love." He flicked his fingers. When she hesitated, he laughed again. "You've already denied me once. I won't suddenly change my mind when your bracelet is showing."

Reluctantly, Aesylt peeled the robe away. A nude attendant tried to take it from her, but she wasn't ready to part with it. It was her break from all of it, as Proctor had explained, and without knowing how the night would go, she couldn't guess how often she'd need a moment to herself.

"You are a vision, love." The man licked his lips. "But I am a man of my word. May your evening provide infinite rewards. Find me again at the first snow." He sashayed off.

Aesylt had never felt so exposed. The need to be robed again was almost stronger than her determination.

Men and woman alike eyed her like prey, a feeling both unsettling and seductive. She'd never been the woman who commanded a room. Never had needed to be. Yet *something* about her was enough to stop conversations as she glided slowly down the hall, wearing a level of confidence she had yet to earn.

Right as she was looking in on a room that seemed to be filled with only the color yellow, powerful hands gripped and tugged her hips from behind. She gasped, trying to turn, but the man's hold was like iron.

"Wait," she croaked, but he marched her to a settee against the wall and bent her forward over the arm, then smashed her face into a cushion still warm from when someone had sat there.

Rahn kept finding her and losing her.

For such an apparently secret society, it seemed like half of Wulfsgate was in attendance. He could tell a lot about people by the way they stood, how they held themselves, and there were enough naked highborns in the hall for a proper scandal.

He spotted her talking to a tall, naked man and pushed through a crowd to get closer. But by the time he was free of the tangle, she was alone again and continuing down the hall.

Without her robe on.

His pulse hastened as he moved faster, determined not to lose her this time. He was smashing into so much flesh, he no longer bothered to apologize. Before... Years ago, Revelry would have lighted every one of his unusual sexual appetites, but his blood and bones were ice, his mind consumed with a single purpose.

Protect her.

Rahn gasped when a man grabbed hold of Aesylt from behind and dragged her. Rahn led with his elbow, pushing and shoving until he ran smack into a nude woman dangling two drinks.

"I suppose this one's for you, seeing as you clearly need it!" she teased, shoving some bubbly concoction under his nose. He tried to get past her, but she matched his side steps like it was a game.

"I need to—"

She nudged the glass to his face, clinking it against his teeth. He shoved it away, right as he saw something that made every nerve in his body stand on end and the ice in his blood turn to fire.

This is happening. This is really happening. This will really, actually happen unless I rip off my bracelet.

But this is what I want, and it's why I've come here.

The man's hand shifted to the small of her back, holding her in place. His cock slapped her ass a few times before he lined it up against her.

Who are you? she wanted to ask but wouldn't. What was happening in that sordid moment was the entire point. Why she'd come. Her notes would be magnificent, and her heart would mend, but she had to relax.

Aesylt crushed out a gulp when the stranger penetrated her. Her hands slid down to the cushion and wrapped beneath the sides, bracing her through every vigorous thrust, her robe pressed between her body and the cushion. He grunted different variations of *yes* and *so good,* but they sounded absurd. None of her interludes with the scholar had prepared her for it, because the two things were nothing alike at all. That had been intimacy. Being taken by a stranger was carnal. Empty.

"You want me to fill this cunt, girl?" He moaned.

She tried to answer, but her voice creaked.

The man gave one final, forceful shove, and it was done. His warmth spread through her, sending her heart into palpitations, but she was risking nothing. She was already late, already in trouble. If she couldn't get ahold of her vedhma's tea soon, she'd be in an entire world of it.

The man patted her back like she'd done well, helped her stand, and disappeared like a thief in the night. She glanced around, worried what others were thinking about her brash affair that had been over as quickly as it had begun, but everyone had their own explorations to occupy them.

I just laid with another man. A man I'll never know or meet again. A man incapable of breaking my heart.

And I want more.

"Up for some illusions tonight, beautiful?" She was still reeling from the encounter with the man whose face she'd never even seen the whole of, and she didn't at first realize the man speaking to her was one of the two who had nodded at her in the green room.

Rahn rolled his tense hands over the arm of the settee where *that man* had... had...

White-hot rage seared the back of his eyes. How savage had handled her... like she meant nothing... like she was merely a hole for him to exploit. Like she wasn't a talented, clever, beautiful creature deserving of everything.

I don't care what she says.

I don't care if she hates me for it.

I'm getting her out of here before this place swallows her whole.

The room was lined with plush cushions of violet, cerulean, and gold. The walls, too, were painted in these colors, art with no pattern. One of the men slid his hands along her shoulders and cleared her hair from her neck to kiss it. The other grabbed her chin and lifted her mouth to his. She moaned at the dual sensations of the men behind her and in front of her.

"You can call me A, and he's B. When the light goes out, you'll know me by the scar on my chest," the redhead, A, said. She finally got a good look at them both—the other had hair as dark as night—and realized they were brothers. "And you are, beautiful?"

"Ella," she said, her eyes on their cocks, both of them hard. *Two more ways to forget.* "But you can call me whatever you want."

The men exchanged lustful glances. "Put this on," A said and handed her a blindfold.

Aesylt turned the silk cloth over in her hand. "Will you be wearing one?"

A grinned. "No, beautiful. We need to see you."

"All of you," B replied.

Aesylt didn't want the men to think she was hesitating from lack of interest, so she removed her mask and tied the blindfold as best she could. One of the men came up behind her and tightened it, but he pulled her hair aside so it wouldn't get caught.

"Comfortable enough?" A asked.

"More importantly, can you see?" B laughed.

"Yes, it's comfortable enough. And no." She smiled and waved her hands in front of her eyes. "Not a thing."

"This is your first time at Revelry," B said. "Hopefully not your last, *Ella,* so we'll go easy on you. This time."

"This time," A stated, and they both laughed.

They were being kind and considerate, two things she hadn't expected after the crude way the other man had fucked her on the couch and left without a word.

But kind and considerate wouldn't obliterate the pain.

"Actually," she said, tilting her head back. "I'd prefer you didn't."

Rahn searched every room. He was chased out of two and yelled at by revelers in three others. He mumbled hollow apologies as he looked behind couches and turned over cushions, dodging swats and objections. He reached for anything he could find, anything to erase the image of Aesylt being manhandled by that degenerate.

He was as much looking for that cretin as Aesylt.

Rahn couldn't catch his breath. Every one was too short, too strained. He wheezed, dark spots teasing his vision.

He closed his eyes and reminded himself what was at stake if he couldn't pull himself together.

Aesylt was led to a pile of cushions that seemed higher than the others, with A holding one hand, B the other. They gently laid her back, spreading her legs as she was nestled into place. Being blindfolded was so disorienting that when a tongue lathed the center of her, she realized she was only surprised because she'd been expecting something else.

"You taste like another man, Ella." A sounded almost reproving. "We'll remedy that."

Despite the nip in the air, she wasn't cold, because the warm hands of the men were tracing every inch of her. A caressed her thighs as he licked at her. B ran his hands down her arms... her torso.

She cried out when she was close, but A's laugh rumbled against her core.

"Not yet, beautiful."

The air shifted. Both men had stepped away, but she could still hear them.

A hand at her ankle signaled the return of one of them. He lifted her leg high in the air, almost pulling her off the cushion, and slid his cock in slowly. His groan lasted the length of his thrust.

Something strange and delicious washed over her, like she was being carried to another realm. A wave of euphoria ripped through her, and she cried out in delight.

"Feels incredible, doesn't it?" B, close to her face. Flesh slapped her mouth. His cock. She flitted her tongue out to catch it, riding the delirious high that had come seemingly from nowhere.

"You feel it too?" She panted, shifting back against the cushions with every thrust from A.

"We slather it on our cocks to heighten the experience for all of us." He parted her lips with his head and silenced her when he slid himself down her tongue, toward her throat. "We don't know what it's called, so don't ask—ah, *Guardians*... Your mouth is so fucking warm. I might fill it until you choke, beautiful."

Aesylt reached above her head to grip the base of B's cock as he worked her mouth. The push and pull of each man's desire had the rough fabric of the pillows burning her sensitive skin, but she craved more blissful release. More pain. Anything to heighten the experience, to drag her further from the past few weeks.

Rahn's face jumped into her thoughts. Her chest caved, her breath catching. Tears sprang so suddenly to her eyes, she could hardly make sense of them. *No, I don't want to feel like this. I don't want him. No one should ever want someone who cares more for their own illusions than the person they love.*

"You want more, Ella?" A asked between thrusts. "Just nod, beautiful. Your mouth is going to stay full for a while."

Aesylt nodded profusely, hoping neither of them had spotted the tears trickling beneath her blindfold.

Two stunning women appeared, one on each side of him. Rahn smiled curtly, amazed they couldn't read the tension in his body language screaming for everyone to just *get away,* and said, "Excuse me, ladies, I'm in a hurry. I'm looking for someone."

One of them pulled up his robe and nodded. "Kaya, he's yellow. I told you."

"No, *I* told you that there's no way this sweet hunk of man would ever be depraved enough to wear *red.*"

"That is not what you said at all!"

"Ladies—" Rahn breathed deep and hard when they kept bickering. "Please excuse me—"

"Well, yellow, red, he must be open to some adventure," the first one said, laughing. "Or he would have stayed in the green room."

Rahn stumbled away in exasperation and faced them directly. "Please. I'm looking for a woman, about twenty. Long, pale hair. She isn't... isn't wearing her robe. She was going this way."

"Red or yellow?"

He swallowed. "Red."

The ladies looked at each other and laughed again. "Oh," the second one said, "you poor dear. She your wife? I almost regret to tell you that there's no doubt in my mind she's being properly fucked in one of these rooms."

"She's not my wife," he stated, threading his words through gritted teeth. "But I believe she's in danger."

"Here? At Revelry?"

They laughed harder.

"Danger from a good, hard ride," the other cajoled.

Rahn spun away from them and continued down the hall.

A finished, taking some of his spend with him when he pulled away. He spread her wide and moaned at whatever he saw. Aesylt could only guess. She could see nothing beyond the barest hint of light at the center of her blindfold.

He crawled atop the cushions until he was closer to her head and parted her mouth to make room for his cock. It was soft and salty, and she understood he was looking for her to restore it to life. She reached up to grab his ass, tugging him farther in and sucking him as far as her throat would allow, and the sound he made told her she was doing well.

When she paused for breath, he removed himself, and there was more confusion of activity. She was lifted gently at the waist, shifted, and placed in the lap of who she assumed was B. With one hand on her face, the other between both of their legs, he slid inside her and said, low and rough, "Ride."

The word alone was enough, but the surreal nature of the evening, the bizarre high she couldn't explain, turned her pace into a frenzied series of movements that had B asking her to slow down and be 'one with the moment.' But he was bigger than A, bigger than—*no, don't say his name, don't even think it*—and the pain broke through in short, stinging waves that made her unexpectedly erupt into an orgasm that came from deep within her.

"Fuck *yes,*" B moaned, slapping her ass to urge her on. "A, get over here."

A wasn't far. She'd felt him nearby, watching. He slid his hand down her back and between the crack of her ass, then dipped even lower as he slid his finger inside of her, running alongside B's cock. She couldn't figure out what he was doing until he withdrew his wet finger and slid it into her ass.

Aesylt lifted from the shock of it. She had never... Well, she hadn't even been touched there.

"You don't like that?" A asked, withdrawing.

"I don't know if I like it," Aesylt replied, slowing her stride so her nerve endings could catch up. "I've never done it before."

"We usually start with a finger. Work our way up," A explained. "Sometimes women say they can feel both of us touching."

"Oh," she said, breathless, feeling B swell inside her as he drew close to a finish. A was working up to fucking her... back there. At the same time, she was riding B. Imagining it drove her wild again, but something was nagging at her. It was just beyond the reach of her thoughts, swimming yet disconnected and floating away from each other.

Twelve rooms he'd checked, but it was the thirteenth where he found her.

If the entire night hadn't been so dreamlike, he'd have been rooted in place at the sight of Aesylt riding one man while another had a finger inside her ass. But with only the slightest relief, he realized he'd actually been expecting worse, after some of the scenes he'd barged in on.

"Oy! Get your own room!" the man under Aesylt cried.

She hadn't seen him because she was blindfolded.

Rahn moved in farther. Both men stared at him in disbelief, wondering if he was stupid, arrogant, or both, but they could wonder until dawn for all he cared. He was there to get Aesylt *out*.

"You hard of hearing, pretty boy?"

Rahn cleared his throat. Aesylt had stopped moving but was still hinged over the man's lap. He couldn't explain why it cut so deep. Why it *hurt* the way it did, like something immense was sitting on his chest and wouldn't relent. "Ella. Do *you* want me to leave?"

Aesylt's back straightened. Her head darted his way, her mouth parted in alarm. "Ra—Gerald?"

"I've been looking for you, Ella."

"Who is this? Your husband?" one of the men asked with a dry laugh.

"Just a friend," she said. Her pale throat moved with a swallow. "What are you doing here, Gerald?"

"I came to take you home."

"I'm not going home."

"Come on, B, let's get him out of here."

Rahn took another decisive step inside. "No. I'm not talking to you. I'm talking to Ella."

"Ella, tell this yellow bracelet how things are," one of the men said, his tone testy.

"I want... this, Gerald," Aesylt said carefully. She adjusted on the man's lap, her bare back twisting, like she was embarrassed. "I'm not doing anything I didn't ask for."

"We can talk about this at home—"

"No," she said. "No. You can go, but I'm staying."

He started toward her, and the man who'd been playing with her ass stepped between them.

"It's all right," she said, and the man relented. "I'll handle this."

Rahn crouched beside her. He couldn't look at the man beneath her... at what they were doing. He couldn't even fathom her giving and receiving pleasure with someone else. He had no right to feel so *angry* about any of it—no right to feel anything at all about what she did with her own body.

His hand came up to cup her face. "I don't believe you really want this. I know you."

A single tear rolled down from a gap in her blindfold. "If you knew me..." She didn't finish.

"If I knew you, what?" he asked.

"I'm not doing this with you right now. If you want to stay, then... then enjoy yourself, as I am."

Rahn's voice broke. "How?"

Aesylt turned in the direction the other man was standing. "Can he join?"

"Ahh..." The man scoffed, snorting in annoyance. "I don't know. B?"

"She has three holes, doesn't she?"

Fresh wrath exploded from his every pore to hear them speak of her like that. "Ella..."

"I want to try something new tonight," she said, lowering her chin and tilting her head. "But I would prefer it be with someone I trust."

Rahn shook his head, despite her inability to see. "What do you want to try that we haven't already?"

Aesylt glanced behind herself. He suddenly understood.

"You want *that*?"

She nodded. "I want that, and I'll have it. But if you stay, you could... be the one. The first."

Taking a woman that way had always been a desire of his, but whenever he thought of broaching the subject with Aesylt, the timing always felt wrong. He loved the way she invited his pain, so it wasn't that. Truly, he didn't understand his reticence at all.

And she wanted him to do it while *another man* was inside of her.

"I can't," he said and kissed her cheek, brushing his thumb along the same spot. "I'm sorry."

Why, why had she asked him to stay? The whole intent of the evening had been to drive him *away* from her thoughts, to replace every brush of his hand—every thrust of his affection—so whatever power he held over her would be neutered forever.

But she wanted it. Wanted it badly. Wanted *him* to be the one behind her, keeping her safe while she lived out a dark fantasy she might not get to experience again.

And he'd refused.

"Stay and play or leave," A barked. "You're killing the mood."

B grabbed her hips and urged her back into motion. Aesylt lifted and did as he asked, but nothing was the same anymore. The spell had been broken, and all she felt was lost, her thoughts spiraling down a dark corridor.

"Come home with me."

"Close," B groaned.

"Ella. Look at me," Rahn pleaded.

Dizziness punched her in the face. She rolled off B. Her hand clawed at her face, ripping at the blindfold, and the assault of light left her nauseated. The room spun, and it seemed no matter where she landed her hands or her knees, she was crawling into nothing... nowhere.

"Ella?" Rahn went to her.

"I don't feel so—" She gripped the seams of two cushions for support and vomited.

"What did you give her?" Rahn demanded. He gathered her hair at the nape of her neck.

"Nothing that would do this," A said. "It just heightens the experience. That's all."

"It wasn't..." Aesylt hurled again. *It wasn't the serum. I don't know what this is. It's the stench. It's the... I don't know what's wrong with me.*

"She's done here," Rahn said. He slowly stood. "Ella and I are here as guests of Pieter Dereham. If that doesn't cool your blood, there are swords in the rack by the entrance."

"The... fuck..." B whistled. "We're not here to force anyone to do anything! She came here on her own. Ella's free to leave if it's what she wants."

"Got what you wanted, did you?" Rahn retorted.

"Rahn..." Aesylt vomited through fresh tears. For years she'd been too broken to cry, and twice now she'd done it in as many days. *It's finally happening. I'm breaking into a million pieces.*

"What did she say?" A asked, confused.

"I have you, Squish," Rahn whispered, closing her in an embrace from behind. "Don't think about anything else. It's just you and me now."

"Come on, let's go, B."

She didn't begin to fully sob until both of the men had left.

"I don't know what's wrong. I wanted this, but now I feel so..." Aesylt went limp when he shoved her robe back through her arms. "You should have stayed away."

"You should know by now I'd never leave you alone in a place like this," he said and lifted her into his arms as he stood.

"Rahn—"

"Tell me about the stars, Aesylt."

"What?" Her tears stained his robe, but his words brought her momentarily to life. That night in the tree came swimming back to her... the way he'd climbed for her, risked everything for her.

"Just press your face to my chest, close your eyes, and tell me about the stars, Squish."

Rahn was aware of the concerned and curious eyes following them down the red-carpeted hall as he carried a weeping Aesylt, but he was singularly focused on getting her the bloody hell out of there. They could think whatever they damn well pleased.

When he stepped into the green room with her, relief crept in. They were close. He would find the guards and get her safely into the wagon, and they could put the night behind them.

His gaze locked onto the door, but Pieter stepped in front of him.

"Whoa. Did something happen to her?" He was either a better actor than Rahn was aware of, or his concern was genuine.

But Rahn didn't care about that either. "We're leaving. Move."

"Is she all right?"

"A bit late to be asking that," Rahn muttered and shoved past, marching through a thick silence that followed him all the way to the welcome rush of fresh air.

Aesylt blinked languid and slow, like the world as it passed by at half the pace it should be while she bounced in Rahn's muscular arms.

Rahn. Adrahn. Her scholar. She'd been running away from him all night, only to land right back where she'd started.

Tell me about the stars, Aesylt.

The trees bowed and bent, consumed by flames. But no, that wasn't right. They weren't on fire. The flickering was from the bonfires, and the bonfires were in the—

Aesylt blacked out.

Rahn had been gently smoothing the sponge against Aesylt's tender flesh for the past hour. She'd woken intermittently, long enough to mumble gibberish before succumbing back to her heavy slumber.

She slept against his chest in the bath. The whole night seemed like a fever dream. Nothing else explained the gentle peace he felt listening to her inhalations and exhalations as the snow fell in soft flakes outside the window. It was a jarring departure from the fear and anger that had carried him down the long hall.

The bathwater had gone cold long ago, but the fire was keeping him warm enough.

He closed his eyes and kissed the top of her head, lost for what to do about any of it.

Reluctantly, he broke the spell and lifted her from the tub. She stirred in his arms but didn't wake, not even when he dried her and slid her nightgown over her clean body, or when he laid her in the bed.

"Are you... Are you mad at me?" Her soft voice drifted from the bed. Her eyes struggled to open.

"Mad? Squish..." Rahn sighed, burying his face into his hands. "No. No, I'm not mad. You've done nothing wrong."

"If you're not mad, you're... You're something."

"Confused," he said after a soft pause. He sighed. "Worried. They drugged you, and you *vomited,* and—"

"They didn't drug me, and that's not... It's not why I vomited."

He shook his head. "Then why?"

"You don't think I was coerced, do you?"

"Why did you vomit, Aesylt?"

"Because I wasn't coerced."

"If you were, those men would be dead, and I would be in jail."

She drew the blanket tight to her neck. "I don't regret it, so if you're waiting for me to say I am—"

"I wasn't—"

"But I never, ever want to do that again." Her eyes welled with more tears.

Rahn tried to breathe deep, but it came short. "Why?"

She rolled her head to face away. "I thought I could be the kind of person who could enjoy a casual encounter and still be me. I thought maybe..." She shook her head tightly. "And you... Did you have your own... fun... tonight?"

"No." Rahn cleared his throat and smoothed some lumps from her blanket to keep his hands busy.

"Why not?"

"I didn't go there for that."

A distressed frown knit her eyebrows together. "When I asked you to stay and participate with those men, you said no."

Rahn jumped to answer but realized he needed to think first. "I *wanted* to share it with you, Aesylt, just not... not in that environment. Not with those men."

Aesylt considered all of that for a while. Their silence turned from careful to comfortable, and he was priming himself for the inevitable retreat to his own bed when she finally had something to say.

"Scholar, I... I think we've done enough. In the coitus curricula, I mean. I think we've done all we can for it, and it's..." She rolled her lips inward, sucking in through her nose. "I think I'm done."

Rahn squeezed her leg through the blanket, fervently nodding through a powerful impulse to cry. "I agree, Squish. We've done more than enough. No one would dare say otherwise."

TWENTY-THREE
ALL HAIL THE END OF DAYS

Aesylt guessed it was an ambush the minute she saw her brother sitting to the right of Lord Dereham in the Great Hall. His unannounced visit wasn't what put her nerves on edge though, nor the strange, almost fatherly looks passed between Rustan and his son. It was Imryll's face, reddened from a good long cry, that had Aesylt pausing midway to her brother and saying, "All right, someone is going to tell me what's going on *right now.*"

"It's good to see you too, cub," Drazhan said dryly. He was smiling, broader than the general mood seemed to require. "I'm sorry for not sending word first. My movements are closely tracked. Couldn't take the risk."

"You know damn good and well that wasn't my question, wulf."

"Why not begin with some cider? Aesylt, you do recall that all cider we consume here at the keep is in fact made by the Dereham men themselves?" Rustan poured six mugs and slid them to each of those in attendance.

"I recall," she said tersely, glaring daggers at her brother. She chanced a brief look at Imryll, but her obvious distress only inflamed Aesylt more.

"Adrahn, good to see you," Drazhan said. "Will you both sit?"

"Not sure that I will," Aesylt said, right as Rahn took his seat. She shouldn't be surprised he would cow to Drazhan's intimidation. He was a rule man through and through. "Not until you tell me what's upset Imryll."

She had another reason for not wanting to sit. The soreness of her evening antics had caught up to her when she rose that morning, achy and nauseated.

"Aesylt, please," Imryll said, sounding far more passive and defeated than Aesylt was accustomed to. Whatever had happened had done more than upset Imryll. It had broken her spirit. "You need to hear this. And prepare yourself. It will hurt, perhaps more than it should."

Rustan whistled. "The bad news first then?"

"What bad news?" Rahn asked. "Has someone been hurt? Have things in the Cross escalated?"

"Nothing in the Cross is any better or worse than you left it," Drazhan said, his eyes on Aesylt. "Marek remains a craven fugitive. We are still divided, and war seems to be the only weapon we have left to break it." He blinked hard and snapped his gaze at Pieter. "I think the young Lord Dereham should be the one to explain his betrayal."

"Betrayal?" Aesylt shifted her attention between her brother and Pieter. "What betrayal?" *What betrayal could be important enough to drag my brother away from the most important days of his stewardship?*

He couldn't have told Drazhan about Revelry, or Drazhan would be far from calm.

"It's our hope you'll hear what Pieter has to say with an open mind," Rustan said with a strained smile. "Betrayal requires ill intent, and Pieter has, for all his faults, always been well intentioned in his choices."

Pieter folded his hands with a hard look at the pitcher. "I suppose the only way to begin is to answer a question posed to me on the day you all arrived." He looked up and into the distance. "I told you about my time in the Seven Sisters, Aesylt. But what I didn't tell you is it put me on the path to meet a man named Fair Douglass. Fair is—"

"The archminister of the Reliquary," Aesylt whispered. Imryll's pulse pounded in her anticipation.

"He is now," Pieter said slowly. "But at the time, the men who conceived of the Reliquary, a place of faith and learning in the name of our Rhiagain kings, had only an old abbey to conduct their work from. The great towers of Riverchapel, most of which are, even now, still in construction, did not exist. He was searching for like-minded men to join him in his vision, and he invited me to become one of his ministers." His hands unfolded and rejoined. "I accepted, followed him to Riverchapel... and that's the truth of where I've been for two of these past eight years."

"Now explain to Aesylt why you kept this from us," Imryll spat. She reminded Aesylt of the woman she'd been when she had come to the Cross to marry Drazhan.

But Aesylt knew what he was about to say. And if he told the *full* truth, then both Drazhan and Imryll would know her and Rahn's secret, which could never, ever happen. "So let me see if I can fill in the details for you, Pieter," she said, sneering as she paced her side of the table. "Your father... what, wrote to you, to tell you we were coming? You told Douglass, or maybe someone else who was equally bent on edging us out, and he ordered you to come spy on us?"

Pieter offered a penitent shrug. "Yes... and no, Aesylt. You're right about Douglass. He never wanted you involved, but he knew if he just removed you without cause, there would be repercussions. Truth is, I think he's nervous there are two Duncarrow residents living in your village, because he can't know for sure what their relationship is with the current crown." His eyes closed through a long sigh. "I did tell him about all your work with...

astronomy." He locked her gaze, the secret passing between them in silence. "I *did* send along your notes, just as I told you I had. But... He wrote yesterday to inform me that Witchwood Cross may no longer take part in any of the Reliquary's research, at least not in the current conditions."

Aesylt's heart pulsed so hard, she finally had no choice but to sit. She pulled the chair out and perched on the side of the wooden seat. "*Our* research. *Our* vision."

"And you wonder why I left Duncarrow," Imryll retorted with a sniff. "The same kind of men who run that rock run the Reliquary. There is no mystery in those men's hearts. They're all the same."

"Did you know, my lord?" Aesylt turned her ire on Rustan.

"No, cub," Rustan replied, no longer pushing his joviality on the table. "We were disgruntledly aware of his association with Douglass, but not that he'd joined their efforts."

"*Why* though?" Rahn asked, scooting to the edge of his seat as he leaned in. "What *cause* do they have to make such a decision?"

Pieter lifted his shoulders in another shrug. "He didn't see fit to tell me."

Aesylt watched him lie and read the truth in it. Everything Pieter knew, the Reliquary knew. Using names of other cohort members on their reports had only worked when no one else knew they were the ones actually submitting. Whether intentional or inadvertent, Pieter's own version of events could not possibly match the one she and Rahn had sold in their reports.

It meant they'd known almost from the very beginning of their submissions from Wulfsgate, and yet had let them continue on and on, like fools.

"Doesn't matter the cause." Imryll wiped her eyes. "What's done is done. It was always going to end this way, once they decided themselves the arbiter of right and wrong."

"Gods," Rahn whispered and flopped back in his chair.

Aesylt had been waiting for this day, but it was no less crushing to watch, to *feel,* her passion slipping from her fingers. There'd be no more research. No more joy of discovery alongside others who were just as curious about the ways of their world. No more building something that everyone could benefit from.

She buried her face in her hands.

"All is not lost, cub," Rustan said, almost tenderly. "Pieter did what he could to save your projects, but this battle was unwinnable, even for him. But it does not need to end here, does it? Your passions can continue." He nodded briskly. "Not just continue, but go further than they ever could have in the Cross."

"Just tell her," Imryll said, looking away.

"The stewardess is understandably upset," Rustan said. "And we will make it right for her. As for you, Aesylt and Duke Rahn, the Reliquary has extended an invitation for you both to join their ranks, where you'll be part of all future research efforts."

Aesylt snorted and shifted her eyes toward the side. "Have they now?"

"That doesn't ring true to me," Rahn said. He squeezed his eyes closed, shaking his head. "If they wanted us to be a part of the research, they would have allowed us to continue as we were. This feels more like..." He clicked his tongue.

"Well, I wouldn't go to the Reliquary and lick their boots if they held a sword to my throat." Aesylt could hardly breathe. *They know. They know. They know, and the whole dirty secret could come crashing down on us at any moment.*

"No, you always have a choice, cub." Drazhan rapped his knuckles on the table. "And I... I was wrong, for not listening to you when you told me what you wanted. I can't protect you forever, and you don't need it, do you? If you want to be a wife, then I will no longer stand stubbornly in your way." He smiled—a phenomenon so rare, Aesylt knew whatever he said next would be the best or worst thing that had ever happened to her. "When Lord Dereham sent word to me, I was surprised. Not that he's fond of you, because who could know my sister and not be?" His smile faded. He seemed himself again. "Lord Dereham has proposed a match between you and Pieter. You will be the next Lady Dereham, Aesylt. You."

Aesylt slapped both hands onto the table. "I'm sorry, *what*?"

"He's your childhood friend. He shares your interests. He's a good, respectable man, and your children will inherit one of the greatest legacies in the kingdom. He can help you achieve what you want the most, to continue your research." Drazhan bowed his head over his folded hands. "If you're still thinking about Val—"

"I never *wanted* to marry Valerian!" Aesylt swung her gaze along the table, looking for an ally but finding only pity. "I made him a promise I never expected I'd be held to, because I wanted to keep him safe. That's all! Yes, I wanted to marry, but that was before... before the scholar showed up, and everything changed."

"Cub, you're not seeing the full picture here. You can wed a man who shares your passions and, at least until he becomes Lord Dereham in his own right, can study *at* the Reliquary, where they have every resource imaginable."

"Because they're crown sycophants. It's all crown gold," Aesylt replied. Her spittle landed on the table, and she sat back down. "You, *you,* the man who sacrificed a decade of his life to bring them down, are the last person I would ever expect to be licking their boots."

Drazhan's mouth drew into a tight pinch. He scoffed and snapped his head back. "Aesylt, from the moment—from the *very moment*—the Reliquary took over my wife's work and invited her to 'participate,' I was ready to raze the cursed institution to the ground. But it wasn't what she wanted. I have battled my own anger, set it grudgingly aside, because Imryll is one of the most brilliant women in this kingdom, and a hundred of their men couldn't hold a candle to our one of her." He inhaled an unsteady breath. "All of that, I could say about my little sister as well. If... If *studying* kindles your spirit, Aesylt, then I want that for you, even if it means holding my nose while you consort with their tainted ilk."

Aesylt sank lower on her chair, lost for words. Drazhan truly believed he was doing right by her, and she couldn't even argue with his reasoning. Pieter was an ideal mate in most ways. Highborn. A scholar like herself. A friend from childhood. And despite the way he'd played both sides, in his own way, he'd protected her and Rahn. He'd kept their secret, when he had no reason to.

Except he *did* have a reason. It wouldn't do at all if everyone knew his future wife had been rutting around with other men.

Especially if my moon flow continues to evade me.

She whipped her head upward to see how Rahn was reacting to the shocking betrothal, but his eyes were fixed firmly on his own lap.

Pieter was doing the same.

Cowards. Both of them.

"What your brother isn't saying, sweet cub, is that this arrangement would put an immediate end to the insurrection in Witchwood Cross. The moment you become a Dereham, it's no longer up to Drazhan whether Wulfsgate gets involved." Rustan clamped a hand atop hers with a quick, firm squeeze. "He won't say any of this because it's not why he did it. He wouldn't sell you out to save your village, even to his ruin. He wouldn't broker any marriage he didn't think would improve your life. But I don't need to tell you that, do I?"

Aesylt could only shake her head. Tears threatened, but she had no idea if they'd fall. The past few days had thrown everything into question, and she could be sure of nothing anymore. "Then prove it, Drazhan, and let this be my choice to make."

"It *is* your choice," Drazhan affirmed. "You don't want this? Then we're done here." He held out his hands. "The only thing I will ask of you, Aesylt, is to sleep on it, so you can be sure you're answering with a clear mind. Whatever your decision in the morning, we'll consider it final."

"Thank you," she said, though she didn't feel grateful.

"This is not some coup to corner you into something you don't want, Aes." Pieter finally spoke again. "I had no designs on marriage myself, which is why my poor mother had to bring another child along in her middle years. But a partner, one I could share passions with? An equal? A friend? That's something I could look forward to."

"Friends don't... They don't lie to each other." Aesylt closed her mouth when an involuntary sob crept up. "They don't deceive."

"I thought I was helping you by acting as a mediator. I swear."

"Quite helpful, Pieter, seeing as you got us thrown out of our own work!"

"I hope we haven't misread the situation." Rustan frowned. "I had spoken with Duke Tindahl before sending word to the Cross, to ascertain whether this would be an acceptable match."

"You spoke to the scholar about this?" Aesylt was stunned.

Rahn tilted his head, shaking it. "My lord, I never said—"

"And you said *nothing* to me?"

He sighed and turned his eyes downward. "It wasn't my place, Aesylt."

"It doesn't matter," Imryll stated, cutting in. "As my husband said, this is Aesylt's choice. She has the information before her now, and she can decide for herself." She pushed back from the table. "I need some time with everything. Excuse me."

Aesylt watched her leave and spun on her brother. "What Lord Dereham said, about saving the village..."

"I've refused his men every time he's offered them," Drazhan said evenly. "That should tell you where I stand on it."

"And if I turn down this betrothal?"

"Then we will do what we have always done. Handle our own business."

Aesylt threw her head back with a laugh. "All hail the end of days then. No pressure whatsoever. No, this definitely will not haunt me to my very last step. Save the village or think only of myself and what I want? What kind of choice is that?" She staggered back from the table, tripping over her chair as she tried to stand. "I need..." Her hands flew to her mouth. "Some air. Don't follow me!"

Aesylt emptied her belly into a crop of bushes at the south entrance to the Wintergarden. Shaking, she rose to her feet and wiped the back of her hand across her mouth, staring into the lush escape beckoning only a few steps away.

But she didn't crave the comfort of beauty.

Aesylt turned her back on the Wintergarden and moved instead toward the livestock pens.

For the second time in her life, she was at a crossroads.

She couldn't fathom how everything had slipped away from her so fast. The mess with Val and Marek, the tangled web of lies she'd spun with Rahn, her broken heart... a complete miscalculation of the risks in the celestial realm and never considering the possibility she could become impregnated there and carry that affliction into her own world and life.

But it all had started with Val, she thought as she traced her hands along the thin wires of the chicken coops. It had started with Val and the empty promise she'd made, which had launched her village into the verge of a civil war.

Aesylt wrapped her cloak tight and slipped into a nearby barn. She settled onto a pile of hay in a dark corner and drew her knees to her chest.

If she was the one who had gotten them all into the mess they were in... then she was the one who had to guide them safely out of it.

Pieter waited in the library for the scholar. He readied himself for the inevitable skewering, which he deserved but was still not looking forward to.

He hadn't always been so secretive, but one of the crueler lessons he'd learned was that it was a dangerous gambit to put one's faith in one person or belief system. *Always keep your feet in both ponds,* an old friend had said, and it had stuck with Pieter, even before he'd really understood the meaning.

He believed in the work the Reliquary was doing, and they were the only institution in the realm with the funds and sponsorship to do it properly. But he abhorred the way they'd pilfered the stewardess's ideas and then slowly, and wrongly, had edged her out of it altogether.

And while he *had* been sending regular reports to the archminister about Rahn and Aesylt's doings, he'd arrogantly believed his endorsement of their commitment was enough to protect them from being extricated.

His old friend had failed to mention that if one straddled two ponds for too long, they tended not to notice they were drowning in both.

The library doors whooshed open. Rahn appeared within the opening, his face as red as the apple Pieter had eaten at breakfast. With his shoulders lifting in hard breaths, the scholar released the doors, and they slammed closed.

Here we go.

"Scholar." Pieter held his smile, his only visible defense. "I know what Aesylt means to you, but let me assure you—"

"You are not fit to even speak her name!" Rahn stormed in, his voice thundering. He wore a look bordering on confused, like even he couldn't discern where all the fire inside of him was being stoked. "You know *nothing* except treachery, Pieter. Save your hollow truths for those more susceptible to your lies."

Pieter inhaled slowly, tempering his own reaction. He hadn't expected anyone to be happy after the revelations in the Great Hall—including himself, though no one would waste their tears of pity on him—but he was surprised Tindahl had it in him. The man was absurdly intelligent but woefully disconnected from his emotions. It seemed unlikely he'd ever acknowledge his feelings for Aesylt, but maybe Pieter had been wrong. "Hollow truths?

You said nothing at all in the Great Hall, so what good are your words now?"

"It wasn't my place to speak. And this isn't about an arranged marriage. It's about your role in stealing the most meaningful thing Imryll and Aesylt have ever been a part of."

"Not about me marrying Aesylt, is it?" Pieter raised both of his brows and moved to the drink cart to pour them both a tumbler of mead. "So you're fine with that? You don't have any particularly strong personal feelings on the matter?"

"Personal feelings?" Rahn sputtered. "My only concern is that she is allowed to choose for herself, and Drazhan has... had made that clear enough. She'll choose what's right for her."

Pieter spun around, holding both drinks. "Oh, and what choice is that?"

Rahn's face was a portrait of pure hatred. Disgust. "You threw away any chance of her accepting your betrothal when you betrayed her."

"Betraying her would have been to tell my father and the steward what the two of you have *really* been doing in the tower."

"You want me to believe you had altruistic motives? That you aren't holding onto the information for another opportunity?"

The information *was* useful. But Pieter had no intention of using it. Nor did he expect Aesylt to accept the betrothal, even if it was the prudent choice. That didn't mean he had the stomach for indulging the scholar's delusions though. "You're entitled to your fears, Scholar, but it wouldn't do at all to have my wife's fidelity called into question before we're even wed."

Rahn narrowed his eyes in disgust. "You're mad if you think she'd ever marry you."

"If she's smart, she will."

"You cannot even fathom intelligence such as hers."

"If you truly cared for her, you'd convince her to accept, Scholar. She'll never get a better offer. She can save an untold number of lives by averting a war her brother is too proud to accept help for under any other condition. Aesylt knows, once she peels away the shock and anger, that I would make a suitable partner. I don't want someone to bear my children and make my home; I want someone who will challenge me, every day. She could live whatever life she wanted." Pieter emptied his drink and set the scholar's on a nearby table, preemptively grinning at the scholar's reaction to what he was about to say. "It isn't as if she has a heart match waiting for her."

Rahn pressed his fingers to his temples with a bracing sigh. "What, exactly, is your game, Pieter?"

"It was never a game." Pieter crossed his arms and leaned against his mother's abandoned pipe organ. The thing was older than all of them and was seldom used, but she refused to get rid of it. She held onto things long past their expiry; it was why it had taken her so long to come to terms with her own son's defection. "I'm not in love with her, but I've never been in love and can't say it holds much interest for me. It seems... distracting. Marriage was my father's idea, and I recognize the merit in it. I see a future where she and I could do great things together. Even love can't compare to that." Pieter propped his elbows on the smooth mahogany surface. "A value I assumed you and I shared. The research has to come first, no?"

"You know nothing of me and my values." Rahn scowled, scoffing, and turned toward a long shelf full of weathered journals. "And you know nothing of *her*."

"Not like you, you mean?" Pieter peeled away and started toward the scholar. "You could still have her, you know. My father doesn't know this, and he wouldn't hear it if I told him, but I won't be having any children. Aesylt can bed whoever she wants, and I'll never begrudge her for it because I intend to do the same."

"You," Rahn said, horror spreading over his face, "are disgusting. A foul excuse for a man. How can you look at yourself?"

"I seem to recall that Duke Rahn Tindahl had the Reliquary in mind as his own destination, before he was waylaid in the Cross for... research." Pieter laughed. "Or whatever excuse you're using now. You could have that again, Scholar. *That* is the future you've been offered. And she'll be there. You don't have to give up anything. The only person with the authority to care is me, and I don't."

Rahn continued to stare at him with the same aghast scowl, his head moving in one long endless shake. "You think you're describing freedom? What you offer her is just a cage of another metal."

"We're all caged, Scholar, if we're brave enough to admit it."

"I was only headed for the Reliquary before I knew who they were. How low they'd stoop to get what they want." Rahn straightened, his lip hitching. "I wouldn't join them now for all the gold and renown in the world. And you really don't know Aesylt if you think she feels any differently."

"So says the man who showed her the sun and then took it away." Pieter slowed as he neared Rahn, who was practically radiating with heat and fury. "Only her husband and her blood have the right to such a stirring defense on her behalf. You're just the man who saw an opportunity to have her without commitment and took it."

Rahn raised a hand, then clenched it. His head passed slowly back and forth. "Say whatever you want about me. *Do* whatever you want to me. But if you ever do another thing to harm her, say a single word that even slightly fades her smile..." His laugh was almost sinister. "I may not appear to you to be a violent man, but I only value the lives of those who value the lives of others."

Pieter flinched when the slamming door shook the furniture. He chuckled to himself when it settled.

The problem with men like Rahn Tindahl was a surplus of vision but a lack of grit. All the threats in the world wouldn't resolve his anger or address the gap already forming where Aesylt had once fit.

Pieter might not be in love with her, but he did love her, in the same way he loved his family—enough to fight for her and even die for her, if matters called for it.

It was more than Rahn would ever allow himself to offer her, and Pieter could live with that.

Aesylt waited for Rahn in the tower for over an hour, plenty of time to devise all sorts of reasons he might be avoiding her. Every one made her feel worse.

She'd already decided what she needed to do, but she couldn't until she looked Rahn in the eye and asked him how he could just *sit there* while others talked about marrying her off to another man. How he could... how he could dare suggest to Lord Dereham that it was the right move. How he could whisk her away from Revelry like a protective lover and then abandon her like it had meant nothing at all.

When he finally opened the door—wearing a pathetic, defeated look that only made her angrier—she was so exasperated, she had to close her eyes and remind herself that he hadn't yet had the chance to explain himself.

"You're here," he said. Her heart added a tone of accusation to it.

"You sound disappointed," she retorted, not fast enough to quash her annoyance. *I might never see him again. If I want answers, a fight isn't the way to get them.*

"I'm sorry you feel that way." Rahn closed the door and went straight to his bed. It creaked when he dropped onto it.

I'm sorry you feel that way? Aesylt was astounded at how quickly his concern for her had shifted to apathy. She braced herself on the back of the chair. "Now I'm another man's problem is what you really mean."

"If that's what I meant, Aesylt, I would have said it."

"Well," she said, throwing up her hands. "Now I understand why you sat there and did *nothing* when they tried to sell me off to the man who betrayed us."

Rahn didn't speak for so long, she pulled back the curtain to see if he was still listening. "It was not my place to offer an opinion. And... Maybe this will be good for you. Your brother knows your needs better than I."

"*Good* for—" Aesylt inhaled a gulp of cool, musty air. Had the room always smelled that way? Had it always felt so... so small and cloying? "Are you punishing me for last night?"

"What a ludicrous suggestion. I already told you I wasn't upset." The disgust in his voice was callous and wounding.

She ripped back the curtain and found him sitting at the edge of his bed, bent over his lap. "What's ludicrous is you becoming someone else entirely without so much as an explanation. Is it so easy to shut me out of your life?"

"Like you did at Revelry?"

"Excuse me?"

"You're the one who declared our research ended."

Aesylt reared back. "That's not what I'm talking about, and you know it's not."

He shook his head at the floor, lifting his palms. "What should I have said to them, Aesylt?"

"The truth maybe?"

"What truth?"

Everything inside of her was screaming to just go. Just let things lie. Preserve some shred of dignity. But she couldn't. She needed to know, even if it shattered her. "That I cannot marry Pieter Dereham because someone else already holds my heart in their hands. That you're... that *you're* in love with me, and it would be impossible to watch me wed another man."

Rahn's back lifted in a hard breath. He bowed his head lower and dragged his hands through his hair and down to his neck, gripping it. "Oh, Aesylt... That would not have been an accurate claim for me to make."

She staggered back, her boot catching against a stone. If he'd screamed the words, said them in the heat of the moment, she'd know he hadn't meant them. But his calm delivery—his utter exhaustion of her—was evident in every tense of his muscles.

"Well I don't believe you, Adrahn. I don't believe your actions, your words, add up to such careless disregard of me."

"I care about you... You know I do." He released a long exhale. "But everything you've weighed and estimated about me has been misread. Our research required a level of intimacy, so I may have enhanced the depth of my own emotions to achieve what we needed. Hurting you was never my intention, but I was clear, and we agreed, from the beginning, what it was, what it wasn't—"

"Nothing is anything until it is! That's how all relationships begin, as nothing." Aesylt turned and paced, grappling for some semblance of control. But she was truly losing it. Inch by inch, she was slipping away. "No, I don't believe you."

"It's the truth."

"I don't *believe* you!" she screamed.

He pulled his hands down his face. "I can't do anything about that, can I? I have been nothing but who I said I was. I'm not a family man. I'm not *made* for that kind of life. And even if I was..."

She saw the strained flex of his jaw... the white of his knuckles as he tensed his hands over his face.

"I don't feel that way about you. I'm sorry."

"You cannot possibly—" Aesylt gripped her sides, fighting through the pain of her heart shattering. "You cannot possibly want to see me with another man."

"Well, I've already done that, haven't I?"

She shuddered in a breath, stunned he would go there. "That was cruel. And unfair."

"Life is cruel and unfair, Aesylt. You know it better than most."

"You're *trying* to wound me, so it will be easier to walk away—"

"Stop. This is pointless."

Tears spilled from her eyes. She reached a shaking hand up to wipe them, but there'd be more. Rahn had awakened that in her, like so many other things, and she'd never be able to put her heart back in a box. It would never be safe again. "If you're going to lie to me, then look at me when you do it. Look me in the eye and tell me you don't love me."

"You're the one forcing my hand here—"

"Look at me, Adrahn, and tell me you feel nothing for me!"

His hands clenched into fists before they slid away. He seemed to fortify himself before sitting up, but she could see, before he ever opened his mouth, that no matter how he felt, he would hold fast to his meaningless convictions. They were all he had.

His face and eyes were red, but he locked both on her, just as she'd asked, and said, "I do love you, Aesylt, but not like that. I'm deeply sorry if I inadvertently contributed to your belief otherwise."

Aesylt nodded, at first slowly but then faster, her movements gaining speed and courage as she took one last look at the room where she'd returned to life. She could hardly breathe for all the effort it took, her thoughts a scattered tempest of where she'd been before and where she needed to go next.

She'd already packed a small bag, though she almost hadn't. A part of her had believed Rahn would, faced with the finality of it all, finally break down the walls keeping them apart. But it was not to be, and there was nothing left to the wreckage but more groveling... more pain.

"Well, uh... Thank you, I suppose, for your honesty," she said, blinking the spots from her eyes as she reached for her knapsack. "I won't trouble you about it again."

"Where are you going with that?" Rahn pointed at the bag.

"Do you care?" She swung it over her shoulder and took another look around the room to be sure she had missed nothing critical. But she didn't need much where she was going. Her gowns would be sent home with her trunks. "My brother's here now. Whatever promise you made to him has been fulfilled."

"I care." His voice broke, but she knew without looking that it meant nothing, beyond how tired he was. Of her. Of their research. Of all of it. "You don't have to go on my account."

"I'm going to sleep in the keep tonight, and I'll stay there until either Drazhan lets me go home or my new husband decides I belong somewhere else. With our research concluded, there's no reason we ever have to see each other again."

"Aesylt." He sighed. "I don't want to leave things like this."

"You were quite clear where you want to leave things." She paused at the door. Beautiful, painful memories flashed through her mind. Their first time. The way he'd taken to sleeping in her bed when he could see she felt unsafe. How he watched her at supper when he didn't think she was aware. The little ways he looked out for her. Maybe he was right, and she was the fool after all. The whole point had been to prove to herself she could separate emotion from her work, and she was the one who'd fallen in love anyway. "I should apologize for not respecting the rules, for falling for you against all my better judgment, but I find the words impossible to say." She closed her eyes and rolled her hand with the doorknob. "Pieter was right. You're a coward, Adrahn."

"Wait—"

Whatever else he said was lost with the slam of the door. She heard a crash in the room, but she was already running down the steps, shoving her memories of Rahn Tindahl into the past where they belonged.

Lord Dereham didn't question her request to sleep in the keep that night. There was already a room made up, and they were more than happy to offer it to her. She saw relief in his eyes when she asked, the lord probably thinking about how it would look to others to have his future daughter-in-law shacking up with her scholar.

She had no intention of sleeping, however.

Not in Wulfsgate Keep.

Maybe not at all, depending on how the night went.

It was past midnight before she slipped out of the room, armed with the lies she would tell to slip from one place to another.

Another half tick of the moon passed before she made it to the stables, dressed in Rahn's clothing, hooded in his cloak. It was easier than it should have been to join a caravan leaving through the gates headed north. No one even looked twice at the smallish "man" huddled in the back of one of the wagons, holding tight to the stupid wooden squirrel she should have left in Wulfsgate.

Two hours later, she rode into the tiny village of Voyager's Rest, on the back of a horse she'd stolen from the caravan when they'd stopped to fill their waterskins.

It was a town for travelers, a row of inns lining the main road. She'd been there once before, when her father and Hraz had been alive. They'd taken her and Val along for a trip to Wulfsgate, but a storm had waylaid their arrival, so they'd been forced to take a room for the night.

Val would remember. He had to.

She paid double for the room and asked where she might find a ravener. The pubkeep directed her to a tower at the end of the road, and she made her way down there, her hood drawn and her dangerous letter in hand.

Sending a raven to Witchwood Cross came with significant risk, but even if her words fell into the wrong hands, no one would be able to read them—no one except Nik and Val, who had learned the language of Old Ilynglass same as she had, from Rahn. The rest of the cohort hadn't been interested in such a daunting endeavor, but Nik and Val had relished the idea of knowing something no one else in the village did.

If she sent the message straight to Val, it would be burned before he even knew of it. But it might reach him if it made it safely to Niklaus first.

Aesylt pulled Nik's handkerchief from her satchel and handed it to the ravener. "This has his scent on it. But here are the coordinates that will get your bird close. Is that enough?"

"It's enough," the ravener replied and accepted her coin.

She stayed to watch the raven fly away and didn't leave until he disappeared into the stormy night sky.

The final words of her appeal played in her head, over and over, as she stared at the clouds settling over the village.

Tell him it was where my ota, Hraz, and the two of us spent a frosty night. Val will know the place. If he's inclined to come, he needs to come now, before they find me. You're the only one I can trust with this.

Don't forget the grimizhna tea.

"Please," she said, wiping away the last of her tears as she walked back to the inn to wait.

SLAYER
OF MONSTERS

TWENTY-FOUR
A FUTURE YET TO BE DECIDED

Until Niklaus anxiously slipped him the coded letter from Aesylt, Valerian hadn't realized it was exactly what he had been waiting for all along.

He'd been chasing her all their lives. As toddlers, in their shared nursery. As adventurous children, through the safe parts of a forest that was almost never theirs. As adults, into a future yet to be decided.

Valerian had never questioned that future would lead to Aesylt as his wife.

Not because she was a Wynter and a political catch.

Not because he was one of the few young men in the Cross worthy of her.

Not even because she was beautiful.

Because he loved her, and she loved him.

And yet, he'd known her promise in the barn was less about love than fear. He hadn't expected to survive his trial, but he wouldn't have held her to her word. That was how he knew he loved her, because he'd never shied away from taking what he wanted. All the beauties of the Cross he'd availed himself of in corners and shadows—who kept coming back for more, even after the thrill had subsided—had been delightful reminders he had something worth offering, something more than being the son of Baron Esker Barynov and the spare heir of Hoarfrost.

The name would take him no further. His father had chosen treachery with his whole heart. No matter how the current conflict resolved, the Barynovs would fall, and far. Valerian didn't care where he landed, only that he was likely to lose what mattered most.

He'd already *been* losing Aesylt, inch by inch, ever since the scholar had ridden into town, offering the things Valerian could not. Oh, how he'd tried though. It wasn't even pretending, because he'd desperately *wanted* to share everything with Aesylt; he needed to understand her curiosity about the world, her passion for discovery. And if he hadn't wanted any of it so badly, he never would have learned Old Ilynglass, and he wouldn't be riding to Voyager's Rest on the heels of her desperate plea.

It all had to do with the scholar somehow. When Valerian had learned she'd been sent away with Tindahl, he'd never known such raw jealousy in his life. Such animosity.

But in the end, Aesylt had called for *him*.

And he hadn't, not for a second, debated whether he would answer.

Drazhan wasn't blind. Nor was he a fool, at least not a great one. He hadn't missed the longing glances passed between his baby sister and the scholar, nor Imryll's almost amusing neutrality on the matter.

Until Rahn had stormed into his bedchamber in a panic, stammering about his "gut feeling" that something was wrong with Aesylt—a gut feeling that turned out to be suspiciously accurate—Drazhan had just never dreamed the man was foolish enough to act on any of it.

It reminded him of how he'd behaved when he'd thought his revenge against the crown had cost Imryll her life. Ten years of careful restraint had shattered at the thought of a world without her.

But Drazhan had let this man *into his home* and trusted him with Aesylt's safety.

He would deal with the duke later.

Aesylt was missing.

Her note said only *I will no longer let our village suffer. If you feel the same way, you'll let me go.*

"She cannot... She cannot *possibly* think..." Rahn rattled the chair he held tight to.

"Why was she sleeping in the keep?" Imryll asked as she fastened her robe. She was unsteady on her feet, having only fallen asleep a bit ago. No chance, however, he could convince her to go back to bed.

"She said..." Rahn's mouth tightened as he inhaled through his scrunched nose. He flicked his fingers. "We had an argument."

Don't kill him. Don't kill him. Don't kill him. "About..." Drazhan braced. "What?"

"She was upset. I... I wasn't as supportive as she wanted me to be." Rahn released the chair. "Does it *matter*, when every minute she's gone is a minute we lose? She could be anywhere by now."

"Draz already sent for Lord Dereham," Imryll said. "But there's no reason we have to wait for his men to assemble." She abandoned her robe on the bed and started for her bureau, but Drazhan reached for her arm, shaking his head with as much calm as he had left in him.

"Imryll. Please. For me," he pleaded. "I need to know you're safe. You and Aleks—and the baby."

She squeezed her eyes closed in annoyance, but nodded. "How can I help from here then?"

"Wake Uli Castel, and let him know he and my men need to be ready within the half. Then find Lady Dereham and get her to rouse her best chambermaids. We don't—*can't* know what Aes will need when we find her." Drazhan's head felt ready to implode. Imryll would know what to say to ease it, but that wasn't what he needed. "We have to be ready for anything, love."

Imryll slipped a dressing gown over her shoulders, swiftly kissed him, and whispered, "I don't know what's going on, but he knows her better than we do right now. Listen to him."

She was gone before Drazhan could respond.

The scholar stood at a window, bent over the frame. He looked stiff and aged and lost, all of which reminded Drazhan that the man was too old to be lusting after Aesylt.

On my Ancestors, it will never, ever be this man.

Drazhan rubbed his temples. "Tell me more about this fight."

"It wasn't a fight, it was a difference of opinion." Rahn straightened, his head falling back. "She was upset I didn't speak on her behalf, but it wasn't my place to position my voice above yours and Lord Dereham's."

Clipping his sword belt into place, Drazhan asked, "And if it had been your place, what would you have said?"

Rahn turned. His eyes were shot with pink and red. "You wait for your men, I'll go ahead—"

"No." Drazhan checked his sword. Sharp enough. "We'll go together. What, *exactly,* did she say that led you to believe something had happened?"

Rahn tilted his head back again. "It was... a feeling. After she left, the feeling didn't go away. I talked myself into checking on her. She was gone. That's all I know."

"An accurate one, ostensibly. So tell me, what are your *feelings* telling you now? Where is she? Back in the Cross, you think?"

Rahn lowered his eyes to the ground and shook his head. "I don't know." He glanced up in hopeless defeat. "If I did, it's where I'd be now."

Drazhan laced his boots, thinking ahead to the search. The snow and darkness would be significant impairments to progress. She could already be halfway to Witchwood Cross by the time they saddled and mounted, but if she was still on the road, those same perils would reach her too. "My wife says you know my sister better than all of us. Silence hurts her more than any confession you'll make."

"There's…" Rahn's voice cracked. He glanced away, straining. "If I thought anything I could say now would help us find her, I would hold nothing back. Marek… Marek is still *out* there, and now, she's… I wish to the gods I knew more. I wish I'd listened, that I'd heard what she wanted me to hear. She was angry and determined when I saw her last, and you and I both know Aesylt is capable of anything."

Drazhan dipped toward the window and checked the sky. It was just past midnight. They still had a full night ahead. Rahn was right about one thing; every minute they spent talking was a minute she slipped farther away. "When Aesylt is safe, you're going to be forthcoming about what's gone on between you two, or you can be sure you will *never* see her again in this life."

The person standing before Valerian was the most exquisite woman he'd ever seen—and also a complete stranger.

She answered the door to her room at the inn with her hood pulled tight. After casting suspicious glances into the hall, she yanked him inside and bolted all three locks before throwing herself into his arms.

And she was crying.

Sobbing.

The last time he'd seen her shed even a single tear had been on the worst night of their lives.

"Hey, Aessy. Aessy, I'm here." Valerian pulled back, holding tight to her shoulders as he choked on his own well of complicated emotions. Right away he could see she'd been through something she might not be willing or able to explain. She seemed older—no, not older, but wiser somehow. The kind of wisdom he attributed to the adults of his life, who had lived through the cycles of peace and war and were always ready for either. In her eyes were a hundred confessions she might never offer.

"You're alive. You're really, truly alive. V, I..." She stepped backward and sank onto a chair, burying her face between her legs. "I wasn't sure you'd come."

"I had to satisfy my curiosity about why Aesylt Wynter is holed up in an inn under an assumed name, sending coded messages through a war zone." Valerian dragged a chair in front of her and sat on it. She was still staring at the floor. "Aessy. Come on, it's all right. I'm here now."

"I used to wonder if I would ever cry again," she said, swiping her face on both sleeves before looking up with a drowsy smile. "Now I wonder if I'll ever stop."

Valerian had wondered the same thing. Memories of that night were never far from his mind. Nor Nik's. The two men had only spoken of the Nok Mora a handful of times since, but every time had been about Aesylt. Their worry for her. The fear of what suffering and denial turned into when buried so deep. "There's nothing wrong with crying, beautiful. Makes your eyes bluer."

"My..." Aesylt's hands flew to her face, which crumpled in playful annoyance. "Did you... have much trouble getting out of the Cross?"

"Hardly any." Valerian shrugged and sat back. It burned him to think of how easily he'd slipped away actually. If he'd ever questioned his role as a pawn in his father's games, he needed to no longer. All the talk of dozens of guards in the halls outside of his room—the show of nursing their baby boy back to health—was just theater. In fact, the only thing his father had done since he'd awoken, aching and confused, was threaten him into swearing fealty to their cause. "Hoarfrost is pretty well guarded, but they mostly leave me alone, unless they need to parade me around town to send a message."

"V." Her expression fell. "How are you feeling?"

"Better. Physically." He breathed deep, blowing out a sharp breath. "Angry otherwise. Aesylt, you need to know that I *never* told Marek what we talked about that day before I went into the forest. I *would* never tell him. He's my brother in blood only, always been my tormentor. My lifelong bully. You know that. I wouldn't feed him a secret unless I wanted the world to know."

"I believe you," she whispered, finally peeling her hood away. He was startled at how much she looked like her mother, Sonia, who had been known as much for her nontraditional beauty as her quarter-Medvedev ancestry. Her portrait hung in the Great Hall of Fanghelm, and he had always been taken by it. "But how did he know? The betrothal could have been a fortunate guess, I suppose, but the starwalking?"

"He had help. Feist, my father's koldyna." Even from Aesylt he'd kept his family's darkest secret. He'd wanted to tell her, but for all his father had failed him, Valerian still didn't want to see the man executed. "She and Marek have… a special relationship. I don't know the all of it, Aessy, but she's given him access to magic he has no right knowing. He was *there,* somehow, we just couldn't see him. And I know this is true because he told me, when he thought I was sleeping. Right before he informed me…" Valerian swallowed and pointed his gaze away to find the words. "That Father wouldn't rest until Marek and you were the new stewards of the Cross. And while no one will admit this to me, I believe it was the koldyna, under the direction of Marek or maybe even my father, who cursed me so the wulves would bring me back." He pursed his mouth. "I just don't think they were expecting me to be alive when it happened."

"Ancestors keep us. Your father…" Aesylt laughed bitterly. Her tongue caught the tears rolling over her lips. "I shouldn't be surprised, but I am."

"Sadly, me too."

"And I *would* have married you, V. I made that promise because I was afraid for you, but it doesn't mean I wouldn't have followed through. They must know I would gouge my own eyes out and run myself into my sword before I would let your brother anywhere near me though."

"They're not interested in your compliance. They might even be happier without it." Valerian shrugged. "I wish I could tell you when my father went from an ambitious man to a vile one, but the transition was so subtle, I didn't see it until we were already embroiled in a civil war."

"So that's what they want, is it? To topple my brother and take his place?"

He nodded. "If I had known where you were, I would have come to you the moment I woke up."

"Oh, you say that now, but..." Aesylt sucked her teeth with a heavy look at her lap. "It's only because you don't know."

"Don't know what?"

"What I've done."

Valerian leaned in. "And what do you think you could have done that would make me turn away from my favorite person in the world?"

She met his eyes with a bracing look. "Fell in love with another man. Gave myself to him, body and soul."

Her words landed softer than they should have because he'd been expecting them. Some of them anyway. "You've been in love with Scholar Tindahl since the day you met him." He shook his head. "But I didn't think the monk had it in him, honestly."

"Oh, he only 'had it in him' in the name of science. I never got the chance to tell you, but Imryll gave our cohort one of Jasika's curricula. Coitus." She snorted. "I think she hoped Rahn would come up with some clever alternative to actually *performing* the experiments, but there wasn't one. It was either find a way or the Reliquary would win. If she had known the two of us... She never, ever would have reassigned it." She sawed her teeth along her upper lip. "I was the idiot who thought it was more. *He* made himself perfectly clear what it was. What it wasn't. But everything that happened before Wulfsgate seems like an entire lifetime ago, and now I don't know which way is up anymore."

"Aesylt, if you think I would judge you for what you did with the scholar... That would be rather stupid of me, considering how many women I've been with."

"It wasn't just Rahn." She wrung her hands until they were marked with red and white scores and then told him about a place called Revelry.

He'd heard of those secret societies of course, had even considered visiting one. But unlike her confession about the scholar, he was stunned to hear her relate what she'd done in the old abbey. He would cut out his own tongue before letting her see it though. "Ah, well..." He cleared the clog from his throat. "If I had someone who could get me in, I'd have done the same."

Aesylt's eyes narrowed slightly. "You haven't even asked why I needed the grimizhna tea."

"It only has one purpose, Aessy. Well, two, but you wouldn't have requested it now if you weren't already in trouble." He nodded toward the door, where his bag rested on the ground. "I brought it. Niklaus got ahold of some, from a Petrovash vedhma, so you can thank him. I'm supposed to tell you it's more likely that stress has affected your, um, moon flow. If you drink it and you feel fine after, then there was nothing to worry about. If you drink it and get sick..."

"I know." Aesylt nodded solemnly. "I know how it works."

"Do you really think..."

"I'm not only late; I'm unwell. Could also be from stress, but..."

"Right." Valerian's head was swimming. He'd been honest enough about not judging her, but it didn't mean he wasn't shaken by her confessions. Aesylt *had* lived another lifetime in the months since he'd seen her last. She'd fallen in love, had her heart shattered, and explored her desires with four different men. It should hurt. It would, he suppose, if he allowed himself to dwell on it. But he was her friend first and foremost. "You didn't bring me all this way just to unload your conscience."

Aesylt pushed out of her chair and paced to the other side of the modest room. "I had to tell you everything before I made my proposal. It would have been wrong and unfair to say what I'm going to say next when you still know me as who I was before."

Valerian stood but didn't immediately go to her. "You want to get married, right? To fix what others can't."

She whipped her head up in surprise. "How did you guess?"

"Aessy, Aessy, Aessy." He clucked his tongue, grinning. "Why else would you send for me, huh? Why else would you risk making things worse, unless you had a plan to make them better?"

"I..." She sagged against the wall. "All right. Yes. That's my proposal, that we handle this ourselves. But you need to know what you're getting into if you accept. I do care about you. I *love* you. You're a part of me, and... You always will be. I will *not* deceive you, especially about this. I shouldn't love him still, V, but I do. I love him so cursed much, I feel like..." She raised both hands to her chest. "Like I'm cracking open, splitting from the inside."

Valerian went to her and gathered her in his arms. Nothing she'd said had hurt as much as the heartbreak in her voice when talking about the man who had broken her. If there were time, he'd deal with the man himself, knock some sense into him. "He has no idea what he's walked away from, Aessy. No idea. But I do." He kissed the top of her head, sliding his mouth down to her temple.

"It's my fault for breaking the rules. I *knew* why we were doing it. I knew, and *I* broke the rules. Me."

"Aesylt, the only question is how he could experience all that with you and *not* fall in love." On the many hours it had taken Valerian to ride to her, he'd run through every scenario he could imagine, and all of them led back to Aesylt and Rahn. The moment Valerian had met Rahn Tindahl, it seemed as though the man had been made for Aesylt, and Valerian hadn't been able to compete with that. The scholar was everything Valerian was not, but Valerian knew what he had. "I'm not threatened. Not by what you did at Revelry. Not even by the man you love more than... well, more than you could love me. I don't need you to love me that much. I don't believe we're *meant* to feel that powerfully about anything for long. Marriage is less about love, in my estimation, than companionship. Respect. I respect your love for him, and I respect you. That's enough for me." He cupped her face in his hands with a soft laugh. "So I accept, Aesylt. Because both of us could do far worse for ourselves than a good friend, aye?" He kissed the corner of her mouth. "And you don't need to drink the tea. I'm here for whatever comes."

TWENTY-FIVE

THE CONSEQUENCES OF THEIR REBELLION

By noontide the following day, Aesylt was Valerian Barynov's wife.

Those were not the names they'd given the local minister, but all they needed was a signed, legal document they could take back to Witchwood Cross as evidence. They'd offered twice the coin for Minister Elfreth to leave their names blank so they could fill them in themselves later.

They'd paid for discretion but received so much more. Minister Elfreth and his sister, Faustina, had invited them to their modest home for a celebration meal, and it was Valerian who'd insisted they go and enjoy at least one peaceful meal before they returned to the Cross and faced the consequences of their rebellion.

The siblings brimmed with so much unexpected warmth, Aesylt couldn't decide whether to be suspicious or grateful. Smiling, she watched them shuffle in and out of the kitchen, laughing about some story from their youth they'd obviously revisited many times from the way they were finishing each other's sentences.

Valerian had a soft, hazy glow on his cheeks as he observed their easy way with each other. A great sadness came over Aesylt when it struck her that his family had never been anything like that, at least not since the Nok Mora had taken both of his sisters from him.

"The two of you seem to have such a special relationship," Aesylt said as everyone settled at the small table in the partitioned room.

"Twins," Elfreth explained when they all had their stew and cider. "Though Fossy is ten minutes earlier, as she's wont to remind me."

"Only when you're being a self-righteous ass," Faustina teased, pointing her thick wooden spoon at him. "What you really want to know is... Why are two old bats like ourselves living together and not with families of our own?"

"Well, no, I wasn't—"

"I'm not admonishing you for curiosity, dear. I'd want to know as well." She locked eyes with her brother. "Elfreth chose a minister's life, of course. And I *was* married, you see, many years past. I was a different woman then, and so was my husband. Nothing ever troubled us overlong, and we believed there was nothing we couldn't overcome, until we realized my body couldn't carry a healthy child." She smiled wistfully. "The one thing he wanted more than me was a family, but even that wouldn't have made him leave. So I did it for him. Told him what he needed to hear to hate me, so he could find a better future for himself. And he did, last I heard. Moved to the Southerlands and even has great-grandchildren now."

Aesylt had not been expecting such candid disclosure. No one in her life had ever been so open with strangers, and certainly not about pain. "That must have been very hard for you."

"Hm? Oh, at the time, I suppose." Faustina waved away the suggestion with a gentle laugh. "Not all heartaches age with us."

"Planning a big family of your own?" Elfreth asked between sips of stew.

Aesylt glanced at Valerian, both of them grinning through their awkwardness. Most marriages started with such questions already answered, but there'd been no time to consider any of their dreams or wishes. The only thing they *had* discussed was Valerian's willingness to father Rahn's child, should there be one. Discussed wasn't quite the right word though, because while he'd offered, Aesylt had never answered. Children were not in any vision she had for her own future, and she'd been so overwhelmed, she hadn't factored in Val's wishes on the matter.

The question only reminded her that while she had left the scholar, and her heart, in Wulfsgate, a part of him was still with her.

"Gonna start tonight," Valerian said, giving her a soft elbow. She turned her eyes on her bowl.

"That's the spirit!" Elfreth exclaimed and clinked his mug to Valerian's. "I like a young man who knows what he has. Women are the fabric of this world." He turned toward his sister and started in on some recollection about a traveling organist who had come through the village several seasons past.

I'm married. To V. Possibly carrying the child of a man who wants nothing to do with me.

"Aessy?" Valerian whispered. "Everything all right?"

Aesylt swallowed, nodding and trying to smile. *Married.*

He cradled her neck in one hand, leaning in for a soft kiss. It was gentler than the exuberant one he'd laid on her when Elfreth had announced their union sealed, and more intimate than she would have expected in the home of others. "We did the right thing."

She nodded. "I know."

He glanced at the squabbling siblings. "It's not how I imagined this day would go, but I'm happy. Are you?"

Aesylt had made a vow to herself that if Valerian agreed to her harebrained idea, he would do so knowing the full accounting of her truths, past and future—even if they hurt. "To be honest, I don't know what I feel right now. I have this sense of being disconnected..." She sighed and scanned the room. "Like I'm here but not."

His smile faded. "You're not having regrets?"

"Not regrets, no." She kissed him. It reminded her of the excitement of childhood, not the womanhood she'd discovered under the stars of the Wulfsgate bell tower. "I just think I'm still in shock, V. My head is looking to the future, but my heart is still lagging." Her smile felt almost real. "It'll pass."

Valerian pressed his forehead to hers. "I know what will take your mind off of it. But..." He squeezed her leg. "Not here."

Her heart inched toward her throat. She'd known what she was offering Valerian was more than a piece of paper. But her belly turned at the thought of intimacy with anyone. It reminded her either of the hole inside her or the emptiness deeper still. *Know truly what you ask for before you ask, or you'll be poorer after receiving it,* her father used to say, and oh, how she understood the words finally. Like an arrow to the chest. "Not here," she agreed.

"Now, we're accustomed to a lovers' need for discretion, but I can't help myself wondering if the two of you are Vjestik," Elfreth said.

Aesylt startled, adjusting herself on the rough bench. "Why do you ask?"

"It's in the eyes," Faustina said knowingly, waggling hers.

"Nay, you sow, I was gonna say the *accent.*"

"Oh, the *accent*, like you're some kind of expert now!"

"And just what do you know about eyes then, more than most folks having two of them?"

Aesylt shifted her gaze to her lap with a grin. Valerian chuckled to himself and patted her leg before reaching across the table for the pitcher of sharp cider. She was already a little tipsy when he poured her a second mug, and she knew it wouldn't be her last.

"Drink up, mates," Elfreth said, raising his own glass. "The nights are cold here, and there's more than one way to warm them."

Their midnight ride produced only futility. A squall had formed before the men even left Wulfsgate, making travel so perilous, they'd eventually had no choice but to turn back and wait for it to clear.

Going against the counsel of Dereham's top men, Rahn and Drazhan had pushed on anyway but found themselves lost, snow-blind, and near hypothermic. Drazhan had suffered a sprain in the melee, but they'd narrowly avoided anything worse.

But nothing worked against them as much as having no idea where Aesylt had gone... whether she'd fallen into trouble of her own. Her trail had gone cold just beyond the keep. They'd questioned the north and south gate guards, but they'd claimed no single riders had left, only a caravan headed north.

North then, Drazhan had grumbled, but they'd already guessed as much.

Rahn slipped into a daze watching the blacksmith sharpen his sword. He hadn't ever owned one until Drazhan had had one made for him. Rahn faintly remembered holding his father's steel, which had been far heavier than it had looked. As a six-year-old, he'd tried to hoist it only to fall, sword and all; his father's tender chuckle had lessened the sting of embarrassment as he'd helped him up. *About six more years on you, and we'll be ready to visit the forge.*

Sometimes those memories were his to revisit, and sometimes they were lost altogether. But whatever access he had to them were only glimpses of time. Vignettes of what might have been, not what was.

Uli had shared there'd been a confirmed sighting of Marek in the night. The roads had been cleared, and their group would depart again soon, except their second attempt would have a more defined radius and at least an hour of daylight.

No one said what they thought, but no one had to.

If Marek was out there, and Aesylt was out there, the rescue effort had become a race against time.

Drazhan and Rustan's men had gathered at the other end of the courtyard and were waiting for the signal to ride. They didn't need practice. Men like them had more training on a midweek day than Rahn had garnered in his entire life. The one and only time he'd killed had been—

A bolt of violent pain split his head, and he went reeling into a post.

The faces of Calder and Dacian Rhiagain materialized, as clear as they'd been that day.

Rahn shook his head and lifted his sword, but the flash behind his eyes had him lowering it again.

"Let go! There's only room for two of us!"

"We'll drown, Calder. We can all make it to shore!"

"You're not a Rhiagain. Our father will have all your heads if you don't let go!"

"Tindahl?"

Rahn's eyes rolled upward to look at the cloud-darkened sky from one side, the wood beams of the forge on the other. Vertigo crashed over him, his ears ringing so loud, there were no competing sounds. He was on the ground. Half in the structure, half out.

"He's all right! We're fine," Pieter said. He shooed onlookers with his arms, and the guards drifted away, muttering in confusion. "Any reason you're on your back?"

Rahn eyeballed the man's hand with distrust but took it, worried he might fall again and draw even more notice. "Thank you," he muttered, dusting himself off. When he blinked, he saw the White Sea again. The utter nothingness. "A dizzy spell is all."

"Dizzy spell..." Pieter squinted in suspicion. "Some wine?"

"No need." Rahn glanced at his hands to find them shaking. He shoved them under his cloak and turned his attention back to the blacksmith, who was completely unfazed by Rahn's episode. The ringing in his ears droned on, a gentle buzz. "Time to leave?"

Pieter laced his hands over his torso with a pained look. "I came over to apologize to you. And... to offer my help."

The man's groundless nerve flared Rahn's nerves back to life. "You and your help," he retorted, turning to reach for his abandoned scabbard.

"I never intended to harm your work, Rahn, but to aid it."

Rahn whipped the belt around him and fastened it in a rush. The beady, calculating eyes of Calder and Dacian stared him down, waiting for him to return. "And Revelry? Was that *aiding*?"

"Did you know the Barynovs had been communicating with Aesylt behind her brother's back?"

Rahn coiled in anger, but it was directed more at himself, for indulging Pieter at all. "Your presumptions about Aesylt have done nothing good for her. Even the suggestion that they could get a letter to her without Drazhan finding out is madness."

"I saw the letter. It was from the baron, Esker." Pieter stepped closer, lowering his tone. "He appealed to her sensibility, offered a quiet end to the civil war if Aesylt surrendered herself to them. Presumably to marry one of his sons, though he didn't say so specifically. *That's* what I was reading the day she attacked me."

"Attacked you? You mean defended herself against an unwarranted assault on her person and property?" Rahn retorted. "Your delusions are almost impressive."

"And she was *really* upset I'd read it. More than was warranted, if she wasn't taking the offer seriously. She definitely didn't want her brother to know. Or *you*, as I recall, since she failed to mention it when you asked her what was going on."

Rahn turned his eyes back toward the blacksmith. He would know if they'd written to her, because she'd been with him almost exclusively since the problems had begun. But for it to be a lie was equally strange. And when Rahn weighed what he remembered of that day with Pieter's explanation, her behavior made much more sense.

And rendered their final confrontation all the more crushing.

"I thought she was marrying you," Rahn managed to say.

Pieter laughed. "We both know that was never going to happen. I wish my father had consulted with me, or I'd have saved him the breath and trouble. Curious how *you* counseled him into the idea though. A little counter to your own self-interest, isn't it?"

"I didn't—" Rahn drew a bracing breath. He'd already humored Pieter more than he should have.

"Drazhan doesn't want to send a raven to Witchwood Cross and risk alerting them to our whereabouts, but I've suggested we send a faction there ahead of us instead. My gold is on her riding home to follow through on the letter's offer, and I'd hate to be right... and too late to do anything about it." Pieter whistled through his teeth.

"Then you don't know Aesylt." Eager to get his sword, to leave, Rahn lifted his scabbard from where it rested against the post.

"You never said what happened to her the night at Revelry."

"What do you *think* happened to her?" Rahn didn't release his sword. Day turned to night, the ground to sea and storm. He blinked, recalibrating himself to the present. "Exactly what you intended. And now she's gone, and the brute who put his hands on her neck is..." Never had he known the depth of regret he owned until that last debilitating conversation between himself and Aesylt. If he'd only—

"I said I wanted to help, and I do. I'm going to tell you something that could have my family arrested." Pieter checked to be sure they were alone. "We have our own collective of magi here in Wulfsgate. They aren't registered with the Sepulchre, and no one knows about them beyond those who need to." He reached into his cloak and withdrew a familiar nightgown. "I've already given this to our seeker. They're meditating and will have a location soon. We *will* find her. And when we do, I'm bringing our best healer, just in case."

Rahn's breath caught at the sight of the thin fabric. His hands clenched at the tactile memory of smoothing his hands along it...

lifting it away from her skin. Oh, but what had he come to regret more, the intimacy or the betrayal of it? "Pray when we do that she's unharmed and undisturbed, or no amount of penance will absolve either of us."

"Time to move!" cried a loud, booming voice.

"I don't expect penance would ever trifle with me, Scholar, but I hold no hope for her forgiveness either." Pieter clapped a hand atop Rahn's shoulder. "As for you... First you'll have to forgive yourself."

Valerian stifled a laugh as Aesylt stumbled over the threshold, skittering into the room. Her giggles trailed into the hallway, drawing the judging eyes of the more subdued drunkards in the tavern below. He quickly pushed himself inside and locked the door before collapsing into laughter.

Aesylt was half draped over one of the rickety chairs, gripping her head and shaking it. "I survived *years* of Barynov wine, only to be taken down by an old man's backyard cider?"

"You're trying to make this an insult against our esteemed varietals, but really you've just validated my entire existence." Valerian picked her fur up from the floor and hung it. He stumbled in trying to remove his own but eventually got it. "You, uh, struggling with those boots there, princess?"

With her tongue wedged between her teeth and her eyes narrowed at her laces, she raised a hand in an offensive salute.

"My, you've become vulgar." He lowered before her and peeled her hands away so he could loosen her laces. "I like it."

"They were interesting people, weren't they?"

"Squabbled like an old married couple," he said, pulling one boot off.

"That would have been Drazhan and me if he hadn't met Imryll."

Valerian chuckled. "Never. You'd have always had me."

"I know, but... He would still be so broken, and I wouldn't have had the heart to leave him." Aesylt flagged over the table. She flexed the toes on her free foot. "Why is it that men are the sigils of strength in this realm but are always the ones more easily shattered when it matters most?"

Valerian fumbled her laces. Anytime she veered too close to speaking of what had happened the night and following morning of the Nok Mora, he and Niklaus had always steered her back to safe waters. She'd never been ready to face all she'd been willing and able to do in the shadow of the king's horrors. He didn't know how to get her there. "Men are just expected to be strong. It's assumed. We're only playing the part given us. But most of us aren't born that way."

She scoffed, nestling her face into her arm she'd folded atop the table. "Women are expected to be strong too, but not *too* strong, or we're trying to assume the man's role. And if we're not strong enough, the world is too much for us. But if we're... If we're *just strong enough,* to... raise families, to lead villages... No one has anything to say about it at all."

"I know you don't want to hear this, but we're married now, so I'm saying it anyway." Valerian pulled off her second boot and chucked it across the room. "The way Drazhan protects you just reeks of guilt to me. He knows you did what he couldn't, and now he thinks he's making it up to you, like those ten years didn't happen. He doesn't want to see you as you are because then he'd have to see who he was."

"I just wish he'd hear me when I say I don't care about the lost years anymore. We both dealt with things in our own ways, and at least he—" Aesylt hiccupped with a sour-faced frown. "We should have left after supper, V. I'm going to be tasting this for days."

"At least he what, Aessy?"

"Found his happiness at the end of it all." She planted her hands on the table and pushed to her feet, faltering.

Valerian quickly gathered her from the side and guided her to the bed. He sat at the edge, mulling her words. *At least he found his happiness at the end of it all.* Ancestors, how it stung, but what had he really expected, riding through the night to answer her desperate call? He'd rightly guessed why she'd sent for him, and he'd known, even before accepting, he wasn't her first choice. Then. Now. Maybe ever. She'd always kept him at arm's length, the space between them filled with a love more familial than ardent, and he'd pushed to narrow the distance inch by inch, blurring and perhaps even disrespecting the lines she'd established. It was always him pushing the boundaries. Always him making the moves. And she loved him too much to refuse.

And what good is love if it leaves her like this?

"Volemthe, Aessy." He leaned in and kissed her forehead. "Volemthe auvjek."

"I love you evermore too," she whispered, her eyes struggling to stay open.

Valerian had never been so nervous around her. Hadn't thought twice about what to say or do. Before everything had gone so badly, he wouldn't have hesitated to kiss her. Inebriated though he was, it hadn't been enough to kill the desire raging within him. "Aesylt, I have to say something."

She opened her eyes and met his.

"I want—badly—to touch you, but I'm scared it's not what you want."

"Oh..." Aesylt strained to rise onto her elbows. She scooted aside to make room for him. "We're married now, and you shouldn't have to feel like—"

"Don't. Don't finish that thought." Valerian lay down beside her. "You've been through the wars, and you need time."

Aesylt sighed, turning her face against the pillow. "You shouldn't have to wonder whether it's appropriate to touch your own wife on your wedding night."

"I can wait." He shrugged, hoping he looked more indifferent than he felt. "And I was thinking, about the child... You know, the scholar and I have similar features. Both have dark hair, for one.

No one should question it, other than the timing, but women give birth early all the time, don't they?"

Aesylt peeled back from the pillow. "Valerian, I don't want children."

"Understandable that you wouldn't want *this* one."

"You've known this about me since..." She swallowed. "Since we were children ourselves. I would never have been so reckless with Rahn if I hadn't truly believed we were exempt from such consequence in the celestial realm." Her head shook. "There was one time we were not so careful, but it was near the end. By then I'd have already been gone with child."

Valerian cringed at the visuals this produced, but her revelation disturbed him more. She'd been repeating the line about a childfree life since the Nok Mora, but so did most Vjestik, and yet still they had families. It wasn't uncommon for them to have five or six or even seven children, to compensate for what they would sacrifice in the Vuk od Varem. "I understand your fear, because everyone in the Cross shares it, but most people change their minds. You're only twenty."

"And when I am thirty, forty, fifty, there will still be a Vuk od Varem. Still a son, every single year, who must give all for our village. *Every* family must provide one." She sucked in, her head shaking. "I won't do it. Call me selfish, cold... I don't care. But I have already sacrificed almost everything for our people, and I won't give more. You, of anyone, should understand that after what you endured out there."

"I do *understand,* but..." Valerian chewed his lip, lost for what he could or should say next. It was unfair to suggest she had been dishonest because she hadn't. "We don't have to decide now."

"Valerian, I *have* decided. You're a good man for wanting to step into another man's responsibility, but I'm not asking you to."

Valerian struggled with her confession, though he knew she wouldn't think differently of him. He wasn't less of a man for what had happened to him, but it felt that way. The vedhma had tried and tried to make it right, but his wounds had been too grievous to return all his function. His family was indifferent to his disfigurement, but he expected as much from the parents who had passed over their eldest son for the Vuk od Varem to send their second in his place. "I can't have children. My internal injuries... Not everything could be saved. I can still... you know... but if you change your mind about children years down the road, it will be too late. This child will be our only chance."

Pity flashed across her eyes—fleeting, but he saw it. "Then you chose your wife wisely, for I have no expectations." Her smile faltered. "I'm sorry, V. I really am. And I know your relationship with your own family is convoluted right now. But Drazhan and Imryll are generous with sharing Aleksy, and will be with all their children. Being his teta is such an honor. One day I'll have to watch him..." Her voice caught. "Go into the forest as well, and that will be the hardest day, hard enough without making it worse by adding the only child I would ever have to the pain."

"It doesn't have to be a death sentence."

"But it almost always is." Aesylt looked away. "The year Drazhan won his bid against the wulf, he had help. The sorcerer Mortain intervened... the *same* creature who put Witchwood Cross in the sights of the king. Imryll's real father, who put them on the path to each other. We'll never know if my brother would still have won without it, but my heart knows the answer."

He'd heard that rumor, but Aesylt verbalizing it gave the claim veracity. Of course he'd thought about what it would mean to send his own child into the forest, but it was their way of life, and Drazhan wasn't the only son who'd conquered the wulf, help or no. The first one had actually been a Barynov.

"V, the very last thing I would *ever* want is for you to regret this." Her eyes had glazed. He could see she was drifting. "Once we've returned to the Cross and put an end to all of this, we could undo what we've done. I would understand. You'd still be my dearest friend."

"Just rest now, Aessy." Valerian kissed her temple and rested his mouth there. His thoughts were spinning in so many directions, wild and detached, and he needed time with them. "We have a long day ahead of us tomorrow."

Aesylt woke abruptly in the night. She glanced at Valerian, snoring softly beside her.

Spirits had always affected her strangely. Exhaustion visited on the front end, followed by wicked insomnia hours later. But the thoughts she'd held as she'd drifted to sleep were still as fresh several hours later, and there was no chance of returning to sleep with her mind so full, so she slipped carefully from the bed and tiptoed to her knapsack.

Aside from the clothes she'd stolen from Rahn, she'd packed only a couple of outfits, both practical: trousers and blouses appropriate for the long ride.

Aesylt dressed quietly and shrugged Rahn's bulky cloak over her shoulders. Valerian hadn't stirred at all and probably wouldn't until morning. She blew him a kiss, unbolted the door, and exited into the hall.

A handful of patrons were still cozied up at the bar, but the tavern was otherwise empty. The pubkeep nodded at her as she descended the stairs, and she nodded back, bracing for the biting cold waiting for her.

An icy gale swept the night. She pinched the cloak tighter, lowered her head, and made for the stables. It would be warm enough for the privacy she needed to make sense of not only the past day but the past season. Her heart was still too sore to visit the celestial realm.

She passed no one on the short walk. The stables were empty, other than the horses boarded there. Just to be safe, she threw the wooden bolt once inside and made her way down the row to the beautiful mare she'd stolen. *Exelcius,* her saddle had said, but she didn't look like an Exelcius, so Aesylt had taken to calling her Bella.

Bella immediately moved to the opening to say hello.

"Dobranok, Bella," she said as she reached up to pet her snout. "We have a long ride ahead of us tomorrow, but I'll make sure you have a fine breakfast in the morning before we go."

Bella snuffled and nudged her mouth across Aesylt's forehead, making her giggle.

"You like that word? Breakfast? There's also noontide meal and supper and—" Aesylt stuttered a breath in when cold steel pressed against her throat. She couldn't speak or turn. She held her breath as her thoughts sped through the possibilities.

"Move before I tell you to, and I'll kill you. Run, scream, or fight, and I'll kill you and my brother both." A tug on the knife broke her flesh.

"Marek." Aesylt's fingers twitched, thinking of the dagger she'd foolishly left in the room. She had no excuse for the slip beyond exhaustion. "Just tell me what you want."

"I'll show you," he said. "Not here."

She remembered what Hraz had taught her about dangerous men. *Never go anywhere without a fight. Once you leave the unknown, no one will be able to follow you.* "You can show me here."

He gathered her hair in his hand and ripped backward until she was staring at the ceiling. "I said *not here.* You know your choices. Make one."

Blood trickled down her throat and into her blouse. A cautious glance revealed nothing close enough to help her. Marek had to know where she was staying, because he'd been waiting for her in the barn.

Which meant he knew where to find Valerian.

Aesylt wasn't ready to die, but there'd been enough suffering. She was still the only one with the power to avoid more. "Okay, Marek." She slowly raised her hands to her sides, to demonstrate compliance. "I won't fight you."

"Good girl," he hissed in her ear just before he shoved a hood over her head.

TWENTY-SIX

WHATEVER YOU NEED TO BELIEVE

Twenty long minutes they trudged through snow and ice. The counting protected Aesylt's sanity, calmed her mind enough to apportion itself between putting one foot in front of the other and manifesting a way out of an increasingly bleak situation.

Valerian wouldn't realize she was gone until morning, and by then, there'd be no tracking where she'd gone. Even if he could, she prayed he wouldn't. Marek wanted his brother dead and was looking for a reason. She felt it in her bones, and her instincts were the only defense she had.

Aesylt felt something falling from her pocket. She couldn't reach for it without drawing Marek's notice, but when she realized what it was, she let it fall. Another push from her instincts.

With a hard shove from Marek, she went stumbling forward, out of the cold. The ground was solid but covered in something soft and dry. Hay, perhaps. The nearby bleating of goats gave her guess further credence.

A door slid closed with a rattling thud and a thrown bolt. Her hood was ripped away.

Aesylt squinted to adjust to the addition of light. Five or six lanterns were all there was to brighten the small barn, but it was enough to see they weren't alone.

There was a woman, young and vibrant, radiating with chilling energy. Behind her were five stoic guards and a man in a minister's robe.

She met the cold, dead eyes of the woman, who seemed to be the real one in command. "So it's true," Aesylt whispered. "All this time you were accusing me, and you had your own koldyna."

"Feist has been in our family for generations, you dumb bitch. The Wynters aren't very clever, are they?" Marek tossed the hood into a corner and stepped around until he towered over her. Her hand traveled to her neck in horror.

"Your corruption is not our shortcoming." Aesylt's artificial impudence was swiftly outpaced by her instincts, which were screaming at her to act or die. But she wouldn't get more than a punch in before his guards, or the dark witch, took her down. "Our misplaced trust in your father is a reflection of your poor character, not ours."

The slap happened so fast, she felt the sting before she saw his hand slice through the darkness. "You know, I dream about that day I almost killed you. Touch myself to it, on chilly nights. Never come harder in my life than when thinking about standing over your dead body, cock in—"

"You're a sick, depraved fuck." Aesylt spat the copper filling her mouth. Her cheek throbbed. "And you should have killed me that day in Val's room, because you have no idea what I'm capable of."

He slapped her again, harder, sending her skittering back. "I know what you're capable of, little *cub.* The men you slaughtered in cold blood. Aye, they deserved it, but the entire village knows what's in the dark little heart of yours." He poked her chest hard enough to unsteady her footing. "I'm grateful to that insolent little brat, Niklaus. If I'd killed you, Aesylt, I'd never be the steward of Witchwood Cross, would I?"

The revelation was another smack to the chest. The minister. Of course. She looked at the group standing quietly like specters, waiting. "A marriage isn't valid without consent, and I'll never sign that paper." Her windpipe abruptly constricted, her attempts to breathe through both her mouth and nose denied. She clawed at her neck in a panic, catching, briefly, the koldyna's grin.

Air returned to her lungs just as fast as it had been stolen.

"Say that again, cub?" Marek cupped his ear with a perplexed look.

"All that did was..." She erupted into a coughing fit. "Did was... fortify my preference for death over even a minute with you."

Marek nodded at Feist.

A quill appeared in Aesylt's hand. She released it, startled, but another appeared, and then another. Her hand lifted on its own, scrawling phantom words in the air. She tried to pull it back, but it was no longer under her own command at all. "Typical weak man, needs a woman to do what he cannot—" Her words were swiftly killed by a kick, which sent her flying to the barn wall. The sharp pain on impact knocked her breath away again, sending a dark explosion into her vision.

Marek's stormy footfalls echoed through the barn, nearing. Aesylt squirmed, slapping blindly for purchase and fighting the overwhelming call to close her eyes and drift away. *Drazhan,* she thought, trying to find the old channel in her mind, the one place she could always reach him. But there was nothing. The path was blocked, and she knew by whom.

"I'm not going to kill you, because I need you. But *all* I need is a signature and your cunt. And I will have both, whether you're conscious... whether you still have all your fingers and toes and limbs and teeth. I'd be content to tie you up and leave you that way the rest of your life, feeding you just enough to keep you alive, visiting only to take what I need, as you grow child after child to strengthen *my* legacy."

Wheezing, Aesylt spat at his feet. More blood. Everything hurt so much, she couldn't discern what the worst of her injuries were, but there was only one way to heal them, to restore herself to fighting form and turn the situation. That she hadn't considered it yet was a testament to how much danger she was truly in, but she was Aesylt Wynter, afraid of nothing except losing the people she loved. On the matter of her own fate, she was tragically indifferent.

"You're such a dumb—"

"I can't marry you, Marek, even if I were inclined to subject myself to a lifetime of disgust and shame." Nauseated and dizzy, she used the wall to slide her feet toward her torso. But she couldn't shift until she had her wits back. "Because..." She closed her eyes, straining her breath through what she assumed was a punctured lung. Sticky blood coated the front of her. She wasn't ready to know what it was from. "I'm already married to your brother."

Aesylt whispered her command and winked from their world into hers. The moment she saw the shift in the air, the muting of colors, she clambered to her feet in relief.

A shrill whoosh sounded. She looked up and saw *Marek*, standing in the same place he'd been in the real world.

"Surprise," he said, a macabre grin splitting his face.

Rahn urged his horse to the limit, chasing Drazhan's grueling pace as they stormed the Compass Road on their push north. The deafening thunder of hooves drowned out the sharpest points of his imagination, which had been on a wild tear.

Voyager's Rest was their destination, the seeker had claimed, with more confidence than Rahn thought appropriate for someone who had merely sniffed a nightgown, rolled their eyes back as though possessed by the mythical demons themselves, and spit the words out with a snake-like hiss that had half the room cowering in alarm. But it was all anyone had, and he wasn't opposed to calling upon the darkest magic out there if that was what it took to find her.

The soothsayer believed Aesylt wasn't alone. At least two men were with her, one who loved her and one bent on her destruction.

The second had to be Marek. Everyone assumed the first was Valerian, which gave startling validity to Pieter's disturbing claim.

Drazhan had sent a dozen of his men back to Witchwood Cross and another dozen south on the Compass Road, just in case. The other twenty-five joined them on their hard ride to Voyager's Rest.

The village was a waypoint stop approximately midway between Witchwood Cross and Wulfsgate. Drazhan said he'd stayed there once with his father, and so had Aesylt, on another trip. Her familiarity gave the seeker's proclamation further legitimacy.

Drazhan raised a hand, and the contingent came to a sliding halt. He spun his horse to face everyone, wiping snow off his scarf, and waited for the rabble to subside. "We've reached the outskirts of the village, and in another half a mile, we'll be within the border. The town itself is small, but the farmland extends for miles. If Marek Barynov *is* there, Aesylt is already in danger. I, Tindahl, and four of my guards will approach the main road *quietly* and search the inns. Uli will lead a company to the south, Lord Rustan to the west, Lord Pieter to the east, and Baron Augher will hold a barrier in the north. No one is getting in or out of this village without coming through us, and anyone who resists leaves us with but one choice and no hesitation. Clear?"

Everyone gave their enthusiastic assent.

"Uli, you divide the men for the perimeters."

"Tak," Uli said. "On it."

"Pieter, send the healer with us. Keep the others with you."

Pieter nodded.

Drazhan looked at Rahn. "I made you that sword because all men—all women—should have steel. But if you don't know how to use it, then keep it sheathed, unless you want it taken and used against you."

Rahn's head was swimming. Pain. Confusion. Gods, was he soaked—to the very bones of the bones, as his mother would have said, but his mother wasn't there. Neither were his father or Jemma, because they were still in the inky-black sea all the others, bobbing for something to hold onto. Rahn had been right there with them, until a wave had carried him away, sending him crashing into the rocks.

He reached for his side and pulled back blood. That was when the swoon hit.

"Mama," he moaned and stumbled onto his face. "Papa. Jemma." He threw up into a tangle of mossy weeds.

"Jemma!" His mother howled, but it was the following sound, the feral, guttural cry coming from his father, that gave Rahn the strength to rise to his feet.

He squinted against the moon's blinding reflection, because he couldn't trust what his eyes were seeing. Dacian Rhiagain, Carrow's eldest, was wielding a wooden plank. He smashed it to Jemma's head, and she slipped off of the wreckage and into the sea.

Rahn raced down the slippery rocks to the sound of his own screams. He looked up right as his mother went flailing into the sea... and then his father and then... Calder Rhiagain staring directly at him from the piece of wreckage he'd wrested from Rahn's loved ones. Smiling. Laughing. He pointed, and Dacian looked up as well. Smirking.

"Adrahn?"

Shrill ringing shook his balance. "Lost myself for a moment." Not just for a moment but for the second time that day. Aesylt had been enduring the same experience with her own dark history, and she'd linked the resurgence of memories with her heightened physical and emotional state as a result of the physicality of their research. She'd shared that with him for a reason. She wanted him to understand her and had felt comfortable enough to be vulnerable. And instead of telling her how proud he was of her courage in self-reflection, he'd given her space. "I understand."

Drazhan looked ahead as he spoke. "You're with me because I can see in your eyes something I've seen in the mirror. I recognize a man intimate with desperation. I know what horrors can follow." He swung his sharp gaze back to Rahn. "Nothing reckless, Adrahn. If not for me, then for her."

Rahn felt as though he and Drazhan had conducted an entire conversation in the spaces between his words.

No, no, no, no, no. Rahn screamed the words with his lungs. He battered them into the rocks. Mama, Papa, Jemma!

He bore down to shove the thoughts back.

But even at eight, Rahn knew what he'd seen. He knew what had been done. And he knew he was alone in the world.

He could hardly hear himself speak at all when he said, "I respect your lead, Drazhan."

"How?" Aesylt demanded. She balled her hands at her sides, thrusting out her arms to make herself bigger, as Drazhan had taught her.

"How?" Marek flicked his head back. "You used to be smarter than your own good. Not anymore, aye?"

Aesylt swept back a step when he drew nearer. She commanded her body to heal, as she'd always done when the celestial air filled her lungs, but nothing happened. "If you could starwalk, I'd have known."

"Like you knew I was there that day you sent my brother into the forest?" Marek tilted his face to the side in mockery. He shuffled to the left and right in a series of taunting skips, arcing closer with each series of movements. "All that time I was accusing you of being a dark witch and the truth was *right there*."

"Tell me!"

The dark air beyond the barn whistled, rattling the boards, breaking their concentration.

"The answer is sitting right behind you, in our world. Because *this* world, little cub, never belonged to us. You must have some koldyna in you after all, or you'd never have reached this place on your own." He grinned and waved beyond her. "I know you've been taking Val here since you were littles. Feist told me. We kept it from my father, but the man is all vision, no backbone. She knew I'd be leading us soon enough. Every time you pulled my stupid brother into this place, Feist would say, '*The little idiot has taken him again.*'"

Aesylt went rigid. It had always been hypothesized that the celestial realm belonged to the koldynas, the crones and warlocks born of the demon realm. Their father certainly believed it, which was why he'd made Aesylt vow never to return. He didn't know her toes had been curled when she'd said the words, the Vjestik way of resisting a vow made unwillingly, and she'd only deceived him because she'd believed he was repeating old superstitions. He'd not been there, always refusing her offers with fear. He didn't know what a wonderful place it could be. How she'd learned to fight, to kill, and to defend, and how she had given her brothers a safe environment to do the same.

Either it had been true all along that the koldynas controlled the celestial world or Feist had the gift and ability to share it, but nothing changed the fact that Marek was there or that her only priority was figuring out how to escape a situation seeming more and more inescapable with each passing second.

"Ahh. I wish I could see your tiny little mind working the problem." Marek moved closer and Aesylt inched back, step by step in a careful dance. "It's unnatural, what you are. You're too pretty to lock yourself away in dusty libraries with dusty scholars, rotting your brain... filling it with nonsense. None of it helps you now, does it?"

"You wanted to kill me that night at Hoarfrost. Now you want to wed me?" The pain had caught up, but there was nothing she could do about it. She required all her energy to stay alert.

Marek snickered. He cupped his crotch in a grotesque gesture. "You don't inspire the 'romantic' in me, but I need legitimate Wynter heirs, not bastards."

Keep him talking. Keep his mind busy. "You almost *did* kill me. If not for Niklaus, you would have. You insult my intelligence, but you're the one who tried to annihilate your entire plan."

"It wasn't my plan. All that time, Father had been pushing Val to the stewards. Never me. Until he did say it. And then it was all I could think about. Always should have been me, as the eldest, but Val had a fancy for you, and my father always gave the pissant anything he wanted."

Aesylt carefully examined the space, searching for ideas, for anything useful. "If your revelation about me came *after* Val returned home, it doesn't explain why you would curse him when he took *your* place in the forest."

"My father wanted a war. Feist helped me give him one."

"Why?"

"You ask a lot of questions. You won't need this curiosity where you're going." Marek reached behind himself and withdrew a hunting knife.

"Have the Barynovs always been planning a coup against us?" Aesylt's chest locked from the pace of her heart. Every bruise and laceration on her body stung to life. She'd given up healing herself. Marek or Feist or both were blocking it. The world had only been hers to command for as long as others had allowed it.

"Coup?" Marek slowed his approach. His expression contorted in repellence. "The seat was always ours, and *you* stole it. The Barynovs were *first* to the Cross. Darek Summerton was a grifter who couldn't even best a wulf, never mind talk to one. Changing his name to Wynter in some ridiculous tribute, like he was the keeper of the seasons themselves? Your entire bloodline is built on weakness."

"How compelling, from the man who needed five guards, a witch, and a minister to keep a little girl from killing him." Aesylt braced after her impulsive gaffe. Whatever reprieve she'd bought was over.

"Do you see them now?" Marek flung his arms wide. A ripple passed over him, turning to a shimmer. His dark hair lengthened. The broad form he was known for reduced to the frame of a strong but average man.

Standing before Aesylt was Hraz.

No, not Hraz. It's not my brother, no matter how I might desperately wish it were.

"Hey, cub." But it was Hraz's crooked smile. The half wink he always saved for her.

Aesylt shuddered through a sob. Both of her hands flew to her mouth but not quick enough to curb her tortured scream.

Then her beautiful, beloved frata lifted a hand and sent her flying to the barn wall.

There were thirteen inns along the main stretch of Voyager's Rest, but it only took four to uncover where Aesylt had been holed up. A bag of gold was all that had been needed to get the "discreet" taverners' tongues wagging.

"Aye, sounds like th' one who checked in, oh, not long past, I ken. One I'm thinking of ha' a fella join her though." The taverner's thick Southerlands brogue had both Rahn and Drazhan straining to make sense of his words.

"Describe him," Rahn commanded, drawing Drazhan's instant annoyance.

"Young, 'bout her age, I'd ken. Pretty boy, if ye like."

Not Marek. Rahn nodded, relieved. "Show..." He lifted his palms in submission to Drazhan, who was still glaring in warning.

"Show us," Drazhan said, turning back toward the older man.

"Aye, but the girl slipped out an hour or so back. Alone."

"Slipped out? Where?" Rahn asked, leaning in.

"Cannae say. Didnae ask." He chuckled, nervously glancing at Drazhan. "People pay for discretion."

"Yeah, you're real discreet, taverner," Rahn muttered, shaking his head.

Drazhan checked the door, then his sword. "You follow the taverner to the room and see what you can get out of Val or Nik or whoever is up there. If it's Val, we need to know whether he's on our side or Marek's. If ours, get him to the caravan safely. If Marek's, find some chains. There's a flare in your bag that will signal Baron Augher if you need aid."

Rahn hesitated. The past hours, wondering and waiting, had already been unspeakable, but now they were close and Drazhan wanted to pull him away?

"There a problem?"

Rahn tapped the bar. The truth would not help the situation, and if Aesylt had run into danger, Drazhan was the best person in their entire contingent to be there. "None. No."

"I'll let my men know the search has shifted. Find us when you can. I'll leave a trail."

Rahn watched him leave and followed the taverner upstairs. The man dug into his pocket and withdrew a massive key ring, unlocked the door, and was already halfway back down the steps before Rahn could thank him.

Valerian sat on the bed, still half-asleep. He stared at Rahn like he were a ghost.

"Where is she, Val?" Rahn closed the door and stood in front of it.

"Scholar Tindahl?" Valerian squinted and wiped his eyes. "Some fucking dream. The infant king here somewhere too?"

"Where *is* she, Valerian?"

"I don't even know what you're talking about."

Rahn flipped the bolts on the door and marched toward the bed. Valerian cowered, his eyes widening in a slow return to reality. "Tell me where the fuck Aesylt is or I'll—"

He whipped around, searching for a friendly face, but there were only others like him. Orphaned, abandoned, screaming for all they'd lost. Teleria Farrestell was the closest, rocking and sobbing with her knees drawn to her chest.

Time became as fluid as the sea. He replayed the terrible events in reverse and tried to imagine them ending another way. He did so until shrill shouts drew his eyes back toward the sea, where the Rhiagain brothers were trying to anchor themselves to the rocks. They each grasped in desperation, but they'd landed not where Rahn had, at an outcropping of rocky beachland, but farther down the island, where the rocks were cliffs.

He blinked, watching them struggle and fail. Calder must have seen him, for he waved both hands over his head, screaming for Rahn to come to their aid.

"And she was *fine* and *here* when I fell asleep, which couldn't have been... Scholar?"

Gods deliver me. Rahn shoved his hands under his cloak and pumped them in and out of fists to ground himself. *Here. Now. Not then. Never then.* "Just..."

Rahn slowly picked himself back up off the rocks and stared at the boys who had killed his family. Calder had been his friend. They'd played every manner of game a thousand times together. Laughed, cried, fought. Calder had loved Rahn's mother's winter soup, enough that she made it even in the summertime. He'd even called her Mother when his own had neglected him.

Both boys brightened when they saw Rahn coming their way. He had nothing to help them. He searched his pockets, but there was only the broken quill he'd had just enough time to stuff into his pockets when the ship had collided with something and—

His father's dagger.

He didn't remember sitting on the bed. Falling either. Valerian's stricken face stared down at his.

Why is this happening to me? Why now?

You know why, Adrahn. My beautiful boy.

I can't do this right now, Mama. I have to find her.

Right now is when you must do this. For her.

Rahn gripped the sheets and bolted upright. "Where's Marek?"

"Not here." Valerian plopped back on his heels. "Why... Why are you asking me where Marek is?"

"Because he *is* here, Valerian, and you and I both know why."

"But..." Valerian's head shook and shook. Dread spread over his expression, down his cheeks. "No. *No* one followed me here, and there's no one who could read the letter she sent me. It was written in Old Ilynglass, and who knows that except her and me and Niklaus and you? And I suppose Duchess Teleria, but why would she—"

"She wrote you a letter in the old language?" The inky White Sea hit him with a wallop of seasickness, but he stopped fighting it. Too much of his focus had been consumed with stopping it, and it was just as Aesylt had said. There could be no light without dark. No love without hate.

"It's like I told you; she sent for me, and so I came, and we were married, and—"

"*Married*?" A flame ignited deep within Rahn, in a part of himself he'd believed long dead. *That rogue Pieter was right. He was fucking right.* "Don't murder him, Adrahn. He doesn't know. He doesn't—"

"Who are you talking to?"

"Cut the ropes for the rowboats!" he'd cried, folding his dagger into Rahn's hand before disappearing into the desperate throngs.

There hadn't been time to cut anything. A few had been launched by the time Rahn arrived on the starboard deck, but most had sunk with the ship. Everyone grabbed hold of what they could and then the cold had come.

*Rahn saw more people he knew, prostrate and howling for the lost, but he was still thinking about the dagger. His father was a soothsayer—*had *been a soothsayer, but he was gone, gone... they all* *were—and liked to say he didn't always know why he did what he did, but a part of him knew.*

Maybe Esteban Tindahl had known Rahn would need the steel for something else.

"We don't have time for this. Come with me," Rahn commanded, shoving Valerian into motion. "*Now.*"

Aesylt wanted to close her eyes and drift off somewhere the pain couldn't reach her. The fear she loathed more, because it reminded her she was a fraud, weak and powerless, just like others always suspected.

Choking on a whimper, she looked up and straight into the eyes of her father.

She could withstand any physical torture Marek had planned, but gazing into the past was paralyzing.

"You're not Ezra Wynter." She folded an arm over her face, only for it to be ripped away by some foul magic. "Ezra Wynter would never act like an alleyway thug."

"Ezra Wynter was as much a pretender as his ancestor Darek." Marek was again himself. "But he *should* be here tonight, don't you think, Aesylt? To watch his little girl get married? Hraz could come in for a minute or two from time to time, I think." He swayed with a cheeky grin. "Only one missing is Drazhan. I could be him too, but then I'd deny myself seeing *his* face after the way he led my father on."

"He didn't lead anyone on. He's just as impossible as you all think he is." Aesylt's vision doubled again as fresh nausea rocked her. She averted her eyes, in case he tried to get into her head again with painful images. He already knew the tactic worked. She hadn't had a chance to hide her shock. "He was never going to agree to Val and I marrying because he was never going to let me marry anyone to begin with."

"Didn't stop you, did it?" Marek crouched before her, smirking at her flinch. "I don't care that you're not a virgin. I'd just as soon piss on you as fuck you. But I won't be touching you at all until we've returned and given you the tea, be sure anything that crawls out of you later is mine and only mine, so you can save the terrified-damsel act for our honeymoon."

No one is coming. The revelation crashed into her like a barrel of flour. She hadn't been expecting help, but until the words raced across her frantic consciousness, she'd been unaware of the part of herself dreaming that some villager had seen her being hauled away and had run for help.

But Voyager's Rest wasn't that kind of village. Even the pubkeep had paid no mind when she'd left in the middle of the night, alone.

There was nothing in the celestial version of the barn with which to defend herself. She had no control there, not anymore. For the first time in her life, it wasn't an escape but a prison.

The door wasn't far, but even if she weren't so injured, there was little chance she'd make it there and clear of danger before Marek or one of his entourage stopped her.

But little chance was still better than no chance.

Aesylt shivered as her head came up. One of her lungs seemed to whistle. Something thick and warm spread along her left gut and back, and a dark flash of her landing on a dull tine when she'd hit the wall the second time popped into her head. *Not a knife, not a sword, not—*

A pitchfork.

Not everything traveled from world to world. But it *had* been there in the real one. And if she'd *landed* that way and had not moved before shifting, it meant when she returned, she'd end up exactly where she'd left herself... impaled.

This world isn't mine anymore. It never was.

But if tonight is the night I greet the Ancestors, I go where my family can get closure. Justice.

I'll be with you soon Hraz. Ota. Oma.

She spat another wad of blood into the hay beside her and winked herself back to the real world.

"Scholar, you really look green." Valerian skip-jogged to match his pace. "Like you haven't slept in a quarter century."

Rahn swatted him away. The memories were coming fast now, and he'd stopped fighting them. Since he'd given in, they had at least still been gracious enough to let him think, to keep his senses tuned enough to recognize the trail Drazhan had left for others to follow.

When he reached the cliff's edge, he clambered down as far as he could without slipping into the sea. Calder and Dacian hollered for him to hurry, that their makeshift boat was sinking. His vision doubled, blurring and spotting, his thoughts torn between a dozen perfect memories from his childhood and the horrors tearing the lives of everyone he'd ever known asunder.

"No, that way," Rahn muttered. A hazy film came over his eyes. His nose filled with brine.

Dacian's hand appeared on top of the cliff. Rahn looked at it as fresh rain and wind whipped him sideways. He peered over the edge and found Calder not far behind, scaling the serrated wall with his fingertips.

"Grab my hand, you imbecile!" Dacian cried, his other hand reaching over and slapping but sliding away from the stone.

"Red cloth. Another one," Valerian said, excited and catching on to Rahn's observations.

"You killed them," Rahn said. Saying it aloud gave it the sharpest teeth, and he couldn't believe the words. He couldn't believe Dacian and Calder had done it.

"It was them or us, and you know..." Dacian grunted when his hand slipped again. "You know why it had to be us, so give me your cursed hand!"

Rahn shook his head, though no one could see him. He shook it and shook it, still staring at Dacian's straining hand. Lightning split the sky. Everything was muddled. Nothing was right anymore.

Nothing would ever be right again.

Rahn stepped on a misshapen rock and almost continued on, but instinct had him kneeling to check anyway. His hand jerked, and the wooden squirrel landed back in the dirt. With a ragged inhale, he reached for it again. Turned it over. *Squish.*

Was it murder on his mind when he inched closer to the edge... when he toed Dacian's hand with his boot and then... and then stomped on it, hard enough that the boy released his grip and went hurtling into the darkness below?

"What is it? Some child's toy?" Valerian asked.

"Adrahn!" Calder bellowed. "What have you done?"

Rahn squeezed the statue in his fist before slipping it into his pocket. "No, it's Aesylt."

"Don't climb any higher, Calder." Rahn unsheathed the dagger and held it out in his shaking hand. His tears blended with the rain. The screams with the roar of the unrelenting sea.

"You know she loves you... Don't you?"

"Maybe he's all right. We just need to—"

"Calder. Stop. You can't come up here."

"Gods! What's wrong with you? Help me!"

Rahn squinted against the moonlight at the split in the path. Had they gone east or west?

"You killed my family." Rahn shoved the words from his chest. "You killed them. All of them."

"I'm the future king, Rahn. I can't die. You would have done the same thing if you were me."

"Scholar? What's happening with you?"

"Can't?" Rahn knelt and watched Calder struggle against the slimy stone wall. "Go back, Calder. Please, I don't want to do this."

"Valerian, are you prepared to kill your brother tonight?"

"Don't want to do what?" Calder screamed and tugged himself up onto the final shelf. "Give me a hand, you dolt."

"We don't even know if he's here—"

Rahn leaned over the cliff and waved the dagger, his voice a trembling, scratchy mess. "Don't come any closer."

"He's here." Rahn closed his eyes, and Aesylt filled the space of his mind. A soft peace cut through the tension, and an involuntary smile spread across his face. *East.* "This way."

"Adrahn, look at me. I'm your oldest mate. Get me up, and we'll fix this!"

"But I don't see any red fabric."

"You called her mama. You called her mama and then kicked her into the sea and killed her."

"Doesn't matter," Rahn said and started down the east path, one hand clenched over his bulging pocket.

"Nearly everyone is dead, look around!"

"How do you know this is the right path?" Valerian sprinted to catch up.

He was right, but most of them hadn't been murdered. Rahn pointed the dagger downward. "I mean it. Not another inch."

"I need to know you won't hesitate."

"Hesitate?" Valerian cackled in frustration. "Scholar, I'm fucking lost."

"Where the devil am I supposed to go?" Calder snorted with a tentative look over his shoulder before hoisting himself up with more strength than his brother had shown. Both of his hands gripped the cliff. Rahn's heart raced as he stared, contemplating his own worth, his own capabilities.

Rahn felt the dagger from that night with the same tangibility of the squirrel in his pocket. Both were equally real. Both opened a door into who he truly was. "Your sword. I know you know how to use it. But will you hesitate to take it to Marek?"

"Almost. There." Calder grunted, and Rahn decided those were to be his last words. He saw his sister's face, felt his mother's arms, and heard his father's raucous laugh, and they gave him the last bit of courage to drive the dagger straight into the center of Calder Rhiagain's scrawny neck.

Valerian slowed. "Wouldn't even have to think about it."

The boy's eyes widened, in fear... in shock, but he had nothing left to do except fall.

Rahn saw again Aesylt's pale face, flushed from excitement. She nibbled the corner of her mouth and flitted her eyes upward as she laughed at something he'd said that wasn't funny to anyone but her. She'd always given his words more weight than they deserved.

Rahn, shaking, released the dagger, and it disappeared into the abyss with his old friend.

"How did you know this was the way?" Valerian asked.

He fell himself, but soft arms enclosed him from behind.

"Magic brought us to the village." *You are as imitable as the stars in our interminable sky.* "Aesylt will take us the rest of the way."

Weeping, he looked up and saw the young Duchess Farrestell, seventeen and fresh off her own grief.

"You poor dear," she whispered.

Aesylt didn't give herself time to register the pain, already sliding forward and gurgling through the extraction of the thick tine. The koldyna noticed first and narrowed her expression, staring through her beady eyes as Aesylt wavered to her feet.

Marek snapped into the real world. He charged, but Aesylt rolled out of the way, and his fist crashed to the wall, rattling the wood.

"No! I can handle her!" Marek screeched when his guards moved to alert. He squared up, swaying his balance from one foot to the other. "You must really, *really* like pain."

"You know, I really do," Aesylt replied, grinning through the blood filling her mouth. "But you refuse to give it to me."

Marek snarled, his focus whipping to the gaping puncture in her abdomen that would probably kill her soon. She might have stood a chance if she'd left the tine stuck into her, but it was too late for that. It was too late for anything.

"You're a sick little bitch, aren't you?" He rushed her again.

She had nowhere to go, so she dropped to her hands and knees, crawled through his legs, and dove for the shaft of the pitchfork. Her fingers wrapped around the splintered wood just as she landed on her back, which was a mistake, for it felt so good to lie there, to let the world slip away.

Just a little more, Aes, she heard Hraz say. The real one. The one who had taught her, played with her, loved her. Died for her.

Marek stumbled over. She brandished the pitchfork. His eyes widened in warning. "You couldn't hurt me with that on a good day."

"Is that why you haven't taken it from me yet?" Aesylt steadied her grip when a tremor seized her hands. The ink blots in her eyes dilated, spreading. She was fading, faster than she wanted, and Marek wasn't wrong. She no longer had the strength required to run the tines through him. Holding it aloft was already too much.

But there was one thing she could do. She would fail, but she would die a warrior's death. "If you're not afraid of me, prove it. Draw your sword, and we'll settle this as men would."

Marek's mouth flashed wide in a cackle. "You want to...*fight* me with *that*?"

"If you're so confident, why isn't your sword out?" She knew exactly why he hadn't drawn it. The brute wasn't wearing one at all. Only his guards were armed with steel, and they were across the barn, where she needed Marek to be.

"I don't have to fight you."

"Because you know I'll win, even as I am now?" Aesylt resisted the swoon with everything she had. She held tighter to the pitchfork. *Come on, come on, come on.*

"You're delusional, just like the rest of the Wynters."

"And your fear of me is all over your face." Aesylt lashed her tongue across her lips. "Right there, corner of your mouth."

Marek's hand traveled there before he realized, grunted in disgust, and swung it away. "You want me to carve you up like a wintertide boar? Fine. Feist will heal the parts I require." He stormed away, his boots crushing the boards with booming stomps.

"Be quick about it, Marek. She's lost a lot of blood." Feist spoke with all the warmth of a post.

"Aye, but the bitch doesn't need arms or legs to bring a child, so give me a fucking moment, Feist, and then you can have her."

Aesylt pursed her mouth and breathed in shakily. She whispered the names of her ancestors, loud enough for her own ears only.

"Fucking *give* it to me," Marek demanded, wrestling with a guard's belt.

She squirmed until she was leaned up against a bale of hay, shifting her legs until they were under her. Onto her knees, she rose. She transferred the pitchfork to her other hand and, wincing and trembling, lifted it over her shoulder. Tears rolled down her face as she strained to draw her arm back, fighting the overwhelming need to just let go.

On the wings of this life or the bones of the next.

Marek turned.

Aesylt's mouth peeled back in a scream that exploded from deep in her belly. It was the very last of herself. Flesh ripped and peeled as she stumbled to her feet and released the pitchfork in a roar of fury that sent her hurtling back into the darkness before she could see where it landed.

Steel and shouts sounded from a barn ahead. Valerian started to run, but Rahn snapped him back.

"Look," Rahn whispered, watching a lone, hulking figure ambling down the hill in a hurry. Valerian said something under his breath, something like *oh no* or *oh fuck*, or maybe that was Rahn filling in the silence with his own internal monologue.

But Valerian definitely said, clear as a whistle on a cool night, "Marek."

Rahn fixed himself on Marek's location. It didn't seem the man had noticed them yet. He was wrestling with something long, like he was trying to pull it out of himself. "Go to the barn, Valerian. Drazhan and the others will be there."

"You asked me if I would hesitate," Valerian stated, glancing from Rahn to his brother's harried shuffling. "I told you I won't."

"And I'm not asking you anymore. Aesylt needs you. Go. *Go!*" Rahn wrapped his fingers around the hilt of the sword Drazhan had made him, but it was the wet leather of his father's dagger under his palm. In one single stroke of fate, Rahn had changed the history of the Rhiagains forever, and no one but he and Teleria knew. Had the boys lived, the crown would not be in such conflict, because there would have been three heirs, not one insufficient one. Sweet Torian would be alive because he would have been nowhere near the ascendancy. Whether Imryll would have still been put in the prince's path, and therefore Drazhan's, was unknown, which meant so was Rahn's eventual landing in Witchwood Cross and his fateful meeting of Aesylt.

But Rahn had not then nor ever had the gift of foresight. He wasn't thinking about the crown's future that night on the cliff of the Isle of Duncarrow, but of the one stolen from him, and gods knew how many others. It had never been a question whether he would kill the boys who had killed his family, only how fast he'd realized his potential. For some, there was no justice suitable but death.

Marek *would* have justice, but Rahn was leaving nothing to chance.

Rahn skittered down an embankment and followed a stream at the bottom, aiming to head Marek off at the fence line. He bent as low as he could go and still move, holding his position and his sight of Marek. Water splashed onto his trousers when he slipped into the riverbed. The sound alerted Marek, who perked and swung around in search of the source. When he did, the moonlight caught the side of him, revealing a darkened spot on his abdomen.

Rahn ducked low and waited. Marek pushed on.

No one ever has to know, Teleria had said as she held him on the rocks, both of them sobbing for all they'd lost.

What if I want them to know?

They'd kill you, Adrahn, and we're not going to let that happen now. We've both lost all we can handle, haven't we?

Sweat turned to shaved ice on Rahn's face. It frosted his eyelashes. His trousers fused to his flesh where the stream water had landed. His heart was under an intrinsic pull to go to the barn and be with her, but no one else was coming for Marek. No one else seemed to have notice him slip away. There might not have been another chance, and it wasn't Rahn she wanted to see at the end of a trialing night, but her husband.

Rahn keeled over to retch into the snow.

He continued, closer to where the fence crossed the stream. Marek picked up speed as the incline steepened, and Rahn had to push twice as hard on flat ground to keep up. He dug deep, dredging the final memory of the cursed night that had shaped him and his life forevermore.

When you remember tonight, Adrahn, think not of yourself as a monster but a slayer of them.

Rahn tripped but kept his momentum, half running, half flailing as he narrowed the last of the gap between himself and Marek. Marek paused at the fence line, bowled over in respiratory distress, and Rahn used the brief reprieve to draw his sword and shove the tip between Marek's shoulder blades.

"The fuck?" Marek turned with a yelp.

"I should have done this the night you put your hands on her neck. You don't deserve a trial. There is no fairness in you, and I'll deliver none."

"Tindahl? You self-righteous fuck—"

Rahn pushed on the blade to shut him up. His hand already ached from the weight—the force. He remembered Drazhan's words. "If she doesn't survive this night, I will find you in the afterlife, where there are no limits to the deaths you will die."

What's the difference between being a monster and slaying them, Duchess?

"Whatever you need to believe it is," Adrahn answered, driving his sword at an upward angle, straight through the monster's heart. His hands shook against the resistance, but he held his ground, baring his teeth through the excruciating effort it took to turn and twist the sword until the blade was pointed upward.

Marek moaned and staggered away, then crashed into the fence with the twisted sword still stuck through him. His hands flailed as he looked at the steel tip protruding from his chest and then, with a slow, distrait look back at the scholar, he pitched forward over the fence and collapsed.

Drazhan surveyed the carnage in breathless astonishment. Seven dead, none of them his. One was still missing, the one who mattered the most.

Never in his life had he regretted anything as much as not killing Marek Barynov when Aesylt had come home with the man's handprints on her neck.

He'd sent Uli and the others to search the fields for Marek, holding Pieter and Valerian behind to help with Aesylt, who couldn't wait another minute for the aid of Dereham's healer.

They'd arrived mere moments too late.

Pieter and Valerian had wrapped Aesylt in as much cloth as Pieter had in the satchel he'd brought. She was unconscious, her breaths shallow and further apart with each passing minute. What he needed to do was lay hands on her and take it all away, but without knowing all the ways she'd been injured, he'd risk making it worse. If there was even a shard of a sword or dagger or that bloody pitchfork inside of her...

"You done?" he asked from the door, searching the field for any sign of progress.

"We need to bring the healer here," Valerian cried. He sniffled and wiped his face in the crook of his elbow. "We can't move her."

"There isn't time," Pieter said. He sat back, scanning Aesylt, and exhaled. "We could make a stretcher from wood and one of our cloaks. Or..."

Drazhan marched over and descended to a crouch. "Where's the wound entrance? Exit?"

Valerian pointed at two spots, one in Aesylt's abdomen, the other inferred to be directly behind it on her back.

Drazhan slipped an arm above the penetration spot and hoisted Aesylt into his arms. Her head flopped back, her arms to the sides, and Pieter quickly folded them into place over her chest. The fury in the man's eyes was the same that had been there when he'd quietly dispatched the koldyna while she was trying to melt one of Dereham's guards with her dark magic. Aesylt might not want to marry him, but he'd earned Drazhan's grudging respect.

"Valerian." Drazhan moved to the door and checked both sides before turning back. "You have a choice to make."

"Never them," Valerian said, his head high. "I didn't know Marek was here, Drazhan, or I'd have gotten Aesylt out of Voyager's Rest the second I arrived."

Drazhan wanted to know how Aesylt had convinced the boy to come at all—and why—but it could wait. "Both of you cover me. We move fast. We *run.*" He adjusted Aesylt in his arms, avoiding looking at her. That could wait too. It had to. "Go!"

Rahn was sitting on the wagon's gate when Drazhan came sprinting down the path, Pieter and Valerian a pace behind. He pushed slowly to his feet, his heart expanding with hope when he saw Aesylt dangling from her brother's arms, her face tucked to his chest.

"Healer!" Drazhan cried. "Healer!"

A young woman who had just finished looking over Rahn's minor, pointless wounds leaped out of the wagon and ushered them over.

Rahn helped her spread the blankets out and climbed in beside them to assist Drazhan and the girl, Seala, in sliding Aesylt into place. Seala shoved everyone out of the way and climbed over Aesylt to straddle her, mouthing indecipherable words as she withdrew a dagger and sliced through the patchy swaddling covering her midsection.

"Guardians keep us," Lord Dereham cried and turned away, his arms crossed over his chest.

One quick look was all it took to leave Rahn in question of Aesylt's fate. "Squish," he whispered, crawling behind where her head rested. He knelt forward, over her, and pressed his lips to her temple. "This is not how it ends for you. You are as..." A sob choked his throat. "You *are* the stars, Squish. You *are* the sky. That's what I should have said when you asked me... when you asked me..."

"Adrahn," Drazhan barked. "Get out of her way."

"He's not in the way, sir," Seala said, looking back. "His presence is calming her." She fluttered her hands over Aesylt's belly and resumed her silent chanting.

"Marek's body is just over there, Steward," Rahn heard Uli Castel say. "The scholar dealt with him."

"On purpose?"

"Unless he accidentally ran his sword clean through the man's heart and twisted, I'd say so."

"Someone keep watch on Valerian. I want everyone to see he's with us when we reach the Cross." Drazhan groaned. "Healer?"

Palm over palm, measuring his breaths as he needed her to, Rahn smoothed Aesylt's hair away from her face. *Stay with me. Stay with me, Aes, and I'll make up for all of it.* He kissed her again, anyone watching be damned. *Any part of me you need is yours.*

"The bleeding has stopped. I sense no foreign objects inside of her. I'm working on restoring her now," Seala said. "She's steady enough to get the wagons moving, sir."

"I'll stay with her," Valerian said, rattling the gate as he started to climb.

"You ride with Uli. Bound, until we clear the Fanghelm gates," Drazhan said. "The scholar will stay with her. Riders, mount up!"

Rahn looked up, catching Drazhan's stony gaze when he passed.

"Is she your wife?" Seala asked as the wagon creaked to life. She uncapped her waterskin and took a deep sip.

If I wasn't such a coward. Rahn shook his head. The wagon jerked as it crawled up a short hill toward the road.

"Huh." Seala tossed the skin aside and lifted her arms in a deep breath.

TWENTY-SEVEN
A BETTER MAN

Rahn hovered at the doorway, his hip anchored to the frame. Niklaus and Valerian were piled onto the bed with Aesylt, leaving a respectful enough distance to keep Drazhan from defenestrating them into the snow. They hadn't left her side. Valerian had a right to be there, Rahn supposed, because he loved her, but Niklaus loved her too. Both had been loving her unconditionally her whole life, even when others had failed her.

Love like theirs was something Rahn only understood with the tragedy of hindsight.

She hadn't woken at all, except her panicked rise from the wagon four nights ago, when they'd passed through the village gates of Witchwood Cross after the stress-filled ride home. "Hraz!" she'd cried, pitching forward, only to teeter back into Rahn's arms.

Four vedhmas had been coming and going regularly, but they all said the same thing.

Her body is mended. Her soul is still searching for a way back.

Rahn understood the statement so much more now than he ever could have before. He also finally grasped the true, fundamental difference between himself and Aesylt. They were both rooted to their traumas, but Aesylt had been actively searching for the joy hers had stolen from her. Rahn had run as far from his as his legs could carry him.

And then he *had* found joy—and ruined it. Ruined her. He'd seen the moment the dazzling light had winked from her eyes that day in the tower. It had been blazing so bright, in hope. For him. All he'd had to do was reach out and take it—take her—in his arms and forget the past, cast aside the thin reasons he'd given for why his life had room for just one passion and embrace the fear. The last time he'd loved deeply, he had watched everyone in his heart sink into the ocean. *To love me is to know death,* he'd said to Teleria back then, and while she'd comforted him, she hadn't corrected him.

But love was more than a feeling. It was more than joy. It was pain and sacrifice and choice. It was knowing when that love was too big to do anything but suffocate. Letting go was the ultimate act of love because there was no reward for the loneliness that followed.

"Adrahn." Drazhan rapped the wall behind him. "We need to talk."

Rahn breathed deep. He'd been waiting for "the talk." Drazhan had divided his time between Fanghelm and Hoarfrost over the preceding days, and everyone was waiting for him to announce the outcome of his negotiations with the Barynovs. "Your office?"

Drazhan turned without an answer, and Rahn, with one last longing glance at Aesylt, followed.

Drazhan pointed at the smaller chair in front of the desk and dropped into his. "Before we get into it, my gratitude is necessary." His eyes flitted upward as he pulled a steady inhale, his fingers wrapped around the chair arms. "If you hadn't known something was off with my sister, we might—we *would* have been too late to help her. She's alive and will eventually recover. Marek is dead, and will not, also thanks to you and your unexpected justice. Nor will the Barynovs, who now have no sons to force into my chair because Valerian is one of us now. Esker will be stripped of his title of baron and of his ownership of Hoarfrost, both of which will be passed to Valerian. Should Esker 'reveal' there are other boys running around conveniently bearing his blood, they are ineligible for inheritance as a condition of the penance. He has until tomorrow to leave the Cross on his own, or he'll never again leave it alive." He reached for the carafe of wine on his desk but changed his mind. "When Aesylt wakes, I'll tell her that her marriage to Valerian has been undone. The minister hadn't filed the documentation yet. I have the original in hand and will show it to her, before burning it." He seemed to grow taller in his chair. "If she still wants to be Mrs. Valerian Barynov when she's recovered, then we'll give them a proper ceremony."

Rahn tried to make sense of the massive amount of information Drazhan had shared in just a handful of breaths. "I see. The worst is behind us then."

"Not quite." Drazhan opened his drawer. He set a muddy wooden squirrel on the desk and sat back. "Uli found this in the wagon. I believe it belongs to you."

Rahn's breathing slowed, but his heart soared at the sight of it. "It was a gift. To her."

"But it was on you."

"I found it when I was looking for her that night. She must have dropped it on the way to the barn, where Marek..."

"Well, it's either yours, Adrahn, or it belongs to the filth pile, because it's not hers. Did you know..." Drazhan's nose flared. "I debriefed with Valerian. He wasn't very forthcoming at first. He's loyal to her. And you. But when he realized the only trouble ahead of him would be if he lied, and that he was a part of this family now, he opened up. More and more, I'm beginning to understand what drove my sister from Wulfsgate in such desperation."

"You'll get no denials from me." Rahn spread his sweaty hands down his pant legs. He'd never imagined the day he'd be left confessing to Drazhan about the weeks he'd spent entwined with his sister, but he wasn't afraid of the aftermath, not anymore. "I left her confused and hurt and then said things, horrible things, that I knew would make her hate me. I thought it was what she needed to... move on. That I was helping her. It was only after she was gone when the dread sank in, and I realized I'd gone too far."

"Perhaps it wasn't just your words," Drazhan said after a grueling pause, "but the fact she believed you'd gotten her with child and then abandoned her?"

Rahn's chest constricted. His flesh erupted in head-to-toe tingles. All those times in the land of no consequence replayed in a frantic jumble, mixing. Only in the end had they... but that would have been too soon for her to know. "She never..." Rahn brought his hand to his mouth, fighting the onslaught of emotions swelling from deep within.

"Because you fucked her in the celestial realm, you thought you could do whatever you wanted to her because it wouldn't count?" Drazhan's entire face seemed to flare. "Well, she's not pregnant, glory to the fucking Ancestors. She never was, and if she had been, her injuries would have seen to it. But she's not the same, is she?"

"You're expecting me to defend myself," Rahn said slowly, no longer tethered to the seat, to anything. She'd come to him, scared and needing reassurance, and he'd offered only pain and rejection. Of course she'd sent for Valerian, because he'd never let her down. And he'd married her, knowing the potential child wasn't his, because he was a better man than Rahn had ever given him credit for—a better man than he himself could ever be. He cleared his throat. "To do so would insult us both, and enough damage has been done."

"I wasn't expecting you to be stupid enough to defend yourself, but *explain* yourself? I'll take even a smidgeon of *that*."

Two truths existed in Rahn: the one he'd fed himself to quell his swollen conscience, and the unadulterated truth, without qualifiers or self-deceptions. He'd given too much power to the first, at the expense of the second... at the expense of the only woman he'd ever let into his heart. "It began as a way to save the curricula. I don't know when exactly, but at some point, perhaps at different times for each of us, it became more. Too much more. I think Aesylt believed that if we both wanted it enough, we might find a way, that... *love* would find a way, but I knew what she refused to see. Even if you'd have blessed our union, I'm not..." Tears stung his eyes. "I cannot give her what I cannot even find for myself."

"Love." Drazhan stretched his arms to the corners of his desk with a steely look at the stack of papers in front of him. "You aren't the first man to hurt the woman he says he loves. But *this* woman has someone stronger looking after her, and I don't care if your love is bigger than the fucking White Sea, Adrahn. It's harmful. It broke her. And you won't get a chance to mend it, because by the morning, I want you gone. I don't care where you go."

Rahn shook his head wildly. "Drazhan, I need to stay at *least* until she wakes up. I have to apologize, to make things right—"

"I'll send you with any resources you need to take you where you choose. But you will not return. You will not see my sister again. And when she asks where you've gone, I will tell her the truth. That Adrahn Tindahl is a coward who *could* have sat here in this room and fought for her but didn't."

"I won't deny any of that is true, but I failed her once, and I won't—I *can't* let her down again. I need her to hear it from *me*."

Drazhan didn't seem to hear him at all. "Aesylt will never have to settle for *any* man who wouldn't lay it all down to protect her." He stood. "If you're wondering why I haven't killed you, my wife would call it character growth." He snorted. "Or maybe I just don't want to look my baby sister in the eyes again and confess yet another way I've hurt her. But if you're not gone by noontide tomorrow, character growth can go fuck itself."

Rahn pushed to his feet with a shaky breath. "Then kill me."

Drazhan rolled his eyes. "Don't leave on my account, Adrahn. Do it for her. She has everything she needs here, but she'll never see it as long as you're here. You're a millstone about her neck, blinding her from what's real, only offering ephemeral glimpses into what happiness *might* look like. That isn't love. It's selfishness. If you are actually capable of love, this is how you prove it."

Rahn balled the letter and hurled it into the hearth, where it landed next to a dozen others that weren't remotely adequate.

Say little. But say enough. Every attempt had borne those objectives in mind, and they'd all come miserably short of what he needed to say. Drazhan had agreed to deliver the letter in place of a more meaningful good-bye, but only if he approved of the contents.

I see myself now so clearly. You gave this to me. You opened my past, so I could have a future. Nothing I taught you over the past year comes close to all you've taught me. You have such a brilliant mind and—

He discarded the thirteenth attempt.

Drazhan was right. Rahn was a selfish coward. And to bear his heart fully, on the eve of offering her freedom of all they'd done together, would be the most craven act of all.

Rahn tossed the fourteenth try into the fire.

You are as imitable as the stars in our interminable sky. And I am not fit to stand in your shine.

He tore his hands down his face and let them land on the desk with a defeated thud.

Only a fool would walk away from a love as powerful as ours, so I must be the greatest fool to have ever walked this realm.

"No, no, and no," he muttered, starting over again.

When you asked me if I loved you, I have never told such a lie as that one. And had I not worked so hard to hide it, to fight it at every step, you'd have seen the lie as clearly as if I'd claimed not to require breathing for survival. You'd have known that only the mind can deny what the heart has decided. I know all this now, but it means little when I have hurt you more than I could ever atone for. I have hurt the person I love most in this world. You. Only you. Always you. And it is with love that I leave your life forevermore, so you can step into your promising future knowing you deserve so much more. Never settle, Aesylt. Never compromise on what you need. If I was a better man, I'd have met you right where you needed me to.

Rahn groaned and threw the balled attempt at the wall.

To offer his raw honesty was not kindness. It was selfish. Love would be giving her just enough to find peace and move on, without him.

He withdrew the last piece of vellum and went to work.

Aesylt watched the attendants add logs in her hearth as Drazhan spoke. He'd filled in the parts lost to her—some of them anyway. He was still withholding something.

Marek was dead. Her marriage to Valerian had been nullified, but he had become an honorary member of the Wynter clan for his loyalty. The Barynovs had offered a full and unconditional surrender, though Drazhan had his own conditions, which, as far as Aesylt was concerned, were the most gracious he'd ever offered anyone. He'd always had a soft spot for Esker, she thought, for like Fezzan, he'd stepped up for Ezra's kids after the Nok Mora, and it might have been the only reason the man was still breathing.

Best of all, Drazhan had said, smiling at her from his awkward pose at the end of her bed, she was going to make a full recovery. And the village would have a wonderful year ahead, thanks to all the meat she'd secured in her hunt with Lord Dereham.

Aesylt pulled herself up against the headboard. She tried to smile. She wanted to, for him. As light and happy as his words seemed, there was trepidation just under the surface, like more foul business was waiting around the next corner. "You said Marek was killed. Was it my doing? With the pitchfork?"

"That might've done him in, with time." Drazhan looked away briefly, but Aesylt noticed. "The scholar took his sword to him. Right through his heart."

"Rahn killed him?" Her pulse rocketed from gentle to a resounding thud at even the idea of what Drazhan had revealed.

I do love you, Aesylt, but not like that. I'm deeply sorry if I inadvertently contributed to your belief otherwise were not the words of a man who had slayed a monster for her.

"Tak." The veins in his neck were taut enough to pop.

"Why are you..." Aesylt wasn't even sure what her question was. She had so many.

"He's gone, Aesylt. Left this morning. And it's for the best. For you." She angled forward to object, but he reached for her ankle and wrapped his fingers around it, steadying her. His stare was on the window. "I know what happened in Wulfsgate. I'm not angry, cub. Not at you. I *know* why you..." His face scrunched into a scowl. "I just wish you'd talked to me."

The truth was out then. Had come out while she was sleeping, giving everyone a chance to sit with it—everyone except her. Curiously, his even-keeled words matched his temperament. He didn't seem angry. He seemed sad, like he was losing her.

For the first time in over a decade, Drazhan was asking her to open up to him.

"He left?" She wrapped her robe tighter, crossing her arms over her chest. "Why?"

"It was the right thing to do."

"*Why*, wulf?"

"I told him to." Drazhan faced her. "He could have fought me. He didn't."

"No one would dare fight you, Drazhan!" Aesylt exclaimed, but her heart was shattering. Rahn had come back for her. He'd murdered for her. And according to Valerian, he had ridden in the wagon at her side, refusing to leave until they'd unloaded and carried her to her bedchamber, and he'd only left when Drazhan and Fezzan had forced him out.

"You can believe this or not, but he didn't even try, cub. He sat there, defeated and weak, and agreed it was the right thing to do." Drazhan ground his jaw in disgust. "The smartest men are often the greatest fools. He failed you. And... so did I."

Aesylt couldn't help but laugh. "You think I had an affair with Rahn Tindahl because of a lack of strong male influence in my life?"

Drazhan balked. "I said nothing of the sort."

"Your fault?" Aesylt leaned in. "Draz, I'm two decades along in this life. My girlfriends are all wed. Most of them have children of their own now. Imryll is only a year my senior and is blissfully married, readying for a second child. Either I'm too young for any of it or I'm too old to not have a strong prospect lined up, but I'm *tired* of being seen as the little girl who watched her brother and father murdered in front of her and has been through 'so much.' Why does no one see the one who guided the restoration of her village? The one who never gave up and still found fulfillment through her own interests? Her own experiences?"

"I don't see you that way, cub," Drazhan said, shaking his head at the bed. "I don't."

"No? Then you'll believe me when I tell you I have done *nothing* with Rahn that I didn't choose for myself, and..." She pressed a hand to her chest to suppress a sigh. "I regret none of it. I fell in love with someone incapable of loving me back, but I see now that this isn't *my* failure. He's the one who has lost. I wish I'd never dragged Val into this, but I thank you for seeing the goodness in his heart and bringing him into our family. He's not like his father and brother. He's one of us. In a way..." The next words would hurt worst of all. "Rahn never could be. And didn't want to be."

Drazhan sat with that long enough she thought he might get up and leave. It gave her time to steady her heart, still so shattered no matter what she'd said. But if she said it enough, she'd believe it. She had to believe it. Otherwise, she'd be conceding that the greatest happiness of her life was already behind her.

"I know Hraz was your favorite," he whispered. "He would have known what to say."

Aesylt was stunned at his choice of response. "Hraz was *everyone's* favorite, wulf. He wasn't like anyone else, was he? But he's not here." She closed her eyes to shut out the horrible recollection of

Marek's illusions. "You are. And maybe it's *you* I need. Did that ever occur to you?"

"He's not here, cub, because I tricked him into my taking his place in the Vuk od Varem. He wouldn't let me volunteer as his replacement, so I went against his wishes and signed my name in blood with the kyschun while he was sleeping."

"You think you're to blame for..." Aesylt's breaths trailed off. "Drazhan, no. *No.* Mortain sent the king to our village because he wanted *you.* You can envision any other outcome of that night, and they all lead to the same damnation for all of us. And that night..." Aesylt choked up. "That *night* belongs to both of us, but you can't know it because you won't listen when I try to talk to you about it. And I need to, wulf, because if I don't, it will never end. It will have nowhere else to go. I never feel more alone, ever, than I do when I think about what happened."

Drazhan swiped the backs of his hands against his eyes and looked up. "I'm listening now, cub."

The midnight bell stirred Aesylt. Blinking through her grogginess, she rolled over and saw Drazhan stretched out beside her atop the blankets, snoring away. He'd earned his exhaustion, just as she'd earned hers over the hours they'd talked and talked.

Aesylt slipped out of bed and stumbled a bit as she found her footing on the way to her writing desk, which the vedhmas had co-opted for their materials. A carafe of nettle water was calling her name. Her throat was parched from all the talking. Her body ached from everything that had come before.

She was still shaky, so she sat to pour herself a half mug. It felt so good going down, she poured another half and then sat back in her chair, watching snow paint the world beyond the window.

Aesylt didn't know what to think anymore. She was tired of doing it. The unburdening of the Nok Mora had been a desperately needed catharsis and the mending of a crumbling bridge between her and her brother, but there was nothing left to say.

To feel. To do. She'd dammed one river, only to watch the other flood the banks. She'd never believed herself a romantic, so it was embarrassing to look back on how easily she'd fallen into the trap of love conquering all battles, closing all wounds.

Some wounds weren't meant to close.

One in particular never would.

She glanced back at her brother, passed out on the bed. All these years, she'd only thought she knew him. And now he knew her too. Everything she'd done that night belonged to him as well, and his pain and shame and guilt was hers to help absolve. It wasn't the end but a beginning.

Yawning, she pushed her chair back when she saw the note sitting next to the carafe. It was folded far too neatly for Drazhan, or even Val, but it wasn't the fold that froze her in place. It was the handwriting. *For Aesylt.*

Carefully, she opened it and read.

Aesylt,

By now you're aware of my departure. I leave knowing you will survive this ordeal and that your life will go on. You are poised for so much greatness. I need not see the future to know it holds nothing but accomplishment for you.

You are not after hollow bromides though, so I will say what I must so you can move on. You asked me to tell you I didn't love you, but in the end, it matters not how I feel at all, only what it has done to you. Forgive me, Squish, for being the coward you rightly called me. You deserve the world and more.

You were then, and always, the best of us.

With care,
Adrahn

Aesylt folded the letter and crushed it to her heart. Her head rolled back, sending her tears sliding down the sides of her cheeks. *I hate you. I hate you, Adrahn. I hate you. I hate you. I hate you.*

With a cry, she wrenched her arm back and hurled the letter into the fire. Stunned, she watched his words burn, every black singe stealing the past.

She fell to the floor and crawled over, bawling as she raked through the embers to retrieve what was left. All she could rescue was the upper corner, where her name had been written.

Aesylt.

"I hate you," she whispered, rolling onto her side on the warm stones, the corner of his letter bunched in her fist.

TWENTY-EIGHT
THE CHAMBERS OF HIS HEART

By the time Rahn stopped in Voyager's Rest, both he and his horse were practically foaming at the mouth. He led her to a trough to rehydrate and then settled her into the roomiest stall available in the stables, with as much feed as he could fill the bin with. He brushed her down, enjoying the gentle mindlessness of the act while thinking of his next move.

He had options. Wulfsgate. The Reliquary. There was an entire kingdom waiting for him to explore. He could even return to Duncarrow, for he'd left on congenial terms with Queen Adamina. His potential landing points were limitless.

But there was only one her.

Rahn strolled through the sleepy village, counting the candles in the windows. When he ran out of those, he counted the shingles and eaves, and before he knew it, he was standing in front of the inn where he'd found Valerian.

There were only a handful of patrons inside. The pubkeep was busying himself drying glasses.

Rahn neatly stacked his coin on the bar. "Room three for a night, and a bowl of whatever you're serving, please."

The old man tossed his rag with a nod and moved to the uneven hooks on the wall. He reached for the key to room two.

"No. I want *that* room," Rahn stated, pointing at the paddle painted with the number three.

"Aye? Still need to clean tha' one, if Tessa ever shows herself this week. Newlyweds, so cannae guess what we'll find." The pubkeep's hand hovered between two and three, waiting.

"I prefer it as it is," Rahn said and added another coin to his stack.

The pubkeep slid the key across the bar with a skeptical tilt, but his eyes were on the gold. "Aye, I remember ye now. Cauldron's on the back hearth, still some stew. Serve yourself, much as ye like."

"Thank you," Rahn said, but as he imagined himself scooping the stew—eating the stew—he realized he wasn't hungry at all. He headed upstairs instead.

The room was just as he'd left it. Bed unmade... old dishes gathering crust and dust on the table. Someone had collected Aesylt's and Valerian's belongings, but in the rush, things had been left behind. Woolen socks peeked from under the bed, and there was a nightgown hanging from the side of the privy curtain. He traced his hands over the familiar, soft fabric, misery splitting his chest.

Sleet hammered the frozen panes. Ice had already been forming on the trees when he'd crossed the village line, and it was getting worse. He cracked the window and grabbed the nearest chair and a blanket from the bed and dragged them over to watch the world frost over.

First, he counted the branches. Then the stars. One, two, a dozen, five hundred. His fingers ticked through the exercise, leaving room for nothing unwanted to creep in.

Adrahn, aren't you tired of running?

"Five hundred and six. Five hundred and seven..."

You've been running since you were eight. You're nearly thirty.

"Five hundred twelve..."

You know who you are now. This truth is yours. There's no putting it back.

Rahn rolled his hands along the sides of his seat. His mother's gentle admonishments continued, unaffected by his counting. But it wasn't his mother, and he wasn't the type to pretend. A man of science either believed in it wholly or not at all.

"I know it's mine. I know there's no putting it back," he said. His breath curled in the icy air.

His mother went silent, but his inner monologue returned. *Always running from, never to.*

Rahn closed the window and left the chair behind. He paced to the table and back, the table and back. He watched Aesylt's nightgown slide to the floor and dove for it, feeling properly foolish the moment he had it in hand. It was just fabric. Just a gown.

And she was just a girl.

"And I loved her." Rahn wrapped his fists in the thin gown, bringing it to his face. "I loved her imperfectly, but I loved her utterly."

Pack only what matters to you, Adrahn, his father had said the morning before they were set to leave on the massive ships in Mellendha Harbor. He'd never seen their like before or since, and the whispers among the adults had suggested there was magic involved in their swift construction. They were built on the instruction of the four Meduwyn sorcerers who knew all and could do anything. *There will be a great fire,* they'd told Carrow, *and only those on the ships will survive to tell of it. Here, you are merely a duke. But there, you can be a king.*

The following morning, snuggled between his parents, Rahn had watched his entire world burn from the deck, his baby sister sobbing her fear and confusion against his vest. Three nights later, they were all property of the ocean, and he was a murderer.

A murderer twice over. Now thrice over.

He regretted not the acts but the necessity of them—how smoothly he'd cut all three of them down without reluctance or remorse. It wasn't natural. Men were supposed to revere life, not destroy it. Not one of his kills had been an act of self-defense. Not one had been necessary beyond his desire to see their lives end for what they'd done. But who was he to decide their fate?

And who were they to decide the fates of your mother, your father, your sister? Aesylt?

Aesylt understood him better than he understood himself. She'd blocked her own violence from her mind, not from remorse but from the same guilt Rahn had only just seen in himself. Survivor's guilt. He was no more or less worthy of life than the ones who had lost theirs.

It was the night he'd arrived at Fanghelm that was the most vivid. She'd been cuddling Aleksy by the hearth while Drazhan and Imryll were warming their bedchamber. She and Rahn had exchanged a few awkward jests about it, but in her eyes, he'd seen the whisper of her own lust for life—her desires, unrealized, still forming. She was a puzzle, and he, a missing, orphaned piece that had clicked soundly into place, but only she had seen it then. She'd known it that very night and waited, unwearyingly, for him to catch up and find her. The closer she came, the deeper he stuck his nose in the books that had kept his heart safe and dormant for so many years.

But no quantity of books or stars or classes or curiosities came close to lighting the flame within him as the warmth of her face in his neck or her arm bent over his chest as she cupped his cheek... the sound of her soft but deep voice whispering, *And another with me*, barely getting out the last word before she was in his arms, where everything, for once, felt like hope.

When they were together, he'd known fearlessness. He'd known what it meant to be alive. There was pain too, in the inevitable end of all things, but anything beautiful enough to mourn was worth whatever agony followed.

Rahn reached to scratch his temple and realized he was crying.

You cannot possibly want to see me with another man.

Well, I've already done that, haven't I?

The first inch of the blade pierced his flesh.

That was cruel. And unfair.

Life is cruel and unfair, Aesylt. You know it better than most.

You're trying *to wound me, so it will be easier to walk away—*

Stop. This is pointless.

Another inch.

If you're going to lie to me, then look at me when you do it. Look me in the eye and tell me you don't love me.

You're the one forcing my hand here—

Look at me, Adrahn, and tell me you feel nothing for me!

I do love you, Aesylt, but not like that. I'm deeply sorry if I inadvertently contributed to your belief otherwise.

Kill shot.

If you love her, Adrahn, then love her. Perhaps learn to love yourself in the doing.

"I left her *because* I love her," he thundered, shooting to his feet. The chair slammed to the floor. "Do you not understand? Do you not see? A selfish man would stay and ruin her. I cannot fathom a love deeper than the one that gave me the courage to leave so she can live."

You know what's even more courageous, my sweet boy? Staying. Fighting for what you want. Letting go.

Rahn screamed into the crook of his elbow.

He was losing it.

Talking to himself.

Answering himself.

Whatever last vestige of control he'd left Witchwood Cross with had disintegrated, and there was nothing left except to surrender to the dark call of insanity that had always been within earshot.

He plopped onto the bed, only to pop back up when something dug into his hip. He reached into his pocket and withdrew the squirrel. *Squish.*

With a shaky breath, Rahn set it on the bedside table.

He should throw it in the bin. It was a token of what was, not what should be.

A twisted symbol of the happiest time in his entire life.

Rahn lay his head on the pillow, his eyes fixed on the statue. It was then he realized he was still holding Aesylt's nightgown.

He rolled it under his chin. His eyes glazed, from tears... from the loss of focus, but instead of counting to clear the pain, he let it wash over him like an icy wave on a stormy night, and the thoughts he'd spent a lifetime damming flooded in.

Imryll hadn't felt so helpless since her days in Duncarrow.

Sometimes she read to Aesylt from a book of poems Rahn had purchased somewhere in the Easterlands, on his way to the Cross. She couldn't remember where. It only seemed important now that she couldn't ask him. The vacancy he'd left behind wasn't only Aesylt's to bear.

Aesylt seemed to listen, whether Imryll was reading or rambling. Aesylt had spent the day huddled by the fire, staring intensely into the flames as though she might discern the great mysteries of the universe. Her pain was readable in the tension pinching her shoulders back, in the soft murmur she made every time she changed position, and in the rare times she actually looked at Imryll and all she'd lost pooled in the depths of her glossy eyes.

The hopelessness Imryll had felt when Drazhan had been exiled from Duncarrow was fresh again, sitting in the flicker of Aesylt's subdued grief. Her sister-in-law was strong. She'd pull through and be stronger yet. But there was a certain tragedy to collecting strength through despair that chipped away at the light, and Imryll was filled with a terrible sadness as she envisioned Aesylt growing dimmer with each passing year.

"Tasmin has sent word, Aes. She'll be home by springtide," Imryll ventured aloud.

"Ah."

"Niklaus is taking his trials soon to become a formal member of the kyschun. Did he tell you? Drazhan said we would throw him a fete before he goes under the mountain, but he was hoping to consult with you on some ideas."

"Mm."

"Did I tell you the vedhma's have conferred and believe my second child will be another boy? He'll be here just in time for Tas's return."

Aesylt drew her knees tighter against her chest. "I know what you're doing, Imryll. I appreciate it. But why not say what you really mean?"

Imryll sank into the chair across from Aesylt. "What do I really mean?"

"That I should be ashamed for what I did... how I feel. My inability to just... move on."

"Aesylt, I am the *last* person who would ever..." Imryll laughed. "I married the man who trained for ten years to, among other things, destroy me. And if you mean the age difference, well, your brother and I have nearly the same amount between us as you and Rahn. There are young women all over this kingdom promised to men twice, three times their age. Age was never the barrier between you two."

"His position of authority then."

"What authority could anyone ever have over Aesylt Wynter?"

Aesylt's mouth twitched. "He wrote me a letter. You're right that it wasn't age or authority. He's a broken man who has no desire to be reassembled, and I need... I *deserve* someone who loves themselves enough to confront their demons and conquer them."

Imryll leaned in and squeezed Aesylt's foot. "You said it perfectly, my love. You deserve that and more. Rahn is one of my dearest friends, and it brings me great sadness to see him deny himself a chance at happiness. But we are not put on this realm to fix others, Aesylt. Everyone can only be responsible for their own completeness. If we're lucky, we find the person who is uniquely able to take the journey with us. But unfortunately we often meet the right person at the wrong time."

Aesylt smashed her lips together and turned her teary eyes upward. "What painfully perfect wisdom. In another life, another time..."

"I know." Imryll sighed and released her. "And *none* of that is your fault. But in your short life, you have been loved by two great men. Imagine what the rest of your years hold."

"I just don't understand some of it, Imryll. Why did he kill Marek? Why ride with me in the wagon? Why... Why any of it? I can't make sense of his behavior, and I feel like I'm going *mad* trying." Aesylt wiped her eyes with aggravated swats. "And *mad* with all the cursed fucking tears. I suppose my body is playing catch-up from all the dry years."

Because he's a great fool who loves you but cannot say the same for himself. "I haven't been able to find the right words to say this to you, so forgive me if they come out wrong." Imryll folded her hands, praying what she said wouldn't push Aesylt further into her self-torment. "If you two had come to me with your plan for the curricula, you would have received a predictable answer. I knew from the moment the Reliquary intervened in our project that it would one day be torn from our hands, and every day it wasn't was a day stolen. I might have told you exactly that, had you come to me. Saved you a world of heartache."

Aesylt looked up, her expression darkening.

"But damn if I don't respect you for doing it anyway. For storming ahead fearlessly. For convincing the most unflappable man I know, save your brother, to put the science ahead of feelings he most certainly had long before the two of you were ever intimate." Imryll's heart swelled for the girl who had become dearer to her than any sister she might have had. "You are the most incredible woman I've ever known, Aesylt, and I need you to know that you didn't kill our project. You gave it life for a little longer, and you proved to those craven men in their freshly built towers that there's *nothing* we wouldn't do for our passions."

Aesylt traced her hand down her throat. "Thank you, Imryll."

"And I wouldn't blame you nor think less of you if that passion took you to Riverchapel, to the Reliquary."

Aesylt burst into laughter. "After what they did to us? After what Pieter—"

"If I remove my emotion from it, Pieter wasn't the problem. Nor was he wrong to offer you and Rahn a position there. You both belong in that world, if you still want it."

"You think it's where Rahn went?"

Imryll shook her head.

"Why not?"

"For the same reason you'll never go. It would remind him too much of what he lost."

Aesylt nodded and returned her gaze to the fire. "What will you do now?"

Imryll was hoping she'd ask. "We still have our academy in the village. Books of All Things has had an explosion in interest since the civil war ended, and in speaking with Lord Dereham, he's offered to become one of our principal patrons. He's also going to encourage the families of Wulfsgate to send their children to us to board and teach, like the universities of Oldcastle, except only a day's ride from home instead of a fortnight. Drazhan is already working to find us a suitable location for the boarding, and we'll need to expand our staff, of course, if we're to become more than a day school."

"Imryll that's... That's incredible," Aesylt said, smiling for the first time. "It may not seem like it now, but you'll make more of a difference here locally than anything we were doing for the compendium. You'll change lives for the better. So many lives."

"*We* will, because I need your help. I can't do this alone."

"Drazhan will have no shortage of people for you lining up to be a part of this."

"And I will review everyone who applies," Imryll said slowly. "But I need someone with experience to partner with me."

Aesylt nodded to herself. She picked at the blanket covering her knees with a small sigh. "Can I think about it?"

"Of course you can. We have time. Gods know none of this can happen tomorrow."

Aesylt's lips curled. "You know you slip into Duncarrow sometimes. I've noticed it when you're excited about something."

"What?"

"'Gods.'"

"Ah." Imryll laughed. She'd never understood the gods of Ilynglass the way those who'd lived there had, but she'd been raised on the idea of them. The Ancestors felt more real but were also unreachable for a foreigner, no matter how warmly the Vjestik had embraced her. "Do you think you might join us for supper?"

"Not tonight."

"Take your time." Imryll rose from the chair. "It's going to be icy tonight. They're already closing down the mountain roads. Shops are shuttered. Drazhan said they may even close the taverns, if you can believe it."

"Nien," Aesylt said lightly. "It's been… five, six years since things were bad enough to close the *taverns*. Not even the Ancestors dare come between a man and his vices."

"Well, I don't need to tell a northerner it's best to stay indoors this evening."

"Before I forget, will you ask Niklaus to come see me before his trials? I don't want to blink and suddenly he's gone."

Imryll smiled. "I'd be happy to. Any message for Valerian?"

"Not yet. I owe him an apology, but he deserves the best of me when I give it."

"He knew what you were offering."

"It was wrong of me to offer at all. It would have been like… like Rahn dangling marriage in front of me when his heart wasn't in it. I would have lapped at that like a starving dog… Doesn't matter. Intention doesn't soften hurt." Aesylt's smile this time was forced. "You can tell my brother I'm fine. I *will* be fine."

"You will," Imryll affirmed, feeling, for the first time in days, that the words had weight. "You are so loved, Aesylt. I know you know this is true, but it is my dearest hope you *feel* it is true, because I know how quietly hears a broken heart and how even softer listens a broken spirit."

Undiluted impulse put Rahn back on the treacherous road to Witchwood Cross in the dead of night, amid a powerful ice storm, headed toward his dreams instead of away from them.

He was alone on the Compass Road, his only companion the shrill peppering of ice striking the earth, the blinding fog, and the occasional abandoned wagon in a ditch. His heart was a racing, fitful mess he could not keep time with. Every push he made for speed, his horse resisted, balking and thrashing her head in protest.

Twice he stopped to calm and feed her from the apple bag he'd purchased from the stablemaster—and to allow his logical mind a moment of prominence. The road had been slick when he'd left Voyager's Rest, but there were entire patches of ice forming and spreading, their edges beginning to touch. There was no rational reason not to turn around and wait until morning. It would be safer. Fanghelm would be awake and ready for him. There was no rush. No reasonable person would push on.

Rahn gave the horse a soft kiss on the nose, thanked her for all he was about to ask of her, and swung back onto the saddle before that rational side of him pulled him astray.

For all the chaos of his heart, his mind was at rest. There were no difficult memories to falter him nor the soothing but damning voices of those he'd lost. Aesylt was there—she was everywhere, always—but her ubiquitous presence no longer set his nerves on edge and his conscience spinning. She was an essential part of him, guiding him through the freezing tempest toward either his end or his beginning. She was the fire burning through his veins, scorching the inexorable loneliness of his past. The symphonic conductor of his fearless future.

Aesylt had no reason to forgive his weakness, and he, no argument in his defense that came close to redeeming how he'd hurt her. But where he'd failed her with reason, he would offer vulnerability. All those times she'd mused he was the first person to really see her, and he'd failed to see the mutuality—the mirror she held, not with shame but love. Respect.

I see in you what lives in me.

There were a thousand reasons not to keep riding in the dead of night for a village where he wasn't welcome, in the middle of the worst storm he'd ever seen.

Rahn adjusted his horse's hood, thanked her once more, and made his final push for Witchwood Cross.

Drazhan tapped the letter against his knee, watching Imryll dry herself after her bath. The sight of her soft curves, her belly arcing in the early days of pregnancy, sent butterflies rippling across his chest and down his arms.

To worry her or not, that was the debate. Or might have been, if he didn't know the truth: Imryll worried more when he kept things to himself. It was her judgment he feared, though even that would come sparingly. The lack of it would be more shameful.

He was not a man afraid to be wrong, only the catastrophe of the wrongness. But the *damn letter.* He couldn't help but feel he'd missed something fundamental.

Imryll would know what to say and do. She always did.

"Are you going to tell me what's on your mind, or shall I fuck it out of you?" Her towel dropped to the stones as she turned toward him wearing a cheeky look he was tempted to fuck out of *her.*

Drazhan grunted and thrust the letter out and away from him.

She took it with a little *hmph*, sat on the chair across from him, entirely naked, and read. "'When you asked if I loved you, I have never told such a lie as that one.'" Her startled glance over the top of the page was expected. "Rahn wrote this? To Aesylt?"

Drazhan breathed deep through his nose and nodded.

"Wow." Imryll crossed her legs and continued. "'And had I not worked so hard to hide it, to fight it at every step, you'd have seen the lie as clearly as if I'd claimed not to require breathing for survival. You'd have known that only the mind can deny what the heart has decided. I know all this now—'"

"That's enough." Drazhan thumbed the space between his brows. "Please."

"Where did you get this?" She finished reading and set it on the table between them. "This isn't the letter he left with Aesylt?"

"No. Found it. Half-burnt in his hearth."

"She hasn't seen this?"

He shook his head.

"And the dilemma raging in your head, love?"

"It would be easier to have this conversation if you were not so..."

"Distracting?"

He pursed his mouth, restraining a grin.

Imryll rose and made a show of snatching her robe from the hook. She threw it on, tightened the belt, and flopped back down. "Better?"

"Decidedly so."

"I think I can guess," Imryll said, "but you might feel better if you say it."

Drazhan pitched forward, lowering his fists between his spread legs. "Was I wrong, Imryll?"

He appreciated how she didn't answer right away, though she'd surely had an opinion ready. "Whether you were or not, he still left, didn't he?" She lifted in a sigh. "It wasn't her brother who broke her heart, Draz."

"You're being generous."

"A little." She fingered the burnt corner of the letter.

"I can be... intimidating. But you want to know what really got my temper flaring?"

"What doesn't?" She grinned. "Go on."

"Yeah, well..." He smirked, but it faded fast. "Aesylt is... special. I've turned down every proposal not because I'm... not *only* because I'm difficult, but because I would cut down any man who didn't see her full worth. Who took advantage of it. The last thing my mother said to Hraz and me was 'Look after our cub. She's our resilient one, but strength can be mighty lonely.' I left the Cross as much for her as father and Hraz. I couldn't be the brother she deserved. What does it say about a man who would have Aesylt's heart in his hands, only to choose to crush it?"

"Rahn didn't leave because he was afraid of you. He left for her. In his own way, he left for the same reasons you did ten years ago."

"And is that what she wanted?" He thrust an arm at the wall. "Is that what she asked for?"

"No, but he believes he's protecting her. That she can do better. Deserves better. You know how dear Rahn is to me, so it hurts me to say this, but if that's what he believes, then he's probably right. We live the words we speak."

"He said none of that to me. Not a word."

Imryll glanced away with a thoughtful expression. "He didn't try to change your mind or convince you to let him stay because he'd already made up his own mind on what needed to happen. Aesylt knows this. She knows the man she fell in love with. She knows he alone is responsible for the way things ended."

"I left you once too." Drazhan hated the way the words sounded. That had been the second worst day of his life. But he bore all the blame for what happened to Imryll on the stones of the prince's bedchamber, and when she'd asked him to leave, it had been the least he could do. It had been all he could do.

"But you came back." She folded a hand atop his. "I love you, Drazhan. And I think rather than wondering if you could have made different choices, perhaps it's time to let go of making them for her. Don't place yourself at the center of her heartache. There's only room for one."

Drazhan brought her hand to his mouth for a gentle kiss. "Thank you."

Imryll looked confused. "For?"

He had to wait before answering. "Everything."

"Steward." One of Drazhan's personal guards opened the door. "Stewardess."

"Not now, Elden." Drazhan lifted a hand without looking.

"Apologies, but Baron Castel insisted you'd want to know." He took a step inside. "We've received two separate reports by way of the storm ravens that a man has ridden through the village gates just under an hour ago and is claiming intent to climb the hill to the keep." He cleared his throat. "On foot."

Drazhan spun in annoyance. "Why the fuck would anyone do that?"

"We're being told it may be the duke, sir."

"Adrahn?" Drazhan gaped at Imryll, who wore a matching look. "No. That's a mistake."

Elden shifted in discomfort. "And if it's not, what would you like us to do?"

"Drazhan, do *not*—" Imryll puckered her mouth with a look of self-restraint.

"Get him off the road and inside, of course," Drazhan muttered. "It's fucking freezing out there."

"Sir." The door closed.

Imryll shook her head and clucked her tongue. "Should I wake Aesylt then?"

"Not yet." Drazhan stood. "I'll go see what this is about."

"What are you thinking?"

Drazhan was still getting acquainted with speaking his thoughts aloud, and if not for his wife's regular, gentle prompting, he might never. "I won't be what stands in Aesylt's way of happiness. But if it is Adrahn on his way to the keep, I'm not letting him anywhere near her until he's convinced me that none of what you said still holds true."

Rahn had been stopped the moment he passed through the gates. Most roads through the village were closed, and only one inn remained open. He'd explained he wasn't going to the inn, and to where he was headed, prompting the men to exchange nervous glances before informing him the hill to the keep was too icy for any horse or cart to traverse.

"Then I'll go on foot," he said, dismounting and handing the reins to one of the men. "Will you see she's stabled properly?" He dug into his cloak for gold, but the guard waved a hand.

"This is unnecessary, Duke Tindahl." They huddled at the edge of the meager tent, set up to protect them from the elements.

"I'm paying for the inconvenience I've placed on your shoulders, so it is necessary." He squinted in the general direction of the keep, concealed by a thick cloud of fog. A half tick of the moon it would have taken him to make the climb in good weather, but he had at least an hour ahead of him, if it was even possible.

Impracticable. Not impossible.

"I'll be back for her when the weather clears."

"Sir, even on foot—"

Rahn squeezed the guard's arm with what he hoped was a polite smile. "Any accidents are my own fault, and I'll tell the steward you tried to stop me. Death couldn't keep me from the gates of Fanghelm tonight. Dobranok."

Their fearful chorus of "dobranoks" faded into the night, into the past. Shivering, Rahn tightened the stays on his hood, lowered his face to protect it from the punishing ice, and pushed on through the abandoned village. Storm shutters had been drawn on most of the shops, darkness swallowing the main road like an eclipse. He'd picked the worst night of the year to make his stand, but Aesylt had used challenging situations to test herself, to prove she was capable, and it gave him the burst of energy he needed to make it to the base of the winding mountain road that led to the great keep of Fanghelm.

Rahn peered upward once more, but the keep was still wrapped in fog.

The hill was deceptively steep. He'd walked it before, returning from the village when the weather had been fair enough, but he hadn't been contending with trails of black ice threading through the road. Every step was a gamble, every breath a burden on his lungs. Sometime along the ride, he'd lost feeling in two of his toes. He wondered if he'd miss them.

He conquered the first switchback, but on the climb to the next, his boots failed to gain traction, and he went sliding toward the perilous ravine, so deep he couldn't see the bottom. He grabbed hold of a dense bush, but the snap in his arm was the price he paid for avoiding a bigger crisis. Pain shot to his head like a bolt of lightning. His ankle screamed from the twist he'd put in it trying to right himself.

Rahn used his good arm and foot to slide himself back up onto the road. He stumbled forward, catching another bush, but after a wobble, he was back on his feet.

He'd given no consideration to what he would say if—*when*—he made it to the keep. Overthinking was the connective thread between his greatest failures. Nothing could drive him away except her.

The exhaustion he'd held off for hours crept through his bones and veins with a vengeance. He hobbled, transferring as much of his weight as he could to his uninjured foot, which was burning from overexertion. His arm begged for something to rest on, but if he removed his cloak—if he tried to find something to fashion into a sling—he'd open himself up to more problems.

Time blurred. Sleet changed to snow and back to sleet. He blinked and realized he didn't remember the past quarter mile at all and then it happened again, and he wondered if he was dying.

First it was a tingle, but then it was like fire, spreading through his good hand. He flexed, but the response was hardly a twitch.

Of all the foolish things he'd done in his life, climbing a mountain road in the middle of an ice storm topped them all, but if she wasn't worth such a daunting risk, then why had he come? If he turned back now, turned away from the one perfect thing he'd ever known, then he was as good as dead anyway.

The world winked in.

Winked out.

He was there and then he was not.

When he came to, a dozen men were standing over him with blankets.

"Get him up," Drazhan commanded. "Quickly!"

"Aesylt," Rahn croaked.

"Not much use to her dead," Drazhan said as Rahn was swallowed in a suffocating swaddle of coverings.

When he next regained consciousness, he was startlingly warm. He turned his face, and it landed in a pile of soft fur. He moaned into a restricted stretch, but his arm was no longer broken. Sore, but un-fractured. He worked up the courage to wiggle his ankle, to the same result. Tender, but not like it had been. All ten toes responded.

Drazhan's shadow appeared first, followed by the man, perched on a stool. "Another half tick out there, I'd have been breaking some unfortunate news to Aesylt."

"Where is she?"

"You and I are going to talk first."

Rahn pulled himself up, sending his head into a dizzying vortex. He closed his eyes. Without sight, his other senses were pushed into dominance. The smell of old, cracked leather. The feel of rare fur of an arctic yak. The taste of a fire that hadn't died to embers. Drazhan's office. "We do have a matter of business to discuss."

Drazhan folded his elbows over his knees and waited.

Rahn couldn't have the conversation huddled on the floor of a man's office. He hobbled to a nearby chair. "You have my gratitude for not leaving me out there to die. Would have been a simple solution to the problem for you."

"But an unfortunate one for the women I love."

"I love them too, Drazhan." Rahn fought a wash of pain as he pulled himself higher in the chair. "Imryll is family. And Aesylt is... She's..." He had no reason to hold back anymore. "Everything."

"She was everything before you left her, Adrahn. She always was."

"Some plants survive better in the shadows." Rahn squinted through a stream of consciousness. "Over thousands of years, they've adapted to that preference, enough that sunlight can damage or even kill them. They can outlast their sunnier counterparts because this sacrifice leads them to being hardier for it, almost stubbornly so. There are even those who have developed tougher barks or leaves, like armor."

Drazhan scoffed. "And?"

"I should think even you would see the familiarity. We all do what we think we must to endure. We stand beyond the reach of the light, we put on our armor, and we tell ourselves we have no other choice."

"Why did you come back?"

"A man makes two kinds of mistakes in his life." Rahn squeezed the chair arms. It was Aesylt he needed to talk to, but his relationship with Drazhan had always been one of mutual respect. He would no longer answer to the man, but he didn't want to lose him either. "The ones that are beyond repair, and those we'll spend a lifetime never repeating. It's not the offender who determines which is true. Only Aesylt can decide where mine falls."

Drazhan dragged his elbows against his knees with a bracing sigh. "Where was this fight before?"

"I don't know where it was," Rahn replied. "But I know where it is now." He allowed himself a moment before saying what he'd been waiting to say. "When you sent us on to Wulfsgate, you told me one day, if I should want something, you would grant it."

"That's *not* what was meant." Drazhan sat up. "I wasn't bartering my sister's safety for her person. If you're asking—"

"I ask nothing of you, Drazhan." Rahn braced and stood, gripping the mantle for balance. "It's Aesylt whose forgiveness I must ask. Then she can decide what to do with it."

"And when she turns you away?"

"Your sister told me what she wanted the night she fled Wulfsgate. I didn't listen then. I'm listening now, either way."

The office door flung open and bounced off a bureau. Imryll entered, shaking her head at Drazhan, right before Aesylt flew in, wearing only a thin nightgown. "Someone is going to explain to me what's—*Rahn*?"

Rahn gripped the mantle tighter and stood taller. "Squish."

"Cub, head on into the Great Hall. We'll be in shortly," Drazhan said, but it was clear from his defeated tone he expected to be ignored.

She stepped sideways, distancing herself from all three of them. "What are you doing here?"

Rahn started in her direction, but his shaky muscles had his knees buckling. She surged forward in instinct right as he fell to his knees, but he was up before she could reach him. He shook off Drazhan's offer of help.

"Send for the physician," Drazhan called to Imryll.

She disappeared out the door.

"What's wrong with him?" Aesylt stopped halfway, hovering between Drazhan and Imryll. "Draz, what did you do?"

"Saved his fucking life is what I did."

"Your brother didn't do this," Rahn said. "I made it as far as Voyager's Rest—"

"Why did you go *there*?"

"To be close to you." Rahn's face scrunched in a well of pain. "Aesylt..." He bowed his head with a soft sigh before meeting her fraught gaze. "I tried to carve you from my heart. A thousand cuts weren't enough, for each of the chambers of this dark, damaged organ is made up of your smile, your laugh... your touch."

"It's late, and Adrahn is unwell. Morning would be better for this," Drazhan said.

Aesylt's head shook as he spoke. "No. You said you didn't love me. You said *everything* we went through, everything we..." Her gaze shifted to Drazhan. "Was all a misunderstanding."

"And I can no longer call myself an honest man for a lie of such magnitude." Rahn hobbled closer, using the furnishings for balance. Her eyes followed him, glossing over. "There is *nothing* I don't love about you, Aesylt. There's no morning I don't wake thinking firstly of you. No night I sleep without even the most innocuous of our interactions of the day fresh in my dreams. I could lie further and say I could not see the abyss of my emptiness until you were no longer there to fill it, but I knew from the *day I met you*, my life was forever changed. I will never believe I am worthy of you, but that is not my judgment to make."

Aesylt's lips parted, but no words emerged.

Rahn removed his shaking hands from the chairs balancing him and folded them over his heart. "If you tell me the damage is too great, if you ask me to leave, I will. But if you allow me to stay, there is nothing in this world, or others, that would send me away from you ever again."

Aesylt stood stock-still, her hands at her sides, tears rolling down her cheeks. "And tomorrow? What happens tomorrow, when you remember yourself?"

Rahn inched forward. "I loved you yesterday, Squish. I loved you a year ago. I love you now, and I will love you until the gods come to take me home to the Halls of Ilyn."

Drazhan folded his arms and spun away with a sharp inhale.

Aesylt took her time crossing the room, but the moment she was in reach, Rahn stretched a hand to cradle her face. Weeping, she folded herself into his arms. They melted against each other, speaking no words until she looked up and into his eyes. "*You* are as imitable as the stars in our interminable sky, Adrahn. Please don't ever speak of worthiness. Who is worthy of anything, if there is no objective decider? If I say I love you, then I love you. If you love me, then love me. Stop acting as though we've committed some terrible crime."

Rahn nodded through his own tears. "I'm sorry, Aesylt. I am so very sorry."

Drazhan quietly left the room.

"And I will try to forgive you." She stretched up for a kiss, soft and lingering. "In time."

He gripped her face in his hands and kissed her harder. "I'm an imperfect man, and I will make more mistakes, but never one like this. Never again."

She slowly lowered, frowning as she returned to her feet. "Why now, Rahn? Why not say these things before I left?"

He fought the urge to look away. "Years I've been holding onto something terrible... and it *was* terrible. But in the years since, all I could remember was that the last time I'd loved to the ends of my own soul, all of it was taken from me." A sad smile cracked the corner of his mouth. "So I lied to myself as well, because I've always loved you, and whether I lost you to my own stupidity or to Marek's..." He cleared his throat. "In the end, we're all lost to the inexorable call of time, but we don't have to be dead before it happens, do we?"

Aesylt watched him closely. "You killed him. Marek."

"About eight weeks too late."

"I wouldn't have predicted it."

"Because there are parts of me, Aesylt, that I've not shown anyone." He brushed the back of his hand along her forehead. "But I want to try. For you."

She let the words wash over her in silence. It was another minute before she broke it. "What *did* happen to you out there?"

"This imbecile rode through an ice storm, broke his arm, sprained his ankle, and nearly lost half of his toes." He chuckled without humor at his idiocy, which was so much clearer with the danger having passed. "Drazhan healed me, but I'll need a few days of rest before I'm back to my usual self."

"I'm surprised he didn't leave you for dead."

"I fear he only saved me because he was afraid to face you if he didn't."

Aesylt laughed softly. "Maybe you'll survive another day. Or two."

Rahn gathered her hands in his and lifted them, then pressed them to his chest. "It was never just research to me, Aesylt. I was in awe of your belief you could separate the emotion from the science, but I knew I never could. Every moment with you felt like an insidious betrayal of your trust because every moment with you was the best moment of my life."

"I failed too, over and over and over."

He smiled. "I know."

"What you said in Wulfsgate... I'll try to forget the words, but I don't think it will be so easy to set aside something that caused me so much pain. You were so... so resolved, a different man than the one standing before me now, but I don't understand how."

"He was a man in denial of more than his own feelings. A man who could not address the past, because to do so would bring forward a brighter future, and he didn't think he deserved one." Rahn kissed her hands. "I'd like to tell you what happened to me the night my family died, if you'll hear it. What I did. Not tonight, but... but soon."

"I would like that." Aesylt rolled her lips in, nodding. "And I... I'd like to tell you more about what happened the night of the Nok Mora. Not tonight, but soon."

"It would be my honor, Aesylt." He swayed, teetering and sinking onto a nearby chair. "I'm..."

"A mess," she said. "You've had a taxing night. Why don't we go to bed?" With a sigh and a soft smile, she said, "We can talk more in a few hours when we wake."

"I'm sure my old room is still made up."

"No, Rahn. Mine."

"Go to bed together? Will I wake with a sword to my throat?"

"I always bolt my door, so if you wake with steel at your throat, it will be mine."

"I don't recall *that* being on the curricula..."

"Whatever will we do now that we're not bound by their restrictive rules anymore?" Aesylt's eyes narrowed deviously. "You never gave me your answer."

"About what?"

"Reenacting the Dyvareh, but without the restriction of rules."

"Oh." Rahn's face flushed with heat. The prospect hadn't left the back of his mind since she'd proposed it, but no matter how much of each other they'd explored, there were some lines he was still afraid to cross. "Perhaps I'm still considering your request."

"What's your concern?"

He didn't need to think about that. "Hurting you."

"Isn't that the point?" She blinked. "Is that not your fantasy?"

"There's fantasy," he said, "and there's the bleak reality. I wouldn't ever forgive myself if my fantasy caused you actual suffering."

"Well," Aesylt said, lacing her hand through his. "I'll give you until springtide to think of how you'll make this happen without too much suffering. You owe me, after all." She laid her head against his arm. "Will you take me to bed, Scholar?"

Rahn kissed the top of her head, his heart finally settling. "I'll take you anywhere you want to go, Squish."

Epilogue

Aesylt still couldn't believe the observatory was finished.

Rahn and Drazhan had conspired to have it completed for her twenty-first nameday, months ahead of the original timeline, which would have pushed the grand opening into the last throes of autumnwhile—and they all knew that really meant another year. Any construction in the north was subject to the precariousness of the weather, and the autumnwhile season was as ephemeral as springtide.

Rustan and Pieter Dereham had donated fifty workers to the effort. They'd also sent a lovely bouquet from the Wintergarden for her nameday, with a note declaring their intention to donate half their first thaw hunt to the Cross again.

In a separate basket, Pieter had sent her and Rahn a dozen citron.

Rahn whisked her through the arched doorway. "I know you're not thrilled about wearing a gown, but I'm already a little jealous of all the men who will see you in it for the first time."

"I'll enjoy it more when you're taking it off me later tonight," she replied, taunting him. It was tradition for Vjestik women to wear the ceremonial gowns of their ancestresses on their twenty-first, but the plumes alone had her wondering how many people she would smack in the face before the night ended. Then Rahn had dared her to wear the *hat* too, and she could never pass up a challenge.

Aesylt's haughtiness was short-lived though, cut short by her immediate overwhelm.

There were at least a hundred Vjestik inside, all dressed in the finest they had available to them. Most sat at or on the ten tables hauled up and decorated with cutout stars and carafes of Valerian's special wine he'd crafted for the occasion.

A violinist played a lively chorale that had some dancing between the tables, creating magic under the stars. The auroras—a rarity in springtide—dusted the sky with swashes of emerald and violet, reflecting off the shards and squares of perfectly polished glass.

"What do you think, Squish?" Rahn asked, leaning close to be heard over the music and conversation.

"You must enjoy me speechless, because..." She laughed, exhaling. Everyone she loved was there. Drazhan. Valerian. Niklaus and other Petrovashes. The whole Castel clan and the Voronovs. Maia. Tasmin had just returned as well, later than she'd first said, and Aesylt couldn't wait to catch up with her and hear all her stories about Whitechurch and Lord Quintus.

The only one missing was Imryll, who had given birth to her second son, Torian, two nights earlier. Drazhan would only stay long enough to give a speech and then would hurry back to her side. "Thank you, Rahn. I can't imagine a better present."

"Oh, this?" Rahn glanced around with a contrived look of startle. "This isn't your present."

She laughed, delighted to see his playful side on display. He had slowly been getting more comfortable with it, but he was still a serious man. "No? And how will you top an *entire* observatory?"

"You'll find out. Tomorrow." Rahn winked, his mouth lifting. Aesylt wanted to climb him like a tree and drive them both against a wall, but Drazhan wouldn't appreciate her lack of restraint. "*Tonight*, let's enjoy what is evidently the fanciest fete the Cross has ever thrown."

"By a mile," she said, scanning the room in wonder.

"Just think of all we'll learn here. Together." Rahn squeezed her hand and gently nudged her to the center of the room, where others were dancing. "How much we'll teach others."

Aesylt squinted one eye. "I thought you were opposed to dance, Scholar?"

"It's your nameday. Seemed a fair reason to make an exception." He folded one of her hands in his and slid his arm around her waist, falling into suspiciously near-perfect time with the music.

"You're better at this than you wanted me to know," she said, undecided on whether to be impressed or suspicious.

"I learned very little of use on Duncarrow, but damned if they ever let us miss an opportunity to dance."

Aesylt laughed. "You didn't dance so smoothly with Nyssa."

"I was making a point."

"To me or her?"

"Her." Rahn grinned and spun her. "But it seems you received one too."

Aesylt tilted her head back, her eyes blurring as she watched his dimples form and soften. He seemed on the verge of either smiling or speaking, but something changed his mind, and his head shook gently instead as he watched her. "And what was the point you were making?"

Rahn's hand firmed against her back. "I can see you really want to know."

"Can see that, can you?"

"I've read you more and longer than any book on any shelf." He pulled her closer, more than was socially acceptable for a courting couple, sending her heart hammering against her chest. She'd never seen him so bold. "I wanted Nyssa Dereham to know that Rahn Tindahl was a man acquainted with civility, who couldn't refuse the offer of a turn with a lady of her station. But he only *dances* with the ones he can't bear to keep from his arms."

Aesylt recoiled playfully. "Seeing as I'm witnessing an expert at work here, that does not make me feel special."

"In Duncarrow, I danced with women who were like kin to me. I have never..." Rahn became suddenly serious. "Never danced with someone I was in love with. Tonight is the first."

"I was wrong," she said softly, melting to the floor. "I do feel special."

They were still dancing too close. Everyone was watching. Drazhan was already grumbly about Rahn's intentions toward her. They were in love but not betrothed. Marriage hadn't even come up. Aesylt had heard her brother talking to Brita the other day, and Brita had reminded Drazhan that his sister was happy, which was what mattered. Drazhan had diffidently agreed, but she could see he was still bothered by it.

He'd probably be even more cross when she told him she wasn't planning to have children.

The music shifted to a vigorous beat that started a rolling clap around the observatory. Aesylt reluctantly broke away from Rahn, and they joined in.

She squealed when someone goosed her from behind. There was only one man in the Cross brave enough to do it in a room full of people. She spun, feigning exasperation, and said, "Valerian Barynov, *remember yourself.*"

Valerian gripped her face and planted a kiss on the corner of her mouth. "Can I not be affectionate with my ex-wife?"

Niklaus popped out from behind him. "Your union was annulled, wastrel. Do you know what that means? It never happened." He fluttered his hands in a show of magic, and they all laughed.

"Wasn't even annulled. It was never filed," Aesylt replied, still laughing. "Drazhan burned any evidence it happened at all."

Rahn drew closer to her. Since they'd started courting, he hadn't commented on her closeness with Val and Nik, and he never would. But the two of them brought out his subtle possessive side, and the sex after an encounter like that was... exquisite. Almost enough to make her want him jealous all the time.

"Only the Ancestors know how that night went. And me. And Aesylt." Valerian laughed.

Rahn tensed.

"All right, nothing *choice* happened, but only because I'm a gentleman, who had to *pry* her off of me—"

Aesylt blinked at him in warning, and he stopped.

"Aes, we just came over to say we can't stay long," Niklaus said. "I'm reporting under the mountain at midnight for my trials, and Val offered to escort me."

Her heart fell. "Tonight?"

Niklaus smiled. "I've already put them off long enough. It's time."

"I'll give you three time alone. Find me later?" Rahn said.

She tilted up to kiss him. "Volemthe."

His smile brightened his entire face. "Volemthe." Her gaze trailed him as he slipped into the crowd.

"Never saw you two coming," Niklaus quipped.

"Such a stunning turn of events," Valerian said, his eyes rolling. "So many denials."

Aesylt swatted them both with the backs of her hands. "I never said I wasn't interested in him. He was the one who needed to come around." She tugged on her dress, a little too tight around her hips. She'd gained a few pounds in the past months, since they'd done the fitting. Her appetite hadn't been so healthy since she was a child. "You're going to do *wonderful,* Nikky. I selfishly wish you wouldn't, because I will miss you so, so much."

Niklaus reached for her hand with a quick squeeze. "You can always come visit the kyschun for a dose of wisdom into the past."

"Eh. They like to yell."

Niklaus chuckled. "All part of the experience."

Aesylt looked at the two men who were her oldest friends, her first true confidants, and on one terrible winter night, had been witness to her greatest suffering while still reeling from their own. It was with love they'd withheld the full truth, but their watch was over.

She slid one arm around Niklaus, the other Valerian, and gathered them close. They wrapped her tight, squeezing the air out of her, and she laughed, sputtering melodramatically.

"You are my truest friends." Aesylt choked up. "And the most magnificent pains in my ass."

Valerian snickered. Niklaus grinned.

"And I love you both so dearly. Nikky, you have *always* supported my dangerous ideas, always kept me safe when I wasn't nearly concerned enough with consequences. And Val, my champion. I know..." Her chest shuddered. "I know things didn't turn out between us the way... but losing you would break my heart. I need you to know that."

Valerian's hand shot out and cupped her face. "I'll always be here. And I'll always call you my ex-wife whenever the scholar is nearby, so I can relish the stormy look he wears so well."

Aesylt laughed, glancing back into the crowd to search for the man in question. He was chatting with Jasika and Anton, but he caught her gaze and smiled. "I hope you do, because it gets him *so* riled, and—"

"I cry foul, Aes, at hearing about your bedchamber escapades." Niklaus pretended to retch.

She was still laughing when she saw a brief commotion near the door. Guards were whispering to other guards, until one walked swiftly to Drazhan to whisper something in his ear. He startled and said something terse in return, and one of the guards made their way to Tasmin with a message. Her response was far less measured. She looked positively green.

"What?" Niklaus followed where she was looking.

"I don't know," Aesylt said. "Something's happened, maybe."

Drazhan ran his hands against his face with an apprehensive scowl. He nodded, whispered something back, and marched to the raised area of the observatory, followed by Fezzan.

"Aye! Shut it! Your steward has something to say!" Fezzan boomed, and the silence was so immediate, it drew nervous chuckles.

Drazhan shot him a bemused look and waited for everyone to settle. "Tonight is a special night." His voice was strong, carrying all the way to the back of the crowd, where Aesylt was growing increasingly disconcerted. "*Tonight,* we celebrate the rare and treasured occasion of consuming a Barynov wine and surviving to tell the tale."

Everyone tittered at the joke. Aesylt wanted to laugh at her brother's uncharacteristic humor, but it was only putting her further on edge. She exchanged a glance with Valerian, who seemed as apprehensive as she was.

"And my sister's nameday, of course."

More laughter.

"Something's happening with Tas," Niklaus said distantly and slipped off, following Tasmin on her swift exit from the observatory.

"What is going on right now?" Valerian muttered.

"Wish I knew." Aesylt saw Rahn standing with Jasika Voronov, his arms crossed and his brows joined.

"Aesylt is... Well, you all know her. She's more fiery than any flame. More cool than any glacier." Drazhan shifted, looking down. He folded his hands over his torso. "And when she was eight years old, she became the ruling leader of Witchwood Cross, a role she wasn't supposed to have—never asked for—and was forced to take on because her surviving brother had only vengeance on his mind. Yet she was a natural, one of the best stewards the Cross has ever had. Tonight, when you offer her your felicitations, don't forget to thank the girl who became a woman overnight so our village, our people, could rise once more from the ashes of another's war." He accepted a mug from Fezzan and raised it. "Hvala, Aesylt. And Blessed Nameday, cub."

"Hvala!" the crowd cheered. "Blessed Nameday!"

Aesylt wiped a tear on her arm and turned away. Valerian put a hand on her shoulder, sighing. She'd had no inkling Drazhan was going to make his speech so raw and personal. Their bond had never been more solid than after they'd talked about that night, but he'd not acknowledged any of it publicly.

"Cub."

Aesylt turned toward Drazhan. "Are you unwell or something? Feverish?"

"I meant what I said. No reason our people shouldn't hear it." He tugged on her ear but was looking past her, toward the door. "I have to go."

"Of course, Imryll—"

"No." His throat moved. "We have unexpected visitors."

"Who?"

"Do you remember me telling you about Owen Strong and Farradyn Blackfen, my fellow Knights of Duncarrow?"

"The only ones you liked, as I recall."

"My friends. Farradyn took my place protecting the queen after I was gone, but Owen left the service all together... went back to the Southerlands. I haven't seen them since they helped me find Imryll." He pulled at his stubble, still watching the door.

"What's it got to do with Tas? She left in a pretty damn big hurry," Valerian said.

"Tasmin seems to have a history with one of them. I—it's not my place, even if I knew, and I don't."

"Then how did you know to warn her?" Aesylt asked.

"Owen told the guards it would be prudent." Drazhan kissed the top of her head. "Don't waste another thought about it. They're good men, some of the best, and there's no reason to worry. Enjoy your night, cub." He narrowed his eyes with a sweeping glance. "Doubtful we'll have another like it."

Filled with questions, she watched him leave.

"Go dance with your lover," Valerian said. "He's watching me lean in close, whisper in your ear, and he's about to *lose his mind.* Wait... Wait, no, give it another moment. There we are. You can thank me later."

Imryll tapped her foot to keep the chair rocking. Aleksy was curled up on their bed, asleep.

Drazhan paced the length of the room. Little Torian almost disappeared in his broad arms. His thumb brushed his son's head, but his mind was clearly elsewhere.

"How long will they be staying?" she asked.

"Hm?"

"Owen and Farradyn? They are staying, aren't they?"

"Yes. Couldn't say."

"Which is it?"

"I don't know, Imryll."

"Why did they come?"

"I don't know."

"You seem far too worried not to know—or at least have a guess."

"It's not worry." He pressed his mouth to Torian's soft head. "They're our friends."

She stopped rocking and leaned in, but the soreness had her curling back into the soft cushion. "Then what?"

"What can you tell me about Tas and Owen?"

"Oh." Imryll puffed out. She'd almost forgotten. It seemed so long ago. "They had a brief dalliance on Duncarrow."

"What?"

"Wasn't much of a secret. According to Tas, he was completely different the morning after. Pretended like nothing happened and wouldn't even meet her eyes in the halls."

"They had an affair?" Drazhan's frown was full of doubt.

"It was one night. She was hurt by his rejection, but no more was said. She seemed fine after a couple of days. Never mentioned it again."

"Owen never said a word."

"I don't suppose he would have, seeing as he behaved like a scoundrel."

"You mean like Rahn with our Aesylt?"

Imryll stifled a laugh. Drazhan didn't mean it. He treated Rahn like a brother, but he would never stop fussing over Aesylt. "So what if they're not betrothed? The Vjestik are known for courting before formalities are involved."

"But *why* is what I want to know. He has my blessing, Imryll. Does he not want to wed her? How could he not want that?"

"Does he seem like a man who would ever be parted from her?"

He stopped pacing and shot her a pointed look. "You see my confusion."

"Draz, if she were unhappy, you'd know." Imryll grimaced as she stood, wobbly, and headed toward the bed, waving away his concern. "You've never troubled yourself with the rules of propriety. Let them... be what they are. Oh, are you still telling her all of tonight's details were my idea?"

Drazhan snorted.

"So that's a yes."

"Does it matter?"

"She knows the truth." Imryll climbed into bed beside Aleksy, moving him only enough to make space for herself. "I'll go see Tasmin first thing. She's already unsettled from something that happened with Lord Quintus. If I know her, she'll bury it all deep if she doesn't speak of it now."

"I think he's asleep," Drazhan said, tilting down for a careful look at Torian.

"He's been asleep for some time." Imryll's eyes closed. "Set him in his cradle and then you can tell me all about Aesylt's special night."

Tasmin was oblivious to the wind. To the cold. Duncarrow had been perpetually cold, though rarely icy. Never frozen. Though she'd been born on the cursed isle, she hadn't been conditioned for the briny, chill winds, but she had inured herself to them, like all other injustices.

Foreign was the word that stuck in her chest, and it was how she felt, standing without shivers as she stood upon the battlements and lost herself to the passionate swirl of springtide flurries melting through the fog.

"My lady, it's not fit for you out here, the weather in such a state as it is," one of the guards said, a pleasant older gentleman she liked and who had no business being out in said cold at his advanced age. "Should've been a nicer eve, but they say the next few days will be warm enough."

"It suits me fine, Kilgore," she lied, offering the precise smile she knew would work. It was her famous smile, and it had worked on so many, in a diversity of ways. That same smile had caught Owen Strong's eyes from across the ballroom. Had invited him into her bed. And had given him the impression that he was not the first she'd lured with it, though he was. The first and only. An experienced woman wouldn't have thought twice or looked back.

Why he was *in the Cross* was almost too dark a mystery for her, especially on the heels of her visit with Lord Quintus, which had begun with a plea for alliance and ended with a demand for marriage. The events paralleled Imryll's visit to Whitechurch, almost three years earlier.

Imryll had abjectly refused the demand, then had fled, in the dead of night, in fear for her life.

"Can I at least fetch you another fur? A cover?"

"I won't be out here long," she said, extending her smile, which she'd refined to the point it nearly felt natural. Only her mother and Imryll recognized the difference between practiced joy and the genuine kind. "I saw your son tonight at the celebration for Aesylt. He'll be married soon, I understand?"

"Oh." Kilgore seemed to swell with pride in her recognizing such a thing. "Cassius is marrying up, and his mother and I are so pleased."

"A Voronov, I hear?"

"That's right. Baroness Brita's adopted daughter, Tessa. The one she rescued from ahen vodah after the mother drowned?"

Tasmin didn't know the story or the Vjestik word he'd used, but she nodded as if she did. It was better than stealing even a sliver of his delight with a question. "A sad tale with a joyful ending."

"Indeed. Indeed, and now the steward has offered the keep for—" Kilgore swiftly spun away. "Ah, sir, this isn't... I'm sorry, who are you?"

"Donnae ken if yer askin' about my family name or my intent, but ye can call me Owen, and I'm here for a word with Lady Tasmin."

"Don't know the name," Kilgore said hotly. "Don't know the man."

"Aye? Ask Steward Wynter. We're mates. Go way back."

The tension began in her toes, but it shot to her shoulders like a combustible. She'd chosen the battlements because it was the one place no one in the keep ever went if they didn't have to. The one place she'd figured Owen Strong, a salt and sand Southerlander, would not venture.

Only Imryll and her mother knew about the strange night she'd spent with Owen, but neither of them knew the full story. The worst of it.

"If Syr Strong wishes to enjoy the storm, he's welcome to it," Tasmin said, her head down, and started for the metal door leading back into the keep. Owen's thick fist curled around her arm and pulled her to a jarring stop. She looked down, in disgust, but he relented only a little.

"We're overdue for a palaver, you and me," Owen said. His breath warmed her neck, rocking her with a shiver.

"Lady Tasmin?" Kilgore's hand readied to draw his sword.

"You needn't stab him, Kilgore," she said, wincing in pain as she tore out of Owen's thick grasp. "Unless he follows me."

"Tasmina."

Her shoulders pinched back. That nickname. How it had awakened her once. How she hated it now. "You shouldn't have come here," she said and pushed through the door.

Once safely ensconced on the other side, Tasmin lifted her arm and screamed into it.

Rahn could hardly sit still, watching Aesylt enjoy the bread-and-fig pudding he'd spent hours learning to make in the kitchens. But it wasn't the food he was nervous about; it was everything he had planned after.

She was only faintly dubious that he'd borrowed use of a Petrovash cabin at the forest's edge for what he'd sold as a romantic nameday dinner, but she had accepted his thin explanation about privacy.

"Well, Adrahn. You continue to be an unraveling mystery to me," she said, holding her belly with a stuffed look. "Now you're a chef? What will you reveal next, that you're secretly a gilded blacksmith? A ravener?"

Rahn grinned and, for a moment, forgot how fast his heart was racing. "I may have turned on some charm with the kitchen staff." He chuckled at her narrowing eyes. "Or they took pity on me."

Aesylt's cheeks were flushed from the aftermath of an enormous meal. The fullness might slow her in the hour ahead, but it would give her energy too. Stamina. She'd need it. "They're a hardened bunch, so if they took pity on you, you must have *really* left an impression."

"Tears often work in a pinch." He grinned.

She grinned back. Would she still be smiling if she knew what was moments ahead?

She asked for it.

It was time to find out if she meant it.

Aesylt groaned in contentment, sliding back in her chair. "Thank you. It was surprisingly so delicious. I hope you enjoy cooking, because you may be doing more of it."

"Don't get too comfortable." Rahn blotted his face with his napkin and pushed to his feet. *Now. Or never.* "Listen closely. I'm going to give you a head start, Aesylt. Ten minutes, not a second more. I wouldn't squander a single one of them, because I've had months to think about my strategy."

She corrected her posture. "What?"

"A ten-minute head start. You can go anywhere in the woods. You just can't leave them."

A slow, sly grin spread across her face as she caught up. Her eyes twitched. "And then what?"

"You have one hour to evade me." He meticulously undid each button on his vest, waiting until he was done to finish speaking.

She followed his every move, her eyes slowly dilating with interest.

"If I catch you before the hour is up, I decide your punishment. Nothing is off-limits."

"And when I evade you for the full hour?"

"You decide mine. Same rules—that is... There are none." He pulled an hourglass out of his pocket. It dangled on a chain he'd had made, and he slipped it around his neck but kept the glass steady. "You asked for intensity. You asked for violence. Once you leave this cabin, your consent to everything thereafter is implied and will not again be sought. Unless your life is at risk, I won't stop until I'm done with you, and I've had months to think about everything I want from this night." He tilted the hourglass. "Decide."

She slowly stood, watching him closely. With her eyes still following him, she went to the rack and skimmed her hands along the cloaks, choosing an economical one. One that would keep her warm enough but wouldn't slow her nearly as much as the others. Smart.

The rain outside would complicate things, but predators could hunt in any weather.

Rahn lifted the hourglass. Her eyes turned to saucers. She angled herself toward the door, her breaths short and choppy.

I want you to be my wulf again, but this time I want you to catch me.

When he tipped it, something shifted inside of him. "Better run."

Aesylt raced through the forest like she was running for her life.

Not only was the ground clear of snow for once, but the rain was obscuring every step she made, neatly covering her tracks. The advantage stoked her competitiveness, but winning wouldn't satiate her motivation. Rahn had more he was holding back, even from himself. She'd never wanted anything more than to see the dark side of him come out to play. The only way to entice it out of him was to give him a stage where he made all the rules, and she had no choice but to follow them.

The harder I make him work for it, the harder he'll be on me. The realization added flight to her step. She dipped left, snaking through trees, and then right, creating an illogical path he'd never think to follow.

Aesylt paused to catch her breath and listen for any signs he'd caught up. Nothing. He hadn't given her an hourglass of her own, but in her head, she'd been intermittently counting. The first ten minutes had come and gone; she was closer to twenty. A third of the way there.

She pushed on, elation carrying her faster and truer than she'd run in years. Her boots sailed off the ground with every stride, and before long, she was moving like a wulf herself, smooth and elegant and one with the forest.

Aesylt launched into a clearing that was familiar, though it took a moment of orientation to place it without all the snow. It was the tree that surfaced her recognition—the same one she'd sailed into. The one that had offered an illuminating evening with the man now giving her the chase she'd really wanted that night.

She glanced behind her, but there was still no sign he'd gained any ground. The quarry's edge was less perilous when she could actually see where she was stepping, and it gave her the nerve to inch closer to the edge.

The sight was distressing. For as terrified as she'd been clinging to that tree, had she sailed past it instead, the way to the bottom was far enough that she'd have had ample time to contemplate the end of her life before meeting it.

And my quiet, unassuming scholar climbed that tree so I didn't have to be alone. He hadn't hesitated.

She backed away and was evaluating her options when something hard and cold clamped over her mouth. Her feet kicked up, catching air, then bouncing off the ground as she was dragged overland back into the forest.

Her screams were muffled by the smell of freshly cured leather. Gloves. *He wants you to fight,* she thought and peeled her lips back, trying to nip him with her teeth, but he caught on and fastened himself tighter until she calmed.

The forest flew by, blurring. Her boots caught bushes... roots. Stinging pain rocked her when her ankle twisted, but her wulf was oblivious.

The stop was so abrupt, her stomach twisted. She found footing again, but seconds later, she was tripping and running from the force of him pushing her along. Just as she'd gotten a hang of the pace, she was slammed to a tree, and her breath exploded from her chest.

Her face immediately smarted from the scratchy bark. Blood beaded on her cheeks, and she thought, surely he'd address it, because he was a man who went wild when she had a skinned knee. But then he mashed her face against the wood and pinned it there as he tugged her skirt up over her waist with vicious insistence. She spat at the bark, tasting the damp earthy residue as she tried to make words, sounds, but he tensed his hand in warning, and she stopped.

"You thought you could run from me?" Rahn ripped her undergarments off with a single tear, followed by the sharp hiss of spit hitting a glove. He shoved up and into her. "That I wouldn't *catch* you?"

She screeched against the wood as he pinned her with the force of his tearing thrusts, and she realized, with a tiny spark of fear, that he was already *becoming* the wulf. Already shedding the flesh of the sensitive, devoted scholar who had killed the last man who had put hands on her.

He ripped her hair back so her face was aimed at the starry sky. The bowman was out, and she nearly laughed—nearly said it out loud—but then she gulped for air, choking on bark dust. Her groin brushed the tree repeatedly until she was wet, something he noted with a throaty moan.

Rahn bit down on the back of her neck and spilled into her. He held himself there, stilling so the pulsing release was the only sensation... the scorching, ferocious spend of a beast still playing with its kill.

Her clit throbbed in desperation when he ripped her away from the tree and threw her onto the ground.

Aesylt clambered back on her hands and feet, but he was ready for her resistance, stifling it with a bag thrust crudely over her head. She whipped around, sputtering in confusion, but was spun onto her belly with a slam. He yanked her hands up and over her head, thick rope sliding and tightening on her wrists. She tried to catch her breath but then she was off the ground again, thrown over something hard. His shoulder. Bile bubbled up from her throat and dribbled along her face, into her hair. His seed ran down her thighs.

Blind and bound, Aesylt could only watch the world pass by through the threading of the sack. It wasn't enough to even guess where he was taking her, but wherever he had in mind, the savage assault at the tree had only been a taste of the full experience.

With a start, Aesylt realized she *was* scared. He could do anything at all to her, and no one would ever know. No one was coming for her. As recently as earlier that night, she'd recognized she still knew so little about the man she loved, and what if she'd made a terrible mistake? What if she could unleash the beast but not put him back?

Those fears were the single greatest turn-on of her life.

Rahn slowed. The echo of hollow stone replaced the crunch of the forest. He lowered her to the hard ground, cradling her head on the way down—not as coarsely as he'd handled her at the tree, but far from gentle—and moved away. His steps echoed, getting closer… farther. He seemed to be fiddling with something.

"Where are we, Adrahn?"

No answer came. Her arms were extended back above her head, and she slid several feet as he pulled her, then secured her over a rock. He dug out more rope and tethered her bonds to it. Her hood tore away.

Rahn came around the other side of her and knelt between her legs. Her breath caught when he pulled out a knife and slashed it up her dress. The cold steel of the blunt end traveled her flesh as he sliced up into her bodice, until the final snap at her neckline. He ripped the fabric down both sides, exposing her naked body. She tensed in anticipation of the cold, but it didn't come. She was surprisingly quite warm.

A fire. We're in a cave. He really did plan this out.

Rahn stood over her, looking down. Gone was the scholar, the lover… her Adrahn. The wild spark in his eyes made her clench with dangerous desire. "Just remember, Aesylt, it was your idea not to have a way out." He gripped her ankles and spun her, twisting her arms in pain, until she was on her belly.

Aesylt moaned, spitting out rock and dust as she tried to contort to a more comfortable position. He yanked her back until she screamed, his cock sliding in from behind, and lifted her ass at the hips, ramming her into the ground. His thumbs spread her wider, the hurt exquisite and blinding. She no longer had any interest in the celestial realm, after everything that had happened, so explaining her injuries to her vedhma later would be fun.

"This cunt is mine. Mine to fuck. Mine to destroy. Mine to put back together, in whatever way suits me." He pulled out all the way and crashed into her, the piercing collision sending a rush of dark spots into her vision. "You're going to regret asking for this."

"Never," Aesylt croaked, spitting more dust. "Nev—" He silenced her with another vicious slam.

He withdrew his cock with a wet pop, dropping her. She panted, grateful for a moment to catch her breath, but the world moved again, and she was on her back, her arms straight again but so tender, she wondered if they were strained.

She had only enough time to look up before his cock parted her mouth, squelching any objection as he straddled her face, gripped her head, and pumped himself down her throat.

Aesylt thrashed underneath him, choking and trying to catch his eyes. But they were closed, his head thrown back in thrall to the surrender she'd begged for. He abruptly slid out of her mouth, making her wheeze for air, and she noticed a flash of blood on his palm.

There was no forethought at all, just a wave of impetuous desire as she nipped up off the ground and latched her mouth onto it. She suckled, lapping his blood away and locking her eyes on his.

He tore his hand back and nursed it against the other, watching her in astonishment. His eyes skimmed her body, and she followed his gaze and saw she was covered in similar scratches. Her face had to be worse, for all the fire pulsing in her cheeks.

Rahn burrowed his face along her torso, licking and suckling. Aesylt arched her back, but he shoved her down, moving to the next wound, and the next. The suction drove her into a spiral she couldn't unwind from, and a sudden explosion between her legs made her let go and she slipped away, convulsing through the first orgasm of her life that hadn't required direct touch.

His hand seized her at the neck, shearing the pleasure. "I didn't give you permission to come."

Aesylt froze. It was Marek's face staring back at her.

"You're scared," he said, sounding more like Rahn. His hand constricted. "Another man touched you like this, and he died for it. I can still see my sword sliding through his heart from behind, feel it exploding under my blade. I can taste his surrender. Do you want to taste it for yourself? The power?"

She went limp, terrified to move at all. Even her thoughts disappeared.

"Only I can touch you like this. Me. And when you think of a hand at your neck, it will be *my* face you see. *My* cock impaling you until the darkness comes." Rahn unbound one of her hands and forced it between her legs. "Show me how you touch yourself when you think of me. No, don't look away from me, Aesylt. I want your eyes. On. Mine. *Now.*"

Tears trickled from her eyes as she opened them and moved her gaze to his.

"Show me, Aesylt."

Her hand twitched. She shook her head.

"Show me."

She slid a finger down her length. A whimper stuttered in her throat, crushed by his hand.

Rahn nudged her legs wider with his thighs and lined himself up. He pitched his head back and slid slowly into her, then stopped when he reached the end.

Aesylt's eyes fluttered downward and became paralyzed by the sight of his cock holding her open while he choked her. Tremors passed down her shoulders and into her hand, which was still moving, still twisting and flicking the way she always did when she fantasized of him, just as the monster had commanded.

But he wasn't Marek.

The hand at her neck belonged to the one who had ended that fear once and for all.

The one who would deliver no hurt she hadn't asked for.

Rahn's lips peeled back and he rocked forward, finding his pace. Aesylt's shallow breaths came faster as the horrors melted away, as the hand at her neck became not a noose but a means of release. She worked her fingers faster, whining, tears rolling down her cheeks in waves, darkness pulling at the edges of her dimming vision.

His fingers pinched her windpipe. A scream was trapped in her throat, never to be released as she convulsed against the dusty ground. She'd never been pushed so far toward ecstasy. Never been so in love with her wulf as she was then.

He released her neck, and a second orgasm took hold, and she whispered, hoarse, "No. More. Please."

Rahn fastened both hands at her neck and pumped faster, baring his teeth with a threaded howl that bounced off the cave walls. His thrusts were so frenzied, she lost whatever breath she'd gained, and the world slipped into darkness. Warmth surged inside of her, and she came again, her contractions pulling him deeper, solidifying the bond they were always meant to have.

Distantly, she felt him slide out of her. She blinked the world away, but it came back. All she knew was the buzz spreading along her flesh, the utterly stunning awareness she was alive—not just alive but elevated to a higher plane of existence. Another world within her own. One that, unlike the celestial realm, was entirely hers and wholly safe.

Rahn slid a finger between her legs and brought it to her mouth. She wrapped her lips around his finger and sucked, tasting him... tasting herself. She was almost sad when he removed it again, but not for long, for soon his tongue was lapping the same place he'd dipped his finger, and the resulting crash was so much gentler, a soft, palpitating release that nearly put her to sleep.

Her mind registered the pain spreading over her, nearly every inch, but she was beyond that now, in a place where pain had no power unless fueled by love. She had nothing left to give, but he had nothing more to take either. She'd asked him to bare his true self, to trust she could handle it. He'd delivered her of a memory nearly as haunting as the Nok Mora, and she wanted more.

But not tonight.

Tonight she wanted to watch her lover through the haze of her dreamy lucidity and know she was safe.

Rahn was relieved the water wasn't too hot. He'd left it warming over the fire but had removed it when he'd brought Aesylt to the cave, to give it a chance to cool. He wanted the perfect temperature for her tender flesh, which would need healing the moment they returned to the keep. After everything that had happened in Voyager's Rest, they'd agreed the celestial realm was best left to itself.

He hoped there was a vedhma with enough discretion to keep the matter private, but he was beyond such concerns. Shame had no place in their love, however they expressed it.

She was curled up on the furs he'd left ahead of time, sipping from the thermos of cider he'd packed in the bag he thought of as "needs of the aftermath." Until the chase had begun, he couldn't know how far he'd take things. Really, until he'd actually placed his hands on her neck, he hadn't believed himself capable of it—no matter how loving his intentions. There was always a chance she'd react horribly and never trust him again. But Marek haunted his nightmares too. No dead man should have that much power.

Rahn sopped the warm rags atop her flesh, wincing on her behalf when she twitched at his touch. Perhaps he *had* gone too far.

She placed a hand on his arm, with a look that said *I'm fine*, but her eyes told another story.

"This is worse than I meant for it to be." He dug into his satchel for the pot of ointment he'd stolen from the infirmary and spread it over her abrasions. "I should have asked more questions of you, to know what you were looking for."

"This." She scratched her throat, passing over the red rings his hands had left. They'd turn purple soon. He couldn't decide whether to be excited or horrified about that. "This is what I wanted."

Rahn dug out a soft tunic and linen trousers he'd found in her bureau. They were more suitable for lounging indoors than convalescing in a cave, but her skin needed to breathe. At least he'd had the foresight for that. "Here, let's get you dressed."

"Aww," she said and he laughed, relieved he hadn't crushed her humor. She patiently let him dress her and then curled up, nestling her head on his lap, just as she had that fateful night almost a year ago. "So, same time tomorrow?"

Rahn tried to smile. Everything about her tickled his impulse for joy. But if he'd been nervous about releasing his inner wulf, he was petrified to approach the next part.

"What's wrong?" She looked up at him with so much concern gathering in her eyes, he knew he couldn't drag it out a moment longer.

Rahn cupped her face and leaned down to kiss her, just as he'd wanted to do that night in the tree. He'd denied himself so many of life's pleasures, for reasons that made little sense now, if they ever had. "That was the most sensual thing I've ever done. But now my heart is so full of the need to just *love* you."

Aesylt smiled, kissing him back, but he shook his head.

"No, Aesylt. Not just now. Forever." He peeled back to see her expression, but she was guarding it. Waiting for him to finish. "I know you don't want children, and I can appreciate that, for I know nothing of being a son, let alone a father. But how... How do you feel about marriage?"

Aesylt slowly sat up. “Has Drazhan gotten to you?”

“No.” He reached for her face and rolled his forehead against hers. “You have. In only the best ways. And if marriage isn’t for you, it will change nothing. We can go on as we have, and I’ll be perfectly content. I *am* perfectly content. All I want is you. All I *need* is you.” He kissed her, breathing her in. “But if you might consider becoming the wife of a lowly scholar, he could never know a greater honor.”

She pursed her mouth and looked at her lap. “Well, I’ll have to break the bad news to Pieter.”

Rahn chuckled in immediate relief. “Oh, please, let me.”

“You don’t have your heart set on a lavish wedding, do you?”

“Gods, no. Unless it’s what you want?”

“Ancestors, no!”

“Something private then?”

“Just a hundred of our closest friends?” Aesylt slowly grinned. “You know Drazhan will just keep adding names and adding names and adding names, blaming Imryll...”

“We’ve certainly learned the man knows how to throw a party.”

“Who would’ve guessed?” She snuggled against him with a contended sigh. “If you’re serious about this level of commitment, you’re also accepting that you’ve truly set the bar high with this nameday. An observatory, a delicious meal, a dramatic chase, and a proposal of marriage? Impossible to top.”

He wrapped his arm around her and gave her a gentle, careful squeeze, mindful they still hadn’t properly tended her injuries. “I’ve signed up for worse challenges.”

“Well, I accept, on one very sensitive condition.”

“Which is?”

“Forget the nameday challenge. I know what I want every year.”

Rahn kissed her scalp. “I can guess.”

“Save your creativity for the variety you’ll need to keep me on my toes. You won *this year,* but now that I know your game, don’t expect to win ever again.”

"So you *are* issuing a challenge."

"What do you mean, Scholar? I *am* the challenge."

Rahn grinned. "Accepted."

She snuggled back into his lap. "Thank you for tonight, Rahn. All of it."

"Thank *you*, Aesylt." He curled down over her. "Volemthe auvjek, my industrious, resourceful little squirrel."

He felt her chuckle on his leg. "Volemthe auvjek, my sexy, wulfy scholar."

Rahn glanced into the rainy night, his eyes bleary, his heart full. He brushed her hair back and let it slip through his fingers, drinking in the skip in his pulse and the peace in his soul. "Happy Nameday, Squish."

The Book of All Things continues with a new story in *The Flame and the Forsaken.*

ALSO BY SARAH M. CRADIT

KINGDOM OF THE WHITE SEA

KINGDOM OF THE WHITE SEA TRILOGY

The Kingless Crown
The Broken Realm
The Hidden Kingdom

THE BOOK OF ALL THINGS

Blackwood Cycle
The Raven and the Rush
The Poison and the Paladin

Southerlands Cycle
The Sylvan and the Sand
The Flame and the Forsaken

Guardians Cycle
The Altruist and the Assassin
The Belle and the Blackbird
The Virtue and the Vixen

Darkwood Cycle
The Melody and the Master
The Hand and the Heart
The Wolf and the Witchling

Sceptre Cycle
The Claw and the Crowned
The Duke and the Disciple
The Tempest and the Tides

THE SAGA OF CRIMSON & CLOVER

THE HOUSE OF CRIMSON AND CLOVER SERIES

The Storm and the Darkness
Shattered
The Illusions of Eventide
Bound
Midnight Dynasty
Asunder
Empire of Shadows
Myths of Midwinter
The Hinterland Veil
The Secrets Amongst the Cypress
Within the Garden of Twilight
House of Dusk, House of Dawn

MIDNIGHT DYNASTY SERIES

A Tempest of Discovery
A Storm of Revelations
A Torrent of Deceit
A Squall of Sedition
A Chaos of Awakening

THE SEVEN SERIES

Nineteen Seventy
Nineteen Seventy-Two
Nineteen Seventy-Three
Nineteen Seventy-Four
Nineteen Seventy-Five
Nineteen Seventy-Six
Nineteen Eighty

VAMPIRES OF THE MEROVINGI SERIES

The Island

and more

THE DUSK TRILOGY

St. Charles at Dusk: The Story of Oz and Adrienne

Flourish: The Story of Anne Fontaine

Banshee: The Story of Giselle Deschanel

CRIMSON & CLOVER STORIES

Available as a single collection, The Shorts

Surrender: The Story of Oz and Ana

Shame: The Story of Jonathan St. Andrews

Fire & Ice: The Story of Remy & Fleur

Dark Blessing: The Landry Triplets

Pandora's Box: The Story of Jasper & Pandora

The Menagerie: Oriana's Den of Iniquities

A Band of Heather: The Story of Colleen and Noah

The Ephemeral: The Story of Autumn & Gabriel

Bayou's Edge: The Landry Triplets

AS RIVER CHASTAIN
(CO-WRITE WITH ELIZABETH BURGESS)

THE COMPLICATED ROMANTIC LIFE OF ROMY DELACROIX

Silvan

Bastian

Dane

For more information, and exciting bonus material, visit www.sarahmcradit.com

ABOUT SARAH

Sarah is the USA Today and International Bestselling Author of over fifty contemporary and epic fantasy stories, and the creator of the Kingdom of the White Sea and Saga of Crimson & Clover universes.

Born a geek, Sarah spends her time crafting rich and multilayered worlds, obsessing over history, playing her retribution paladin (and sometimes destruction warlock), and settling provocative Tolkien debates, such as why the Great Eagles are not Gandalf's personal taxi service. Passionate about travel, she's been to over thirty countries collecting sparks of inspiration, and is always planning her next adventure.

Sarah and her husband live in a beautiful corner of SE Pennsylvania with their four tiny benevolent pug dictators.

www.sarahmcradit.com

SARAH M CRADIT

WEAVER of WORLDS

www.ingramcontent.com/pod-product-compliance
Lightning Source LLC
Chambersburg PA
CBHW020352310726
48979CB00015B/2571/J
9781958744437